The Kyoto Protocol

by

Joe McGovern

DORRANCE PUBLISHING CO., INC.
PITTSBURGH, PENNSYLVANIA 15222

ISBN-10: 0-8059-7167-X
ISBN-13: 978-0-8059-7167-5
Library of Congress Control Number: 2005937421
Printed in the United States of America

First Printing
For information or to order additional books, please write:
Dorrance Publishing Co., Inc.
701 Smithfield Street
Third Floor
Pittsburgh, Pennsylvania 15222
U.S.A.
1-800-788-7654

Or visit our website and online catalogue at www.dorrancebookstore.com

Dedication

I dedicate this book to my wife, Lisa, whose tireless commitment to family is pure inspiration and whose daily outpouring of love, kindness and charity is unparalleled.

INTRODUCTION

Rachel Carson was born and raised in the rural town of Springdale, Pennsylvania, where she developed an abiding love and respect for nature and all its beauty. Graduating from Pennsylvania College for Women with a degree in marine biology, she went on to write a number of books regarding the wonders and mystery of the sea, including *Under the Sea Wind* (1941) and *The Sea Around Us* (1951). But Rachel Carson is most prominently remembered as single handedly starting a revolution in environmental protection with the publication of *Silent Spring* in 1965, wherein she described how the proliferation of synthetic organic pesticides, including most notably DDT, caused a reduction in many bird species populations. In *Silent Spring*, Rachel Carson demonstrated that certain pesticides were responsible for an uncharacteristic thinning of egg shells, which caused radically elevated levels of avian embryo deaths. The consequentially stark absence of bird song leading to a silent spring was, in Carson's view, a wake up call for humankind to change the way it views the natural world.

The knee-jerk reaction of the United States to Dr. Carson's call to arms was a massive wave of federal environmental laws, adopted on the first ever Earth Day in 1970 and, at the same time, the creation of the United States Environmental Protection Agency to administer and enforce this bold new legal system. Emerging from this nascent body of law is the decidedly ironic admission that environmental protection, at least in the United States, is conceptually founded on a right to pollute. Of the hundreds of thousands of pages of environmental statutes and EPA regulations federally, and the usually equal number at each state level, the vast majority of them have as a theoretical underpinning that pollution is an inevitable consequence of living. It is only the amount of pollution that these environmental laws and regulations seek to control.

Take, for example, the Federal Clean Air Act. The debate is long since over that the breathable quality of North America's air is much better today than it was back in the 1950s and 1960s. That is not to say, though, that current air quality is wholesome, healthy, and vibrant. Quite the contrary. While research data undeniably shows that the level of pollution in the breathable air today is measurably less than what it was in the past few decades, what is also clear is that chronic respiratory problems, especially in our young children, are on the rise. Indeed, there are more children with asthma today than at any time in recorded medical history. This statistic begs the question whether, and to what extent, the Federal Clean Air Act is truly protective of public health, which is the primary and original intent of the statute. What is undisputed is that the Federal Clean Air Act allows millions of tons of pollutants to enter the breathable air each day as a matter of statutory right.

This same policy of a right to pollute applies almost universally. Laws designed to protect wetlands allow them to be filled. Laws designed to protect surface waters allow them to receive and dilute contaminants. Laws designed to protect threatened and endangered species allow their habitats to be erased, so long as the overall number of a species remains unaffected. Laws designed to protect drinking water supplies allow the presence of contaminants in them so long as the concentration of the contaminants will not present a threat to public health.

The human need to pollute to live is no longer the subject of debate. Rather, the only question on the table before lawmakers anymore is how aggressive a standard the regulated community can stomach before that standard creates an undue hardship. It is this question that spawns a singularly unusual interplay of science and public policy, which makes environmental protection a unique, and often times difficult to understand, legal system. At the heart of this legal system is the fundamental issue of what level of pollution is acceptable: the magical level that does no harm to human health or the environment, while at the same time not placing too much of an economic burden on either industry or the public.

The complexity of the scientific underpinning of United States' environmental laws can be seen in the Federal Clean Water Act. Adopted by Congress in 1972, its primary goal is to "restore and maintain the chemical, physical, and biological integrity of the nation's waters." Congress achieves this goal by regulating the discharge of pollutants to surface water bodies through permits that limit and control the amount of chemicals in wastewater from primarily industrial activities. The concentration or level at which that discharge limit is set is a function of, among many other possible factors, the sensitivity of the organisms in the receiving water and that receiving water's ability to dilute the chemical to a harmless level. This dilution capability of the receiving water is, in turn, based on whether others upstream are discharging that same chemical, and at what amount, such that the receiving water already has a background or baseline amount of the chemical already in it. Each of these factors has a particular body of relevant scientific data to aid the government in its decision making process of where to set the appropriate limit on the "right to pollute."

For example, the sensitivity of biological organisms in a surface water body to a particular chemical compound that is going to be discharged to that surface water body can be evaluated with the aid of data from laboratory and field studies. Similarly, the dilution capability of the receiving water can be evaluated based on certain physical characteristics—such as water velocity and volume—and existing chemical content. Combine all of this information together and, at the end of the process, out comes a number or level that theoretically will be protective of human health and the environment. So long as the party discharging to that receiving water does not emit in excess of that magical number, no harm should result.

The complexity arising from this novel marriage of science and public policy underlying environmental protection is compounded by the fact that the environmental sciences are in an embryonic stage. While the long-standing principles of classical sciences, such as physics, chemistry, and biology, each play an important part in understanding how best to protect the environment, as a field in itself, environmental science is only about fifty years old. And, just as at one time scientists agreed that the earth was flat, the theories and principles that modern day scientists agree are protective of human health and the environment may turn out to be sadly mistaken.

Layered on top of this novel environmental protection legal system in the United States is an emerging paradigm of international treaties aimed at controlling pollution on a global scale. While these international standards operate differently in some respects, and on a much broader scale, they nonetheless acknowledge and accept the concept of a "right to pollute." One of the most important and compelling of these newer vintage international environmental protection initiatives is The Kyoto Protocol. Aimed at stemming the tide of global warming, The Kyoto Protocol calls for all member countries of the world to reduce the amount of greenhouse gases produced on an annual basis. Scientists generally agree that, absent immediate and measurable reductions in the amount of atmospheric greenhouse gases, chief among which is carbon dioxide, we will soon witness worldwide ecological changes of potentially catastrophic proportions. In 1999, the United States Senate voted 95-0 to reject any global warming treaty that did not include developing countries, choosing instead to allow the executive branch to devise alternative approaches for the United States that would reduce greenhouse gases on a voluntary, as opposed to a mandatory, basis.

The Kyoto Protocol operates principally on the concept of market-based incentives to environmental protection. Wherever the law provides a legal right, such as a "right to pollute," the marketplace will normally assign an economic value. Critics of the existing method of environmental protection have advanced the theory that, if regulators encourage market-based initiatives, such as an ability to trade the "right to pollute," voluntary environmental protection will naturally follow. The Kyoto Protocol embraces this theory under what is commonly referred to as a "cap and trade" program. It allows participating countries to cut back on the amount of greenhouse gases they contribute to the global atmosphere and receive a "credit" for that emission cut back. The "credit" can then be sold to other participating countries that cannot perform the same or similar cut backs in greenhouse gas emissions. By doing so, the Kyoto Protocol establishes what has come to be known as the "carbon market."

<u>CHAPTER 1</u>

The flame reached out and scorched the protestor's hand as he lit the edge of a torn rag dangling from the mouth of an old wine bottle, filled to the brim with gasoline. His heart throbbed heavily and quickly as the searing heat enveloped his hand and rushed toward his face. As the rag began to burn more aggressively and approached the lip of the bottle, his accomplices, fearing that the hand-made bomb would explode in their midst, screamed to throw it at the police cars barricading the entrance to the United Nations building. As he cocked the bottle back and above his head, streams of gasoline tricked down his arm, bursting into flames. He hurled the bottle just as one of his fellow protestors tackled him to extinguish the flames on his arm. As the bomb arced across First Avenue, streams of flames spit out of the bottle's mouth, attracting a momentary gaze by both sides. Crashing to the ground, the gasoline in the bottle erupted and sent a wall of flames ten feet high. Other protestors, whipped into a frenzy by the explosion, grabbed more gasoline filled bottles from the cardboard boxes sitting behind their own make-shift barrier of cars and plywood. They lit the rags and hurled the explosives at the barricade. Within minutes, First Avenue was a conflagration of searing heat and smoke.

Police ducked and scattered as the bombs hit the police cars, turning an otherwise uneventful, placard-carrying demonstration on First Avenue and Forty-sixth Street into a scene of chaotic lawlessness. Police responded immediately, but weakly, with tear gas in an attempt to scatter the demonstrators. The futility of the initial police response became evident as another barrage of home-made bombs hit the barricade, causing one of the police cars to erupt furiously. Police retreated for cover and waited for orders. Fire trucks came screaming onto the scene almost immediately, as though fire officials had been forewarned of the possibility of this level of conflict. Unlike the police, the firemen speedily exited the trucks, engaged a number of hoses and began dousing the fires, unprotected in the middle of First Avenue, without fear that the demonstrators might target them next.

❧ ❧ ❧ ❧

A half hour earlier, the secretary-general of the United Nations had risen from his seat to welcome the attendees to the Earth Summit.

"Greetings everyone, and thank you so much for taking the time out of your busy schedules to be here. We have a wealth of important and compelling issues to discuss and hopefully resolve over the next few days. But let me start by saying that there has never been so much money in one room at the United Nations. Please leave some behind. We need it. . . ." The secretary-general paused while the audience burst into laughter. "As most of you are aware, the principal focus of this Earth Summit is going to be global warming. I take your presence here as a sign of the seriousness with which you regard the issue. Our panel of distinguished speakers, including former Vice President Al Gore . . . ," the secretary-general paused again until the applause subsided. "Yes, thank you very much Mr. Gore for being here to help us through this difficult issue. We're sure your background and experience with climate change will be invaluable. As I was saying, we have heard from the world's best scientists that serious consequences are looming for the world, and for your own budgets and businesses, if we do not mount a sufficient and immediate response to global warming. It is governments, of course, that bear primary responsibility for responding to the warnings. And many are doing so. The United Nations Framework Convention on Climate Change enjoys nearly universal membership. Almost 120 countries have ratified The Kyoto Protocol. Most countries agree that climate change is a real problem. They want to avoid the potential damages, and to minimize the costs of response strategies while ensuring that they are effective." The secretary-general paused a third time to scan the room for a particular face. "Ah, there you are. Ladies and gentlemen please join me in welcoming Mr. Royce, chairman of the New York Stock Exchange Oversight Board. I am advised by Mr. Royce that we have in attendance at this Earth Summit investors who are responsible for more than $1 trillion. You are the guardians of solemn promises to men and women who have entrusted you with their earnings. We appreciate the weight of the decisions you make every day in directing a significant part of the capital flows that fuel the global economy. And like the United Nations, you are in the business of looking ahead, identifying both opportunities and challenges for the human community. In a real sense, we are all stewards of the future. I thank you for the leadership you have exercised by coming here. Let us do our utmost to ensure a prosperous future for all people on our one and only planet. Thank you very much."

❧ ❧ ❧ ❧

Days before the Earth Summit, the White House distanced itself from a report by its own administration concluding human activities were mostly to blame for recent trends in global warming. The report, prepared by the United States Environmental Protection Agency and submitted to the United Nations a week prior to the Earth Summit, for the first time put the administration on record as saying that burning fossil fuels was the main cause of heat-trapping greenhouse gases. Until that event, the official White House position had been that there was too much uncertainty in climate change research to accurately assess blame. It was on this basis the White House opposed The Kyoto Protocol or any mandatory reductions in carbon dioxide and other greenhouse gas emissions, especially from the power generation industry. The United States president was quoted in his reply to the EPA report: "The Kyoto treaty would severely damage the United States' economy and I don't accept that. I accept the alternative we put out, that we can grow our economy and, at the same time, through technologies, improve our environment." The White House justified its position on the ground that, although the EPA report concluded climate change was most likely due to human activities, the report also stated "we cannot rule out that some significant part of these changes is also a reflection of natural variability."

        ⊰ ⊰ ⊱ ⊱

    The members of Save the Environment Now (SEN) made their political point through terrorism and they had no shame about it. In this instance, it was SEN's frustration with the White House's opposition to The Kyoto Protocol that led to the use of home-made bombs against the police securing the entrance to the United Nations. A week before the Earth Summit, Japan and the European Union's fifteen members jointly ratified the treaty and Russia had committed to do so "as soon as possible." This amount of support raised the likelihood that the pact would take the full effect of law, despite United States' opposition. SEN was convinced that the only way to convince the United States to join the treaty was through the use of force.

    Once the flames from the initial barrage subsided, SEN stood ready for a full frontal assault by armed police. Fearing only that their efforts would not make the 6:30 PM national news, SEN's members did not hesitate to use whatever means they could muster to exacerbate the chaos. Police had been fully briefed before the start of the Earth Summit about SEN's tactics and were given authority to respond with equal force.

    "All right, boys, it's time to bring these commie bastards under control," shouted the police chief to his specially trained group of riot control police. "The EPA Administrator is set to arrive in half an hour. I want every member of this group cuffed and on their bellies in First Avenue in fifteen. Let's move!" A dozen or so highly-equipped and outfitted police officers rushed off in different directions, obviously aware ahead of time exactly where they were supposed to be and what they were expected to do. The police chief shouted warnings and instructions to the members of SEN. "Cease and desist immediately! Armed police are moving into position. We have authority to shoot."

    "Fuck-off, pig!" shouted one of the SEN members, who appeared to be in charge of the protest. "We're gonna burn down the United-fucking-Nations!"

    A few of the younger SEN members watched their leader as he yelled back at the police chief. From the looks on their faces, they were not convinced that their

3

leader's verbal tirade was the correct thing to be doing. Throwing the gasoline bombs had been a rush, but this situation, the younger SEN members realized, was getting way out of control. One of them bolted for an open door in a nearby building and was out of view in a few seconds. A second one followed.

Infuriated by the mutiny, the leader of SEN grabbed another bottle, nervously lit it and stood up from his crouched position to throw the bomb. As he cocked his arm back, a police sharpshooter, who had had his crosshair fixed on this position for a few minutes, pulled the trigger and hit the protestor square in the chest. The bean bag bullet had enough force to knock the protestor off his feet. As he fell, the protestor lost his grip on the wine bottle, which dropped backward into the cardboard boxes holding the other homemade bombs. The bottle exploded into flames as it hit the ground, igniting the surrounding ones. Flames burst into the air as a series of explosions rang out.

The SEN leader was instantly engulfed in a sea of flames along with two other protestors. The 6:30 PM news that night showed a ghastly image shockingly reminiscent of the self-immolation of a Buddhist monk during the Vietnam War.

CHAPTER 2

A wave crested in advance of the tugboat as it pushed its way down river. Small diamond-like patterns of light reflected from the advancing wave: nature's unique signature that it was getting late in the day. You could judge the tug's speed by the size of the wake that followed as it passed by. This one, leaving a set of two foot ripples in the water, was moving at a pretty good rate, probably because the captain knew a Friday evening beer would be waiting for him at the dock. The tug's wake trailed away at an angle, its intensity lessening somewhat with distance, and headed toward the river's bank. The cattail reeds, towering almost ten feet about the water's surface, began to sway as the tug's wake bumped up against them and then slowly dissipated and disappeared into the marsh. Geese and other water fowl scattered, most likely mistaking the movement and noise in the reeds as an approaching predator.

The oppressive heat from the day left a purplish haze just above the river's surface as the sun began to set behind the Philadelphia skyline. Small wisps of high, thin clouds, combined with the heavy center city smog of a late summer afternoon, refracted the angled sunlight into an array of breathtaking orange and red hues. Lights in the windows of the city's office buildings began to take on their own identity as the brightest part of the day gave way to the slow, steady decline to dusk. Small mouth bass and shad breached the river's surface to capture a snack of the insects darting just above, their re-entry leaving a measurable disturbance.

Resting at a point where the Rancocas Creek flows into the Delaware River was a twenty-three foot Grady White with the call name Lucky Streak. It began to rock slowly and rhythmically as the tug's wake finally met the fishing boat's hull. The captain grasped the wheel and dug his toes into the floor of the cockpit to steady himself as he waited for the disturbance to pass. It took only a minute or so. It was then, as the motion and force of the water shifted the boat closer to the reeds, that the captain of the Lucky Streak noticed something unusual floating in the water.

He maneuvered the boat a few feet closer to the reeds, being careful not to run aground, to get a clearer view. What the captain saw was a first for him in his many years on the river: face down in the water was a lifeless human body, a longshoreman's cargo hook punched deep into the center of the upper back.

❧ ❧ ❧ ❧

Seeing the body floating in the reeds certainly came as a jolt to the captain of the Lucky Streak. He carefully thought about his next step, despite the nervousness. He knew he would have to call someone about what he had found. He looked around but found only an empty and still river. The tugboat was almost out of sight by this time. He realized that finding somebody around this late in the day on a Friday afternoon would be nearly impossible. He took a few deep breaths to calm his nerves. Then he realized that the best bet would be to call the United States Coast Guard. He radioed from his short wave aboard the boat.

"This is Toby Middleton radioing from the Lucky Streak, registration number 53-2423. Come in, Coast Guard." No one answered, so he tried again. Static was the only thing audible, so he radioed a third time. "Coast Guard, please respond. This is the captain of the Lucky Streak, Toby Middleton."

"Coast Guard here. How can we be of assistance, Lucky Streak?"

"Yeah, I'm calling from just south of the Rancocas Creek. You may not believe what I'm about to tell you, but I just came across a dead body face down in the reeds. Looks like it's been here for a while, if you know what I mean. It appears to be a man, although I can't be too sure. You should probably send somebody up here to fish him out."

"We're on the way, Lucky Streak. Are you able to stand by until we get there?" asked the Coast Guard dispatcher.

"No problem," replied Middleton. "But, please try to hurry. The tide is moving out and I'm in pretty shallow water as it is."

"We're on the way and should be there in no more than ten minutes." The Lucky Streak rested quietly on the now still water and waited for help to arrive.

❧ ❧ ❧ ❧

By the time the Coast Guard arrived, the New Jersey State Marine Police and the local police force had already arrived. The Coast Guard made the appropriate emergency calls to the local officials on its trek upriver from the Philadelphia main terminal area, which allowed the others to arrive first. Three boats rocked in the river as Toby Middleton talked about the discovery.

The Coast Guard captain overheard Middleton saying something as the Coast Guard boat inched toward the others. "Hey guys, as much as I find this stuff interesting and would love to stick around, the tide and a shallow channel back to my marina have different ideas."

"Okay, Mr. Middleton, you can get out of here now. Just make sure we have your address and telephone number before you leave in case we need to ask you any more questions," cautioned the Coast Guard captain.

"No problem," answered Toby Middleton as he anxiously motored off.

"Any ideas who it might be?" asked the state police officer, directing his question to the Coast Guard.

"Well, we have a report of a missing person from a few days ago," answered the Coast Guard captain. "Some guy who worked for one of the power plants in the Tacony section of Philly. My guess is that's who we're looking at right now." The local police had, by this time, moved a small dinghy over to the reeds and were pulling the body out of the water as the others talked. A wallet in the dead man's back pants pocket confirmed he was the reported missing person, Robert Stark.

CHAPTER 3

The new environmental compliance manager for the Power Systems, Inc. Tacony Electric Generating Plant, Bob Morrone, had been much too busy his first week to meet with the company's environmental attorney. So, he invited him in on Saturday morning with an eye toward capturing four hours or so of uninterrupted time to get his arms around the duties and responsibilities of his new position. Bob greeted his guest at the front door as he arrived, shortly after 8:00 AM.

"Good morning. Sorry to bring you in on a Saturday morning."

"Not a problem. I love nothing more than talking about environmental regulations to get the weekend started," answered the attorney jokingly.

"Can I get you some coffee?" offered Morrone.

"Sounds good to me," responded the attorney.

"How do you take it," asked Morrone.

"Cream and sugar, please," answered the attorney.

As Bob Morrone was preparing his guest's coffee, he heard the sound of several cars pulling up in the parking lot. He was surprised not only by the fact that it was odd for anyone to be in the office at this time on a weekend, but also by the fact that the tires screeched as the cars came to a stop. Morrone interrupted his chore to take a look out into the parking lot. His surprise was magnified tenfold, and soon turned to fear, when he saw the surrealistic scene of four Philadelphia police officers emerging from their cars with shotguns in hand. They were trailed by a number of men in business suits. Bob Morrone rushed to the office door, which had locked automatically after he had let his earlier guest in. He arrived at the door at the same moment as the police.

"What's wrong, officer?" asked Morrone, as he opened the door. One of the men in a business suit walking up behind the police answered.

"Sir, I'm with the Philadelphia Prosecutor's office. We have a search warrant and subpoena here for all of the company's environmental files. Open the door please so we can come in."

Bob Morrone attempted an answer, but was too frazzled to find any words. Looking totally lost, he glanced over to the attorney, realizing that he didn't even know the attorney's name yet. At that point, the attorney jumped up, his heart pounding as he recognized the man holding the search warrant, Charles Sands, the chief prosecutor for the City of Philadelphia.

The attorney meekly asked, "May I see the search warrant please?"

Charles Sands shoved the warrant at the attorney as he pushed his way in the door. The attorney read quickly as the uniformed police now walked through the door, the rubber of their boots making a heavy sound on the tile floor. Their already compelling size was compounded by the enormous shotguns clenched in their fists.

"Looks like they have the right to take the company's environmental files," the attorney said to Morrone, as the prosecutor and the police hurriedly looked around the office. Charles Sands, sensing the uncertainty and fear in the young attorney's voice, decided to set the tone for how the next few hours were going to work.

"Thank you, counselor, for that sharp and compelling advice. Now, what I need is any and all documents related to the company's environmental policies and practices. What I'm looking for are permits, approvals, reports, and so on."

Bob Morrone wasted no time showing the prosecutor the exact location of what he was seeking. "Can I ask, sir, why the Philly prosecutor is interested in our environmental stuff?"

"Sure. A few days ago, the Coast Guard pulled a stiff out of the Delaware. Turns out this guy handled all of the environmental compliance work for this power plant."

"You mean Bob . . . Bob Stark?" asked the attorney, obviously recognizing the name.

"That's right," answered Sands. "Had a cargo hook buried in his back. Just another day in the life for the Philly waterfront. Anyway, we've got absolutely no leads. Seems this guy led a pretty quiet life. He's not the kind you'd expect to see showing up in that condition. Anyway, our only starting point is that he worked here at this plant. So, we convinced the judge that we might find something by going through his work files." By this time, the attorney had located a video camera and was taping the event, following as much of the activity as possible, which Sands found fascinating. "Looks like we got us a regular Perry Mason here," Sands said caustically, leading the police officers to start laughing. The attorney, realizing he was way out of his league, made no response.

Morrone spoke up as a means of breaking the tension. "What do you think you will find in these files that will help you with a murder investigation?"

"I don't know," Sands answered. "But I've got to exhaust all possible avenues. This seems like the best place to start."

9

"Mr. Sands, I think you'll appreciate the fact that the documents you are looking for are my everyday working files."

"I understand," replied Sands. "What do you suggest?"

Bob Morrone understood from his years of experience with government attorneys that it is better to cooperate than to resist. The government could always justify its right to access private records, no matter what kind of resistance you applied, even when doing so was to protect confidential information. In Bob's experience, resistance only caused government retaliation, and, in his industry, that could spell disaster. It was on this background that Bob Morrone made what he thought was the best suggestion to diffuse the situation. "Well, what I'd like to do is make sure that you have a copy of whatever it is you want so you don't have to take the working files with you. Otherwise, I'm going to be totally lost come Monday morning."

"I'm glad to do that for you," responded Sands, "but we're going to be here all day. I don't know if there's enough tape in that video camera to cover that kind of effort." The police officers laughed again, which caused Bob Morrone to gesture to the attorney to put down the camera.

Bob Morrone, the company's attorney, and Charles Sands spent the better part of that Saturday morning identifying files that might shed light on Mr. Stark's untimely demise. Out of an overabundance of caution, Sands took more rather than less. Along the way, he asked Morrone and the company's attorney for a description or understanding of the company's files. The attorney turned out to be useful in that regard—more so than Morrone—because the attorney had been representing Power Systems, Inc. for a number of years.

Sands was admittedly out of his niche when it came to environmental laws and regulations. "Well, these files are all Greek to me," he said to Morrone and the company's environmental attorney. "I'm definitely going to need some expertise to make sense out of this stuff. Looks like a job for Sean Murphy."

The youngish attorney spoke up when he heard the name. "Do you mean District Attorney Murphy with the Department of Justice?"

"Yeah, you know him?" asked Sands.

"Sure. He is famous . . . or should I say infamous, around town," replied the attorney.

"You're tellin' me," said Sands. "I went to law school with Sean Murphy. That's how I know him. He's a character for sure. Played football for Penn State. I heard he was pretty good, although I never saw him play."

The attorney replied, "One of the senior partners of my firm has been involved in a litigation matter against Mr. Murphy for about three years now. As I understand it, Mr. Murphy brought suit against a group of companies discharging wastewater to the Delaware River. It goes to trial next week. I haven't been involved in the case, but two associates have been going nuts on it for the past six months or so. They describe Mr. Murphy as the toughest attorney they've ever come across. The funny thing is, Mr. Murphy treats these guys to drinks like once a month but never invites the senior partner on the case. It's almost as if Mr. Murphy knows the associates are doing all the grunt work and he is responsible for their pain. It drives the senior partner nuts that Mr. Murphy never invites him out for a drink."

"Sounds exactly like the Sean Murphy I know. I always consult him on environmental issues. He's got this stuff down pat. Some folks say Sean Murphy single handedly cleaned up the Delaware River, which, as you probably know, could not have been an easy task."

The attorney replied, "Yeah, I've heard that same story about Mr. Murphy. Well, if he wins this case next week, it will probably be the biggest verdict in his career and a not so good day for my firm."

CHAPTER 4

"I own the Delaware River!" shouted Sean Murphy as he burst through the door of his office. He had just won a significant case in the United States District Court for the Eastern District of Pennsylvania and was riding high on the heels of his victory.

"Twenty companies and their 350 dollar an hour lawyers brought to their knees once again by little, insignificant me." Sean loved to play the self-deprecating role of government attorney, even though in his heart and head he knew better. He had taken on a conglomerate of industries discharging wastewater containing a pollutant known as polychlorinated biphenyls, or PCBs, arguing they were violating the Federal Clean Water Act. The district court judge hearing the case agreed with Sean Murphy and ordered the companies collectively to pay $50 million to a fund to clean up PCB contaminated sediments on the river bottom and to start polishing their wastewater before discharging it to the Delaware River. Adding insult to injury, Sean Murphy convinced the judge to include in the final order an award that the defendant companies reimburse the Department of Justice for Sean's fees in prosecuting the case, a cool $500,000, give or take a few dollars.

The Department of Justice office in Philadelphia always lit up when Sean Murphy won a case. Seconds after Sean announced his win, secretaries and other attorneys began to gather in the reception area.

"This calls for a celebration. I think a round of drinks for all of us is more than adequately covered in the $50 million. How's about the Hard Rock Café?" Everyone in the office was more than receptive to Sean's invitation, considering it was the end of a long, hard week, and hoisting drinks with Sean Murphy on a Friday evening was sure to lead to something memorable.

❧ ❧ ❧ ❧

Sean Murphy was an impressive sight. He stood six feet, two inches tall and weighed in at about two hundred and fifty pounds. His fiery red hair, pulled tightly back from his forehead, was in distinct contrast to his light blue eyes. Although in good physical condition for a man in his mid forties, the heaviness of his chin and roundness of his face—Murphy family traits—revealed his age. His attempt to hide these traits with a closely cut, and well kept, beard was fruitless. Nonetheless, Sean had a distinctive attractiveness that would always warrant a glance by a passing lady.

The fact that Sean Murphy lifted free weights four times a week, bench-pressing his weight, certainly added to his gladiator image. On occasion, he was known to tear the sleeves of perfectly good shirts just by routinely flexing his upper arms during everyday activities. Never could he secure the top button of his shirts to wear a tie because his neck was just too thick. Most people who shook Sean Murphy's hand, even though a cordial event, could instantly feel his compelling size and strength. Sean's bellowing voice was a perfect match for his imposing body.

In stark contrast to his intimidating physical stature was Sean Murphy's boyish good nature, which, when combined with his physical attractiveness, created an irresistible charm. Born into a blue-collar Irish Catholic family of five boys, Sean also developed an unparalleled sense of faith, loyalty, and work ethic from his father and brothers. Unlike them, though, Sean, who was the youngest of the boys, was the only one in the Murphy family to go to college. His size, strength, and athletic ability landed him a football scholarship to Penn State University, where he elected to study environmental sciences. When he was not knocking the snot out of running backs from his linebacker position, Sean kept a keen eye on his studies and graduated in 1977 *Magna Cum Laude* with a Bachelor of Science degree. It was a proud day for the Murphy family.

His interest in natural resources and the environment started at a young age. Growing up during the 1960s in a Camden, New Jersey, neighborhood next to the Delaware River, Sean saw first hand the carnage caused by unfettered industrial pollution. Fish kills from depleted oxygen levels in the river were the rule rather than the exception. Sean was also witness to the river catching fire because of petroleum floating freely on the water's surface. Even at a fairly young age, Sean recognized the irony of a tugboat spraying fire suppressant on a blazing river.

Balanced against these disturbing images was an appreciation of nature's gifts of beauty and balance, which Sean learned from his mother. She would call the Murphy boys out onto the small front porch of their row house whenever a thunderstorm rolled in during hot August days. Mom Murphy recognized that this activity was not only a great way to cool down during the stuffy waning summer, but also a definitive means of building a sense of nature's awesome power in her sons. Regular trips to the South Jersey shore added to the lesson. Sean learned how incredibly complex and surprisingly delicate an ecosystem could be in a simple walk along the shoreline with his mother. Indeed, perhaps one of his fondest memories was seeing first hand the multitude species of life captured in one grasp of wet sand at low tide. Added to this experience was Sean's recognition and appreciation of the serenity that enveloped him with the sight of an empty beach, late in the day.

It was these experiences which led Sean at an early age to decide on pursuing a career in environmental protection. After graduating college, Sean went on to the University of Pennsylvania Law School and joined the ranks of Philadelphia lawyers in 1980, as a member of the United States Department of Justice, Environmental and Natural Resources Division. A group of highly skilled and aggressive trial attorneys, their particular responsibility was prosecuting violations of federal environmental laws. Although it was not the best paying job in town, Sean persevered and eventually became the lead attorney for the Environmental and Natural Resources Division in the Philadelphia regional office.

※ ※ ※ ※

Frustration, helplessness, and despair spawn creativity, innovation, and opportunity. This was Sean Murphy's involuntary life standard. He learned the left side of this equation growing up in a house with an alcoholic father. Pop Murphy's drinking habit was the stuff of legend. He was always a fairly heavy drinker, but the events that led to tales of greatness started shortly after Mrs. Murphy passed away, when Sean was only twelve. Once she died, and there was no longer any form of control in the house, Pop Murphy would regularly start the day by cracking open a beer at five thirty in the morning before going to work "just to take the edge off," as he would say. At least one six pack after work during the work week led to much heavier drinking on the weekends. While other kids were using Lincoln Logs to build their dream fortresses, Sean was crafting five foot high pyramids out of empty beer cans lying around the living room floor on Sunday morning. Although his father was never physically abusive, the complete absence of a formidable and reliable man in the family left Sean confused, frustrated, and empty. These circumstances became exceedingly difficult once Sean became a high school teenager trying to deal with all of the crap that goes on at that time of life. Sean's brothers just assumed that Sean would not make it through high school before either getting hooked on drugs or winding up shot dead in some alleyway. Perhaps it would not have been so bad on Sean if his mother had been around to buffer the effects of his father's drinking escapades. There were many nights, when Sean was young, that his despair would be so intense that he felt anger toward his dead mother for abandoning him in such a hopeless situation. For a young man with no understanding of the world, and in need of daily guidance, there was no other form of relief. Some nights, Sean would wait for his father to pass out from the drunkenness so he could release the tears. Despite the high praise of a good cry, though, it never seemed to help Sean. He knew that, in just a few short hours, his father would be up again for work and popping the top to a fresh can of beer.

The one good thing that Pop Murphy gave to Sean was a strong work ethic. Supporting a family of five hungry boys required no less than three jobs: one full-time and two part-time. From Monday through Friday, Pop Murphy worked as a general laborer for a manufacturing company in Camden. Once that day ended, he grabbed dinner and went to the local high school to mop floors, empty trash, and clean blackboards. Friday night until midnight and Saturday until about 3:00

PM were occupied by selling dried fish and oysters in the bars in South Philly. It was helping his father at the high school in the evenings, and in the South Philly bars on the weekends, that Sean learned the value of hard work. When he was about ten years old, Sean started to accompany Pop Murphy to the high school two nights a week where he would take responsibility for cleaning all of the blackboards. And, although Friday nights were much too rough in the South Philly bars for Sean, Pop Murphy would usually let Sean help out on Saturdays, after which Pop Murphy was always generous with a weekly financial stipend for Sean.

Once, while they were working together at the local high school, Sean noticed that Pop Murphy did not have his trademark sixteen ounce Schmidt's. "Taking a break from drinking dad?" asked Sean, the answer to which he never forgot. "I just want to get my son back," Pop Murphy replied. Sean was elated. He thought that his prayers for an end to the drinking had finally caught God's ear. A few days later, though, Sean and one of his older brothers were picking Pop Murphy up off of the family room floor where he had apparently tripped and fallen after too many beers. The incident confirmed something that Sean knew in his heart all along. Pop Murphy loved Sean and his other sons and wanted to do what was right, but life's bitter suffering was just too much for Pop Murphy to bear.

Lesser young men certainly would have crumbled. However, Sean, most likely by divine intervention, found a way through the chaos. Hard work in school led to the gratification of good grades and success on the football field. Perhaps more importantly, and without Sean really recognizing it, the steady hard work alleviated in part the frustration of an otherwise helpless situation.

The complex dynamic of Sean's young life led to his becoming an unstoppable force. Whenever Sean felt frustrated, he realized that the best thing to do was to work through it. It was no surprise then when Sean eventually was appointed to head a division of the Department of Justice. In that position, he was the first line of defense against polluters and the environmental harm they created, not to mention the principal advocate for the protection and preservation of the United States' natural resources.

When Sean Murphy reflected on his nearly fifty years, an activity which he religiously performed at least once a calendar year, what he saw was an abundance of suffering balanced against instances of incredible good fortune. The unfortunate circumstance of being born and raised in the poorest city in the United States was offset by his God-given athletic prowess, which protected Sean during his young life from the pitfalls of drugs and crime to which many of his childhood friends fell victim. The unfortunate circumstance of being essentially parentless from the time he was a young teenager was offset by the caring of his coaches and, when sober moments allowed, a struggling but loving father, which gave Sean the reassurance he needed to keep moving forward. The unfortunate circumstance of having to care for an alcoholic father was offset by the lessons of responsibility and hard work he learned in the process, which imbued him with an unparalleled work ethic that eventually led him to professional success. For these reasons, Sean Murphy learned to respect the bad times while at the same time celebrating the good times.

CHAPTER 5

Charles Sands waited a week or so to call Sean Murphy for guidance and advice on the Power Systems, Inc. files, during which time Sands had a chance to meet Robert Stark's family and scour his apartment for additional evidence. Sean, still riding high on his recent victory, suggested that Sands bring the files to the Department of Justice office so they could look at them together. Although they were not close by any means, probably because of their disparate personalities, Murphy and Sands stayed in touch on a professional level, given that they both chose the prosecution side of the legal fence and both held pretty high profile positions in Philadelphia.

"Sands!" shouted Sean as the prosecutor entered the office. "I haven't seen you in ages. You get uglier every year."

"Thanks, Sean. It's always such a pleasure seeing you," responded Sands.

"Did you hear about my big win? I'm just kickin' ass and takin' names, Sands."

"Yes, Sean. I heard about your win. It's all over the media. How could I miss it? Congratulations," said Sands, a bit begrudgingly.

"Well, you know, Sands, you get into the news more than I do. Hell, you're in the paper almost every day," Sean said, poking fun at Sands. "I'm not used to it. So, I have to make a big deal of it when I finally get some media attention. Anyway, tell me about this stiff," Sean asked Sands.

"We pulled him out of the Delaware a couple of weeks ago. His name is Robert Stark. He worked for this company by the name Power Systems, Inc., which has an electric power plant in the Tacony section of the city."

"I know it well, my man," interrupted Sean, without any apparent thought or reason.

"Turns out this guy was the environmental compliance manager for the company. We had no leads, other than the fact that whoever did him knew how to wield a cargo hook."

"God damn, man!" exclaimed Sean. "How do you deal with that shit? Makes my skin crawl."

"You get used to it, Sean," answered Sands. "Anyway, like I was saying, we had no leads so I started with the stiff's office. Most of what I came across was environmental 'mumbo jumbo.' You know, stuff that's got you written all over it."

"Let's see what we've got here," said Sean as he started to look through the box of files Sands had brought with him. "Okay, the first set of documents is a bunch of Discharge Monitoring Reports, issued in the name of Power Systems, Inc. These are documents that report how much pollution on a monthly basis Power Systems is discharging to the Delaware River," explained Sean. "It looks like Power Systems has a pretty large cooling system at its facility which both takes in water from the Delaware and then spits it back out," Sean continued as Sands followed him. "Let's see," pondered Sean as he looked more closely at the group of Discharge Monitoring Reports. "Looks like pretty normal stuff in the discharge for this kind of operation. First of all, the water leaving the power plant is a lot warmer than the stuff coming in fresh from the river. That's what you'd expect for a cooling tower. It is supposed to use the river water as a means of cooling down the equipment in the power plant, mainly the furnaces. So, the cooler water from the river takes on the heat from the power plant equipment as it moves through the cooling system. It pisses off a lot of people that power plants are allowed to do that. You know, raise the temperature of the receiving water. But that's why power plants are always located next to large bodies of water. They need vast amounts of relatively cool water to control the temperature of the operating system." Sean continued to finger through the pages of documents in the files. "Nothing out of the ordinary here," he commented generally. "The types and levels of pollutants in the discharge also seem pretty normal for this kind of facility. Nothing too toxic, which is what you would expect for a properly operating power plant."

"What do you mean 'for a properly operating power plant'?" Sands asked.

"Well, all that a power plant does is take a fossil fuel like coal, oil, or natural gas and burns it to produce heat. The heat is then used to convert water to steam, which spins a turbine. Burning fossil fuels is no different than when you and I breathe. What I mean is, if it's done properly, the normal byproduct from burning fossil fuels is carbon dioxide and water. So, you don't get a lot of the more toxic kinds of contaminants that you would see with say a heavy manufacturing activity. Principally carbon dioxide, steam, and some nitrogen and sulfur byproducts. That's about it. Every once in a while power plants will have problems with mercury emissions, which can be nasty stuff. It actually builds up in fish flesh by a process known as bio-accumulation." That comment went right over Sands' head.

"Sean, you lost me on that one. Bio, what?" asked Sands.

"Sorry about that. Bio-accumulation. Sometimes the fossil fuels that power plants burn will have naturally occurring mercury in them. The mercury is not altered during the burning process. It stays intact. As I mentioned, power plants discharge wastewater to the river. If the fossil fuel that a power plant is burning contains mercury, it will eventually find its way into the power plants wastewater. If the wastewater contains mercury, it will settle to the bottom of the river. Little fishies accidentally eat the mercury in the sediments as they are feeding. Bigger fish come along and eat the little fishies, which now have mercury in their system. So, the bigger fish now have mercury in them but at greater levels because they are eating a lot of the little fishies with the mercury in them. Fish don't excrete mercury. It's not like when you and I take too much Vitamin C. You know, we just piss it out."

"Sean," Sands interrupted. "Your analogies always have this tendency to make me sick to my stomach."

"Stop being such a pussy," Sean answered. "Anyway, as I was saying. The mercury stays in the fishies' system and continues to build up over time as they consume the smaller fishies that have been eating the mercury contaminated sediments in the river. That process is known as bio-accumulation. In other words, the mercury accumulates in the fish flesh through the normal biological cycle. That's why you sometimes see public warnings about mercury containing fish. Bio-accumulation. See, Sands, you learn something new every day with me."

"Fascinating," Sands replied mockingly. "Now, can you get back to the Power Systems stuff?"

"No problem. Well, although my mercury pollution lesson was instructive and I'm sure will be helpful to you one day, Sands . . . I don't think. . . ." Sean paused as he looked closely at the Discharge Monitoring Reports in the file. "I don't see any indication here that Power Systems has a mercury problem. Some traces of it, but nothing too serious. So, in addition to the heat component of the discharge, I see some chemical traces of carbon, nitrogen, and sulfur in the discharge, which is normal stuff." Sean paused again as he inspected the file contents closely. "Nothing unusual here, Sands." Sands simply nodded in acknowledgment as Sean shuffled anxiously through the file.

Charles Sands recognized that Sean Murphy was becoming a bit consumed by the contents of the file, so Sands felt it was time for a question. "Sean, you can actually get an idea of what is going on inside of this power plant by looking at what is in the wastewater discharge, is that right?"

Sean answered with his usual swiftness. "That's right. Most chemicals that are in any industrial process will leave some trace in the wastewater coming from that industrial activity. The reason for this is that most chemicals will dissolve to some extent in water. So, by doing chemical testing on wastewater, you can get an idea of what is going on more generally inside of an industrial facility."

"So, everything looks pretty normal at this power plant based on what you see in the wastewater discharge reports?" asked Sands.

"Well, for the most part that's right," replied Sean. "Except," Sean paused for a second to flip through a few more of the Discharge Monitoring Reports.

"Except what?" Sands asked.

"One thing I'm picking up on is a very low pH level in the Delaware River. It says here that, in addition to testing the wastewater, Power Systems, Inc. is required to test the quality of the Delaware River just downstream of where the power plant discharges."

Sands was now lost. "What do you mean by pH?" he asked.

"The pH of a surface water is a measure of its acidity or alkalinity," replied Sean. "The monthly Discharge Monitoring Reports in this file, which cover several years of activity, all indicate a very acidic quality in the river just. . . ." Sean took a moment to get his bearings. "Just south I guess that is. . . . Yes, just south of the power plant. I can't tell why, though, from the reports. Power Systems is apparently not required to test for a specific acid or group of acids under its discharge permit so nothing specific shows up on the Discharge Monitoring Reports. With that said, though, the pH of Power Systems' discharge seems fine, based on my quick review. It's the river itself that seems to have this pH problem."

Sean continued to leaf through the file. Following the group of Discharge Monitoring Reports, he found a letter:

Director, Division of Enforcement and Compliance Assistance
United States Environmental Protection Agency
Region 3
1700 Arch Street
Philadelphia, Pennsylvania 19102

Dear Director:
My name is Robert Stark. I am employed by Power Systems, Inc., which owns and operates a 300 megawatt power plant in Tacony. I serve as the company's environmental compliance manager. Certain information has come to my attention leading me to believe that the Tacony facility is oper - ating in violation of the Clean Air Act. It is my understanding that, under certain federal environmental laws, I may be entitled to a reward of some kind if I provide information to the United States Environmental Protection Agency about this situation.

Please let me know when you have some time so I can get together with you and provide you with the file.

Sincerely,
Robert Stark

Sean noticed the letter was neither signed nor dated, and there was no indication that it had been sent. After reading the letter, Sean said to Sands, "Look's like this guy was planning on blowing the whistle, huh?"

"Yeah," replied Sands. "We found that on the hard drive of his home computer. There was no record of it, as far as we can tell, in the Power Systems' company files. The document in front of you is a print out of the writing on his home computer. My guess is Stark never sent it. Or, never got a chance to send it."

"What. . . . Do you think this guy's death had something to do with his plan to blow the whistle on Power Systems, Inc.?"

"We're not sure," replied Sands, "but it is all we have so far. All of the interviews and research we have done since finding this guy tell us that he was well liked by his family, friends, and co-workers. He had no enemies, as far as we can tell. So, the only logical answer we have so far for his showing up in the Delaware with a hook in his back is that he was planning on blowing the whistle regarding some violation by Power Systems, Inc. of the Clean Air Act. That's where you come in. I have no idea how to relate those company environmental files to the Clean Air Act or any other law for that matter. You're the guy, Sean, who knows all about environmental laws and the Environmental Protection Agency. So, you should feel free to check into that issue as much or as little as you want. My job is to find out who put the hook in this guy's back and that's it. Whether Power Systems, Inc. is violating an environmental law won't come into the equation as far as I'm concerned."

"You mean to tell me, Sands, that you're not interested in what I do for a living?"

"That's not what I said, Sean," replied Sands. "In fact, I have a question."

"Fire away," answered Sean.

"If I came away with anything from this discussion today and what I learned over the past week or so is that our country's environmental protection system is based on a 'right to pollute,' is that correct?"

"That's exactly what I am saying," bounced back Sean. "Pretty much every industrial facility lining the Delaware River has a permit from either the federal or state government granting that industry the right to discharge contamination into the river. I know it sounds 'bass ackwards,' but that's the way it works. And, it does indeed work, at least to the extent of getting some heavily contaminated waters back to a reasonably healthy condition. You take the Delaware about thirty or forty years ago, floating dead fish in the summer were commonplace. But by regulating and progressively tightening down on the amount of crap industries can discharge into the river, we eventually achieved some measurable and noticeable benefits. Shad and other fish species have made an incredible recovery. North of the Rancocas Creek, where you found that body, you even see folks swimming again. Pretty remarkable, huh?" asked Sean.

"Yeah, I understand that the Delaware River is much different today than it was back when I was a kid," replied Sands. "But this idea of a 'right to pollute' is counterintuitive. I mean it still seems like an odd way to go about protecting the environment. Let me put it to you this way. In my line of business, if you want to correct a problem, you outlaw it altogether. If anyone disobeys, you put them in jail. It's a simple equation."

"That's why, Sands, you could never be an environmental attorney. You're too fucking stupid." Sands raised his middle finger for Sean Murphy's observation. Sean smiled and continued. "Environmental protection is characterized by complexity, and the laws I deal with demonstrate that point. You deal all the time with murder, right?"

"Yes."

"Tell me about the murder statute. How many pages?" Sean asked.

"Including the sentencing guidelines, I suppose twenty pages of law," replied Sands.

"See, there's my point. I don't have a single law I deal with that is less than.," Sean paused to consider his point for a second, "less than like one hundred pages.

20

And, in most cases, the law is just setting up the authority for the government to adopt regulations, which is where the real meat is put on the bones. The last time I checked, the EPA had over 200,000 pages of regulations. Almost every one of them is based on a complex scientific principle or theory. Now here is where it really gets interesting. Wherever science is involved, especially a relatively new one like environmental science, you have the opportunity for substantial legislative debate."

"What do you mean?" asked Sands. "Are you saying the laws on the books today may not be protecting the environment because they are based on bad science?"

"It's more than that. The fact that reasonable scientific minds disagree on how best to protect the environment leaves the legislative process open to substantial lobbying opportunity. The Republicans have one idea of how best to achieve environmental harmony while the Democrats usually have an entirely different idea, both of which have what appears to be legitimate scientific reasoning behind their positions. As if that isn't enough, you have the staunch environmental protection community out there, which likewise has its spectrum of thinkers. The preservationists and what are known as 'deep ecologists' want all human kind to die a horrible death and let the planet go back to the bugs and bunnies. The conservationists believe in a more reasoned approach, what they like to call 'sustainable development,' but always want more regulation than both the Democrats and Republicans combined. In the midst of all this mayhem, environmental laws usually come out with some hybrid designed to give a little bit of something to placate everyone, except of course for the 'deep ecologists' and preservationists. Natural selection will take care of them in its own good time."

"Well, I now appreciate the difficulty of your job, Sean," Sands replied sarcastically. "Back to this case. If anything in that box of files gives you a hint as to what may have happened to Robert Stark, give me a call. Other than that, the only reason for me to see your mug again is if you're interested in a beer."

"Me, a beer? Never. You know I never drink. When we were in law school and all you guys were out partying, I was studying and then doing my rosary."

"Yeah, okay. Right. And I love my wife." Sean laughed exceedingly hard at this comment because it was fairly well known that Charles Sands had married a woman from one of the most prominent Philadelphia families probably more because of his political aspirations than his feelings for her.

"Well, Sands, it was great seeing you. I'll give you a call if anything comes up. I think I'll get Steve Cooperhouse involved in this one."

"Where do I recognize that name?" asked Sands.

"He's with the EPA here in Philly. You've probably seen his name in the news media. He's a big mohoff over there, heads up the Office of Air and Radiation. He's been there for, hell, I guess going on thirty years now. He and I roomed together at Penn State. If he can't interpret this file, he'll find somebody who can. Is that okay with you? I mean, do you want me to keep this stuff confidential?"

"No, absolutely feel free to bring in anybody you want."

Charles Sands got up to leave. He and Sean shook hands and agreed to call one another to get together for a drink, each knowing that it wouldn't happen.

CHAPTER 6

April 22, 1970 arrived on a Wednesday. It brought to New York City bright blue skies, light breezes and temperatures in the sixties: perfect conditions to celebrate the first Earth Day. Mayor John V. Lindsey commemorated the day by closing traffic on Fifth Avenue, from Fourteenth Street to Central Park, which immediately prompted a non-stop Frisbee game. Over 100,000 people gathered at Union Square, where folksinger Odetta sang "We Shall Overcome," and a relatively unknown rock band covered the Beatles' anthem "Power to the People." Although Mayor Lindsey planned only a two hour festival, the "ecological Mardi Gras" lasted from noon until midnight.

Earth Day was forged in a time of social unrest and civil turbulence. However, unlike most of the political confrontations in the streets of New York since the mid-1960s, Fourteenth Street was uncharacteristically peaceful and calm on April 22, 1970. It was probably that tone which gave Earth Day its own personality.

In Washington D.C., the weather was equal to that in New York City, but President Nixon kept a regular schedule at the White House. The President was eager to profit from the modern ideal of environmentalism that Presidents Kennedy and Johnson had raised to the level of a political movement. Attempting to create and foster a national environmental consciousness, Nixon established in his cabinet the Environmental Quality Council just four months after his January, 1969 inauguration. Signing the National Environmental Policy Act on New Year's Day, 1970, President Nixon observed that, "the 1970s absolutely must be the years when America pays its debt to the past by reclaiming the purity of its air, its waters, and our living environment. It is literally now or never." Accordingly, when the first Earth Day was celebrated on April 22, 1970, President Nixon was hard at work on Reorganization Plan Number 3, which, among other things, delineated Nixon's desire to create the United States Environmental Protection Agency, the governmental agency that would be responsible for protecting the environment and all its natural resources. Hearings held in July, 1970 were unanimously in support of President Nixon's plan, with Senator Jacob Javitz of New York expressing the prevailing mood of Congress. He testified that the formation of the EPA was a "very strong and overdue effort to arrest and prevent the erosion of the priceless resources of all mankind and also to preserve the most priceless asset, the human being itself, who, in a singularly polluted atmosphere, may find it impossible to exist." It was on this unwavering support that the EPA welcomed its staff on December 4, 1970.

Although he did not join the EPA until several years after its creation, Steve Cooperhouse quickly moved through the rank and file workers on the strength of his scientific prowess and leadership skills. He had been Sean Murphy's roommate at Penn State University and, because they had become good friends there, Steve and Sean continued to room together in downtown Philadelphia after leaving Penn State. Unlike Sean, though, Steve Cooperhouse decided to stick with the science aspect of environmental protection, which the EPA welcomed by offering to pay for his graduate and post-graduate tuition at Drexel University. Whereas Sean needed only three years to obtain his law degree, Steve spent a good deal more time in school because he worked full-time and went to the night school program at Drexel. However, in 1985, he finally obtained a Ph.D. in environmental engineering, which placed him among the elite at the EPA Region III office. It wasn't long before Steve Cooperhouse was appointed to head the Office of Air and Radiation, which oversees all activities of the agency in Delaware, District of Columbia, Maryland, Pennsylvania, Virginia, and West Virginia.

ᴥ ᴥ ᴥ ᴥ

Sean Murphy stared out of the window of his thirty-fourth floor office as the sun rose over New Jersey, the light bouncing off of the relatively new blue paint on the Benjamin Franklin Bridge. Late summer always made for great sunrises, although they came at an exceedingly early hour. Sean could see the sun from his vantage point. He noticed that the western face of buildings in the city below him remained in shadow and darkness, even though the rest of the world was now bright. Sean watched as the deep red sun lifted into the sky, washing away the pastel blue and pink background, eventually becoming too bright for direct viewing. Times of reflection were not a luxury that Sean Murphy could afford, but he normally made a conscious effort to do so a few times a year, usually after the dust settled following a case. Sunrise was a perfect and compelling reason to stop, watch, and breathe deeply.

Traffic was light on the Benjamin Franklin Bridge, most of the vehicles were traveling from New Jersey into Philadelphia, some of them with their headlights still on. It reminded Sean of a habit he had developed when his mother and father were at war, which seemed to happen fairly often because of Pop Murphy's drinking. Sean would escape to the third floor "back bedroom," where he had a perfect view of the bridge. It was quiet room, far away from the shouting and screaming. Late afternoon in the autumn or spring was an especially good time for this escape because it was so quiet that Sean could hear the sound of the tractor trailer tires on the bridge making their way to the ports on the Philadelphia waterfront. Even to this day, watching the vehicles on the bridge had an uncanny ability to calm Sean, much as it did when he was a child.

Staring at the City of Camden waterfront, Sean noticed how it had changed from the time when he was a kid. What used to be the location of RCA's principal record producing factory for decades was now occupied by the New Jersey State Aquarium, a music amphitheater, several new marinas, a beautiful minor league baseball stadium, and The Victor Building, which was RCA's historic manufacturing building converted into luxury apartments. The builder, Carl Dranoff, was careful to preserve at the top of the historic structure the stained glass depiction of Nipper, RCA's trademark Jack Russell Terrier, with its ear cocked next to an early version of a phonograph.

Sean always enjoyed the great memories of his childhood in Camden that bubbled to the surface when he took the time to take in the waterfront from his office. His favorite one was hopping tractor trailers loaded with tomatoes on their way to Campbell Soup Company from South Jersey farms. Because of his speed, Sean was always the one selected to hop the trailer as it made its way north on Broadway. Once on board, Sean would throw the tomatoes to friends running alongside the trailer until they could no longer keep pace. Although the tomatoes that made their way to the Campbell Soup Company were not the best quality, not to mention that loading them on tractor trailers caused a lot of damage, Sean was usually lucky enough to come across a few that were still intact. Sean would pause while riding the back of the tractor trailer and bite into a ripe red one, the juice bursting out of its skin and flowing down Sean's face. His pleasure was usually interrupted by the driver realizing what was happening, at which time he would come to a screeching halt. Rarely did they give chase, though, so Sean didn't worry too much about it. He would jump from the back of the tractor trailer and run for a block or two just to make sure the driver wasn't following. By the end of the day, Sean and his friends would have collected a couple of Hefty bags of tomatoes, from which one friend's mom would make sauce. A couple of pounds of spaghetti was the foundation of one of the greatest feasts of late summer.

The recent case had kept Sean out of his office pretty much non-stop over the past year, except for quick stops between depositions and hearings. Turning away from the window, Sean realized that his office was almost foreign to him. Now that the case was over, and the victory was still sweet, he decided to take a few minutes to reacquaint himself with his surroundings. As he walked around the office, he noticed, most directly, the pictures of his wife and daughter. He missed them so much sometimes it actually hurt. As he put one of the pictures of them back down on the desk, he noticed the two miniature football helmets: one pure white with only a blue strip and the other purple with a gold stripe—Camden City High School Panthers. Sitting next to his computer screen was a funky looking bobble head Tiki guy. Sean never could remember the significance of it or how it got there. Under one of his lamps sat a small jar of sand on which was printed "Beachfront Property," a joke Sean's wife had played on him when she got

24

exhausted with his relentless wailing about being unable to afford a house at the Jersey Shore. In accordance with law office custom and practice, one wall contained impeccably finished and framed degrees and admissions to different courts, along with a few honors notations and academic awards. Another wall was dedicated to pictures of his football career, mainly actions shots from his time on the field as a Penn State Nittany Lion. The third and final wall held various memories: a water color rendition of Sloppy Joe's Saloon in Key West, one of Sean's favorite drinking spots; a horrifying painting of large pink flamingoes at the Philadelphia Zoo; two Nancy Noel angels; and, his most prized possession, a framed crayon note from his daughter telling Sean, "Have a good day with love and luck." Sean spent fifteen minutes or so floating around his office letting the memories flow over him, after which he decided to call Steve Cooperhouse.

Sean remembered that Steve Cooperhouse, much like himself, preferred to start work insanely early in the morning. Sean figured Steve's attention to the new case would be much better first thing. Steve's phone barely rang once before he popped it up to his ear. Steve Cooperhouse's theory on answering the telephone was that taking more than a single ring to pick up was pure slacking. But, as with many things, Steve took this theory too far. He was infamous for leaping dives across his office not to violate the telephone sloth rule, which was a statement more about Steve's compulsive personality than about the absolute and compelling need to answer a telephone before the second ring.

"Cooperhouse here."

"Din head. It's Murph," shot back Sean. "You're soooo professional when you answer the phone. 'Cooperhouse here,'" mimicked Sean in a sort of mousey voice. "I guess I'm the only one who knows better."

"I had an odd feeling," replied Steve, "on my drive in to the office this morning that something awful was going to happen. *Voila!*"

"Kiss my ass, douche bag!" Sean answered. "Say, listen, I have a new case here I would like your help on, assuming you have the time, of course."

"For you, Murph, I always have time. What's it about?" Steve asked.

"You remember I went to law school with Charles Sands, the chief prosecutor for the City of Philadelphia?" Sean started.

"Sure. Real pompous dude, right?"

"Yeah, he can be kind of a dick. I'll have to remind him of that next time I talk to him. He's in to that Ivy League status thing. Anyway, every once in a while he comes across an environmental issue in his cases and he usually sends it to me for a 'look-see.' He came up with a stiff in the Delaware a few weeks back. He mentioned something about this guy being the environmental compliance manager for the Power Systems electric plant in the Tacony section of the City."

"Yeah, I saw something in the Inquirer about that," Steve mentioned.

"Turns out," Sean continued, "this guy, I think his name was Stark, was planning to blow the whistle on the Power Systems Tacony plant regarding some kind of environmental problems. Sands gave me a box of files maintained by this Stark guy. It had a bunch of monthly Discharge Monitoring Reports and some related materials. I looked through the materials quickly while Sands was in my office. So,

I didn't get into too much detail. What I did review, though, seemed to be normal stuff for a power plant. No real glaring problems. However, there was also what looks to be a draft letter from Stark to the EPA where he mentions violations of the Clean Air Act. I can't tell whether it was ever sent. My guess is that it was not. Anyway, long story short is Sands has no interest in what Stark was planning to do in terms of whistle-blowing. Sands is just groping for leads on his murder investigation. He thought I might be interested in investigating the environmental portion of the case further, which is where you come in, Steve."

"Why," Steve asked, "does that name Power Systems ring a bell?"

"It should ring a bell," Sean answered. "It did to me when Sands mentioned the name. After Sands left my office, I decided to do a little Internet research on the company. I'll fax this stuff over to you, but let me refresh your memory a little bit here while I have you on the phone. It'll come back to you—it did me. Anyway, the company website says Power Systems, Inc. is headquartered in Manhattan. When it was formed in 1995, it was one of a small, but growing, group of companies known as independent power producers. Remember how deregulation of the electric generation industry, combined with federal legislation, gave economic incentives to small power producers engaging in market competition with the large publicly held utilities?"

"The name of the law was PURPA, which I think stood for the Public Utilities Rate Protection Act."

"Yep, that's it," said Sean. "That law spawned the creation of small electric generating facilities. If I recall correctly, that federal legislation forced public utilities to buy electricity from the small independent power producers, which gave them an immediate and guaranteed market. From the company's website information, it looks like Power Systems, Inc. originated in and around the time that a bunch of these independent power producers were starting up. Says here that the company was formed by an entrepreneurial group of former utility and petroleum executives—and I'm sure some money guys from Wall Street—with the sole purpose of breaking into the electric generating business by way of these small facilities."

"This does sound familiar, Sean. Anything else?" Steve asked.

"Yeah, I came across this *Philadelphia Inquirer* article in 1998." Sean began to read pieces of the article to Steve. "It took several years for Power Systems, Inc. to get its first facility up and running. But, it did so with great fanfare last week when a 300 megawatt plant located in the Tacony section of northeast Philadelphia started to "wheel" electricity into the Philadelphia Electric Company distribution grid. Bringing twenty new jobs to an otherwise economically depressed area, the Mayor of Philadelphia was more than glad to cut the ribbon on the entrance gate and welcome Power Systems, Inc. as a new taxpayer." Sean continued to piece together information for Steve. "The article then says the Tacony plant went up in record time. 'With the assistance of the state Governor's office and the Philadelphia City Mayor's office, Power Systems received all environmental and building approvals in less than a year: a timetable unheard of by any other business attempting to start a new venture in Pennsylvania.' So on and so forth."

"Okay," Steve interrupted. "This is ringing a bell. It was the 300 megawatt reference that caught my attention. That is one big fucking plant. I remember wondering how it could be built without any air pollution permit. I have a bunch of power plants under my jurisdiction and the most important approval they need is from my office. It can take a couple of years just to get the EPA air pollution emissions permit for an electric power plant because of all the atmospheric air modeling that needs to be done. Not only that, but we take a careful look at the kind of air pollution control technology that the power plant is going to use. So, I do recall being concerned that this plant somehow slipped through a regulatory crack. But, there was more to it, if I recall correctly."

"You're right," Sean answered. "There was more to it. There is another article I found dated 2000, which is when the Power Systems plant started operating. Let me fax it over to you. It has to do with global warming. It's all Greek to me. After you've read it, give me a call back."

❦ ❦ ❦ ❦

TACONY ELECTRIC GENERATOR IS ENVIRONMENTALLY FRIENDLY
by Dan Stiles
Inquirer staff writer

Like many of the large publicly-held electric utility companies, Power Systems, Inc. is engaged in a three-way battle with government regulators, alternative energy providers and the environmental protection community over the realities of global warming and its causes. Because the electric generating industry is a relatively large man-made contributor of carbon dioxide, one of several "greenhouse gases" alleged to be contributing to global warming, it is the first and foremost target of attention in the effort to reduce emissions of carbon dioxide. Although a newcomer to the electric generating field, Power Systems, Inc. immediately stepped into the middle of the on-going and pre-existing debate the minute it "flipped the switch" on its Tacony plant.

Power Systems, Inc. has the upper hand, though, in this battle. Its founders have designed and patented an innovative coal burning technology known as Integrated Gasification Combined Cycle (IGCC), which reportedly creates almost zero air emissions. The only downside to this technology is that it is a much more expensive way to generate electricity, principally because of the extravagant cost to build an IGCC furnace. The question begged is why that is the case. The answer has to do with the way the underlying environmental law works.

The Federal Clean Air Act was enacted in 1970 with the goal of protecting public health and the environment against damaging air emissions from what are known as area, stationary, and mobile sources. The law is designed to meet this goal by establishing and enforcing National Ambient

Air Quality Standards for a number of pollutants. So, for example, the Federal Clean Air Act regulates, and attempts to control, such things as stratospheric ozone depletion, low-level breathable ozone, lead, sulfur and nitrogen oxides, visibility, and acid rain. Interestingly enough, the Federal Clean Air Act never established a definitive program to stem the tide of global warming caused as a result of the emission of greenhouse gases into the atmosphere. Whether the result of gallant and effective lobbying by the fossil fuels industry or the result of legitimate concerns about the potential disaster that would be wrought on the United States economy, the Federal Clean Air Act left for another day the decision of whether global warming is a reality and, if so, what action is appropriate and necessary to reduce or eliminate altogether those pollutants responsible for the condition. Consequently, one of the principal greenhouse gas contributors, carbon dioxide, is completely unregulated under the Federal Clean Air Act. That is, industrial activities, such as manufacturing facilities and power plants, not to mention all forms of vehicles from the simple personal automobile to diesel powered trains and airplanes, can emit as much carbon dioxide as they wish and not be in violation of the Federal Clean Air Act.

Debate has raged for decades now whether global warming is in fact occurring. One side of the table argues that the measurable steady increase in ambient temperature over the past one hundred years or so is merely a remnant of better measuring techniques and data collection. This side opines, among other things, that the current increase in temperature is no more than a blip on the weather radar screen that has occurred a number of times during the earth's four billion year life span. The other side of the table argues that the increase in ambient temperature is indeed a reality and will continue to trend upward unless immediate corrective action is taken. Compounding the complexity of this debate is the question whether this measurable increase in ambient temperature is due to human—otherwise known as "anthropogenic"—activity or is the result of naturally occurring gases. Anthropogenic sources include such things as solid waste landfills, concentrated animal feeding operations, and the manufacturing sector, including the electrical generating industry. An acknowledged natural source of greenhouse gas is volcanic activity. The end result of this debate is that the Federal Clean Air Act left untouched the issue of whether and how to regulate sources of greenhouse gases responsible for global warm-ing, which means that electric generating plants can emit as much carbon dioxide as they want.

However, just like automobile manufacturers are capable of building internal combustion engines capable of achieving 150 miles per gallon of gasoline, so can engineers build power plants capable of "zero emis-sions." It's just a question of how much it will cost to do so and what the market will bear. In other words, what are you and I willing to pay for cleaner electricity? My view is that we should heed the warnings of the *scientists regarding global warming and reach deeper into our pockets to pay for this cleaner electricity.*

❧ ❧ ❧ ❧

Sean Murphy's phone rang a few minutes later. He knew it was Steve calling back. "So, is your memory refreshed?" Sean asked.

"Sure is. It was the 'zero emissions' thing that I was recalling before you faxed me that article. I remember being very skeptical about it. I was frustrated by the fact that we never got a chance to regulate that plant."

"Steve," answered Sean, "you're exactly why government regulators have such a bad reputation. Always wanting to stick your nose where it doesn't belong. What about this global warming stuff in the article? Do you have a good handle on that issue? I haven't followed it so much because it doesn't involve the need for legal enforcement. All I know is what I read in the newspaper, which obviously makes for a dangerous situation."

"I sure do know about it," Steve answered. "The Regional Administrator of the EPA appointed me to a task force to investigate the reality of the situation and to make recommendations about how to deal with it from the standpoint of an EPA regulatory program."

"Great, I need a short course on the topic. It looks like this Power Systems situation is somehow wrapped up in the global warming issue, although I haven't figured out how yet."

"A short course?" Steve replied. "That may not be possible. It's a fairly involved issue, both scientifically and legally, not to mention the fact that it is also a political hot potato."

"I'm game. Fire away," instructed Sean.

"Easier said then done, Mr. Murphy. First things first. Where would you like to begin?"

"At the very beginning, please, Steve. Assume that I am a complete dullard on the topic, which I know is an easy thing to do with me on any subject, right?" Sean said jokingly.

Steve responded in like form. "Sean Murphy a dullard! Impossible. You've got to be one of the smartest people I've ever known, Sean."

"Kiss my ass. Just give me the lesson."

"All right. Well, you want me to start at the beginning. Let's see. That would have to be around 1988 when the United Nations Environment Program and the World Meteorological Organization formed the U.N. Intergovernmental Panel on Climate Change. That year, the U.N. General Assembly adopted a resolution, proposed by Malta, on the protection of the global climate for present and future generations. Then, in 1990, the Intergovernmental Panel on Climate Change called for a global treaty on the subject. After about fifteen months of talks, a consensus of the U.N. members formed what is known as the Framework Convention on Climate Change. If I recall correctly, this Convention was opened for signature at the 1992 Earth Summit in Rio de Janeiro, Brazil, and it took effect March 21, 1994."

29

"That history is wonderful information, but what does it mean?" asked Sean.

"Be patient. I'm getting there. The reason for the history lesson is to give you a flavor for the fact that global warming is an issue that has been around for a fairly long time, even though it is only recently gaining international public attention. In fact, suspicions about the possibility of global warming by meteorological scientists go back a decade or so earlier than these U.N. activities, but it is the U.N.'s attention to the subject that brought about greater awareness of the problem."

Sean picked up on Steve's last comment. "So you agree that global warming is a problem? I thought there was some dispute whether global warming was in fact occurring."

"There was for many years a considerable debate going on," replied Steve.

"It seems," Sean said, "that a good deal of money is being spent to control greenhouse gas emissions, even though there is a debate as to whether global warming is a phenomenon in fact."

"That's correct."

"I'm a bit surprised to see that dynamic," said Sean. "Usually, companies subject to any kind of regulation—be it environmental, OSHA or the like—will react to control a problem only where there is compelling evidence that a problem indeed exists. My experience has been that you're not going to get a regulated industry taking precautionary measures, especially where it may be quite expensive to do so, when there is a substantial question as to whether a problem exists in the first place."

"I agree with everything you're saying," Steve confirmed. "It is a dynamic that I've never experienced before, too, at least not in the field of environmental protection. Usually, the party paying the money for environmental safeguards wants some convincing evidence that a problem exists before opening up the company coffers to pay for the remedy."

"So why is this situation of global warming different?" asked Sean. "Why are companies willing to make the effort to control greenhouse gases when scientist are still doubting the issue?"

"My sense," Steve said, "is that scientists do not dispute the fact that if we continue to allow greenhouse gases to build up in the atmosphere unabated, at some point global warming will indeed occur. It is inevitable, according to scientists in the field."

"So explain to me," Sean pressed, "how we know global warming is occurring. The winters here in the Northeast seem to be a lot colder than they were when I was younger, and they seem to last longer. If someone asked me out of the blue whether the world was getting warmer or colder, I would say colder, just based on what I've experienced over the past twenty years or so."

"You hit the nail on the head," Steve acknowledged. "It's not an easy point to make scientifically. You are talking about what you and I experience locally, but global warming is a much broader issue and one that is very difficult to measure. In fact, scientists predict that for those of us in the Northeast, we will experience just the opposite of a warming trend."

"What's that you say?" Sean asked, obviously surprised to hear that comment.

"What I said is that you and I will probably experience colder than average temperatures in the Northeastern United States. Global warming, according to scientists who have developed complex computer models on the subject, is not going to be warming at all locations on the planet. Some places will be warmer, some cooler, and some will remain the same. Instead, what scientists are predicting is a change in the annual average temperature. As best as can be determined, the annual average temperature of the earth's atmosphere measured from equator to poles is about 57.01 degrees Fahrenheit. The average over land is 47.4 degrees, and the average over the oceans is 60.9 degrees."

"Who came up with those numbers?" asked Sean.

"The National Climate Data Center," replied Steve. "But the Center admits that the world's climate monitoring network has many deficiencies. So the way they come up with these averages is by using mathematical algorithms to fill in data gaps. Combined with these measuring difficulties is the fact that we have good and accurate measurements of temperatures going back only 125 years. That is not a very long time, when it comes to the question of earth's temperature trends. Another problem with the 125 years of temperature records is that many of the data points have to be discarded, especially where that data comes from urbanized areas."

"Why throw out potentially good data?" Sean asked.

"Well, take Philly for example. Meteorological scientists generally agree that urbanization contaminates data, at least when it comes to the question of whether the earth's atmospheric temperature is increasing. Urban areas have a tendency to retain heat more so than natural areas and thus give unrealistically high temperature readings. In Philly, the ambient air temperature readings are taken at the Philadelphia International Airport. What worse place to take temperature readings? It's nothing but hot asphalt. Because of this bias or prejudice in the measuring location, scientists on both sides of the debate about global warming agree that this data should be junked. That means even less reliable data over a fairly short period of time. At the end of the day, no one is certain of the world's temperature. It's not like sticking a thermometer into the Thanksgiving Day turkey, if you know what I mean," explained Steve.

"Yeah, I see what you're saying," Sean acknowledged. "And, I'll bet changing temperatures over the course of any given year probably add to the problem of getting an accurate measurement."

"Now you're getting the picture," Steve confirmed. "One thing that is happening, though, is that scientists agree on the fact that a more accurate measuring system is needed to come up with some baseline upon which to develop an accurate opinion, for once and for all, that the earth's temperature is rising. All of these issues have resulted in the topic of global warming being the subject of scientific debate now going on twenty years."

"So how much warming is occurring?" Sean asked, getting frustrated with Steve's circular explanation. "Does anyone have a gut call on that question?"

Steve continued, "The National Climate Data Center says that 2003 was the second warmest in the past 125 years, behind 1998. The Center reports that 2003 was 1.01 degrees Fahrenheit above the long-term average and 1998 was 1.13 degrees above that same average."

"One degree!" Sean exclaimed. "Is that it? In 125 years? How is that a warming trend?"

"Now you're getting back into the science war. I can't go there. The one degree means about as much to me as it does you," Steve admitted. "I agree that it's meaningless, but groups of scientist seem to agree that even a few degrees increase in the average global temperature could mean catastrophe."

"Like what? Armageddon type shit?" Sean demanded.

"Well, that depends on your definition of Armageddon. To me, it means the end of the world, so the stuff I've heard about global warming is not quite that bad. More intense storms on a more frequent basis are probably the most significant consensus. Melting of polar ice caps resulting in rising ocean levels. A combination of these things could lead to reduction of agricultural yields. Poor countries would probably suffer the most. For countries like ours, we have the financial means to compensate. We would just have to pay more for our food, move our homes away from the current shoreline, and so on. Some scientists say we are already seeing the effects of global warming in the form of an increased incidence of drought, floods, and extreme weather events that many regions are experiencing."

"Do you agree with that assessment?" inquired Sean.

"I have no reason either to agree with it or dispute it."

"Wimp! C'mon, take a position," prompted Sean, showing his legal training and a need to advocate a position.

"I'm being honest," Steve replied. "I haven't seen any data to support those conclusions. So, I can't go one way or another. One of the things that has come to light recently is a concept of dramatic or abrupt change. In other words, these Armageddon effects, to use your phrase, may happen much quicker than the average Joe expects."

"I'm not following," Sean admitted. "What do you mean?"

"Well, ecological changes, especially those on the global scale, are usually measured in geologic time frames. Not years or decades, but eons. You know, 'eras' or 'ages,' like the Ice Age. Most people expect the same kind of timing rule to apply to global warming. What I mean is that any resulting ecological impact will occur slowly and progressively."

"But that's not the case?" Sean asked suspiciously.

"If I was losing you before, Sean, pay close attention now. You're going to love this one. Scientists have demonstrated fairly conclusively now that our atmosphere and oceanic systems are integrally linked. So, this University of California professor comes up with the hypothesis that global warming can impact ocean circulation and nudge this atmosphere/ocean system towards a threshold that could produce an abrupt climatic change."

"I assume the professor has some evidence to support this hypothesis," added Sean.

"I'm getting to it. The journal *Nature* presented an article in early 2004 discussing a paper authored by this professor regarding the deep-ocean circulation system of the North Atlantic and how it is linked to the salt levels in the Caribbean Sea. The paper apparently says that this system controls ice-age cycles of cold and warm periods in the Northern Hemisphere. The paper goes on to conclude that melting the glacial ice of Greenland, which is an accepted outcome of global warming, could quickly and profoundly chance the salinity of the ocean. Here's where it gets interesting." Sean could hear the excitement in Steve's voice. "This professor from the University of California starts looking at the fossils of tiny sea creatures in the Caribbean known as 'foraminifera.' He tracks the fossils back 120,000 years and can show that, as the Northern Hemisphere warmed, the salt level in the Caribbean dropped."

"So," interrupted Sean, not sharing in Steve's excitement, "what the hell does all that crap mean?"

"Well, according to this professor, melting of the polar ice caps could introduce a substantial amount of freshwater into the North Atlantic Ocean thereby reducing its salinity. If that happens, according to this research, history shows that rapid climate changes could follow."

"So," Sean interrupted again, "do you agree with this conclusion?"

"Couldn't say. I'm just the messenger. That's somebody else's conclusion."

"Yeah! Yeah! Yeah! You're still a wimp," Sean repeated. "Well, it seems to me that a good starting point is to have better data, even if it is to make sure that the efforts being taken now to reduce greenhouse gas emissions are effective."

"That is in fact occurring," Steve advised reassuringly. "The United States, for example, invoked two million dollars to set up a brand new observation network in undeveloped areas. Other countries are following our lead. At some point down the road, this measuring system will result in unimpeachable data about the earth's average temperature and whether we are in a warming trend."

"So," Sean inquired, "I assume all of this data is what led to the U.N. forming that Framework Convention on Climate Change that you mentioned earlier?"

"That's correct," confirmed Steve. "On the tenth anniversary of the Convention, the U.N. Secretary General made a pitch to all countries to carry out more intensive efforts to limit greenhouse gases emissions and he targeted developed countries generally and the United States in particular."

"Why developed countries?" Sean inquired.

"My guess is that the U.N. Secretary General wanted to wrap up full support for The Kyoto Protocol, which lost momentum when the United States withdrew its support in the spring of 2001."

"I'm glad you mentioned The Kyoto Protocol," Sean interrupted. "I've seen it mentioned in that newspaper article I faxed to you and I see it popping up fairly regularly since that movie. . . . What the hell was that movie?"

The Day After Tomorrow, answered Steve. "In its simplest terms, The Kyoto Protocol is an international treaty which imposes on its participants mandatory reductions in greenhouse gas emissions by 2012. The Secretary General of the U.N. is of the opinion that effective global action will happen only through participation by all countries in The Kyoto Protocol."

"I assume," Sean interjected, "that it's the mandatory part of the protocol that the U.S. doesn't like."

"Yeah, that's right. The current administration, anyway, does not want to be bound to mandatory reductions. Obviously, that position could change if and when a different administration gets into the White House."

"All right, then, Steve. This has been a great lesson. Thanks a bunch. I'll get that Power Systems file over to you. No rush on it. Give me a call or stop by when you're ready to discuss it."

CHAPTER 7

Steve Cooperhouse first met Sean Murphy at freshman orientation at Penn State University. As fate, and good fortune, would have it, they were roommates. Whenever talking about how they met, Steve would invariably turn to the story about being in his dorm room, setting up his stuff, and hearing a bellowing voice in the hallway: "Who's on MY floor!" Sean Murphy walked into their room, and Steve was initially shocked by Sean's massive size. Steve had never seen anyone quite that large before in his life, and probably not since, except for perhaps some professional athletes. Sean walked into the dorm room in a tattered flannel shirt from which he had completely removed the sleeves. Steve would later learn that this sleevelessness was a matter of necessity for Sean Murphy: his biceps were too large to fit into any off the rack shirt. Sean dropped the baggage he was carrying, which Steve happened to notice were plastic trash bags filled with clothes and shoes, walked up to Steve and shook his hand, causing Steve's whole body to shake. "Sean Murphy, damn glad to meet ya!" Sean's hand wrapped around Steve's like a glove. Before Steve could return the greeting, Sean Murphy was already walking back out of the dorm room. Steve noticed how Sean ducked slightly as he passed through the doorway so as not to hit his head. Then, Steve heard Sean bellow again "I said, who's on MY floor?" Steve could hear Sean's voice as he walked into each room on their dormitory floor and introduced himself to everyone.

At the time, Steve Cooperhouse had no idea Sean Murphy was a football player, although Steve thought he recognized Sean's name when he introduced himself. Steve's father, who was an avid high school sports fan, reminded Steve that Sean Murphy was one the most heavily recruited linebackers in the history of Southern New Jersey. Although Steve was never much of an athlete or sports fan, he recalled his father mentioning Sean Murphy's name when Steve accepted his invitation to Penn State. "I'm impressed," Steve's father said, "with how this young man, Sean Murphy, passed up invitations to a number of prominent football programs in favor of being loyal to a more local school." Although Penn State's football program was obviously no slouch situation, which even a non-athlete like Steve was well aware.

It wasn't long before Sean and Steve were good friends, despite their diametrically opposed personalities. Sean was the quintessential strong and outgoing type. Steve, by contrast, was classically introverted and quiet. Their close friendship was probably the result of the fact that Sean and Steve shared a lot in common because they both grew up in South Jersey. However, saying that they grew up in the same area does an injustice to the fact that Sean and Steve came from entirely different backgrounds. Indeed, their up-bringing was as polarized as their personalities.

Steve Cooperhouse was raised in the affluent suburb of Haddonfield Borough, which is populated mainly by professionals who work, and make big salaries, in Philadelphia. Steve's father was a staff physician at University of Pennsylvania Hospital and provided for his family very well, including a six bedroom Victorian home on the town's main street. Despite their financial ability, Steve and his younger sister never attended private schools, like most of the other Haddonfield children of professional parents. Instead, they attended public schools all the way through high school, which in Haddonfield was a great financial deal, considering it was a National Blue Ribbon School of Excellence. Steve did well academically and was quite capable of admission into the Ivy League. He opted instead for Penn State, wanting to stay with a public education institution, but at the same time wanting to get some reasonable distance from his family. It's not that Steve's up-bringing was stifling in any way—although Steve was always making the comment that the suburbs are nothing but "a massive wave of self-validating boobism"—it's just that Steve saw getting away from his family and home, even if for a few years, as a way of testing himself.

Sean Murphy, conversely, grew up in one of the toughest and poorest cities in the country, which, interestingly, is only a fifteen minute car ride from Steve's hometown. The city of Camden, like many other urban areas throughout the Northeast, was besieged by race riots during the 1960s, when Sean was just a young boy. It was a combination of these riots, and other unfortunate business circumstances, that changed Camden from a thriving manufacturing center following World War II to a burnt out economic mess by the time Sean graduated from Camden High School in 1974. Like Steve Cooperhouse, Sean graduated with honors, which allowed him to go to just about any collegiate football program he desired. Unlike Steve, though, Sean did not have the benefit of financial comfort when he was growing up. Sean's father, although a hard working man, spent a number of years working with Sean's grandfather in what was colloquially known as the New York Shipyard in the south section of Camden. Their home was just a few blocks away. Once the shipyard closed, which happened while Sean's father was still fairly young and well before Sean was born, Pop Murphy became a laborer at a local manufacturing plant. It did not pay well, but it was enough to keep the Murphy family afloat, which is precisely how they lived: day to day.

Sean and Steve realized, soon after meeting at Penn State, that perhaps their most significant common bond was spending summers at the Jersey shore. However, Steve's experiences were full summers at the family's exquisite vacation home in the exclusive community of Avalon, while Sean's were for a week (or two in a good year) at the less expensive resort areas. Nonetheless, their mutual love of the beach was undoubtedly the start of a strong bond. During the summers while they were in college, Sean spent the entire season with Steve and his family at their summer home. It was during these summers together—when the pressures of school and Sean's football life would be lifted, and they were free to talk about what most people would classify as lesser important things—that Steve learned exactly the kind of tough neighborhood Sean came from, and the equally tough young life he had.

Sean Murphy, Steve would soon learn, was a master storyteller. Sean's stories about his childhood fascinated Steve. It was Sean's uncanny ability to recount, in a colorfully vivid fashion, the events and milestones of his younger years that led Steve to conclude that the poor live much more interesting and fun lives than do the wealthy. The lesser financially fortunate are forced by their circumstances to create their fun while the wealthy wait for it to happen to them. Steve's favorite story was the one about "Blackie," a neighborhood dog that was reportedly nastier than even Stephen King's "Cujo." As Sean would start out the story, he and his friends had a daily tradition on their walk home from grammar school.

⊰ ⊰ ⊱ ⊱

"The first thing we did on the way home was hit the playground in the schoolyard. There would be a mad rush to the monkey bars. A few of us were courageous enough to hang upside down from the top rung. The way you did it was to grab the top rung and then swing your legs up between your chest and the top rung. Then you would put your legs up over the top run and bend at the knees. After that, you would let go of the top rung with your hands and your head would swing upside down. It was a great rush. One time, this friend of mine, Dave, who definitely had a few screws loose, slipped and he bounced off of each layer of monkey bars on his way to the ground. There was about a six foot drop from the last layer of bars and the asphalt pavement below. He slammed his back onto the pavement. I remember he was knocked out for a few seconds. Then, he jumped up and climbed back up the monkey bars as if nothing had happened.

"After the monkey bars, we would make a visit to the swings, where we would take turns doing back flips. Timing was important on this drill. First, you had to push the swing to nearly a thirty or forty degree angle from the ground; second, you had to thrust your head back and bring your knees up to kiss your chin. At least one of us would botch the method and either skin our knees on the asphalt or slam down on our butts with the back of our head to follow. Despite the agony, though, it was the ecstasy of the rare 'stick' that kept us returning for more punishment.

"Our last and final stop was the steps of the First Methodist Church. From this vantage point, we could safely tease the Maloncy's dog Blackie. It was a special talent, I'm proud to say. Blackie was a horrible terror on three and a half legs, one of them riddled with arthritis from years of chasing after the neighborhood kids. The way this process worked was we collectively yelled out his name until we got his attention. Then, one of us, normally selected by a process of drawing straws, would stand at the edge of the Maloney's property just out of Blackie's view. When he appeared at the front gate, we would signal the target, who would then have to run from the Maloney's gate, across 6th Street, and then to the church steps. Every so often Blackie wouldn't be interested, but most of the time he would chase, which was a true measure of one's speed and agility. The end of the process was for the unlucky target to run past the side of the church steps where the rest of us, on a landing about six feet above the street level and safely out of "Blackie's" range, would reach down and grab the sprinting meal as he ran by.

"John Strong was always the most athletic one in our group and by far the fastest. He welcomed the small straw. Indeed, John would even agree to accept somebody else's unfortunate draw in exchange for a bit of change. Unlike the rest of us, who would always make a direct run for the church steps, John would often times give Blackie a workout by a running zigzag. Those who risk greatly, though, must suffer at one point or another, including John Strong. One afternoon, John was having his way with Blackie. But, I noticed that John seemed to be a bit sluggish. As John finally approached the church steps, I could see Blackie closing the gap quickly. Although we were all screaming for John to run faster, Blackie caught up to John just as we were grabbing hold of his arms. When we lifted John up, Blackie came too, his teeth clenched on John's ass. We yelled and screamed at Blackie to let go, hoping that the higher we lifted John off the ground, Blackie would get scared and let go. From what I recall it took about ten to fifteen seconds of John's screaming and Blackie's thrashing before it was all over.

"The best part of the story is this, though. John Strong's mother was a nurse and a particularly 'hands on' one at that. We carried John to his house and yelled for Mrs. Strong's help. The next moment is one I'll never forget. She lifted John up on the dining room table and told John 'I need to get a good look at the bite mark.' She proceeded to yank down his pants, underwear included, in front of all his friends and some neighbors. The color of red in John's face, as he reached down to cover his 'package,' rivaled the sunset over the back bay on a hot August day. Although it must have been utterly horrible for John, it was all that I could do to keep myself from laughing. John got three stitches in his ass and we never bothered Blackie again."

❧ ❧ ❧ ❧

Sean Murphy was admittedly rough around the edges, and it was a trait that came through glaringly in his storytelling, but even Steve's parents admitted that Sean Murphy was good for Steve. While they were at Penn State, Sean forced Steve to join Sean on his social forays, which was a life Steve was unaccustomed to and something he never would have done on his own. It didn't take long for Steve to overcome his extreme shyness, a character trait that was the equivalent of mixing oil and water when around Sean Murphy. It was liberating for Steve. Defeating his fear of social situations, with the aid of Sean Murphy, also gave Steve insight to an infinite ability to crush all of his fears, including chief among them a paralyzing lack of confidence that had haunted Steve since he was quite young.

By a similar measure, Steve was good for Sean Murphy. He was completely devoid of self-control, especially when they first met at Penn State. In fact, Sean was a bona fide lunatic at that time. Steve, however, had plenty enough self-control for the both of them, and then some. Steve was convinced that Sean's lack of control was a direct result of his years of playing football. Based on what Steve could surmise from Sean's description of coaching, pounded into Sean's head every day for the better part of his young life was a standard of hostility and violence that is like nothing most people ever experience. It was no wonder, then, that all Sean knew how to do was kick ass and take names. Chief among Steve's memories in that regard was one Saturday during the off-season he made Sean join in on some studying at the library. The concept of doing anything on a Saturday other than partying was completely foreign to Sean Murphy. By about 9:00 PM, Steve thought Sean was going to put a gun to his head. "Steve Cooperhouse, what the fuck are you doin' to me? I should be having nasty sex with about six different women right now . . . and all at the same time, man." Sean Murphy definitely operated at a much higher energy level than the average, normal human being. After a few years, though, and Steve and his parents working on Sean over the summers, Sean achieved a modest level of balance, which thankfully carried through to the present.

The closer you get to someone the greater the likelihood you will get to meet their demons. Unfortunately, Sean Murphy had more than his fair share of them. Although Steve could never pinpoint exactly when it happened, probably because it was an evolution rather than an epiphany, what became clear to Steve was that Sean Murphy had a difficult childhood. While Sean told stories about his father's drinking escapades jokingly, at some point Steve realized that this was a method designed to shield his emotional pain. The lyrics of Sean's life rolled out like a painful Puccini opera. His mother died before he even reached his teens. His father, although a proud and good man, couldn't escape the traps of alcohol. His brothers, all whom were older than Sean, left home while Sean was just starting high school, leaving him to take care of his drunken father alone.

When Steve reflected on these tidbits of information about Sean's life, he was pretty sure the turning point in his understanding Sean Murphy's demons was one night in their junior year. Sean had played a horrible game and both the coaches and the press were pointing the finger at him for the loss to what was nationally recognized as a weaker team. Sean started drinking early that day: Jack Daniels right out of the bottle. Steve had maybe a sip for each ten slugs just to show some solidarity and support, all the time realizing that he couldn't risk being incapacitated because of Sean's likely condition later on. Around midnight, Sean started telling Steve stories, but they were not like the happy ones he had become accustomed to. He mentioned the awkward feeling of staring at his "mother's cold dead body in a coffin when I was just twelve," followed by some horrific experiences with his father, like having to direct him to the toilet when he was too drunk to find it and started pissing all over the living room floor. One Saturday night, according to Sean, he fell asleep on the sofa in the family room and was rudely awakened by the feeling of water splashing on his face. Pop Murphy had once again forgotten where the bathroom was located and was relieving himself on Sean's head. *It's a miracle Sean didn't just up and leave,* Steve often thought to himself after hearing these stories. The most horrifying story, though, and the one that seemed to haunt Sean most deeply, was Sean finding a group of kids laughing at and taunting his father when he was passed out in front of a bar. According to Sean, his father had obviously fallen down the steps of the bar and didn't bother to get up. "I beat one of the kids so badly that he wound up in a hospital for three days," and Sean wound up in a juvenile detention facility. "He didn't have much size to him, so it was easy for me to beat on him. I pounded his face until it was raw and he couldn't stand up any longer. I remember hearing his head hit the blacktop with a thud. That wasn't enough for me, though. I kept punching him in the face when he was down on the ground until he looked like pulp." The regret and sorrow in Sean's voice for never having apologized to the kid was unequivocal and had a lasting impact on Steve.

Layered on top of this kind of troubling experience, which seemingly was a rather common thing for Sean as far as Steve could tell, was Sean's oldest brother, Tom, who was a violent drunk. Although Sean's father, when sober, and his other brothers successfully kept Tom out of the house, one night in Sean's sophomore year of high school, his luck ran out. Sean described to Steve waking up out of a sound sleep one night to a sensation of pain in his head, only to realize that Tom was on top of Sean punching him in the face. Thankfully, Sean's screams roused Pop Murphy out of a drunken sleep, distracting Tom and giving Sean a chance to escape from the house and run all the way to the police station. The fractured jaw Sean received from that pounding almost cost him his football career.

Sean exorcised his demons with wildness, and no one, not even Steve, could blame him. The best Steve could do was show Sean a different way to live, which the summers at the Jersey Shore seemed to do. Sean's troubles didn't end, though, after he left home for college. In his senior year at Penn State, he suffered a serious knee injury that, in an instant, ended not only his college football career but also any prospect of a professional offer, which most experts before the injury predicted would be a certain opportunity for Sean. Midway through his senior year, Sean decided to take the Law School Admissions Test, much to many people's surprise, and eventually accepted an offer from University of Pennsylvania Law School.

Sean and Steve continued to room together when they relocated from State College to Philadelphia for their professional degrees. As both Sean and Steve were known to say, the stories could fill a book. However, none of them came close to, or prepared Sean Murphy and Steve Cooperhouse for, what they were about to experience together.

CHAPTER 8

Since his telephone discussion with Sean Murphy, Steve Cooperhouse solicited the help of one of EPA's crackerjack investigators, Tom Roth, both to review the file that Murphy sent over to Steve and to drum up any other information that might be out there on Power Systems, Inc.

The first thing Tom Roth did when he received the assignment from Steve was to review EPA's internal files on Power Systems, Inc., which included most or all of the materials the city prosecutor had acquired under the subpoena, and then some. The central files room at the EPA offices in Philadelphia was in a cavernous basement of the agency's headquarters at 1700 Arch Street. Dimly lit and heavy with the musty smell of damp old paper, the small area set aside for reviewing files was cramped with a few small desks, each usually containing scattered papers and trash left by the last occupant. Tom had called ahead to make sure the file clerk would leave the Power Systems, Inc. files out on one of the desks, so Tom would not have to waste half a day searching for them. Tom was surprised to find that the file clerk had actually done what Tom asked. The files, about a foot deep, sat on a desktop across the room.

No one else was present when Tom entered, considering it was well after normal business hours. Tom poked around to see if he could find some additional lights to complement the few that were on. After a minute or two, Tom realized that one of the desks had a built-in light, which he turned on. While it didn't add much to illuminate the dreary room, it at least provided Tom with some light under which to peruse the Power Systems, Inc. files. He grabbed them from the desk where the were resting and began moving them to the desk with the light. As he transferred the files, he heard the sound of footsteps some distance down the hallway from which Tom had entered the file review area. It was the only hallway leading in or out.

Tom called out for the file clerk, "Maurice, is that you?" No answer followed. Tom heard another noise, like a file falling to the floor. "Hello, Maurice. You down here?" Nothing. Tom walked a short distance down the hallway and called out a third time, "Maurice, you're starting to piss me off!" Tom waited a second or two and, hearing nothing but dead quiet, turned back toward the file review area.

Tom sat down and pulled out the first file in front on him. Opening it, he came across a report introduced in Congress by Power Systems advancing voluntary reductions in carbon dioxide, one part of which was an explanation of a new technological approach to power generation called Integrated Gasification Combined Cycle (IGCC), touted by Power Systems, Inc. as being essentially "zero emissions." According to this report, Power Systems, Inc. designed and patented a new type of coal combustion chamber or furnace that heated the coal, without actually burning it, in such a way that the coal was transformed into hydrogen, which was then burned to power an electric generating turbine. The report went on to explain that Power Systems, Inc. also had a patented recycling system that reused the exhaust gases such that the only waste product was a material identified as "coke" and some other trace elements. The report finally mentioned how the process allowed carbon dioxide to be separated, a point which was lost on Tom as he read the report. He turned to a specification sheet for the combustion chamber that was attached to the report.

Let's see how this thing works, Tom pondered. *It looks like a traditional coal burning system. Creates high-energy steam to spin a turbine, which then produces electricity. Let's see what's different here. Okay, a typical power plant has a tremendous volume of exhaust gases. This system has no stack for exhaust gases. How the hell do they do that? Where do the exhaust gases go?* Tom paused a moment to see what was attached to the specification sheet. He noticed a diagram. *Okay, this is helpful. No stack. Instead, the exhaust gases are piped back to the combustion chamber. Okay, here we go. This next part looks a bit different than what I'm used to seeing with power plants. The temperature in the combustion chamber is much higher than other plants. And, then, let's see here, there appears to be a secondary and then a tertiary combustion zone, where a little more fresh air is injected. Got it! All they are really doing here is burning the gases at much higher temperatures until all that is left is pure carbon.*

It had been many years since Tom Roth's college chemistry courses. But, he remembered the basics of combustion. A certain amount of oxygen was required to burn a known amount of fossil fuel. Energy, in the form of heat, was the byproduct.

Okay, now I see, Tom thought. *By restricting the amount of fresh air coming in, the combustion process is forced to use the remaining oxygen in the recycled exhaust gases until nothing is left. That's why they have to burn at such high temperatures.*

Those in the business of electricity production know that the economics are a function of the temperature at which the steam is produced to turn the turbine. The greater the temperature in the combustion chamber, the higher the cost of the electricity coming out of the tail end. Tom Roth had some general familiarity with the concept. He realized at once that the cost to burn the coal in the Power

42

Systems, Inc. plant must be astronomically high compared with that of traditional power plants. That was the trade-off. In order to create the benefit of a "zero emissions" power plant, Power Systems, Inc. had to both pay an greater amount of money to build the coal gasification furnace in the first place and, in the second, increase the cost of production so as to superheat the facility and be able to combust completely the exhaust gases so that the only thing left at the end of the day was a solid material. Because carbon dioxide emissions were unregulated, traditional power plants could burn fossil fuel at lower temperatures and simply allow the carbon dioxide to go up the stack and back out into the outdoor air. This was not the case with Power Systems Inc.'s patented IGCC system. It actually used the oxygen bound up in the carbon dioxide compound to support the combustion process.

Kind of like Nos, Tom pondered. He better understood what Power Systems was doing when he compared it to his experience with drag racing. One of the ways to increase a drag car's speed was to use nitrous oxide as a combustion supplement. The three oxygen atoms in the nitrous oxide compound boosted the combustion reaction when compared with trying to squeeze oxygen out of everyday air, where there was only about twenty percent to begin with. So, then, what Power Systems was doing was splitting the carbon dioxide compound back down into carbon and oxygen and then using that oxygen to support the combustion reaction.

Tom Roth continued to ponder the technology. *So, all that this patented "zero emission" system does is use very high temperature combustion to use up all of the oxygen in air. Even the carbon dioxide, which has two oxygen atoms, is bro - ken down and the oxygen used up in the burning process. Let's see, that would mean that what's left over from this process is pretty much pure carbon.*

Tom looked back at the specification sheet to see what it said about waste by-products from the technology, and sure enough, there at the bottom of the page was a reference to "coke" or pure carbon as an end product.

The only other thing that caught Tom's eye on the diagram and specification sheet was a reference to a nitrogen stripping stage before air was injected into the combustion chamber. This made perfect sense to Tom because he knew ambient air was nearly seventy percent nitrogen which would wreak havoc on this patented closed combustion system if it were allowed to enter into the process. If nitrogen interacted with moisture in the IGCC system, it could create nitric acid, which would eat away at the system components.

Following the diagram and specification sheet in the file was a report from the Power Systems, Inc. engineering staff indicating that the Tacony plant was encountering problems during the first year of operations. The power plant kept shutting down, almost as if the flame in the initial burning chamber was being drowned out with a fire extinguisher. The purpose of the report was to identify the reasons behind, and propose a remedy for, these unexpected and unexplainable interruptions in operations. Reading the engineering report, Tom noticed that the power plant would operate fine for a handful of days and then, for no apparent reason, the flame in the burning chamber would slowly fade out. After a few days, during which Power Systems, Inc. would clean out the burning chamber, the flame would re-engage with no apparent difficulty, only to be followed by another shut down a few days later. Interestingly, the report was left undone because after one of the shutdown events, and while the engineering investigation was still underway, the facility restarted and continued operating without incident.

Tom pulled the next file. It was labeled "Emission Reduction Credits." He flipped through a few pages and, realizing he had no idea what the documents pertained to, Tom closed the file and decided it would be a topic he and Steve could study together at a later time.

He then came across the company's Discharge Monitoring Reports. Tom thought to himself, *Power Systems must have some kind of wastewater going into the Delaware River.* At that point, Tom remembered his discussion with Steve where he shared with Tom a comment made by Sean Murphy that the pH of the Delaware River just downstream of where Power Systems, Inc. discharged its wastewater was very low. He looked at the most recent Discharge Monitoring Report: Sure enough, the Discharge Monitoring Report showed that the pH of the Delaware at the test location was four. *Why so acidic?* Tom thought. He noticed that the sample point upstream of Power Systems, Inc. discharge pipe had a fairly normal pH. Tom then looked back at a number of earlier Discharge Monitoring Reports to see if this low pH was a one-time "blip," remembering other cases where laboratories had made mistakes. If this reading was indeed a "blip," Tom would expect to see a normal pH on most or all of the earlier Discharge Monitoring Reports. Much to his surprise, every monthly report going back over the past two years demonstrated this same low pH. The data was intriguing from the standpoint that the pH of Power Systems, Inc.'s wastewater was a perfect seven, indicating that it had neither acidic nor basic qualities. *How then,* pondered Tom, *is the pH of the river water just downstream of the discharge pipe so low?*

Tom pushed his way a little further into the file. Power Systems, Inc.'s wastewater discharge permit clearly stated that Power Systems, Inc. could not discharge anything to the Delaware River that would bring the pH any lower than six. It was no surprise to Tom, then, to see an EPA investigative report into the cause of this low pH just downstream of Power Systems, Inc.'s wastewater discharge pipe. The report documented a detailed level of research by the EPA of Power Systems, Inc.'s operations, including most importantly its waste products and the quality of the company's wastewater. This research confirmed Power Systems, Inc.'s own data, already reported to the EPA in the monthly Discharge Monitoring Reports, that the company's wastewater was neutral. The investigative report concluded that the EPA could not issue a fine or penalty against Power Systems, Inc. because there was no proof that could withstand a legal challenge that Power Systems, Inc. was the source of the low pH.

Tom looked at his watch: 9:43 PM. He had been at it for over three hours now. His brain could not assimilate any more technical data. He decided that his next step would be to visit the Power Systems, Inc. facility, based principally on the well-worn theory that "a picture is worth a thousand words."

He tidily arranged the files on the desk top, save for the Emission Reduction Credit one, which Tom decided to stealth away in his briefcase for his later meeting with Steve Cooperhouse. As he moved through the hallway, he realized that the floors above him were probably empty, given the late hour. He wondered whether the elevator back up to the ground level would still be working. If not, he would have to search out a stairwell.

As Tom walked, he felt the proximity of the old files lining the hallway, looming over him like tall, dark oak trees. Every couple of steps brought about a glance left and right as Tom peered into the aisles running perpendicular to the hallway. Midway between the file review area and the elevator, Tom looked back over his shoulder, feeling a little anxious now about the alone-ness he was experiencing. Turning back, Tom quickened his pace and slammed into the body of another person who had just stepped into the hallway from one of the aisles. Tom's heart jumped out of his chest, and he let out a girlish little scream as he dropped his briefcase.

"Tom Roth!" shouted the figure, shadowed by the lack of light in the hallway. "What the hell are you doing here at this time of night?" Tom, gaining his composure and recognizing the figure for the first time, shouted back.

"Maurice! You scared the fucking shit out of me, asshole!"

"Nice to see you too, Tom. I saw you packing up and knew you were goin' to be spooked walking out of here. Thought I would add a little fuel to the fire," joked Maurice.

"You always had a weird sense of humor," said Tom as he fixed himself and picked up his briefcase.

"C'mon, I'll walk you out, you big pussy," offered Maurice. "We have to use the stairs. The elevators have been shut down for the night."

As they walked, Tom asked Maurice if he had been in the file room earlier in that evening. Maurice responded that his running into Tom was the first time that day Maurice had been to that part of the building.

CHAPTER 9

About a week had gone by since Steve Cooperhouse gave the Power Systems, Inc. assignment to Tom Roth. He figured it was about time to check in with Steve. Tom stopped by unannounced to Steve Cooperhouse's office on Friday evening. As usual, the door to his office was wide open. Steve was sitting at his desk behind a pile of papers, feet up, and telephone connected to his ear. Tom popped his head through the open door and looked at Steve for a second to see if he would acknowledge Tom's presence. Steve immediately responded with a wave for Tom to come in and sit down on the leather couch at the far end of Steve's office.

From the sound of Steve's voice, he was in the process of wrapping up the telephone call. Tom glanced around Steve's office. Not much had changed since the last time Tom had visited. Tom always found it interesting how Steve kept each one of his case files in individual piles stored randomly around the office, most of them on the floor, though. With a full wall of windows facing west, Steve's office provided a spectacular view of the Schuylkill River, with its popular boat house behind the Philadelphia Art Museum and, at this particular time of day, the sun as it was setting behind the city. Tom recognized the eight man crew team from his alma mater, Saint Joseph's University, taking their skulls out of the Schuylkill River after their daily workout.

Like most professional offices, Steve had his mandatory wall of degrees and honorariums, one of which Tom recognized as a joke, and a pretty good one at that. Tom could never pass up the opportunity to read the inscription on the piece of metal laid against a background of oak: "To Steve Cooperhouse, the 'Sultan of Sludge,' awarded in recognition of his singular contribution to the quality of the City of Philadelphia's waste." Below it was a picture of Steve as he was being pulled out of a tank full of sludge at the city's Southeast Regional Wastewater Treatment Plant where Steve had accidentally fallen in during an EPA inspection. Steve's office had a unique academic quality to it because of his being an adjunct professor at Drexel

University. From floor to ceiling along two walls were bookshelves loaded with textbooks and course instructional materials. Over the years, Steve had built a private library, albeit small and focused, based on what references he needed to perform his daily work activities and to teach his class a couple of days a week. Writing was a passion for Steve. So, when he could squeeze a little time out of his hectic schedule, Steve published articles in professional trade journals and even contributed chapters to a handful of books on environmental regulation. His bookshelves, of course, contained a special section dedicated to his publishing efforts, which frankly was impressive. All in all, it was a scholarly and plain office, most of the available surface area covered with files and documents.

"Give me until close of business on Monday to get back to you on that one, okay?" asked Steve to the party on the other end of the telephone. "Great, I'll talk to you then," he said as he hung up the telephone and glanced over to Tom.

"Hey, Steve, how's it goin'? You look pretty busy," chimed Tom.

"It's been one of those days, Tom," replied Steve. "Did we have a meeting scheduled for this afternoon? I don't show anything here on my calendar."

"No," answered Tom. "I just thought you might want to hear about my research on Power Systems so far. You remember, the company Sean Murphy at the Department of Justice asked you to take a look at?"

"Oh yeah, that's right. I had pretty much forgotten about that in the rush of all the other stuff I have goin' on," said Steve, as he stared at the stack of papers sitting on his desk. "Yeah, now's as good a time as any to catch up. Let's sit over by the coffee table so we have some room to work." Steve and Tom moved across to room to a sofa sitting next to a relatively neat and clean table, save for the circular stains from countless cups of coffee.

"So what have you come up with?" asked Steve.

"Well, first of all, I noticed the abnormal pH that I think Sean Murphy mentioned to you," Tom replied.

"That's right, I seem to recall Murph saying something about that when he called me. What do you think is the cause?" Steve inquired of Tom.

"That's the problem," answered Tom. "The records clearly show an extraordinarily low pH just downstream of the discharge pipe, but upstream of the pipe is neutral and the actual wastewater coming out of the plant is likewise close to neutral. It's the damndest thing."

Steve probed a bit further. "Can this be a naturally occurring condition in the river? Some sort of low pH pool because of something at that location? You know what I mean. Remember that time when all of those tree-huggers were blaming the acid conditions in the streams in the Northeast on power plants? The environmentalists were claiming that the sulfur and nitrogen emissions from the power plants was mixing with moisture in the atmosphere and forming an 'acid rain.' It turned out, though, after we did a bunch of studies, that the low pH in a good number of those streams was due to natural conditions in the underlying soil and rock."

Tom thought for a few seconds and said, "Well, I guess anything is possible. In the twenty years I have been doing this work I have learned never to say never, but I've got to tell you that this situation would be like none other that I have seen when it comes to pH conditions in water. Most times when you have an upstream sample that is neutral and a nearby downstream sample that has a pH as low as four in some cases, there has to be some significant acid discharge in between. Especially with a water body the size of the Delaware. It will neutralize a low pH very quickly just because of the volume of water that passes that one point with the tide keeping the water almost constantly in motion. That's why I lean toward saying that this is not a naturally occurring condition."

"So, what do you think?" asked Steve.

"There's gotta' be some source of acid in that area," replied Tom.

"So, what's the next step?" Steve continued.

"I wanna take a first hand look at this place. Give it a good once over if you know what I mean," he said.

"Thought so," Steve replied. "You always were a 'hands on' guy, Tom."

"Do I need a search warrant or some kind of permission before I go?" Tom asked.

Steve advised, "I don't think so. We have a couple of laws that say where a business has one or more environmental permits, like Power Systems, we have the authority to inspect the site at any time. I'll check with legal on that, but if you don't hear from me by the end of the day on Monday, assume it's a go."

"All right. I just hate to show up unannounced," Tom said. "I always wind up in an argument with a security guard or plant manager. Especially after 9/11!"

"I don't have a problem with you calling Power Systems to let them know that you are coming. In fact, they are probably expecting it. Sean Murphy told me that the city prosecutor and some police showed up at the place a few Saturdays ago and executed on a search warrant for some of the files we have been reviewing. I'm sure the folks at Power Systems, Inc. are just waiting for follow-up inspection."

Tom indicated his agreement with Steve's analysis by giving him a quick nod. "Okay, I'll give them a call and get out there early next week."

"Anything else of interest in that musty file room?" asked Steve.

"Aside from Maurice playing his usual games? He popped out of the files and scared the fucking shit out of me," Steve laughed with a tone of recognition about Maurice the file clerk. "I came across some documents I did not recognize in something called. . . ." Tom paused for a second as he shuffled through his briefcase. "Let's see, what did I do with that file. Okay, here it is. Emission Reduction Credits. Does that ring a bell with you?"

"Oh, sure. I'm familiar with the concept," Steve answered.

"Please 'esplain,'" Tom asked jokingly.

"The Clean Air Act," Steve started, "establishes what is known as a 'cap-and-trade' program. It's like a big bubble over, say, an entire city or even over a certain industry sector in that city. Only a certain amount of pollution is allowed within the bubble. So, put the bubble over, say, all of the electric power plants in Philly. The bubble creates a 'cap.' In other words, the amount of pollution in that bubble can never go over a set numerical value. Some power plants will be able to meet the limit on pollution and some won't. Those that can't will buy emissions credits from those that can. This is the 'trade' part of the equation."

Tom looked puzzled. His specialty was digging into the fine details of the science and engineering of environmental controls, not the bigger picture policy and regulatory issues. Steve realized he was losing Tom mentally. "Okay, let's say the total amount of a particular air pollutant that is allowed by EPA to come from power plants within a geographical region is ten. Some power plants, especially those that were built long before the standard was established, won't be able to meet the limit of ten. Those older power plants may be spitting out, let's say, twenty. What that means is these older power plants will automatically be in violation of the Clean Air Act when that standard of ten becomes effective." Steve looked to Tom for some sign of understanding.

"I'm with you so far," Tom acknowledged with some hesitation.

"Okay, the trick then is to figure out how to keep these power plants up and running when they can't meet the standard. Well, the answer is pretty simple. You allow power plants to trade emissions so at the end of the day the total amount of the regulated air pollutant within that bubble does not exceed the standard set by the EPA for that area. The interesting thing about this 'cap-and-trade' program is that it can be much broader than just small areas. The air over our country is not subject to any geographical boundaries. That is to say, the air over California on one day will be over us a few days later. So, if you're looking at the quality of the air nationwide, or over large regions of the country, which is how the Clean Air Act works, then you can do a system of give and take that is geographically expansive."

Tom chimed in recognizing now the significance of the "zero emission" concept of the Power Systems, Inc. Tacony plant. "So, using your example of ten as the standard for some pollutant, a newer power plant may spit out much less than that standard and not be in violation of the Clean Air Act, right?"

"That's right," answered Steve.

"So, if a newer power plant is emitting, say, only one unit of that particular pollutant," Tom started his analysis only to be interrupted by Steve.

"Then, that newer plant can sell those nine credits of pollution under a 'cap-and-trade' program to the older power plant that is in violation. The nine units that this particular hypothetical power plant has available are called Emission Reduction Credits or ERCs. The EPA has a process of documenting them known as 'banking.' We see it a lot where a particular company is shutting down a process or plant. When a source of air pollutants is taken out of service, the company that owns that pollutant source is allowed to 'bank' the emissions that were coming from that source and get a credit for them. Within certain guidelines, these banked emission credits can be used in the future in any number of ways. For example, the company that shut down the source of pollutants can use the emissions credits to build a new plant somewhere else. Or, the credits can be sold to some other party that may be constructing a new plant."

Tom asked, "And that older power plant that we were talking about before will no longer be in violation once it buys enough of a balance from other power plants?"

"That's right," answered Steve. "Remember, the idea under a 'cap-and-trade' system is to make sure that the air quality within the overall bubble does not exceed the standard, not necessarily one or a few particular sources of the pollutant within the bubble."

Tom was starting to catch onto this concept pretty rapidly and could now see its internal weakness. "But, that means certain localized geographical areas within the bubble will not meet the standard because that older facility that is technically in violation of the standard at that particular location."

"No argument there," quipped Steve. "That's one of the typical challenges of environmental groups to the 'cap-and-trade' concept, but by definition, that is what a bubble system of air pollution control means. Some sources will be out of compliance and others not, but the overall air within the bubble should theoretically balance out to meet the standard."

Tom started to flip through the Power Systems, Inc. Emission Reduction Credit file. "Well, this is all starting to make sense now. Power Systems has what is called a 'zero emissions' power plant at the Tacony site," Steve interrupted again.

"Yeah, Sean Murphy sent me some newspaper articles which mentioned that concept of 'zero emissions.' I still don't understand the technology. Do you?" asked Steve.

"Sean Murphy," Tom commented. "That reminds me. How's he doing, Steve?"

"Well, he had a tough couple of years there, Tom, but he seems to be coming through it okay. 'Time heals all wounds' and all that kind of stuff, you know?"

⊰ ⊰ ⊱ ⊱

The casket was painfully small. Colored silver, about three feet long, and poised on an equally small frame, it sat quietly on a hill just above a narrow dirt road near the back of the graveyard. She was alone now, standing beside the grave, with the sun setting behind her on a bitterly cold late February evening. The sun's rays played an oddly peculiar trick of highlighting only her and the casket against a gradually darkening scene. Her head hung lifelessly, chin touching her chest, and her stark pale face stared down emotionlessly at the casket. Her daughter was gone, a mere four short years after she was born.

Sean Murphy and Steve Cooperhouse had been sitting for some time in the limousine, the engine idling to allow the heater to keep the inside of the car warm. Sean finally got out to talk to his wife. Steve rolled down the window ever so slightly, trying not to be obvious about wanting to hear what Sean was going to say to her. Sean approached her slowly, hesitating a few times along the way, trying to figure out what to say.

Mary Murphy didn't move. She had no energy, the events of the past week having drained her completely. Sean, too, was tired. They all were. It had been just about six months earlier that little Kristin was diagnosed with a rare form of childhood cancer. Even though they had been expecting this day for some time, Kristin's death drained a piece of life and happiness from them all. Now that it was over, and they had said their goodbyes to little Kristin, exhaustion set in.

Sean and Mary had been trying for many years to have a baby only to be denied by recurring news of failed attempts, including two miscarriages. Friends and family prayed for years that God would bless Sean and Mary with a child; they were such gentle, loving and caring people who, everyone agreed, would make wonderful parents. When the news arrived that Mary was pregnant with Kristin, they celebrated for months, and just as everyone expected, Sean and Mary were indeed the best dad and mom.

Little Kristin was a complete joy, full of love, happiness, and affection. She was such a bright light in all their lives. No one could recall a moment in her short life when Kristin failed to have a smile lighting up her face, especially Steve Cooperhouse, who, being Sean's closest and dearest friend, got to spend a good deal of time with Kristin. Sean would bring Kristin with him everywhere. She had unending energy, which typically meant that Sean would spend the better part of his time chasing after Kristin to make sure she didn't do any damage. It actually became a joke with his family and friends. It never troubled Sean that he didn't have a moment to relax or talk to his friends when he was with Kristin. She had become Sean's life.

Mary, too, lived for Kristin. There is a special bond between a mother and daughter that transcends description. In the case of Mary and Kristin, that bond was especially strong. Mary would always say that Kristin was a gift from God. Mary read into her earlier miscarriages some divine rule that she wasn't entitled to be a mother. Not so surprisingly, then, Mary began to hate God. Sean tried to explain to her many times that she should not be angry with God but instead should continue trying to have a child: keep the faith and all that stuff. It was this history that set the stage for the special bond between Mary and Kristin. One day Mary pulled Steve aside when Kristin was about two years old and told him that God truly does work in mysterious ways, after which she gave Steve the most incredible smile. Steve realized then that what she meant was a bond so strong would not have been forged with any child who came without difficulty and frustration.

Now, Kristin was gone, and Mary's spirit left with Kristin. As Steve watched Mary through the window of the limousine, he could tell she was lost and hopeless. Steve listened as Sean walked over to Mary, standing aside Kristin's grave.

"C'mon hon, it's getting late and cold. You're gonna' freeze to death standing out here."

Mary stood for a moment, before looking in Sean's direction. When she finally lifted her head, and Steve could see her face more clearly, he realized the full extent of her pain and anguish. It looked as though she had aged twenty years in the past few days.

She tried to answer Sean several times, but the tightness in her throat and the approaching tears prevented her from answering. Each time she let her head drift back down to an empty stare. Sean moved closer to her each time she tried to answer. Sean prompted her again, "Mary, it's time to let Kristin go. She is in God's hands now. She is safe and warm. You know as well as I do that God will take good care of Kristin and she will always be happy. In fact, I know Kristin is smiling at God right now."

Mary looked up again from Kristin's grave and finally found the words. "I'm just waiting for the sun to set so I can tuck her in to bed one last time."

Two years later, Sean came home from work to find Mary in a puddle of blood on the family room floor, her wrists slit wide open. She was pronounced dead on arrival at the hospital.

❧ ❧ ❧ ❧

"Hell, Steve," said Tom Roth, "I don't know how Sean recovered from that loss. No amount of time could get me through what Sean had to deal with. God, first his daughter and then his wife."

"Yeah, I know what you mean, Tom. There was a time soon after Mary's death that I thought Sean wasn't going to make it. He was having this recurring dream where he would see Mary and Kristin holding hands. Sean told me that there wasn't any real background or reference point in the dream. It was grey and empty, except for Mary and Kristin holding hands. Sean told me that the feeling or sense of the dream was that he and Mary and Kristin realized they were no longer together. Then, Mary would say 'Sean, we're so cold,' almost like they were asking for Sean's help. If you knew Kristin and Mary the way I did, her saying that kind of thing to Sean would make your jaw drop. They hated the cold. I remember going to their house in the winter sometimes and it would be like a sauna. Mary and Kristin would still be bundled up in blankets. It seemed like they were constantly putting Sean to work to keep them warm in the winter. So, I know what this dream must have meant to Sean, especially the way he would explain it to me. The dream, I think, made Sean feel like he failed Mary and Kristin, even to the point where he couldn't do a simple thing like keeping them warm anymore. I got to tell you, Tom, I thought Sean was going to blow his brains out when he was having that dream. Sean also told me, about a month after Kristin died, that he woke up in the middle of the night and his arm was hanging over the side of the bed. He felt something holding his hand, squeezing it and then releasing, which Kristin always tried to do. I told Sean it was probably just a dream as his hand was falling asleep. He told me it lasted several minutes and he was wide awake when it stopped. He made the mistake of telling Mary about it. I think that was the start of what sent Mary to the land of no return."

"Steve, are you saying Sean really believes that his dead daughter was holding his hand?"

"Tom, I know it sounds crazy, but that's the way Sean is. He believes more strongly in the spiritual world, faith and God, than he does in what you and I consider everyday life." Steve's head was hanging low in his hands. Tom noticed the anguish on Steve's face and decided to change the subject.

"Well, anyway, I'm glad to hear Sean's doing okay now. All right, then, back to the Power Systems issue. I've had a look at the engineering drawings and specifications. This 'zero emissions' concept seems to make sense. By recycling the exhaust gases and using extremely high temperature combustion, Power Systems essentially burns everything back to no more than a pure carbon, which is the only

52

waste product from the plant, and even that material Power Systems sells to steel manufacturers, which they call 'coke' and use as a raw material in their furnaces."

"Here, let me take a peek at that file," Steve said to Tom.

He spent a few minutes turning pages and digesting the information in the Emission Reduction Credit file that Tom had taken from EPA's Central File Room. "I'll be damned, these documents show that Power Systems has a huge amount of credits." Steve continued to flip through the file as Tom looked on. "My God!" Steve exclaimed.

"What? What's the matter?" Tom asked hurriedly.

"These credits have got to be worth billions!"

CHAPTER 10

A couple of days after he met with Steve Cooperhouse, Tom Roth called the new environmental compliance manager for Power Systems, Inc. to ask permission to visit the Tacony power plant. Bob Morrone knew from past experience not to resist the government's request in these situations because doing so had a painful tendency to backfire and make business life difficult. So, when Tom Roth asked for access to the Power Systems, Inc. site, Bob Morrone asked only what day and time.

❧ ❧ ☙ ☙

Tom decided, because of the unexplainable acidity in the Delaware River, he would take the EPA boat as his means of transportation to the Power Systems, Inc. Tacony plant. This would give Tom a chance to poke around the wastewater discharge pipe from the plant and collect his own water samples. It was early morning when he left the dock, which was located in a small harbor marina, just north of the Philadelphia International Airport, within the confines of the John Heinz National Wildlife Refuge at Tinicum. Established by an Act of Congress in 1972, the Heinz Refuge comprises several hundred acres of freshwater tidal marsh and is home to more than 280 species of birds. The serenity and visual beauty of the refuge stand in stark contrast to its immediate industrial surroundings and the bustle of downtown Philadelphia just to the north.

As Tom motored out into the main channel of the Delaware, he angled the bow of the boat into some small waves and punched down of the throttle. The bow lifted up and then slowly settled down again as the boat trimmed out. With only a light breeze blowing and the tide moving upriver, Tom calculated about a half hour ride or so north to the Tacony section of the City.

❧ ❧ ☙ ☙

Charles Kuralt once said, "I started out thinking of America as highways and state lines. As I got to know it better I began to think of it as rivers. Most of what I love about the country is a gift of the rivers. America is a great story, and there is a river on every page of it."

The Delaware, the longest un-dammed river east of the Mississippi, is rich in history and diverse in nature. It extends 330 miles from the confluence of its East and West branches in Hancock, New York to the mouth of the Delaware Bay, along which it is fed by 216 tributaries. The river drains a basin covering parts of Pennsylvania, New Jersey, New York, and Delaware, comprising 13,359 square miles of land altogether. Three quarters of the non-tidal portion of the river has been included in the National Wild and Scenic Rivers System as have several of its southernmost tributaries. The Delaware Bay and the tidal reach of the river have been included in the National Estuary Program.

The Delaware's contribution to the economic vitality of several states is unheralded. Over seventeen million people rely on the river for drinking water and industrial use. The Port of Philadelphia alone reported $335 million in business revenue in 1997. It supports year-round fish populations including a world-class trout fishery, record numbers of shad, bass, walleye, and herring. A recent survey of shad fishing alone placed the annual value of this fishery at $3.2 million.

However, the Delaware was not always so successful. At the height of World War II, the river was dead. The lower reaches were an open sewer and fouled to the point that the water was devoid of oxygen. Fish and other aquatic life could not survive. It was this condition that, in 1961, spurred a movement to bring the river back to life. For the first time since the nation's birth, the federal government and a group of states entered into a compact to work together as equal partners in the form of a river basin planning, development and regulatory agency, without regard to political boundaries. Thus was the Delaware River Basin Commission created with a very specific canon: that the waters and related resources of the Delaware River are regional assets vested with local, state and national interests for which there is joint responsibility. This canon, and other duties and responsibilities of the Commission, were set forth in a Federal Compact, which gave this regional body the force of law. Among other things, the Commission was tasked to address such wide and varied things as water pollution abatement, water supply allocation, water conservation initiatives, regional planning, drought management, flood control, and recreation. Commission members are the governors of the four basin states and a presidential appointee.

It is against this backdrop that the Commission went to work by adopting in 1967 the most comprehensive water quality standards applicable to any interstate river basin in the nation. Perhaps most impressive is the fact that the Commission accomplished this effort years before the creation of the United States Environmental Protection Agency and the adoption of the Federal Clean Water Act, making the Commission a pioneer in environmental protection. The foresight and effort paid off. The restoration of the Delaware River is hailed as one of the world's top water quality success stories. Evidence of this success is reflected in the fact that pleasure craft marinas now line the waterfronts where once only commercial vessels could be seen. Old abandoned industrial buildings have given way to luxury apartments and condominiums. Indeed, the Commission has been visited by delegations from Indonesia, the United Kingdom, South Korea, the People's Republic of China, the Czech Republic, Hungary, Portugal, Sweden, Uruguay, India, and Japan for a first-hand understanding of the methods used by the Commission to achieve such a notable success.

With the adoption of various environmental laws in 1970, several other governmental agencies now have oversight and regulatory authority with respect to the water quality of the Delaware, chief among which are the United States Environmental Protection Agency, the United States Army Corps of Engineers, and the United States Coast Guard. These federal agencies work closely with the Commission to ensure a smooth flow to regulation and protection of this unique and vital natural resource.

◅ ◅ ▻ ▻

On the river side of the Tacony plant was a dark wooden bulkhead, almost three hundred feet long, the top of which was about twenty feet above the river's surface when Tom arrived. Fifty feet or so from the bulkhead into the river were three massive pilings, apparently used for docking large vessels. Tom remembered seeing in the EPA file a report mentioning the fact that Power Systems, Inc. received all its coal by barge. Just inland of the bulkhead was a chain link fence, ten feet high, with coiled barbed wire at the top of it. Fifty yards or so beyond the fence was the red brick facade of the power plant, taking up half the width of the property and rising up nearly ten stories. It dwarfed all other buildings within a half mile distance and was so high above the surface of the river that it gave Tom the feeling, as he piloted the boat in closer to the bulkhead, that the entire building was going to topple over on him.

Tom also remembered from the documents he reviewed that the southern limit of the Power Systems, Inc. property was marked by a small tributary, which he now noticed as the bulkhead came to an end. He maneuvered the boat a little past the tributary, which is where the reports indicated the low pH was occurring. Tom noticed at the water's edge some debris with metal components, which had a blackish coloring. Although he could not be sure, Tom made a mental note that the tarnished metal could be attributable to the pH condition. He also noticed on the debris lining the banks of the tributary and the river a chalky white build up, predominantly at the high water mark.

Tom pulled back on the throttle and put the boat's engine in neutral. He scampered to the back of the boat and grabbed some litmus paper from a small chemical test kit that was a permanent fixture on all EPA boats. He leaned over the stern and dipped the litmus paper into the river, moving quickly so as not to be out of control of the boat for too long. The change in color of the litmus paper confirmed the earlier testing data. Although litmus paper was not a precise quantitative test of pH, Tom could judge from his experience that this current reading was somewhere around a pH of between four and five.

Seeing that the boat was drifting with the tide dangerously close to the river bank, Tom stumbled back to the captain's seat and put the engine back in gear. He moved slowly back out to a safe distance and again disengaged the engine. He went into a cooler he had brought on board and pulled out four sample jars. Again leaning over the stern, he dipped each of the jars into the river, capped them and placed them back in the cooler, which he had filled with ice before departing. By this time, the security guards employed by Power Systems, Inc. had noticed Tom taking an unusual interest in the area and shouted to Tom from the top of the bulkhead.

"We need you to clear out of this area! We are scheduled to have a coal barge arriving soon."

Tom yelled back. "Actually, I'm here to meet with Bob Morrone." The security guards did not hear him, so Tom yelled again. "I'm here to meet with Bob Morrone."

One of the security guards pulled a walkie-talkie from his belt and began talking. After a minute or so, he yelled back, "Are you Tom Roth?"

"That's right."

The security guard talked a second time into the walkie-talkie and then yelled out again.

"Mr. Morrone was not expecting you to arrive by boat. Rather unusual."

"People say that a lot about me," responded Tom.

"Okay, Mr. Roth. What you need to do is motor up that tributary. There is a floating dock about fifty yards upstream. Can you see it?"

"Yes. Straight ahead," Tom acknowledged.

"All right, we'll meet you there."

⊲ ⊲ ⊳ ⊳

As Tom glided toward the dock, one of the security guards was waiting for him. The fact that the dock was outside the main course of the river, together with only a light breeze blowing, made it very easy for Tom to pilot the boat. Docking is more art than science, requiring a masterful balance of river current, boat speed, wind, and, most importantly, the availability of a dockhand to compensate for operator mistakes. As he drifted slowly within a few feet of the dock, Tom quickly backed off the throttle and gave the steering wheel a fast spin, which caused the stern of the boat to swing in toward the dock. Tom waited patiently for the breeze to catch the boat port side and push it the rest of the way, which gave Tom a few seconds to scramble for a line and throw it to the security guard. A few seconds later, Tom had tied off lines from both the stern and bow and offered a welcoming hand to the security guard.

"How's it goin'? Tom Roth with the EPA."

"You gave us a scare there Mr. Roth. Under our enhanced security measures, we take a suspicious view of anyone who comes that close to the plant, especially from the river side. You're lucky we didn't start lobbing artillery at you," joked the security guard. "Not to mention the fact that using the 'backdoor' lets you avoid our metal detectors at the main gate. I'm going to need to see some I.D."

"No problem. I understand completely," Tom acknowledged. "I've been to enough power plants, including nuclear facilities, since 9/11 that this has become an expected routine for me." As Tom reached for his EPA identification badge, the security guard waved a hand-held metal detector over Tom's body.

When the security guard had completed his standard check, he and Tom ascended a wobbly set of metal stairs from the floating dock to the ground level at the top of the bulkhead. By the time they reached the top of the stairs, Bob Morrone had exited the building and was making his way toward Tom and the security guard. The loud hum of the plant, combined with the noise from a near-by coal transfer belt which had been muted by the bulkhead and vegetation when Tom was in the boat, caused Bob Morrone to shout an introduction to Tom. "Hello, Tom. Bob Morrone. I'm the environmental compliance manager for the site. You and I spoke on the phone the other day." Bob Morrone's nervousness was immediately recognizable to Tom. The last person an environmental compliance manager likes to see is an EPA inspector. The fact that this visit followed closely a government search warrant had put Bob Morrone in a visible state of panic. "What's your pleasure, Tom?" asked Morrone.

"Well, I'd like you to take me on a 'boy scout' tour of the plant, starting out here with the coal delivery."

"Fair enough," responded Morrone. "As you can see, we are a coal burning plant. All of the coal is delivered by barge. In fact, if you look down river, you can see our next delivery on its way." Tom Roth took Morrone's suggestion and noticed a gargantuan barge being pushed upriver by two tugs. "When the coal arrives," continued Morrone, "it is transferred by specially designed chutes, which direct the coal to those piles alongside of the building." Morrone directed Tom Roth's attention to two monstrous mounds of coal on the south side of the plant. "We always keep several days of coal storage on-site. We use a lot more coal that a traditional power plant, because . . . well, I can't really divulge to you our patented technology."

Tom immediately interrupted Morrone's presentation. "I know you guys use high temperature combustion to control emissions. I've seen the patent background information. It's in the files the city prosecutor collected under the warrant."

Morrone didn't know until that point that Tom Roth's inspection was somehow related to the search warrant. "Okay, so you have some idea of what is going on here then? Well, as you can guess, to reach the kind of temperatures we need to control air pollution emissions, we use a shitload more coal than the traditional power plants." Morrone thought this might be a good time to editorialize as a way of showing his knowledge. "The average Joe doesn't understand that environmental protection in many instances is just a trade-off. We use up more fossil fuel than a normal power plant to achieve greater air pollution control. The general public doesn't see that trade-off. All the public sees is that Power Systems produces 'cleaner' energy. Most schmucks will buy into that theory. They will pay more for what we market as 'green electricity' thinking they are doing a good deed for the environment by paying more for the service. What they don't know is that Power Systems eats up three times the amount of coal that a standard power plant consumes in order to reach the higher temperature combustion."

Tom Roth had heard this argument at least a hundred times before. He wasn't inclined to get into a theoretical debate with Morrone. So, Tom decided to refocus Morrone's attention to the immediate purpose of the visit. "What's next in the process?" Tom asked.

"Oh, okay," replied Morrone. "Well, you can see from here that the coal is transferred by conveyor belt into the furnace. Let's go inside so you can get a better look at the internal working of the plant." As they walked from the rear of the property to the back entrance to the power plant, Tom took advantage of the time to get some information from Morrone.

"Tell me Mr. Morrone, I assume you've seen the data on the low pH out in the river?"

"Please call me Bob," Morrone started out, trying to keep things as informal as possible. "Yeah, I've seen the data. Although, I've been here only a few weeks. So I haven't had a chance to delve into it much to figure out what might be going on. Anyway, it is a weird situation. We have data showing our wastewater is neutral, as is the river just upstream of our discharge pipe. It's the damnedest thing. All I know is the company has been threatened with penalties by both the EPA and the Pennsylvania Department of Environmental Protection, but the case never goes anywhere because no one can figure out why the pH problem is popping up."

"What about that white buildup on the banks of the river? Any idea what it is?" asked Tom.

"I'm not sure what you're talking about. To be quite honest, I've haven't really had the time to do a close physical inspection of the plant grounds. Actually, walking back there to meet you this morning is the first time I have been that far back on the property."

Tom watched Morrone's body language as he answered and realized that Morrone genuinely had no idea what was happening and decided the questioning was not worth pursuing. It is a characteristic that takes many years to develop: knowing when to stop pushing.

❧ ❧ ❧ ❧

As they neared the building, Morrone pointed out the exhaust gas return vents. There were three cylindrical pipes, several feet in diameter, coming off the top of the building and wrapping down along the east side. One of the pipes entered back into the building about half way down while another went almost all the way to the ground. The third pierced the ground and apparently went underneath the building.

"It's a crazy thing, huh? A power plant with no big stack. I'm just not used to the look."

Tom jumped into the discussion. "Yeah, I know what you mean. It was the first thing to catch my attention when I saw the plant from the river. Most power plants use the concept of extra high stacks as a means of meeting the air pollution standards. They discharge the exhaust gases so high above the ground that, by the time those gases have reach the ground surface, they have had the chance to mix with clean air below. Like you mentioned before, the general public isn't aware of this kind of thing. As long as the breathable air at ground level is okay, the government isn't too concerned about what amount of pollution is actually coming out of the top of the stack. So, when it comes to power plants, I'm used to the rule that the higher the better for the stack."

As they entered the building, Morrone mentioned in passing that the exhaust gases were recycled back into the furnace, at different vertical levels, with some fresh air, to support the combustion process. Tom reminded Morrone that he had already seen the patent diagrams and specifications and was aware of the recycling concept underlying the plant's operation. Morrone handed Tom a hard hat, a pair of safety glasses, and disposable ear plugs, which he donned without objection. He had been through the routine before. As Morrone opened the safety door leading into the furnace area, a wall of heat washed over them. Along with it came a characteristic smell, almost like that of a wood-burning stove. Also notable, despite the ear plugs, was the heavy hum of the turbines, spinning away as the superheated steam passed over their baffles. As Tom and his guide walked through the plant, several workers passed, offering a standard form of wave and half-hearted smile. Morrone attempted a few times to talk with Tom but with no success. Tom just shrugged indicating his inability to hear what Morrone was saying. Morrone also motioned with his hand a few times attempting to point out an item of distinction or interest to Tom.

Over his nearly twenty years with the EPA, Tom had inspected many electric power plants and was familiar with the basic design and operating protocol. Plus, in the case of the Tacony plant, Tom had pored over the engineering schematics for hours and had an uncanny ability to recall the particulars of plans when looking at the actual real-life product. So, he was unaffected by Morrone's inability to explain the process as they walked through the Tacony plant. After about a half hour or so of touring the facility, Tom gestured that he had seen enough, after which Morrone led Tom back to the administrative offices.

"Is there anything else you would like to see, Tom?" asked Morrone.

"Not at this time," Tom answered. "As you can expect, though, I may need to come back after I meet with my superiors."

"Can you shed any light for me, Tom, as to why the EPA is so interested in the facility?"

"At this stage," responded Tom, "all I can tell you is that the issue of the low pH in the river popped up on the radar screen in connection with the city prosecutor's investigation into the death of Robert Stark."

Bob Morrone walked Tom back to the boat dock and helped him get underway. It was nearing mid-day by the time Tom reached the main channel. He decided that he had time to get back to the John Heinz National Wildlife Refuge at Tinicum and hand deliver the water samples to EPA's laboratory.

❧ ❧ ❧ ❧

EPA's analytical laboratory in Edison, New Jersey, is one of the most highly specialized environmental testing systems in the country. Tom Roth was a regular customer. He decided a face-to-face meeting with the laboratory director was appropriate in this case, given the uniqueness of the pH situation in the river. In Tom's estimation, an environmental sample, without some background and setting, produced meaningless data. Only where the laboratory director had an appreciation for the purpose of the sample, and the evidentiary point that the data was intended to prove, did the testing process have meaning.

"So, what good stuff are you bringing us today, Tom?" asked Alicia Bittle, the director of EPA's laboratory.

"I have some river water samples from the Delaware, near the Tacony section of Philadelphia, if that helps."

"The location doesn't mean too much, but I've done my fair share of water quality samples for the Delaware. What are we looking for this time?"

"The first thing I want is a good quantitative check on the pH," instructed Tom.

"Easy enough. That's a quick procedure. We can have those results for you in twenty-four hours. Anything else?"

"Yeah, we have some historical data showing an unusually low pH. So, while I'm interested in confirming that data. . . ." Alicia interrupted before Tom could finish.

"I know, you want some idea of the chemical reason for the low pH, right?"

"Exactly," responded Tom. "I took a spin in the boat to collect these water samples and couldn't see anything obvious on the banks that would be the source of acidic conditions. You know the routine. Normally, I'll see some old drums leaking acid right into the water or some other similar obvious source of the problem. Here, I saw nothing like that. The only hint of a water problem was a heavy white buildup along the banks on some of the debris."

"All right, we'll do all the normal tests plus a GC-Mass Spec to try to hone in on what's goin' on out there," offered Alicia.

Tom knew that the Gas Chromatography-Mass Spectrometer, also known as GC-Mass Spec, procedure, while quite expensive, was one of the best ways to evaluate the highly complex area of environmental chemistry. In simplest terms, the GC-Mass Spec procedure is based on the likely physical movement of a particular chemical as a function of its weight. Because different chemicals weigh different amounts, they tend to move at varying distances along a particular course. Heavier chemical compounds tend to move less distance and come to a stop before the smaller, lighter chemical compounds. It's kind of like a long distance foot race. Everyone begins at the same starting line, but bigger and heavier out of shape runners normally fall out early on in the race. The smallest runners who have trained long and hard make it to the finish line. Then, there is a whole spectrum of runners dropping out of the race in between the start and finish, likewise depending on their respective size and conditioning. The GC-Mass Spec is a chemical long distance run.

The distance a particular chemical compound moves along that course becomes a type of unique signature because no two chemical compounds occupy exactly the same spot along the same course. Over the years, the EPA laboratory has developed a set of standards for a host of common chemicals that they test. Using these standards for a known quantity of a particular chemical, EPA's laboratory can test a sample with an unknown chemical in it, and figure out what that unknown chemical compound is by checking its distance of movement from the "starting line" and comparing it against the standards as well. If a sample with an unknown chemical in it yields a mark similar to that of one of the known standards, the laboratory can be fairly certain that the sample has that same chemical in it. So, for example, a particular laboratory may have a standard showing that chlorine moves ten centimeters along a column of a medium. If an unknown sample is tested and the laboratory sees a "fingerprint" at ten centimeters, the laboratory can say that the chemical in that sample is likely chlorine.

In this case, because acidity was the issue, Alicia Bittle could limit the universe of chemicals that the laboratory should focus on, at least as a starting measure. "Well, checking for acids gives me a much more limited task than what I'm used to. Most time I get a water sample from some courier who has no idea where it originated and the label instructs me to check for priority pollutants, which is hundreds of chemical compounds. It's an impossible task, really."

"Well, what we're dealing with here is a power plant on the Delaware River. Interestingly enough, the wastewater discharge from the plant is consistently neutral pH. Right downstream of the discharge pipe, though, is this low pH. I did a litmus paper check when I collected these samples and sure enough got a good indication of acidity."

"Litmus paper!" Alicia said smartly. "That's not an analytical test."

"Hey, I'm not a real scientist like you, Alicia," Tom said smiling at Alicia. "I'm just a simple EPA investigator. Litmus paper still does the job for me."

"Are we looking at full 'Custody and Control' papers on these samples?" Alicia asked.

Tom understood the importance of the question. If an environmental sampling result was going to be used for purposes of an enforcement action or a criminal prosecution, the laboratory had to document, by way of 'Custody and Control' forms, such things as who in the laboratory handled the sample and coordinated the testing procedure along with information about the tuning of the laboratory equipment as well. Only by keeping such a close eye on an environmental sample could a laboratory back up its results as being valid and reproducible, a very important area of attack by defense attorneys.

"Yeah, I think you better give me the full work up on these samples," Tom responded. "I'm not sure that we even have a case yet or how it will go, assuming these results come back with some useful information, but Sean Murphy from the DOJ's office in Philly is somehow behind this case. So, that means to me we have a chance of going to court on this one. Plus, I've been burned too many times in the past by not asking for the full work up. So, even though I know it costs an arm and a leg to do it, please give me all the backup on these samples."

"No sweat off my brow, Tom. It's the taxpayers' money here, not mine," Alicia answered sarcastically.

"Excellent! How long before something is ready?" Tom asked anxiously.

"Four weeks," she said.

"What? How can a simple pH test take four weeks?" Tom demanded.

"We're just a tiny operation in an otherwise gargantuan EPA," Alicia said.

"But, Alicia, dear. It's me, Tom. You and I are best friends, right?"

"Okay. As a favor to you, I'll see to it that the results are ready in two weeks, but don't tell anyone. Otherwise, every sample that comes in will be accompanied by a note asking me to extend a favor."

"I promise. It'll be our secret," Tom answered with a smile.

CHAPTER 11

Sean Murphy was pacing in the reception area of his office, running through an argument in his head, when Steve Cooperhouse dropped into his office, without an appointment, as usual.

"Hey Murph. You're putting together an argument, huh?" Steve knew that Tom got his mental juices flowing by pacing in his bare feet. "Thought I'd stop by to talk about that Power Systems file you sent over last week. Remember it?"

"Yeah, absolutely," replied Sean. "I knew you'd find something in those files that I couldn't. I assume you have Tom Roth on the case."

"Yep, that's right. Tom's the man. Actually he's at the Power Systems plant right now. He found the documents showing that low pH in the river. So, he wanted to collect his own samples and confirm the problem. Knowing Tom, he'll be waiting in my office when I get back to give me a copious report."

"Well," Sean said, "I assume you've come back to me because of some kind of violation that I can prosecute. Can I throw somebody in jail?" Sean Murphy loved the high profile white collar crimes.

"I'm not quite to that point, Sean, but I came across something quite surprising. You remember in the early 80s when you and I were doing a lot of air pollution enforcement work?"

"Hell yeah. We put the entire Pittsburgh steel industry on its ass!"

"That's right. And if I recall correctly, I was the one who had to go to the labor union meetings to explain to the steelworkers that they were going to be out of a job because of the government's lofty plan to protect air quality. Environmental protection was the last thing on the mind of a laborer trying to feed six kids. Hell, man, one of the meetings was on Christmas-fucking-Eve. I'll never forget the look on the faces of those guys when they realized that the purpose of the meeting was to announce a plant shutdown. And, if I recall, you were noticeably absent. "

"Tough shit," Sean bemoaned. "You fell for the industry line. All they had to do was cough up the dough to install air pollution control equipment and the steel workers would still have had a job. It wasn't the government that shut down those plants; it was the tightwad companies that elected to build new plants outside the country."

"Enough reminiscing," Steve prodded Sean. "Do you remember the theory about cap-and-trade? You know, the Emissions Reduction Credit program under the Clean Air Act. Some of the steel manufacturers you so fondly recall were able to meet the Clean Air Act standards by purchasing emissions credits from other manufacturers."

"It's been a while, but yeah I recall the theory generally. What I seem to recall is some of the steel manufacturers paid a hefty price for those credits. Millions of dollars in some cases."

"To be sure," answered Steve. "I'm coming across the same thing with this Power Systems case, only with a slight twist. Our research shows the Tacony plant alone has potentially billions of dollars of emissions credits."

Sean looked a bit surprised. The Department of Justice kept a fairly close eye on the air pollutant emissions trading market to make sure nothing fast and loose was happening. "That's impossible, no single facility, power plant or otherwise, has that kind of value wrapped up in emissions credits. What's the pollutant?" Sean demanded. "Our biggest trades recently have been for nitrogen oxides and sulfur oxides."

"That's the interesting thing about this situation. Power Systems has credits for carbon dioxide."

"Carbon dioxide?" inquired Sean. "It's not regulated by the Clean Air Act, and our lustrous administration has not seen fit to execute The Kyoto Protocol, which would be the only way carbon dioxide would come under a hammer. So, there can't even be a market." Sean was quite proud of his profound legal answer.

"And that's where you are wrong, my good friend," quipped Steve, with a smile coming to his face. "When Tom showed me the file, I had the same uninformed knee-jerk reaction." Steve was pleased to see Sean give him the middle finger. "But then I opened my mind to the possibility that there might be something I don't know." Sean now held up a second middle finger. "Anyway, I did a little research on my own. It turns out that about fifty companies right here in the U.S. of A. have entered into a private deal to reduce greenhouse gas emissions voluntarily. These companies have apparently bought into the theory that greenhouse gas emissions are causing global warming. The voluntary reduction program is the brain child of this guy by the name of Brendan Frisk, who founded something called The Climate Exchange. Those companies participating in the voluntary reduction program that can't reduce greenhouse gases buy credits from other companies with certified reductions on this exchange. And guess who's the biggest contributor of credits."

"Power Systems, Inc.," responded Sean.

"That's correct. Aside from Brazil, that is."

"Brazil? What the hell does Brazil have to do with greenhouse gases in the United States?"

"Well, unlike other air pollutants which create problems either close to where they are discharged or within a certain geographical region, the greenhouse effect is a global phenomenon. The argument, then, is that any action anywhere on the planet that helps to reduce greenhouse gases is beneficial in terms of halting global warming."

Sean interrupted, "That's all well and good, but I'm still not following how Brazil plays into The Climate Exchange." He paused looking for Steve to fill in the blanks.

"If you'd let me finish, chucklehead, you'd get the full picture. You and I are used to the idea of somebody reducing or eliminating air emissions and then getting a credit for it, right?"

"That's how I remember it working," Sean answered. "When those steel plants shut down, they banked and got credit for emissions that would have otherwise been coming out of the plant if it had continued to operate. Then, they sold those credits to other steel manufacturers in the same. . . . What was it we used to call those things?" Sean asked, his memory obviously hazy from the number of years that had passed since he had done any meaningful air pollution enforcement work.

"Air basins, Sean. There were certain geographical and other restrictions on the sale of air emission credits for things like metals, sulfur oxides, and nitrogen oxides. It didn't make any scientific sense to let a power plant in the northeast buy nitrogen oxide emissions credits from a power plant in the southwest. The northeast would never realize any actual environmental benefit from nitrogen oxide reductions occurring in the southwest. So, we put restrictions on those markets. That's the point I was trying to make here. The beauty of a carbon dioxide cap-and-trade market is that it is free of the traditional restrictions because the greenhouse effect is a global phenomenon, but there is one other interesting twist that you and I never heard of with our Pittsburgh experience."

"I knew this was coming," complained Sean.

"Carbon sequestration."

"Seques . . . what?"

"That's what I thought you'd ask. Unlike a lot of the traditional pollutants that you and I are used to dealing with, carbon is a chemical element that is used naturally by many living organisms as a building block. You and I are made up of carbon. We get our carbon from the foods we eat. Some living organisms, like trees for example, get their carbon mainly from carbon dioxide in the air."

"I see where this is going," Sean said to Steve. "Plant a tree in Brazil and a certain amount of carbon dioxide in the air will be 'sequestered' in that tree as it grows."

"You got it, Einstein." Steve lived for moments like these. "So, I checked The Climate Exchange database and found that the principal greenhouse gas credits currently available on the Exchange are those generated by Power Systems. They have cornered the entire market, with the exception of some carbon sequestration going on down in Brazil. My guess is that Power Systems is marketing these greenhouse gas credits to the members of The Kyoto Protocol through some similar kind of exchange."

Sean paced around his office thinking about the information Steve had just dumped on him. After a minute or two, Sean asked, "A few questions. First, how does Power Systems gather such large amounts of credits? They must have some kind of super-duper carbon dioxide control system in place."

"I guess you could say that. Tom Roth tells me Power Systems has a patented 'zero emission' system."

"Impossible. I've never heard of such a thing. It couldn't work. There's just too much exhaust involved with a power plant."

"Unfortunately," Steve answered, "you're goin' to have to wait for Tom to explain it to you. I know I couldn't do it justice. But, Tom tells me he looked at the specs for the Tacony plant and the exhaust gases are piped back into the furnace where it is combusted using very high temperature."

"So how does The Climate Exchange calculate Power Systems' greenhouse gas credits?" Sean inquired.

"I can't be absolutely sure, but what I have been able to glean from this Emissions Reduction Credits file that Tom Roth came across, the Exchange gives Power Systems a credit for the amount of carbon dioxide that would go up the stack with no controls."

Sean was obviously puzzled. "I don't follow."

"Remember freshman chemistry at Penn State? If you completely combust a known amount of fossil fuel, you can calculate through chemical balancing methods the exact amount of carbon dioxide that will be produced."

"Yeah, I remember that technique. But not so well. You're so good for my memory, Steve. You should come by more often and give me refresher courses. What was that chemical balancing theory called again?"

"Stoichiometry," he answered. "Now we're getting down to the nitty gritty. If you recall, stoichiometry tells us that during a combustion reaction a carbon atom attaches to two oxygen atoms. The coal industry can approximate for us the number of atoms in a ton of coal. From that, we can calculate the number of carbon dioxide compounds going up the stack when Power Systems burns a ton of coal. Simply multiply that number by the number of tons per day of coal that Power Systems consumes and you have the basis for a credit."

"Fair enough," answered Sean. "One thing that bugs me, though, is why bother? If the laws don't say you have to do it, why join this Climate Exchange and bind yourself to a costly commitment to reduce greenhouse gases? There's got to be something more than just gratuitous environmental protection in the corporate thinking of these member companies."

"You're so jaded, Murph," Steve said jokingly. "I know what you mean. I struggled with that one too. When did Fortune 500 companies all of the sudden become altruistic, right?"

"Exactly!" Sean exclaimed.

"The only thing I can come up with—and this is pure speculation—is labeling."

"What do you mean?" asked Sean.

"Power Systems holds itself out as the region's primary producer of 'green energy' and the average consumer jumps. Environmental conscientiousness sells. My guess is the members of The Climate Exchange are doing the same kind of marketing. You know, some kind of a label saying that a product was made without contributing to global warming. There's actually a phrase for it now: 'Carbon friendly.' Got to love it, huh? Like I said, it's just a guess."

"I can buy into that. We're seeing a whole bunch of that kind of marketing out there now. Well Professor Cooperhouse, once again you have managed to surprise me."

Steve smiled and said, "I don't know if it will lead to anything, but I thought you were better equipped to investigate this trading stuff. It's interesting to me, but not my strength." Steve continued to talk as he walked toward the reception area of Sean's office. "Let me know if you come up with anything."

"First thing to do is find out more about this Climate Exchange. I think I'll give Becca a call on this one," Sean responded. Steve stopped in his tracks.

"Rebecca Lockhart! My oh my." Sean was already beginning to frown. "Isn't there some ethical rule that says you can't tap the ass of your own expert witness."

"Fuck you, Cooperhouse," Sean blurted back. "But, to answer your question, I'm glad to say no—there is no such rule. Plus, Becca is not an expert witness, she's a consultant."

Steve smiled at Sean's feeble attempt to justify his actions. "Spoken like a true lawyer, Sean."

"Anyway, Becca and I haven't seen each other that way in over a year," Sean replied.

"You're kiddin' me right?" Steve asked. "Why didn't you tell me that before? I figured you guys were still seeing one another. Sean Murphy, you never cease to amaze me. You let another drop dead gorgeous woman slip through your fingers, didn't you?"

"It's not like that. I don't know. . . ." Sean uncharacteristically fumbled for the words, " . . . I can't explain it. So, kiss my ass and leave me alone."

"Oh, I'll leave you alone, all right," said Steve. "But not for long. I want to hear what happens when you call her."

Sean flipped yet another middle finger at Steve as he walked out of the office, to which he returned a smile.

CHAPTER 12

In the wake of all of the corporate reporting scandals, beginning with the Enron, Inc. debacle and the subsequent attack on the Securities and Exchange Commission for failing to pay closer attention to the marketplace, Sean Murphy had gained a heightened level of sensitivity to corporate environmental reporting requirements and decided to keep a close eye on the area. It was an obvious "cover the ass" tactic, but Sean was not about to find himself in front of a congressional panel explaining why and how the Department of Justice missed an obvious fraudulent environmental report. Sean sent a memorandum to all employees in the Philadelphia regional office of the Environmental Protection Agency explaining how the events with Enron, Inc. and similar corporate fraud could easily arise in the field of environmental regulation. He cautioned all EPA employees to evaluate closely all reporting forms that came in from regulated industry and to report to Sean immediately any instances where misinformation appeared on a report, even where a mistake seemingly occurred inadvertently and honestly. Sean's new protocol for improper environmental reporting was to prosecute immediately. It was a hard line that deviated from Sean's usual policy of giving regulated industry a chance to correct an honest mistake, but the fallout after Enron, Inc., including most importantly the 'head chopping' of several government regulators, left Sean no choice.

One of the other precautionary things Sean did was retain a stock market analyst, Rebecca Lockhart, on a consulting basis to monitor air pollution emissions credit trading that was going on within Sean's jurisdiction. It was an admittedly small part of the environmental compliance reporting universe, but it was an area that Sean thought was ripe for fraud, and the environmental harm that could be created as a result of a fraudulent air emissions trade report was potentially disastrous. So, the use of outside help in this case was justified in Sean's estimation. In the few years that Sean had Rebecca Lockhart acting a market watchdog, she discovered a number of cases of improper reporting, which Sean used to send a loud and clear message to industry that the government, and Sean in particular, was serious about maintaining integrity in this relatively new marketplace.

Rebecca Lockhart was raised in the "Main Line" section of Philadelphia, the daughter of one of the most successful businessmen in the city. It was no surprise, then, that Rebecca spent both her undergraduate and graduate time at the Wharton School of the University of Pennsylvania, graduating in 1988 with an M.B.A. She spent the next ten years working for what at the time was one of the Big Eight accounting firms, where she specialized in government bond work. But with the consolidations and mergers of the 1990's that firm eventually became one of the Big Five, and Rebecca noticed that she was just one of several thousand accountants in the firm with an M.B.A. Rebecca's effort to distinguish herself, which she was perfectly capable of doing, was simply being outpaced by sheer numbers of others trying likewise to distinguish themselves.

Early in 2000, Rebecca took stock of her circumstances and decided to make a drastic professional change. She opened her own financial consulting and advisory firm with a niche practice of servicing government clients only. Rebecca had developed a strong relationship with a number of such clients over her years and they were all pleased to follow Rebecca when she left, especially in light of the fact that her hourly rate dropped significantly the day Rebecca opened up her own office. It wasn't long after that event that Sean Murphy met Rebecca Lockhart at a mutual friend's house party. When Sean heard of her background and experience, it was a foregone conclusion that Rebecca was perfect for the assignment of acting as a watchdog on this unusual environmental marketplace of air emissions credit trading.

Rebecca was tall, about five foot eleven, with long straight blonde hair. It matched perfectly her light blue eyes. Her lifelong passion of distance running, which she managed to do five days a week by rising at 5:30 AM, blessed her with impeccably shaped legs, which Rebecca loved to show off by adding on the highest heels she could find. Those who knew Rebecca agreed that her tremendous good looks were equally matched by her sharp wit. Rebecca Lockhart never married, much to her mother's chagrin, but the professional world was where Rebecca was most comfortable. Marriage did not scare her. It was just that Rebecca never saw herself following in her mother's footsteps: a stay-at-home mom with lots of time to volunteer on a wide range of worthy projects, none of which ever put a dollar in her mother's pocket.

As expected, Rebecca quickly learned the air emissions credit trading marketplace and monitored it well for the Department of Justice. Soon after Rebecca took on the assignment, she kicked up some improprieties in the marketplace that, although they were inadvertent mistakes by participants, came as a total surprise to Sean, not to mention the violating companies. He knew that most others in the profession never would have identified the mistakes that Rebecca had uncovered. She was thorough.

Most of the companies that committed the trading errors, though quite sophisticated, couldn't understand the nature of the violation. Frankly, neither could Sean. So, dealing with the market improprieties required Sean to work closely together with Rebecca for a period of about a year. It was during one of their settlement negotiations with an electric power plant operator in West Virginia that Sean and Rebecca's relationship went beyond just the professional kind. Sean agreed with the target company that he would come to Charleston for the settlement negotiations. He and Rebecca took separate rooms at the Hampton Inn on Virginia Street, overlooking the Charleston River. Late one night, as they were pouring over boxes of records dating back nearly ten years, Sean decided it was time for "Mr. Guiness" to make a visit. Rebecca said a glass of red wine would be nice, in response to which Sean told room service to bring the whole bottle. After a few sips of her wine, Sean had already finished his beer and was starting on a glass of wine too. As they drank, their discussion turned from the boxes of records to more personal matters, like what weird path brought them together in Charleston, West Virginia.

They shared some Philly experiences: 76ers games and Big Five basketball at the Palestra; listening to the Philadelphia Orchestra at the Academy of Music, with its beautiful artwork and impeccable glass chandelier and the guy at Sixth Street who sells soft pretzels but has a nasty habit of wiping his nose in the winter while conducting business. Rebecca explained that her new business was going well and was a welcome relief from that feeling of being lost in a big accounting firm. They then talked about their first meeting.

"Do you remember the first time we met, Becca?" Sean asked.

"Yes, like it was yesterday. You came to a party at my girlfriend Rachel's house. If I recall correctly, you and your buddies had gone to a 76ers' game. You had that bimbo with you and she was hanging all over you."

"Not a bimbo, dear. A finely tuned 76ers cheerleader, who, by the way, spent the better part of the evening doing splits for me. And, yes, you're right, she was all over me. You can't blame her, though, right?" Sean said jokingly bringing a modest smile to Rebecca's face. "But then Rachel introduced me to you. And what happened then?"

"As far as I know, you nailed the bimbo, even though she was probably half your age."

"No, I didn't nail her, and you know I didn't. You and I talked for over an hour. I didn't think it was fair to lead that wonderfully spankable young cheerleader on. So, I walked her to her car and said goodnight like a gentleman."

"Wait a minute, Sean. Now that we're talking about it, I seem to recall that cheerleader had to take a pee and she couldn't wait for Rachel's bathroom to get freed up."

"Oh yeah," Sean answered with a laugh. "That's right. She asked me to go outside with her so she could take a pee. She was afraid of the neighborhood."

"Afraid of the neighborhood, my ass. She wanted you there when she pulled up her skirt."

"Minor detail," Sean answered. "Look, I like to think of myself as a gentlemen. If a woman is in distress and needs my help, I make every effort to oblige. Plus, there was no way I was missing out on the opportunity to watch a 76'ers cheerleader take a pee in an alleyway. I got a lot of use out of that story. After she was done, I came back in to talk to you, though."

"I was so pissed off at you, Sean. Rachel asked me to come to that party so she could introduce me to you. Next thing I know, you are watching this cheerleader pull up her skirt."

"Yeah, but I eventually won you over, didn't I?" Sean asked.

"Yes, you did," she answered.

The conversation took a sour turn when Rebecca mentioned how surprised she was that Sean wasn't married. She was horrified to hear Sean's explanation about how he had lost his daughter to cancer and his wife to suicide. Rebecca leaned over to console Sean, seeing that the discussion had brought back some difficult memories. It wasn't much longer before Sean and Rebecca were locked in an embrace on the floor of his room, files and records all around them. It had been a good deal of time for both of them, so they made love until dawn. Sean and Rebecca made the mistake of going to sleep as the sun was rising and were woken up by a 10:00 AM call from the president of the company with whom they were supposed to be meeting.

Sean and Rebecca kept up an informal, but enjoyable, relationship for the next year or so, at which point Rebecca's work for the Department of Justice began to wind down. Their relationship likewise tailed off, without either of them paying much attention to it. Both were busy with their professional lives and didn't focus on what was happening between them. About a year had passed since Sean and Rebecca were last together when Sean decided that he would call Rebecca for help on the Power Systems case.

"Hello, Rebecca Lockhart," she said answering the phone.

"Hello gorgeous, it's Murph."

"Sean, I'm so happy to hear your voice. How are you, sweetheart?"

"Exceedingly well, as always, dear. I hope you're the same."

"Of course. I never have a bad day, Sean. Every day is Christmas around here. I saw you won a big case. You were all over the papers. I'm so proud of you."

"Thank you," Sean paused for a second and then said, "I miss you, Becca."

"I miss you too, Sean," she answered.

"I need your help on a case. Do you have the time?" asked Sean.

"For you, Sean, I always have the time. What do you have?"

"Well, it's a lot like what you were doing before. You know, emissions credit trading. There's this company by the name of Power Systems that operates an electric power plant in northeast Philly." Rebecca Lockhart started to take notes. "They have been trading emissions reductions credits for carbon dioxide on what is called The Climate Exchange. That's where you come in. I need you to gather as much information as you can about this Exchange and figure out how it works." Sean paused and Rebecca picked up with some observations and questions.

"Carbon dioxide credits. That's a first, huh? I assume this has something to do with global warming."

"As always, you are correct," Sean answered.

"The Climate Exchange," Rebecca commented. "I think I read some articles about that a few years back in a few of the trade journals. Brendan Frisk founded it, if I recall correctly."

"Yeah, that's right. You know him?" Sean asked.

"No, not really. I remember his name from the work we were doing together before. He was involved is some air emissions trades that we were watching."

"Well, that's a better starting point than what I could manage. Can you do the typical background research and stop by when you get some time?"

"Sure," replied Rebecca.

"Great. I assume your hourly rate has gone up since you last billed me?"

"Of course it has, Sean, but I'm worth it," Rebecca commented confidently.

"No problem. Just set up a new billing account under the name Power Systems."

"Okay," Rebecca said. "Give me a week or so and I'll be ready with some preliminary information."

"Excellent. See you then."

⊰ ⊰ ⊱ ⊱

As promised, just about a week later Rebecca Lockhart called Sean Murphy's secretary, Kate, and set up a time for Rebecca to stop by for a meeting. Without ever actually asking, Kate knew that Sean and Rebecca were, for a time, romantically involved. The signs were easily recognizable: meetings that invariably carried over to dinner and drinks, less formal but more frequent conversations on the telephone, and a lot of late morning arrivals, which was a material breach of protocol for Sean. And, during the year or so that Sean and Rebecca were seeing each other, Kate became very fond of Rebecca, kind of like a mother-daughter thing, which Kate was inclined to do on occasion.

"Good morning. Sean Murphy's office," answered Kate.

"Hello Kate, It's Rebecca Lockhart."

"Becca! Sean told me to expect your call. How are you?"

"Just keeping my neck above water, if you know what I mean, Kate. I hope you're keeping that maniac in line."

"You know I am, dear. I'm the only one who can. He's scared of me. I hit hard."

"Good. Don't hold back. Sean can use a good whipping every once in a while. You alone can tame that beast, Kate."

"Don't you worry about that, Becca. I've spent the better part of twenty years whipping him into shape. I think I'm finally getting somewhere."

"Good things come to those who wait, right Kate?"

"That's right, dear. So, Sean said you would be calling to set up a time to stop by to discuss a new case. Is that right?"

"Yeah. Anything in the next few days open for him?"

"Actually, Becca, he is free this afternoon if you'd like to stop by."

"Works for me, Kate. I'll be there around three or three thirty, if that's okay."

"Perfect. I'm so excited to hear that you and Sean are working together again. I'll let Sean know you're coming. See you then."

When Rebecca arrived that afternoon, Kate jumped up from her desk and gave Rebecca a big hug. Because of her girth, Kate's hugs were noteworthy to say the least. Plus, because Rebecca towered over Kate, her head squeezed awkwardly into Rebecca's chest when Kate grabbed her. Genuine kindness is not proud, to be sure. Sean walked out of his office while Kate and Rebecca were still in their embrace.

"All right. Break it up you two. Give me a chance." Sean grabbed Rebecca and hugged her, leaning backward as he did so. It was the only way he knew how to hug. Even though Rebecca was taller than most women, the combination of Sean's height and curve in his back caused Rebecca's body to press down on Sean's. Rebecca's initial reaction was to put her palms into Sean's chest, which had the effect of keeping at least her upper body free from contact. But, Sean's strength was so overwhelming that Rebecca, after a few seconds, gave up and fell fully into Sean's hug, wrapping her arms around his neck, her feet about a foot off the floor. Sean made a few grunts, which was a standard part of his bear hug, and then released Rebecca. "So, what have you got for me Becca? Did you pull a rabbit out of the hat for me?"

"The only thing I can say is you and I missed a golden opportunity." They walked into Sean's office and he half closed the door. As Rebecca sat down on one of the chairs facing Sean's desk, she continued with her comments. "We should have started this kind of exchange. These greenhouse gas credits are trading like crazy and the guy who is quarter-backing it makes a fee on every deal."

"What else you got for me besides reminding me I'm goin' to be a poor white man for the rest of my days on earth? You know, Irishmen just don't know how to make money. Never have, never will."

"All of Power Systems' credits are on the up-and-up. I checked the Exchange's verification procedure. Power Systems can prove through coal purchasing records how much product it is burning. I also checked the math on calculating the tons of credits that Power Systems is entitled to under the Exchange's protocol. Everything looks fine. A big chunk of Power Systems' greenhouse gas credits are available right now for purchase on the Exchange. In the first year of trading, all fifty or so companies in the Exchange bought credits, to one degree or another, from Power Systems."

Sean stopped Rebecca's presentation, knowing what was coming next. "Drum roll please. And the grand total is?"

"Twenty five million dollars right to Power Systems' bottom line in the first year of trading."

"Holy shit! That's gotta' be some kind of record, right?"

"Yeah. With the stuff you have had me bird dogging over the past few years, the most I've seen any one company make in the way of profit on a credit sale is a couple hundred thousand dollars."

"But from what I'm hearing, it's legit', right?" asked Sean.

"All straight up. Sorry," she said.

"That's okay. I have plenty to keep me busy," he answered.

Rebecca paused a minute to look back at the records she brought with her. "I did a little corporate archeological digging on Power Systems. Energy suppliers have to register with the Securities and Exchange Commission. So, I had a look at Power Systems' registration statement. Nothing out of the ordinary. The company was organized in 1995. Five owners of record, each holding an equal share of the company."

"Who are they?" Sean asked.

"A couple are guys who have been in the power generation industry for many years. Looks like they brought the industry knowledge to the table. You know, how to actually do the day-to-day work of generating electricity. One of the guys I recognize as a money man on Wall Street. All he does is invest the cash and get the company up and running. He has a position with the company, but that is more a means to watch over his money rather than actually participating in the business. I'm sure he never leaves his office on Wall Street, even though his investment is in Philly. In fact, I'm fairly confident he probably has never even seen a plant. Then, the company's registration statement reports that one of the VP's is an attorney out of Washington, D.C.

"Do you remember his name?"

"Let me see," Rebecca replied as she looked through the file. "Says here his name is . . . Oren Kane."

"Boy," Sean said, "that name sounds familiar." He paused for a second or two to trigger his memory. "Wait a minute, is it Senator Kane?"

"The registration statement doesn't mention anything about him being a senator," replied Stephanie.

"It can't be him. That would be just too small of a world."

"What do you mean?" Rebecca asked.

"Right after law school, I had a run in it with this Senator Kane. At the time he was heading up the Senate Sub-committee on Environment and Public Works, which handles a bunch of environmental legislation. If I recall correctly, this guy was also a practicing attorney and had an office in D.C. Anyway, when I graduated law school, I took a position as a clerk with this congressional sub-committee; you know, doing a lot of research on proposed environmental legislation. So, all's goin' well for about the first six months or so when I hear that this Senator Kane is complaining about my work. A couple of the senators on the sub-committee tell me that I should set up a meeting with Senator Kane to smooth things out."

"Are you kidding me?" Rebecca interjected.

"No, I'm not. As far as I was concerned, everything was peachy and then the next thing I know is I'm expected to 'smooth things out' with this Senator Kane.

Hell, I didn't even know what I was supposed to have done wrong that required a 'smoothing out.'"

"So, what'd you do?" Rebecca asked.

"Well, the first thing I did was go back through my research memos to see what kind of work I had done for Senator Kane. I came across a few things, but nothing substantial. Then, I talked to a few of the other clerks who said that they heard Senator Kane was miffed with me but nothing more than that. So, I had no choice but to go meet with him."

"You mean to tell me you went into a meeting cold, not even aware of what it was that you were supposed to have done wrong?" Rebecca inquired.

"That's right. There was no other way to deal with it. So anyway, I set up a meeting. I go into his office one morning and. . . ." Sean was interrupted by Rebecca.

"Were you scared?"

"Hell yeah. Shitless in fact," Sean replied. "You figure I was twenty four at the time and here's this older senator who has been around for a while. To say that I had dry mouth would do a disservice to my level of panic, but I fought my way through it and just opened up by saying that I heard he was . . . displeased is the word I think I used . . . with my work."

"No way. Really?" Rebecca blurted.

"Oh yeah. So, he proceeds to tell me that he was waiting on a number of research assignments that he had given me a couple of months back and I had failed to report back to him on my progress."

"Is that true?" Rebecca asked.

"No, which is exactly what I said to him. I told him I had nothing outstanding that he had asked me to do. But, then I figured I would do the right thing, and so I asked him to tell me the assignments and I would get right on them."

"So, what'd he do?" she asked.

"He slammed his hand down on his desk, which caught me by surprise—in fact I jumped in my seat when he did it—and then he yelled that it was too late. To use his phrase, 'You dropped the ball.' He had asked another one of the clerks to do the work. So, now I'm sitting there wondering what to do next. Senator Kane was shuffling through some papers on his desk, paying absolutely no attention to me. I didn't know whether to sit and wait for a scolding or get up and leave. So, I sucked it up and asked him what I could do to 'smooth things out.'"

"That was noble of you, Sean," Rebecca observed.

"Yeah, I thought so, but it didn't have the effect I thought it would. Senator Kane proceeds to tell me that he doesn't want to be bothered with someone who can't remember to do a simple assignment. As you can guess, that comment got my Irish blood boiling."

"Oh, no. Here it comes," she observed.

"Yep, you got it." Sean replied. "I knew the guy was wrong about asking me to do the research assignments, and I figured I had made a good faith effort to play along and be the peacemaker. But it didn't work. So I figured fuck it."

Rebecca knew what was coming next, having worked next to Sean in some complex and difficult cases. "What'd you say to him?" she asked.

"Well, I told him again that he never asked me to do the assignments and suggested that maybe he had me mixed up with one of the other clerks."

"What was his answer?" she asked.

"He said something obnoxious like 'are you questioning my memory, son?' I, of course didn't like his tone so I suggested something like I wasn't questioning his memory, but it certainly seemed like he had a convenient one?"

"You didn't," Stephanie responded.

"Oh yeah, I did. Then I walked out of his office," Sean said boldly, almost proudly.

"You didn't. What happened?"

"What do you think, I got fired."

"Sean, you have absolutely no finesse," Rebecca observed.

"Well, I was young and full of testosterone, but it definitely came back to bite me in the ass. Oh well, I came back to Philly and wound up getting a job with the DOJ about a month later. It gets better, though. Turns out that Senator Kane had a son-in-law graduating from Georgetown Law Center at the same time he is working this scheme on me."

"How do you know that?" Rebecca asked.

"A few months after I was fired, I got a call from one of the other clerks who started right around the same time I did. He told me that Kane's son-in-law filled my slot. So, as far as I'm concerned, Kane worked this scheme to have me fired so he could make room for his kin."

"WHAT . . . A . . . DICK," Rebecca said gallantly.

"No doubt. I remember this shithead had a habit of folding his hands together and rubbing them back and forth while he talked. I got the sense he did a little too much masturbating when he was younger and it was his subconscious way of cleaning years of residue off of his hands, if you get my drift. He was a typical short guy, which means to me that none of the high school girls wanted to touch his pee-pee. So, he had to resort to an inordinate amount of jerking-off."

"Only you, Sean, could come up with something like that from a hand rubbing habit."

"I know it's pathetic, but it makes me feel better to think that's why he was doin' it, instead of just some random nervous tick."

"That is a weird story, but to be honest Sean, you have a lot of weird ones. You just seem to attract them."

"I know, but that's what makes me so special. You know Becca, I've come to a conclusion," Sean offered.

"What's that, Sean?"

"People either love me or hate me. There is no middle ground with me and my relationships. Nobody ever seems to feel lukewarm about me. The problem is that the number of those who populate the latter category is substantially greater than the number of those who populate the former category."

"Well, I don't care what anybody else thinks, Sean, I love you." Although Rebecca made the comment jokingly, she immediately became nervous at the possibility that Sean might read more into it.

"Good, that makes it you, the pizza slice guy down the street, Kate—sometimes anyway—and well my dog, but I don't know if she counts."

"So," Rebecca asked, "do you really think this Kane with Power Systems is this Senator Kane that you had a problem with?"

"I don't know, but consider this little bit of weirdness. Last year I went to see Bruce Springsteen at Lincoln Financial Field."

"Oh my God, Bruce," Rebecca interrupted. "Isn't he some kind of a deity in your world?"

"Kiss my ass. Anyway, Bruce was touring to market his music on *The Rising*. You know, the one he came out with after 9/11."

"Oh, yeah. Great CD," Rebecca admitted painfully.

"So there's this song on *The Rising* where Bruce is talkin' about meeting up with someone who has done you wrong and talkin' about getting revenge. You know the one I'm thinkin' of?"

"I think so. I'm pretty sure it was called 'Further On Up the Road.' Let's see now: 'Further on up the road, Where the way is dark, and the night is cold, One sunny mornin' we'll rise I know, and I'll meet you Further on up the road.'"

"That's it!" Sean yelped. "When I heard that song, it immediately brought back memories about how I felt after getting fired. I was so pissed off, but there was nothing I could do about it. So, I reverted to the age-old form of satisfaction of thinking that some day he and I would cross paths again and I would have no choice but to kick his sorry ass. That Bruce Springsteen song brought all those feelings back, instantly. It was like I was sitting on the train back to Philly right after getting fired. It got my blood boiling, and I started swinging punches in the air. It was great!"

"You are one pathetic creature, Sean," Rebecca said as she shook her head. "Well, I wonder if this Kane affiliated with Power Systems is the same guy."

"As far as I'm concerned," responded Sean, "it's a sign from God. And, I never resist divine justice. I think we should do a little more digging on Power Systems."

"You really are a weirdo, Sean, but if the Kane in the Power Systems registration statement is your friend Senator Kane, no wonder Power Systems has been so successful. The company has everything it needs: industry savvy people to run the plant, plenty of Wall Street money to fund it, and a power broker in Washington. I couldn't think of a better combination."

Sean pondered, "This company just keeps getting more and more interesting. I can't explain why, but it just does."

"As I said, though, Sean, these guys seem on the up-and-up. Everything looks kosher."

"Yeah, I know. I'm probably just spinning wheels here. But one thing I didn't mention to you is an employee of the company was found floating in the Delaware a few weeks back. This stiff's family thought he was going to blow the whistle on Power Systems because of some environmental problem."

"What, this employee was murdered?" Rebecca asked, surprised to hear the story.

"Yep," he answered.

"So, is the theory that this employee was murdered as a means of keeping him quiet?"

"I don't know that it's an actual theory yet," Sean responded. "More like a nagging undercurrent, if you know what I mean."

"Such drama!" Rebecca observed emphatically. "I can't believe you kept the good stuff from me till last, Sean. I've never been involved in a case with such a dramatic twist."

"Becca . . . be serious. Murder? Drama? We . . . live . . . in . . . PHILLY," Sean blurted with obvious purpose. "Murder isn't drama in Philly. It's routine."

"I can't believe what I'm hearing," Rebecca said flippantly. "Philly's greatest advocate, Sean Murphy, actually has something bad to say about his City of Brotherly Love."

Sean immediately got defensive. "That's not what I meant. I was making the point that you were overreacting."

"Say what you want, but you dissed Philly."

"Whatever."

Rebecca smiled because she knew she had hit a Murphy nerve, not to mention the fact that Sean never let her win an argument with an uncharacteristic "whatever." Sean Murphy was all about fighting to the bitter end, even when he had absolutely nothing left to fight with. "One other thing, Sean."

"What's that, dear?"

"Getting back to this guy Kane. Regardless of whether he is your Senator Kane, the SEC Registration Statement mentions that his income is handled differently than all of the other key employees of the company."

Sean was again interested in the conversation. "How so?" he asked.

"For the most part, all of Power Systems' employees are paid an annual salary and that's it. Like all the others, Kane gets a base salary, which is pretty sizable by the way, but on top of that he is engaged in this interesting bonus program that is linked to the amount of credits that Power Systems sells. My guess is that, considering the company sold $25 million in credits its first year of operation, Kane must be getting some pretty significant cash payments out of the bonus program."

"Why would Power Systems do that? I mean, why would the company treat him differently than all the other employees?"

"It's just a guess, but if this guy Kane is a U.S. Senator and is on the Environment and Public Works Sub-committee, my guess is that he wields a good deal of power in Washington and even across the country for that matter. In my experience, guys like that are brought into companies for one reason: to grease the political wheels so that the company makes a profit. Assuming all that to be the case here, it would make sense that Kane is 'incentivized' with a bonus based on the income into the company by way of credit sales."

"Becca, this company just keeps getting more and more interesting to me." Sean paused for a second or two to think about the next step. "All right, then. Good job so far. Let's get a definitive answer on whether the Power Systems Kane is my old buddy Senator Kane."

"And if they are one and the same?" Rebecca inquired.

"Well, then, you'll get all the drama you can handle in a lifetime."

Sean showed Rebecca to the door, leaned over and kissed her lightly on the cheek. Kate smiled.

CHAPTER 13

The next thing Rebecca Lockhart did after getting the assignment from Sean Murphy was to scan the various trade publications for a seminar or program that would get her mind warmed up and push her up the learning curve. She found one on the Internet labeled "First Annual Carbon Expo" which was being held in Sydney, Australia. It had been some time since Rebecca had broken her daily routine and the bustle of Philly was beginning to erode Rebecca's normally warm and welcoming nature. The change of scenery, Rebecca figured, would be good for her, not to mention the fact that putting the expense on Sean Murphy's shoulders brought an immediate smile to her face. Rebecca cleared her schedule, made reservations, and was on her way to Sydney the following week.

When Rebecca arrived at the Pacific International Hotel, which was where the "Carbon Expo" was also being held, her registration packet was waiting at the check-in desk. Rebecca settled in to her room and began reviewing what was available in the way of learning tools over the next three days. The participants were impressive: the World Energy Council, the European Union, the World Bank, the International Energy Agency, and representatives of just about every country that had ratified The Kyoto Protocol. Rebecca was happy to see the United States represented by way of the Department of Energy and the Environmental Protection Agency. Also present were officers of many of the Fortune 500 companies. By merely reviewing the attendance list, Rebecca realized that the "carbon market" was more than just emerging. It was a robust and truly international marketplace that undoubtedly, in Rebecca's estimation, involved significant dollars.

Rebecca spent the next three days going to hour long seminars on a variety of topics surrounding greenhouse gases and global warming. While the subject matter interested Rebecca, she was more interested in the practical aspect of things, including mainly who were the principal "movers and shakers" in this new marketplace. One afternoon, she met and talked with a number of British and

German businesspeople who seemingly had significant influence over the European Union, which was working aggressively to get full ratification of The Kyoto Protocol. They explained to Rebecca that, without all industrialized nations accepting the terms and conditions of that international treaty, global manufacturing would be on an uneven, and therefore, unfair playing field. The fact that Rebecca was from the United States made these European businesspeople especially interested in her presence at the "Carbon Expo." They saw it as a chance to put pressure on the United States to ratify The Kyoto Protocol. Rebecca explained to them that, while she was from the United States, she was not there as an advocate for the country, but rather as a representative of an small agency interested in the topic. One of the British businessmen in particular, by the name of Byron Russell, took a keen interest in Rebecca' research efforts.

"What agency is it, Rebecca, that you represent?" Byron asked.

"Actually, I am self-employed. I own a firm in Philadelphia that provides financial consulting services to the government sector, at all levels. In this case, though, I am working for the Department of Justice Division of Environment and Natural Resources."

"That sounds interesting," Byron commented. "Is your work on a particular case or is it just research generally?"

"It's on a particular case," Rebecca answered. "We have a power plant in Philadelphia operating under the name of Power Systems. It is specially designed. . . ." Before Rebecca could finish, Byron Russell was interrupting her.

"Oh, I know Power Systems well. They are a large contributor of greenhouse gas credits to the global carbon market through an exchange in London, in which I have an interest. I deal in carbon futures. A lot of my business involves carbon contracts for the Power Systems credits."

"What a small world," Rebecca said. "Here we are in Sydney, Australia and I meet someone from England who knows about the Power Systems plant. What do you mean, Byron, when you say carbon futures? I mean, I'm familiar with commodities futures generally speaking, but I'm new to this carbon market. Can you explain the concept to me?"

"Surely," offered Byron. "You should know that I too didn't understand exactly how carbon futures were going to work when I first got into this market. It is a fairly unique tool that takes some time to understand. So, then, a carbon futures contract is simply a bet on what the price of a greenhouse gas credit will be a few years down the road. Right now, greenhouse gas credits are trading, on average, at say $15 per ton, but the carbon market is like any other market: supply and demand. If demand is high and supply is short, the price for the commodity will increase and vice versa. Simple economics, right?" Rebecca nodded to indicate that she was following Byron's presentation. "All I do by way of a carbon futures contract is bet on where the price per ton of greenhouse gases is going. My current thinking is that the supply of greenhouse gases credits is going to increase rapidly and stay way ahead of demand."

"Which means," Rebecca interrupted, "that you think the price per ton of greenhouse gases is going to drop below the current price of $15 per ton."

"That's correct, Rebecca. In fact, I think that in the next five years or so the price is going to drop to about $10 per ton and will stay at that level for some time, maybe even ten years. So, I have several carbon futures contracts where I'm obligated to buy from The Climate Exchange millions of tons of greenhouse credits over the next five years. If the going price per ton on the market is greater than $10, I will make significant profit because I will be able to resell those credits at the higher market rate in Europe, where many governments are obligated to comply with The Kyoto Protocol. If it is lower than the $10, I lose. In other words, I will have to sell the credits at a lesser price than what I am obligated to buy them. I simplified the deal, of course, but that's the gist of it."

"And you say most of your carbon futures contracts are with The Climate Exchange?"

"Yes, they are, which, as you are probably aware, means that the bulk of my purchases under those contracts will be credits supplied by Power Systems. That reminds me. You mentioned that the Department of Justice is interested in that company?" Byron inquired.

"Yes, that's correct," Rebecca answered and then realized that Byron Russell was probably worried about the fact that the Department of Justice was targeting the company that was at the center of his carbon futures contracts. "Oh, I don't know that it is so much the company in particular that the Department of Justice is investigating as it is the carbon market in general. I'm sure you're familiar with the Enron and Worldcom corporate scandals in the U.S.?"

"Of course," Byron acknowledged. "What a tragedy. I actually was involved in the Enron debacle personally."

"How so?" Rebecca asked, somewhat surprised to hear that a businessman from England had a link to Enron.

"One of the businesses in which I have a financial interest is engaged in the paper manufacturing trade. Oddly enough, one of the assets in the Enron bankruptcy was a paperboard facility in Minnesota."

"You're kidding me."

"No. You'd be surprised to hear all of the different kinds of companies and business enterprises that Enron owned. As I was saying, Enron purchased a paperboard facility that had been family owned for three generations. In fact, this facility had been the primary employer in a small Minnesota town for over one hundred years. I guess this family business fell on some hard financial times and Enron swooped in with a huge cash offer and a promise to keep the plant running. A month after buying this Minnesota plant, Enron went bankrupt and had to shut down all of its businesses, including this small paperboard facility. From what I hear, it was the first time in over a hundred years that this plant shut down. And, because it was the principal employer in this small Minnesota town, it went from a thriving community to an economic disaster area overnight."

"That's a horrible story," Rebecca said dejectedly.

"Indeed," Byron acknowledged. "Wait until you hear this, though. When we petitioned the bankruptcy court to purchase this facility, we were given a period of time to inspect it. You know, perform the standard engineering and structural evaluations to make sure we could put the plant back into production." Rebecca nodded to indicate her understanding of the inspection process. "Well, I was part of the team that went in to the plant to do this work. I was the first to arrive. When I walked into the plant, it was completely vacant and everything was shut down, except for some security lights on. I went into the administrative offices and noticed that desk top computers were still operating. Some of them even had a word processing document up on the screen, almost like the employees were told to get up from their desks and leave immediately. It was eerie. I sat down at one of the desks to start getting familiar with the plant layout and I looked up to the cork board above the desk. It had a sheet of paper, which was labeled 'Enron Code of Ethics.' Someone had taken it and turned it upside down. I'll never forget the impression that image left on me. I can just imagine the poor employee, who had probably been working at the plant for years, probably had a number of children to support, and found out the he or she was out of a job just because executives of Enron were crooks. The only solace that employee had was to make the point that Enron's code of ethics was a lie by turning it upside down."

"Wow!" Rebecca said in a stunned tone. "Did your company get the facility operating again?"

"No. It would have been too expensive to retrofit with the kind of equipment we needed. I wanted so much to give that plant back to the community, but there was nothing my company could do. I lost a few nights sleep over that one."

"I'll bet you did."

"I'm sorry, Rebecca. I got sidetracked when you mentioned Enron. You were saying that the Department of Justice has some kind of interest in the carbon market because of Enron."

"Well, it's not just Enron. You may recall that the Securities and Exchange Commission got some flak after the Enron and Worldcom debacles along the lines that if the agency had been paying closer attention, the financial problems with those companies might not have happened."

"Yes, I do recall that. Along the lines of a watchdog agency not really watching the dog," Bryon observed.

"Exactly. Well, the Department of Justice likes to keep an eye on the air pollutant emissions trading market to prevent that kind of catastrophe. Not just the carbon market, but air pollutants generally. In this case, it is not so much people's jobs that would be impacted by a problem in the marketplace as it is their health, along with natural resources damages."

"I apologize, Rebecca, but you lost me there."

"I understand. It took me a while to grasp at first. In your Enron example, people lost their jobs because the paperboard plant had to be shut down. There is an immediate and real human impact in your example. In the case of the air pollutant trading marketplace, people won't get put out of work if a company improperly reports its trading activities. The worst that would happen is more air pollution than intended, which can cause respiratory problems or adverse impacts to the environment."

"Now I follow you," Byron said proudly. "So, I assume you are learning about how the carbon market works so you can advise the Department of Justice about potential improprieties."

"That's right."

"It sounds like interesting work, Rebecca. Let me know if I can ever be of any assistance," Byron said as he handed Rebecca his business card. "It was a pleasure meeting you, and I hope to see you again soon."

"Likewise."

CHAPTER 14

Occupying the fourteenth floor of 111 West Jackson Street, The Climate Exchange is just a stone's throw away from the Chicago Mercantile Exchange and has one of the best views of the Chicago River in all of the downtown area. The Climate Exchange is a multi-sector and multi-national market for trading greenhouse gas emissions. The goal of the Exchange is to have its members reduce emissions of greenhouse gases by four percent below the average of their 1998-2001 baseline and to achieve that objective by 2010. It is measurably less strict than the goal of The Kyoto Protocol, which calls for a reduction in greenhouse gas emissions of 5.2% compared to 1990 levels no later than 2012.

The Climate Exchange is over fifty members strong, boasting players such as Ford Motor Company, DuPont, Dow Corning, IBM, and Amtrak. The idea behind the exchange is for each member to figure out, based on its own needs, how to achieve the required reduction of four percent: eliminate actual greenhouse gas emissions from their operations, achieve the same effect by purchasing credits from some other member of the Exchange that make an actual reduction, or some combination of these two options. For the few years the exchange has been engaged in active trading, the average cost per ton of greenhouse gas has been around $15.

The Chairman and Chief Executive Officer of The Climate Exchange was Brendan Frisk. Harvard trained with a Ph.D. in economics, Frisk spent fifteen years on Wall Street, starting out as an aggressive young trader. He rose quickly through the ranks of a high risk investment banking firm, eating up as much information as possible along the way. Those around him at that time knew Frisk could not spend the rest of his life making money for others. While he did quite well financially, it was not his goal in life to continue to feed the fat rich white man. He was on a mission from the first day he set foot on the floor of the New York Stock Exchange, which was to own and control a trading company of some kind. Frisk never learned anything for academic sake. Every minute of every day was a chance for Frisk to collect some information or knowledge that would eventually benefit him financially.

His chance came in the mid 1980s when Frisk was reading the *Wall Street Journal* one day. He noticed an article on amendments to the Federal Clean Air Act aimed at reducing acid rain by controlling sulfur dioxide emissions from electric generating facilities. Frisk read that, as the sulfur dioxide gas mixed with water in the atmosphere, it formed a weak sulfuric acid. One of the concepts discussed in the article was a market-based solution to acid rain. The EPA was establishing an emissions trading program, which was to be administered by the Chicago Board of Trade. Frisk immediately abandoned a perfectly lucrative position in New York and headed to Chicago without a place to live or even a job offer, which was and continued to be his style.

Frisk's dream of starting his own trading business came one day when he heard a news report about The Kyoto Protocol. Frisk learned as he researched the issue that, like the sulfur dioxide emissions trading that he had become familiar with through the Chicago Board of Trade, The Kyoto Protocol included a provision encouraging market-based solutions to the reported developing problem with greenhouse gases. Because of the widespread intellectual and political support that had been achieved with respect to sulfur dioxide emissions trading as a means of controlling acid rain, Frisk knew that a similar trading program for carbon dioxide and other greenhouse gases would be wildly successful. The only difference, Frisk realized, was that greenhouse gases were not regulated under the Clean Air Act, and he knew the United States was not going to join in on The Kyoto Protocol, which was the only legal mechanism to impose restrictions on emissions of greenhouse gases. The one thing that attracted Frisk to the area was the fact that the amount of greenhouse gases emitted per year by the electric generating industry far exceeded the amount of sulfur dioxide. This in turn meant more trading, which signaled to Frisk that the value of this market would be substantially greater than that of the sulfur dioxide trading. Frisk also recognized that, even though no legal obligation currently existed for companies to reduce greenhouse gas emissions, it was just a matter of time before the United States either joined in on The Kyoto Protocol or amended the Clean Air Act to impose such reductions. There was just too much public outcry about the government doing nothing in this regard, and something would have to happen to respond to public opinion of the need for controls on greenhouse gases.

Frisk hastily left his position and immediately contacted all of the private investors who had participated in forming the sulfur dioxide trading program. Frisk was one of those people who always made money for his friends. So, it wasn't long before he had significant financial support for his idea of forming The Climate Exchange, which commenced trading of greenhouse gases in December, 2003.

Soon after trading commenced, Frisk announced that the Exchange had joined forces with the London-based International Petroleum Exchange to develop an electronic market for trading greenhouse gas credits in line with European Union directives aimed at compliance with The Kyoto Protocol. The joint venture with the International Petroleum Exchange, which was the leading energy futures and options exchange in Europe, immediately created the world's largest venue for trading greenhouse gas credits and was touted by Frisk as "a truly global marketplace for the reduction and trading of greenhouse gases." Under the terms of the joint venture, The Climate Exchange granted a license to the International Petroleum Exchange to list and market Frisk's products through an electronic trading platform known as the Interchange.

⊲ ⊲ ⊳ ⊳

Given Brendan Frisk's singular expertise in the environmental trading business, he was asked to testify before the Senate Environment and Public Works Committee at its hearings on the Climate Stewardship Act. After Mr. Frisk was sworn in under oath, one of the committee members started the questioning.

"Mr. Frisk, thank you for being here today. As you know, the United States Congress is trying to decide how this country should approach the issue of climate change. Obviously, it is a subject that has many levels, one of which we think touches directly on your background and expertise. What I am talking about is this concept of a carbon market. I was hoping you could explain it to us lesser informed."

"Of course, I'm glad to do that for you, senator. The collection of greenhouse gases in the atmosphere is now acknowledged as an environmental problem. Whether that's a fact or not is irrelevant, at least as far as the marketplace is concerned. What matters is that scientists and the environmental protection community firmly believe that global warming is occurring and is the result of this collection in the atmosphere of greenhouse gases, carbon dioxide mainly. That's all you really need for any market to exist. Let me give you a few facts. The World Bank's Carbon Finance Unit reports that the international trading market for greenhouse gas emissions credits has been growing from its inception. Traded volumes in metric tons of carbon dioxide increased from thirteen million tons in 2001 to approximately twenty-nine million tons in 2002, to approximately seventy-eight million tons in 2003, to one hundred fifty million tons in 2004. And experts predict that the volumes will continue to climb every year almost geometrically. However, in the marketplace, uncertainty stalls action, and we still have a whole bunch of uncertainty in the carbon market. For example, we don't have any clear governmental standards on how greenhouse gas reduction credits should be measured and verified. Even more importantly, though, we don't know how the credits should be priced."

Another committee member interrupted Frisk's presentation. "You lost me there, Mr. Frisk. What do you mean by pricing credits?"

"Sorry about that. If you think carbon—in the form of carbon dioxide, I mean—is the principal source of the global warming problem, then it must have some inherent price. That's one of the things we are struggling with in getting the carbon market fueled up and going. What we really need now is for governments internationally to provide greater regulatory certainty about how companies will be required to restrain their carbon output in the future, if at all. We also need

88

specific norms for carbon trading contracts. The lack of standardization in this nascent market keeps the carbon trading transaction costs high, which acts as a disincentive for growth of the carbon market."

The mention of the costs of trading prompted a committee member to ask, "What is the price of carbon?"

Frisk responded, "Right now prices are highly volatile and can range anywhere between $9 to $30 per ton depending mainly on where you are trading. The Climate Exchange is running right around the middle of that range at $15 per ton."

"So, where do you see this market going?" asked another committee member.

"Actually, I think the carbon market is going to be huge. It has to be if folks are serious about preventing global warming because it is a huge issue that involves a lot of tonnage every year of carbon dioxide. We have everything we need to develop a successful market, not only from a dollar standpoint but also from an environmental protection standpoint. All we need to do is fill in a few of the details."

"Mr. Frisk," asked one of the committee members, "have you been following the latest research and market reports on this new commodity, carbon?"

"Yes, I have, sir," Frisk responded.

"And what does that research say about the marketplace?" asked the committee member.

"The research, sir, says that a lot is happening. I don't mean to sound simplistic about it, but that's the best broad stroke description I can put on it. Now, let me get into some specifics. Right now, because of the requirements of The Kyoto Protocol, there is demand to get greenhouse gas credits, especially in the European Union, Japan, and Canada. Supply is the problem right now, but it won't be for long. Most of the studies say that the carbon market will quickly reach the billions of dollars and it will affect most directly, as you can expect, energy-intensive sectors, the energy sector itself, and industry that is heavily dependent on energy for its performance. Like any other newly created market, sir, we are learning by doing."

"How can the shortage of greenhouse gas credits be addressed, Mr. Frisk?" asked a committee member.

He responded, "I anticipate a number of activities aimed at responding to that deficit. First of all, I suspect those countries subject to The Kyoto Protocol will look to implement clean energy and renewable energy, such as biomass, hydrofuels, and wind parks."

"Excuse me for interrupting you, Mr. Frisk, but what is biomass, please?" asked the committee member.

"Biomass energy," explained Frisk, "primarily comes from transforming organic matter, like vegetation and animal carcasses, into a combustible gas known as methane, which can be used as a replacement for fossil fuels."

"Sounds kind of 'Star Trek' to me," joked one of the committee members.

"I had the same reaction at first, sir," answered Frisk. "However, the World Wide Fund for Nature and the European Biomass Industry Association issued a joint report in May, 2004 that concluded biomass energy production has the potential to reduce carbon dioxide emissions in industrialized countries by as much as one billion tons per year and to replace more than 400 existing power stations. The report goes on to say that biomass sources could power 100 million homes and provide fifteen percent of the industrialized world's energy needs by 2020. Currently, biomass contributes only one percent of the industrialized world's energy needs."

"Mr. Frisk, when you talk about biomass, do you mean growing new vegetation specifically for energy needs?"

"That's the idea, sir," Frisk responded.

"Well, doesn't that use up available land for food production and homes?"

"Yes, it would, sir, but the study also reports that only two percent of land in the industrialized world would have to be set aside for biomass production, which means it would not conflict with the needs of food production and nature conservation."

"So tell me, Mr. Frisk," asked one of the committee members, "is there anything we can do as a legislative body that will get the carbon market moving quickly?"

"Yes, a number of things come to mind," answered Frisk. "But, before I go there, I'd like to set the stage for my comments. As you know, many countries, mainly in Europe, have agreed to adopt the mandates of The Kyoto Protocol, which is a 1997 climate change treaty. The United States is one of the few industrialized countries not to do so. This situation makes it difficult for signatory countries to remain competitive in the marketplace. Take our situation in North America for example. Canada has adopted The Kyoto Protocol mandates. Because the United States has not, it is very difficult for Canada to attract industrial investment when a key trading partner right next door has not made similar climate change commitments."

"But, Mr. Frisk, I thought The Climate Exchange is trading greenhouse gases for companies located in the United States?"

Brendan Frisk could see the political party lines developing in the nature of the questions he was getting. "Yes, you are absolutely correct sir, but obviously I would like to see more substantial trading. Not to sound obnoxious about it, but more trading means more income to the Exchange and to me. So, what I think we need to do legislatively is adopt a mechanism to help the market mature a bit."

"How do we do that, Mr. Frisk?" asked a committee member.

"First of all, we need legislation to establish a registry for tracking carbon dioxide credits."

"What do you mean by a registry, Mr. Frisk?" asked a committee member.

"Well," Frisk responded, "it goes back to the comment that I made at the outset about establishing certainty in this new marketplace. Some kind of uniform standard for certifying greenhouse gas emissions reductions is the important starting point for this carbon market. As I understand it, the Climate Stewardship Act does not have a definitive standard for credits yet."

"You're correct about that, Mr. Frisk. So, do you have a suggestion how we fill that gap?"

"Yes, I may be able to get you started in the right direction. Here's what I did for The Climate Exchange. A coalition of public and private organizations known as the Climate, Community, and Biodiversity Alliance developed a set of standards to certify greenhouse gas reductions. As you can expect, they are known as the 'CCB Standards' and are designed to help companies, conservation groups, governments, and international funding groups identify cost-effective carbon emission reduction projects. Members participating in the projects governed by the CCB Standards include British Petroleum, Conservation International, the Hamburg Institute of International Economics, Intel, and The Nature Conservancy, among others." Frisk took a few seconds to flip through his comment sheets. "The registry should pay particular attention to carbon sequestration or carbon storage."

"Excuse me for a second, Mr. Frisk," interrupted one of the committee members, "but you lost me with that last comment."

Frisk replied politely. "Carbon sequestration. For example, farmers in the United States should get an annual credit for agricultural activities based on the number of carbon tons per acre that are being sequestered in the plant body. These credits could be a tremendous financial resource to farmers who, as we all know, have a difficult enough time as it is just making ends meet, even with subsidies. These agricultural related credits could be traded for value to manufacturers in need of a way to balance out their carbon dioxide emissions."

"Do you really think agricultural activities can store that much carbon, Mr. Frisk?" asked a committee member.

"Frankly, senator, I'm getting out of my area of expertise. But the research I've seen indicates that U.S. agricultural activities could result in 100 million to 150 million tons of carbon sequestered per year. Assuming that number is reliable, that is a huge amount of trading, just from U.S. agriculture."

"What else, Mr. Frisk, do you consider a priority to get the carbon market going?"

"Well, I don't know that this is something that can be done legislatively, but another thing that would be very helpful is some way to boost consumer demand for 'climate friendly' products."

The committee chuckled when they heard the phrase. "Climate friendly, huh? I don't know there is much Congress can do about advancing that ball, Mr. Frisk."

Frisk answered with a question. "How about a 'Carbon Fair'?"

"A what. . . ?" answered one of the committee members.

"A 'Carbon Fair.' The World Bank sponsored the first ever 'Global Market Fair & Conference,' which was held in Sydney, Australia. I went. It was great. Some folks refer to it as the 'Carbon Expo' or 'Carbon Fair.' The purpose of the fair was purely educational, but the idea is to get buyers and sellers of greenhouse gas emissions credits together to encourage deal-making. Interestingly, even though the first 'Carbon Expo' was intended to be educational, I am aware of two carbon contracts that were negotiated during the meeting. I guess the idea I'm suggesting to you is to encourage the creation of an international platform for the exchange of greenhouse gas credits. Another idea is for Congress to figure out a way to connect with the World Bank and its prominent Prototype Carbon Fund."

"I'm sorry, Mr. Frisk," said one of the committee members. "I missed your last comment. What was that about the World Bank?"

"The World Bank has launched several funds aimed at encouraging or catalyzing carbon dioxide emissions trading and investments in emission-reductions projects, the most prominent of which is the Prototype Carbon Fund. Countries looking to comply with the requirements of The Kyoto Protocol can pay into the fund, which then can be used to invest in emission reduction projects. Again, I'm being a bit self-serving because if Congress works into the Climate Stewardship Act some mechanism to connect with the Prototype Carbon Fund, my exchange will likely benefit financially. I'm sure I will see an increase in trading as a result."

"You've given us a number of suggestions and insights, Mr. Frisk. Where do you suggest we start?" asked a committee member.

"I'm glad you ask that, senator, because I can give you a starting point. Historically, energy producers, like most other companies, have focused on short-term profits, leaving long-term policy issues to governments and environmental groups. That old model can and must change."

"I don't follow you, Mr. Frisk," said a committee member.

"What I mean is energy producers need to start involving government and environmental groups in strategic corporate planning right from the outset. Instead of those groups being merely protestors, energy producers and other companies need to make them allies and decision-makers. Open and honest collaboration is the key."

"I just don't see that happening, Mr. Frisk," a committee member blurted. "No way will energy producers, or any company for that matter, invite government and environmental groups into private chambers to make decisions."

"Interestingly enough, senator," Frisk answered, "there is support for the proposition that doing so can lead to increased profits. I've seen recent comment and analysis in the financial world on the issue of liability disclosures in the wake of the ENRON and Worldcom scandals. The dispute surrounding accurate disclosure of a company's financial health includes whether and to what extent to make information available about environmental risk. The accounting community now generally agrees that a company's obligation to disclose business risks and uncertainties should include environmental issues, even that of potential impacts by a company on climate change. For example, Nova Scotia Power was criticized because the company failed to disclose a deal in which it decided to sell off its supply of natural gas for a short-term financial gain and shifted to burning coal to generate electricity. That action drew the attention of a market analyst who downgraded the utility's stock on the basis that the short-term profit gain was more than offset by the environmental damage caused by greater greenhouse gas emissions attributable to burning the coal."

One senator interrupted and said, "So if I understand what you are saying, when consumers and shareholders begin to pay closer attention to long-term environmental impacts of company's decisions, the pressure to meet short-term profit goals will fade away. Is that correct?"

"Close enough for government work," Frisk quipped back, which didn't make many of the committee members happy.

"Yeah, but still," another senator continued, "in your example about Nova Scotia Power, so what? Who cares that this market analyst downgraded the utility's stock? Does it have any meaning in the real world?"

"Absolutely," Frisk quipped again. "Insurance companies are starting to refuse to protect corporate officers and directors unless they adequately address environmental risks. Not only that, but banks and other investors are increasingly reluctant to invest in corporations with poor environmental reporting. Finally, there is no question but that shareholder activism on environmental reporting is on the rise. So, the end result is that doing business on a day-to-day basis can become extremely difficult without the confidence of insurers, banks, and shareholders."

"Mr. Frisk," said the chairman of the committee. "One of the difficulties we have here today is resolving a dispute among the committee members about the cost to industry of the Climate Stewardship Act. Some time ago, the Senate voted to reject the measure because of the reported high cost to industry, which was based on certain mathematical modeling typically used for evaluating proposed legislation. We are thinking of modifying the bill in a way that we were hoping would reduce that compliance cost to industry. Can you comment on the mathematical model we are using to evaluate this bill?"

"I prefer not to comment, Mr. Chairman. The reason is that by merely commenting on the process, I may lend credibility to it, which I don't want to do. I don't think the kind of modeling the government does on proposed environmental legislation is a credible barometer from which to assess the economics. For example, Mr. Chairman, the Senate has a long history of not being able to do an adequate job of using assumptions that reflect the innovation of advanced technology in the environmental field. The Department of Energy has an entire department dedicated to the advancement of technology yet the agency does not use the concept in its modeling."

"I appreciate your candor, Mr. Frisk."

The committee appeared somewhat stunned by what Frisk had to say. Things became accordingly quiet, which prompted the Chairman to speak up. "Mr. Frisk, thank you for your time and testimony today. It has been quite enlightening. We will take your comments under consideration as we deliberate this issue."

"You're certainly welcome, Mr. Chairman and members of the committee. I applaud the committee for what it is doing here and wish you the best of luck. Thank you."

CHAPTER 15

Tom Roth's visit to the Power Systems plant hadn't yielded much in the way of useful information. He was still waiting on the testing results of his river water samples from the EPA laboratory, which put him at a standstill. This kind of downtime was nothing new for Tom, though. It happened in almost every case. He thought about calling Steve Cooperhouse, but decided against it because Tom didn't want to give Steve an incomplete report. And, for some unknown reason, that's what Tom felt about his investigation so far. Something was missing, leaving him with a sense of his task being incomplete.

As a means of keeping the process going, Tom decided to rummage through some old aerial photographs of the section of the Delaware River where the Power Systems facility was located. Tom had developed a unique knack of ferreting out useful environmental information from aerial photographs, which provide a "bird's eye" view of the landscape over time. While simply comparing and contrasting a number of chronological photographs yielded a wealth of information, like changes in land use and vegetative growth or decimation, Tom Roth was one of the first to take the process to the next level by way of an instrument known as a stereoscope. This process employed a pair of specially designed glasses placed over a pair of mirror-image aerial photographs, slightly askew. The end result was a three dimensional image of the photographed site that allowed the viewer to pick out and distinguish changes in topography along with things like building heights and excavations. Even though this process had been used for many years in intelligence and defense, Tom Roth was one of the first to apply it in a way that was helpful in the context of environmental protection. In fact, the EPA regarded Tom as one of its top investigators based mainly on a couple of cases where Tom came up with indicting evidence using only aerial photographs.

Tom Roth could put together a property history by finding aerials in the craziest places. The EPA maintained its own database of aerial photographs, but Tom would scour through historical society files, local library records, and other unusual sources to patch together a pictorial chronology, sometimes having photographs for each year going back in time twenty, thirty, and even forty or fifty years in some cases, especially urban areas. The defining moment in Tom's use of this tactic was when he found a series of aerial photographs showing a dye manufacturer burying fifty-five gallon drums of waste on its property over several years in the 1980s. When the EPA investigated the property in the early 1990s, there was no evidence of any environmental threat or problem on the property, even though neighbors were complaining about taste and odor problems in their drinking water, which came from private wells. When the EPA tested dozens of wells in this neighborhood, they were contaminated with various solvents and metals. The only significant industrial activity in this particular neighborhood was a dye manufacturer that had been operating since the turn of the century. It, thus, became the focus of the EPA's attention in trying to answer the question how the drinking water became contaminated. Although EPA's site inspection of the dye manufacturer did not uncover any problems, Tom was convinced something was going on at the property, mainly because he noticed some discoloration of the Delaware River near the dye manufacturer. He found aerial photographs dating back to the 1940s. About a dozen photographs spanning from 1950 through 1980 showed the property maturing through various stages of vegetative growth and forestation, as he expected. All of the sudden, on the 1982 photograph, Tom noticed a large chunk of the vegetation removed. When he looked at the area through the stereoscope, which not only created a three dimensional image but also magnified it, Tom noticed heavy machinery on the site. He could also tell, because of the three dimensional aspect of the stereoscopic image, that the machinery was excavating a pit in the cleared area. The aerial photograph for 1983 had, in the excavated area, hundreds of little circles lined up next to one another, much like it looks when one stands over top of a box of glasses or jars. This same pattern appeared on the aerial photographs for 1984 through 1987, after which the cleared area was graded out and re-vegetated. Tom surmised that the circles were the tops of fifty-five gallon drums containing waste and convinced a Federal District Court Judge to give the EPA a search warrant to perform some test pits on the property. By simply measuring distances off of the street and river, Tom identified a handful of test pit locations, each one containing drums about five feet below the ground surface. The case ended with Sean Murphy getting two convictions under the Federal Resource Conservation and Recovery Act, with jail terms of eighteen months each for two corporate executives and a corporate fine of one million dollars.

This groundbreaking effort led to Tom winning an EPA award that year, but more importantly it gave support to what Tom had long advocated about the use and value of aerial photography searches, even though Tom was the first to admit that many times the documents wouldn't yield any useful information. But, like that one good tee-off shot, it was the periodic windfall from aerial photographs that kept Tom coming back to them, which he decided to do with the Power Systems facility. He had collected a couple of shots for each year since the plant had been built and an annual one for five years prior to construction.

Okay, let's see what we can see here, Tom thought as he looked at a 1995 photograph. The site was what he expected it to be: vacant with typical river front vegetation and debris. He saw pretty much the same thing on every yearly photograph up through 1999, which showed the beginnings of the site being graded and readied for development. Through 2000, the photographs showed the site in various stages of construction, which caused the site to take on an appearance that Tom recognized from his site visit. *What's goin' to jump off the page at me here?* Tom was an avid believer that the longer you patiently study something, whatever it was, the more likely your chances of finding something significant or meaningful. Most people did not appreciate the fact that good quality research and results, in any field, does not require a "rocket scientist" or an otherwise superior intellect. Rather, it is more about patience and calmness, with an unyielding attention to detail. Those are what inevitably lead to good results, and Tom had become a master of it. The trick was to wait until studying an item took you to the point of frustration. Soon after that, assuming one had the ability to stick with it, an unusual sense of peace and calmness would take over, which is when the real, high quality studying of a subject could happen. It worked for Tom Roth anyway. *What's here? Anything hiding?* Tom shifted his attention back and forth between the aerial photographs and the schematic diagrams of the power plant that he had studied before. The trick was to compare the two documents section by section, inch by inch, and wait for some discrepancy or abnormality to pop off of the page. He was a detail oriented guy.

⊰ ⊰ ⊱ ⊱

Once Tom had written an article for a trade publication. It was one of the few times that the trade publication had received a written piece without a single typographical error. The trade journal's editor called Tom to ask him to reveal his secret of perfection.

"I proofread my articles backward," said Tom.

"What?" asked the publisher.

"I start proofreading at the right side of the last sentence and work my way backward through the article. It forces me to focus on the spelling of each word."

"You've got to be kidding me?" the editor asked in disbelief.

"Nope. Works every time," Tom said proudly. "I don't think I've had a typo in any of my written materials in years."

Some called him anal. Tom, however, liked to think of himself simply as thorough.

⊰ ⊰ ⊱ ⊱

Tom now had about half dozen aerial photographs scattered around the table, all of them circling the plant schematic in the center. He had been at it about and hour and fifteen minutes. *Somethin's not right. I can feel it, man. What the hell's wrong in these photos?* He shifted the stereoscope from one photograph to another, in no particular order, every once in a while peering back at the schematic drawing. *There's the top of the plant. Looks to be about the same size as the drawing. The exhaust pipes appear to be the correct size.* Tom slowed his pace now. He felt something amiss. *Exhaust pipes. Exhaust pipes. There were three running down the side of the building that I saw.* Tom focused his attention in on the exhaust pipes coming out of the top of the building. During his site inspection, he could not see the top of the building, but he recalled the three huge exhaust pipes running down the side of the building and re-entering the building at different elevations. He looked back at the schematic drawing for some detailed information on the exhaust pipes. *Okay, what've we got here? This is the exhaust system schematic. Shows the exhaust pipes venting out of the top of the building.* The schematic on the Power Systems exhaust design was a couple of sheets, so Tom turned the page and there it was, jumping out at him. *What the hell? This shows only two exhaust pipes. I know I saw three.* He shifted his head back to the stereoscope and peered again at one of the aerial photographs. *I'll be god-damned! There it is.* What Tom saw was an aerial photograph right after the Tacony plant was constructed, showing the facility with two exhaust pipes as called for by the plans and specifications, but another aerial photograph about a year later showed three exhaust pipes coming off the facility. *Looks like they built the plant as 'spec'd' and then later modified it to include a third exhaust pipe.*

Tom knew now that he had something to report to Steve Cooperhouse. He wasn't sure exactly what, only that Power Systems had modified the exhaust system for some reason after plant start-up. Tom suspected that this information, plus a report of the EPA laboratory data for the water quality samples he collected during his site tour, would be of some interest to Steve Cooperhouse.

◁ ◁ ▷ ▷

"Hello, is Alicia in?" Tom Roth asked the receptionist of the EPA laboratory who had answered the ringing telephone.

"Yes, who's calling, please?"

"It's Tom Roth."

A few seconds later, Alicia's voice was on the other end. "Hey, Tom. Callin' 'bout those water samples, I bet."

"Yes. Sorry to push, but you know me."

"You are a pit bull, Roth. You'll be happy to know that I came up with a whole bunch of good stuff."

"Oh yeah? Let's hear about it," Tom said in a perky voice.

"Well, I'm goin' to e-mail you the hard data report, but let me give you a quick overview. We ran a phenolphthalein test on the water." Tom recognized that testing procedure as a much more accurate way to get a read on the pH of a sample than the litmus paper check he did when he collected the samples. "You checked the river with litmus when you were out there, right?"

Tom answered, "Sure did. I almost took a dip into the river, too."

"What'd you get?" Alicia inquired.

"pH of between four or five, or thereabouts."

"Not too shabby for a field grunt. We ran the pH test a couple of times and came up with 4.3 on one and 4.4 on the other."

"What else you got for me? Any explanation for the low pH?"

"Carbonic acid," replied Alicia.

"What?"

"Carbonic acid is what I said. It's not surprising or unusual to see this kind of thing happening in water quality. We have some streams in Pennsylvania and West Virginia that have a pH as low as three."

"Because they're contaminated, though," Tom said.

"Not necessarily," answered Alicia. "We've seen some situations where the water gets acidic because of naturally occurring conditions. One situation that comes to mind is water that flows over limestone, which is calcium carbonate. Under right temperature conditions, the carbonate can dissolve into the water and cause carbonic acid conditions. It's a relatively weak acid, but it can get the pH of water down to what we are seeing here."

"So this area in the Delaware River is a naturally occurring acidic condition?" Tom inquired.

"Might be," she responded, "but not likely. I've tested hundreds of samples over the years from this part of the river and never saw this kind of pH condition. Don't get me wrong. We've seen our fair share of acidic conditions in the river, but when it is localized, like this one seems to be, we can usually find some source of the condition."

"Anything else?" Tom inquired.

"No, that's it."

"What do you suggest as a next step?" he asked.

"Well, I think we should follow our normal protocol. First, we will organize a more extensive water quality testing of the area. We need to confirm the data we have so far and then gather more samples. It will be done in a way that looks for a possible source of contamination. Who knows? We may get surprised and find that there is some natural source of carbonic acid out there, but my roll of the dice is that we'll come to the conclusion this is related to some kind of on-going spill."

"Is there anything further you need from me, Alicia?" Tom offered.

"No, we'll take it from here. I'll let you know when the additional data is in and what it shows."

"Thanks for all your help as usual, dear."

CHAPTER 16

Steve Cooperhouse reached quickly for the telephone receiver, making sure that the silence after the first ring did not evolve into a second one. Steve could tell from the four digits showing up on the LCD display on his telephone that it was a call from one of his colleagues from inside the EPA, which meant he didn't have to be overly formal in his manner. "Hello, Cooperhouse here."

"Hey Steve, it's Tom."

"What's up, Roth?"

"I wanted to give you an update on that Power Systems case. I've come up with a few interesting things."

"What've ya' got for me?" Steve inquired.

"The low pH in the Delaware is coming from carbonic acid."

"Carbonic acid? It's got to be naturally occurring. Where else could carbonic acid possibly be coming from?"

"I was just about to say," Tom answered, "don't ask me what it's doin' there, but you beat me to the punch. The EPA lab was emphatic about the fact that carbonic acid is the culprit. They are going to do some further investigation."

"Oh hell, I don't want the EPA spending a lot of money chasing after a ghost, Tom. I'm going to call the lab and ask them to hold off on any additional sampling, assuming you're okay with that, of course."

Tom replied, "Not a problem. Give Alicia at the Edison lab a call and let her know we talked about it. I tend to agree with you that a bunch of sampling probably won't yield any useful results." Tom paused to look at his notes. "In addition to the carbonic acid finding, I noticed a glitch between the construction drawings for the Tacony plant and the actual layout of the facility."

"What do you mean?"

"When I was out at the facility, I noticed three exhaust return pipes. I didn't really remember it until I was looking at some aerial photographs and comparing them to the construction schematics. That's when I noticed that the schematics called for only two exhaust pipes, not three."

"You and those aerial photos, Tom," Steve interjected, knowing Tom's passion for detail. "But I'm not surprised to hear that there is an extra exhaust stack. We see that kind of stuff all of the time. Large projects like power plants are always tweaked a bit during construction because of oversight by the designer or any number of other reasons."

"I don't disagree with you on that point, but this would be a huge oversight relative to what we are used to seeing. It is one thing to forget a door here or there, or to change the layout of bathrooms or a cafeteria, but these exhaust return pipes are massive, integral parts of the operation. I would have expected to see something in the records about a substantial design change, which probably would have required the EPA's approval before Power Systems could have included that third exhaust pipe."

"Okay, how about you take another look at the plant and try to figure out what's goin' on?"

"Will do," Tom answered.

"Thanks for the report, Tom."

☙ ☙ ☙ ☙

Tom Roth decided to call Bob Morrone about the third exhaust pipe in case there was an easy explanation that Tom had simply overlooked.

"Hello, Bob, this is Tom Roth with the EPA. I visited the plant a few days ago."

"Yes, Tom, what can I do for you?"

"I got some lab results back on water samples that I collected in the river where that pH condition is popping up. The lab rats tell me that the culprit is carbonic acid. Any ideas?"

"I couldn't even begin to guess. As you know, I've been here only a few weeks and everything that I've reviewed to come up to speed with the operation says that we have nothing troublesome in our wastewater discharge. It must be a naturally occurring condition or maybe a continuing release of some kind on the river banks. I've seen a number of landfills located directly on a river that leach out contaminants underground and degrade the river water quality. Maybe there's an old closed landfill or dump nearby that is releasing carbonic acid."

"Well, the EPA lab tells me that this condition is an unlikely candidate for some kind of natural source of carbonic acid. You may be correct about the other point, though. Anyway, I also found another interesting discrepancy in Power Systems records."

"I knew this was coming," Morrone responded shakily. "My first suspicion was getting served with a subpoena for all of my records two weeks after I started this job. Then you come out for a site visit. That's why I haven't signed anything since I filled this position."

Tom could sense the nervousness in Bob Morrone's voice and thought he would accomplish more with a calm and cooperative person on the other end of the telephone. "Don't jump to any conclusions, Bob. I'm not sure this discrepancy means anything yet. That's why I'm calling you. I thought you might be able to give me a simple explanation that will make this thing go away."

"Okay, fair enough. Sorry to get upset like that, but I've seen guys in my position go away to jail. A lot of people don't realize that risk. One thing I'm always aware of is putting my signature on a mistaken environmental report that can lead jail time, even if I didn't intend to commit a crime."

"I know what you mean, and I assure you my investigation is not a criminal one. I'm simply trying to figure out this pH anomaly in the Delaware. That's it," Tom asserted in a way that reassured Bob Morrone that his ass was not on the line here.

"Well, I'm glad to hear that. Frankly, though, I don't know how much help I'm going to be. I never had a chance to look at the construction drawings for the plant. The city prosecutor came and took all the files before I had a chance to go through them. We made copies of most of the stuff, but the construction plans were an odd size and couldn't be copied, so the prosecutor took the originals. You probably know more about those plans than I do, Tom."

Another dead end. Tom Roth believed Bob Morrone was truly lacking knowledge. Tom figured he and Bob Morrone would learn together.

"I understand you're operating from a position of weakness in this case given your newness to the job and that all of the relevant files are in the government's possession. So, let's try to figure this one out together. I'll stop by the plant tomorrow with the construction drawings. In the meantime, you will see three large exhaust pipes running down the east side of the plant. Try to figure out their origin and destination, okay?"

"I'm very rushed today, but I'll do my best to find a couple of maintenance guys to check that out," Morrone offered.

"Sounds good. I'll see you tomorrow."

"Okay." Morrone hung up the telephone with a sinking feeling that he was being greeted by a tempest just about ready to blow. Tom Roth uncharacteristically interrupted the process of hanging up his telephone and brought it back up to his ear, after hearing what he thought was a clicking noise.

"Hello? Bob? Is anyone there?" The line was silent.

CHAPTER 17

Following her meeting with Sean Murphy and the trip to Sydney, Rebecca Lockhart decided the next appropriate and necessary step would be to the office of Power Systems, Inc.'s principal shareholder, which was a corporation by the name of Alternative Energy and Environmental Investment, Inc. Rebecca checked her research materials and found the address for Alternative Energy and Environmental Investment, Inc.'s offices—West Twenty-second Street in Manhattan—and the name of its chief executive officer and managing director, John Braddon. Through some additional research, Rebecca learned that John Braddon held an M.B.A. from Harvard University. When Rebecca contacted John Braddon, he was cordial and receptive to the idea of meeting with her to discuss the Tacony plant.

❦ ❦ ❧ ❧

When the Amtrak Metroliner pulled into Penn Station, Rebecca exited the train and was immediately swept into a mass of humanity, which caused her heart to start pounding a little quicker. Rebecca worked in Philly, which was a busy city in its own right, but no matter how much time she spent on Philly's streets, they never prepared Rebecca for the pace of Manhattan. It was an entirely different ball game. Although it made her nervous, Rebecca loved the idea of doing business there. New York City took her to an entirely new level, even if that level was a temporary mental fabrication. So, as was always the case when she exited the train, Rebecca knew that so long as you followed the crowd up, you would eventually reach street level.

Once there, Rebecca could not prevent herself from staring upward. The buildings in Philly were tall and impressive, but the ones in Manhattan were different. They took up whole city blocks and stretched skyward almost to heaven.

Rebecca loved the process of following a New York City building line from the ground all the way up to its peak, but Rebecca would always caution others that you have to do it slowly, otherwise you tip backwards and fall on your ass, which was no doubt the most distinctive way of singling yourself out as a visitor.

The offices of Alternative Energy and Environmental Investments, Inc. were conveniently just across from Penn Station. Once Rebecca had finished her touristy check of a few buildings around Penn Station and the Madison Square Garden marque, she jaywalked across Twenty-second Street into a routinely nondescript building on the other side. After passing some minor security measures, Rebecca took the elevator up to the thirty-second floor. The elevator opened directly in the offices of Alternative Energy and Environmental Investments, Inc., where an attractive, young, and noticeably large-breasted receptionist, replete with the fashionable telephone headset, was waiting to greet Rebecca.

"Good morning. How may I help you?" she inquired.

"Good morning," Rebecca responded courteously. "I'm here to meet with Mr. Braddon."

"You must be Ms. Lockhart, then," commented the receptionist.

"Yes," replied Rebecca, impressed by the fact that her appointment accorded such a high priority.

"Please have a seat, Ms. Lockhart, and I will let Mr. Braddon know you are here."

"Thank you kindly," Rebecca answered as she walked into the reception seating area. It was decorated with dark mahogany walls and equally dark colored, but fashionably soft leather seats. A large rectangular glass table was centered in the middle of the leather seats. Floor to ceiling windows provided a spectacular view north on Fifth Avenue. From the thirty-fourth floor, Rebecca noticed how the mass of people on Fifth Avenue flowed like water escaping a dam with each green light. Looking back toward the receptionist's desk, Rebecca noticed that the mahogany walls extended down a long hallway on the other side of the reception area toward what appeared to be a number of offices.

Rebecca melted into the welcome-ness of one of the plush seats and picked up the mandatory copy of National Geographic Magazine sitting on the fingerprint-free glass table. Before she could start reading, though, a tall, slender gentleman approached and introduced himself as John Braddon. Rebecca guessed from his looks, including his full head of silver hair and the beginnings of some arthritis is his long hands, that Braddon was in his early sixties. His European cut charcoal grey suit contrasted sharply, but tastefully, with a bold red tie. Rebecca noticed how the length of his pants measured to a precise match with the top of his black wing tip shoes, convincing her that Braddon kept an updated version of GQ on the table next to his bed. After the usual introductions, Braddon led Rebecca down the hallway on the other side of the reception desk.

"How's the City of Brotherly Love these days?" Braddon asked as a means of showing his local knowledge more so than any genuine interest in the well-being of Philly.

"Doing great," Rebecca replied.

"I get to Philly maybe twice a month on business. I love it there. It is a much more quaint setting than New York. You can get lost in the pace here, if you know what I mean."

Quaint? Rebecca thought to herself. She wasn't sure if this description was a snobbish jab or an accurate characterization in the eyes of a visiting New Yorker. Either way, Rebecca considered Philadelphia as deserving a much more substantive and better rating than merely quaint. "Yeah, I love Philly too," Rebecca decided was the more judicious response, but was quick to add. "Make sure you check out the Avenue of the Arts the next time you're downtown. It's getting international acclaim." Maybe that would give Rebecca's hometown a little more respectable footing in Braddon's eyes.

"I'll be sure to do that," Braddon answered, totally oblivious to Rebecca's mental gyrations behind the suggestion. As they walked along, Braddon started to point out a number of gadgets and tools carefully preserved in glass cases. Each one was artfully illuminated by single lamps attached to the wall above. "These items here, Rebecca. Is it okay if I call you Rebecca?" Braddon asked in a rote way but respectfully nonetheless, to which Rebecca acknowledged an okay by smiling and nodding her head. "These items that you see down the hallway are a number of Thomas Edison's inventions. We—when I say we I mean myself and the other investors in Alternative Energy and Environmental Investments—we have spent a load of money restoring and preserving them. My partners and I have been involved in financing the electric generation industry in one way or another over the past twenty-five years now. So, we figured with Edison's contributions to the industry overall, we would acquire and preserve as many of his inventions as possible, as a means of giving back to an industry that has been so good to us. You'd be surprised the shape we found some of these items in. It took a lot of money to restore them and then take measures to store them in a way that we were sure would preserve them for future generations to enjoy. We have one of the largest collections of his inventions. Some of the local schools have field trips to our office to see them. Some appraisers have valued the collection at five million bucks. All of my partners and I love Edison's quote that goes something like 'Be courageous! Whatever setbacks America has encountered, it has always emerged as a stronger and more prosperous nation. . . . Be brave as your fathers before you. Have faith and go forward.' That last phrase obviously took on a whole new meaning around here after 9/11. "

Rebecca was truly impressed. What appeared at first to be a typically superficial investment company now took on a whole new meaning. Before Rebecca could say anything, Braddon was directing her into a conference room at the end of the hallway. Much like the reception area, the conference room had floor to ceiling windows making up an entire wall. Centered in the middle of the room was what appeared to be an antique table with a dark cherry wood top and thick ornately sculptured legs. A single piece of large artwork on each of the three remaining walls, which carried the same mahogany feature as the rest of the office space, left Rebecca with a singular impression in her mind as she glanced around: *impecca -ble!* Braddon asked Rebecca if she would like some coffee as he walked toward a small side table wafting the smell of fresh brew into the conference room air. Rebecca could not resist.

Braddon commented as he delivered Rebecca's coffee in fine china. "So, Rebecca, I understand you want to talk with me about the Power Systems Tacony plant."

"Yes, at the request of the Department of Justice in Philly, I've been doing some background research into Power Systems generally and the Tacony plant in particular. What I'm looking for is some of the basics about the company, like how and when it was created, for what business purpose, and who the principal players are in the operation."

"Can you share with me Rebecca why the Department of Justice is so interested in that facility?"

"Honestly, sir," Rebecca answered respectfully, "I'm not entirely sure what the investigation goal is here. What I *can* share with you is that I've been brought in to gain an understanding of the carbon dioxide emissions credits and how they play into the carbon market. That's my background, market research and analysis."

"A market analyst working for the Department of Justice," Braddon commented charmingly. "I guess nowadays the government needs outside experts in just about every field."

"I actually specialize in government bond deals and that marketplace. So, this air emissions trading market is a natural outgrowth for me," commented Rebecca.

"I see. I see," Braddon said contemplatively. "Well, Rebecca, it is a much different business world out there today compared to when I started out, which by the way was a long time ago." They both laughed. "To be sure, the marketplace is exceedingly complex and highly specialized. Back when I started, you had to be sort of a 'jack of all trades,' which was both good and bad. It forced you to learn and understand things that perhaps you weren't otherwise inclined to handle, which naturally brought a good deal of stress and difficulty to the business. But, in the long run, that forced learning rounded you out as a business person. Process was as important as the ends. Now it seems the business world is characterized mainly by specialization."

"Not to be flip, sir, but specialization is the kind of market that I grew up in." Braddon chuckled at the collateral dig on his age. "Frankly, I don't know any other kind of marketplace. The interesting thing about being a specialist, though, is how the market defines that term."

That comment by Rebecca caught Braddon's interest. "And how is it defined?"

"In the marketplace, a specialist is simply the person who has done something one more time than all the others." Braddon laughed heartily at that comment, recognizing and appreciating Rebecca's rebellious attitude in it. "The trick, assuming your goal is to get rich, is to recognize a niche and establish yourself as a specialist early on in the process. A good example is intellectual property generally and computer software programming in particular. The few businesspeople who anticipated the real economic growth potential in that field have made fortunes because they got in the field at the early part of the learning curve."

"And, how about you, Rebecca? Has your expertise been lucrative?" Braddon asked in a matter of fact way.

"I do okay," Rebecca responded in an equally matter of fact way. "But my area of specialization has been around for a long time. You can make a good living doing what I do, but I'll never get rich. That's for sure."

"Well, Rebecca, thank you for indulging an aging businessman in market chit chat, but I don't want to keep you from your purpose here today. Time is money after all, right?"

"No, that's okay, sir." Rebecca responded. "I actually get a good deal of pleasure out of 'shop talk.'"

"Rebecca, please return the favor by calling me John instead of sir. As between the two of us, formalities work more of an injustice on me than they do you." Braddon smiled again. Rebecca was pleasantly surprised by how at ease Braddon made her feel, especially considering he knew that Rebecca's objective in being there was to conduct an investigation for the DOJ. Reflecting on it even further, Rebecca realized that Braddon's appreciation for Rebecca's potential apprehension was exactly why he was intentionally conducting the meeting is such an informal way, which caused Rebecca to gain a instant respect for Braddon. He had artfully taken Rebecca's initial apprehension, and by simply handling the first few minutes of the meeting in a cordial and haphazard way, he had made Rebecca completely at home. She was ready to begin.

"Okay, then, John it is," Rebecca acknowledged. "As I was saying, John, I'm under contract with the DOJ—Sean Murphy in particular—to gain some insight into this carbon market and how Power Systems fits into it."

"That's easy enough," Braddon observed. "I formed Alternative Energy and Environmental Investments about thirty five years ago. The company mission, as you can tell from the name, was to support the development of commercially available energy technologies that did not rely on fossil fuels. You may recall that, back in the 1970s. . . ." Braddon considered where he was going with his comment. "Then again maybe you don't recall. Anyway, back in the 1970s, the country went through an energy crisis of almost biblical proportions. So, I had the idea that things like solar energy, wind power, and geothermal power were going to take off and make a bunch of money. I convinced about six major Wall Street players to pony up a bunch of cash and I added my fair share in. Hence was born Alternative Energy and Environmental Investments. The problem was that the energy crisis passed, fossil fuels became amply available and affordable, and the alternative energy technology market never really got started. We actually wound up investing in a number of nuclear power plants because the solar and geothermal ideas just weren't taking off. I mean, we always had some money in those technologies, but the true return on our investment was in the nuclear power industry. Then, Three Mile Island happened and that market dried up because it got too expensive to build nuclear power plants."

Braddon paused for a second, which gave Rebecca an opportunity to speak. "I'm surprised to hear that you invested in nuclear power. I thought that was the worst thing going because of the inability to dispose of the radioactive waste materials."

"Well, Rebecca, Alternative Energy and Environmental Investments got into the nuclear power industry because, frankly, we are in the business of making money. Solar power and the like weren't bringing in any bucks. So, we had to make some adjustments to our investment strategy. And, if you think about it, at the time, nuclear power was a viable and commercially available alternative to fossil fuel fired power plants. So, the idea of investing in nuclear power fit within out mission statement. Quite frankly, Rebecca, sitting here today, I'm still convinced that nuclear power is the answer to our energy needs in this country. It is cleaner and cheaper."

"So, if that's the case, why hasn't nuclear power taken over the market?" Rebecca asked.

"Well, Three Mile Island dealt the industry a huge blow, unfortunately. What people don't realize is that the public health problems associated with allowable air emissions from fossil fuel burning plants far outweigh the actual dangers associated with nuclear power plants. But once the public got whipped into a frenzy of opposition after Three Mile Island, there was no chance for nuclear power."

"I don't follow," Rebecca said. "How can one event like that control an entire industry?"

"The general public doesn't know how to evaluate risk. You and I deal with it all the time in the business world in the context of financial risk. What I mean is we take a studied approach to investing in a particular business by weighing the likelihood that our investment will go bad and we will lose money. The general public seems unable to make that kind of assessment when it comes to risk of threat to their health. If I had to roll the dice on it, I would say that if any one person of average intelligence really studied the actual risk of nuclear power, he or she would reasonably conclude that the reward far outweighs the risk, including most importantly the environmental benefits to be gained."

"Which are what?" Rebecca inquired.

"Like I was saying, no air pollution, mainly, which in and of itself is huge. Hell, if I had my way, every furnace in the country would be nuclear based. Not just power plants. I mean every furnace in an industrial process and even home heating furnaces. Nuclear is the cleanest way to go. But you can't defeat popular public opinion, no matter how misinformed it is. Maybe some day. Anyway, I think we got a bit sidetracked there, Rebecca. What were we originally talking about?"

"The origin of Alternative Energy and Environmental Investments," she answered.

"Right. In the mid 1980s, we began investing in small independent power producers. A few maverick business people saw an considerable financial opportunity under some federal legislation advancing these small power generation plants that were supposed to burn waste."

"Come again?" Rebecca interrupted.

"Well, the original idea behind the federal legislation favoring small power plants was to encourage the construction of facilities that burn waste to generate electricity, as opposed to burning fossil fuel. The so called 'waste-to-energy' plants were supposed to take care of the mounting solid waste disposal crisis, mainly here in the Northeast, while at the same time providing a useable byproduct in the form of electricity and reducing the country's reliance on fossil fuels. You know, the classic 'win-win' situation."

"I assume you're going to tell me it didn't work," Rebecca commented.

"Bingo. Once again, public opposition to these kinds of facilities got in the way. The 'waste-to-energy' plants were what gave rise to the concept of NIMBY, which means 'not in my backyard.' Unlike the death of nuclear power, though, many 'waste-to-energy' plants were built because there really was no alternative. Landfill space was running short and Lord knows people weren't going to stop generating waste. So, we made out pretty well financially on those facilities and indeed continue to finance their construction even to this day, but not at the rate we did back in the 1980s and 1990s. Then, in 1995, I think it was . . . yes around 1995 . . . one of our contacts in the Southwest who had been operating fossil fuel power plants in that region for various utility companies for over twenty years came to us with what we thought was a kooky idea . . . at first, anyway. This guy is a bit of an eccentric. You know, one of those Albert Einstein types: wears the same outfit everyday so he doesn't have to waste brain power thinking about his clothes, can't carry on a normal social conversation because his brain is so hopped up all the time. He's also got the classic frazzled hair in a constant state of disarray. Anyway, this guy came to us out of the blue one day with a furnace design that he tagged as zero emissions. Of course, we thought at first that this idea of his was pie in the sky stuff and didn't give it too much attention. But, in our line of business you have to be careful about dismissing ideas hastily. That practice can come back to bite you in the rear, if you know what I mean. So, we invited him to New York to show us his plans. Don't you know, he shows up with not only the design for the system, but also a ten year business plan showing how just one of these plants could be generating scads of money in a couple of years. We did our usual exhaustive research and, lo and behold, came to the cautiously optimistic conclusion that this idea was sound. After funding the initial patent approvals and some small scale pilot tests, we were convinced that this technology had a good shot at being competitive and making some serious money. So, over the next few years, we invested $100 million, in round numbers of course, to get the Tacony plant up and running."

"If I understand," Rebecca interjected, "Alternate Energy and Environmental Investments is the sole shareholder of Power Systems, is that correct?"

"I'm glad to hear, Rebecca, that you have done your homework. Yes, that's correct. In fact, that's how we structure all of our business. For each new venture, we set up a new corporation and it becomes a wholly-owned subsidiary of Alternative Energy and Environmental Investments. Power Systems, Inc. is one of about a half dozen operating subsidiaries owned by Alternative Energy and Environmental Investments."

"Tell me, then, are there any other investors in Power Systems besides Alternative Energy and Environmental Investments?"

"No, we're the money backing up the operation," Braddon answered.

"You know what, I think I asked the question the wrong way. You mentioned before that you and a half dozen or so 'Wall Street' guys are the money behind

Alternative Energy and Environmental Investments. Are there any other investors in that company?"

"Good point. Yes, there are. When we first started out it was just myself and a handful of others, but once the Tacony plant became operational and our bottom line started glistening, we have had an infusion of money, mainly from state employee pension funds."

"You lost me there, John," Rebecca said. "Explain that please: pension funds?"

"Oh sure. Public employee pension systems are some of the most substantially financed investors in the country. Think about it. Probably one of the largest single groups of employees is state and federal employees. You know, compared to, say, any single private enterprise. So, the amount of cash in the pension systems for those governmental employees is almost endless. For example, the California State Employees Retirement System has billions of dollars it is looking to invest. When the market got wind of Power Systems' novel technology, combined with the fact that it was making serious money a few years after start up, hell, the investors were lining up handing us cash for the next generation of Power Systems facilities."

"That's interesting. You would think with the government bond work that I do I would have known about the public employee retirement systems." Rebecca smiled at Braddon to acknowledge her appreciation for the information. Learning is indeed a continuing process. "Let me ask you, John, how is Power Systems set up corporately? I mean, I understand now where the money comes from, but where does it go? Who's on the payroll?"

"Getting down to the meat and potatoes now, huh, Rebecca?" Braddon said jokingly. "We, of course, gave a substantial equity interest in the company to the guy who developed the technology and let him organize a team for operating the Tacony plant. So, he is identified as a VP of the company. He brought in some long time friends from other electric public utility companies, mainly in the Southwest. In addition to his team, I have a long-standing relationship with Senator Kane in DC. He and I actually met at Harvard. He was in law school at the same time I was getting my M.B.A. Senator Kane serves on the board of directors of a number of businesses in which we have made investments, and we value his professional opinion and capability. So, when this opportunity came along, I asked him to become an officer of Power Systems, instead of just being on the board."

"How's that working out?" Rebecca asked.

"He's working out great so far. It never hurts to have some political juice in DC, if you get my drift."

"Absolutely," Rebecca acknowledged. "Lobbying is the name of the game these days. I'm glad you mentioned Senator Kane, John, because I notice in the company's SEC filings that his total annual salary is not disclosed. It mentions a bottom line number, around $100,000 if I recall correctly, and then mentions something about a bonus program on top of that salary." Rebecca waited for Braddon's reaction.

"I'm genuinely impressed now, Rebecca. In fact, you're starting to make me nervous," Braddon appeared visibly shaken by Rebecca's last comment, almost as if the conversation had immediately gone from one of informal discussion to interrogation. "You're right, Senator Kane is on a bonus program, which is quite normal and customary for this kind of business." Braddon paused for a second and seeing that Rebecca wanted to know more, he continued. "I suppose you would like the detail on the nature of the bonus program."

"Yes, if you could please," Rebecca answered politely.

"Well, it's a performance related bonus program. We give Senator Kane a bonus based on the amount of revenue generated from the sale of carbon dioxide credits in any particular fiscal year." Braddon would not yield on the answer that Rebecca was obviously waiting for.

"Can you tell me, John, what Senator Kane's salary was last year with the bonus included?"

"I think he made close to one million."

"Ten times his base salary. That's a sizable bonus," Rebecca commented.

"That's the way it always works with bonus programs. They're designed to encourage revenue generation. So, Senator Kane got what we promised him: no more, no less."

"I understand," Rebecca conceded, then continued. "By the way, what are Senator Kane's duties and responsibilities for the company?"

"Well, he is an 'all-purpose' kind of guy. As I mentioned before, though, mostly he is responsible for keeping an eye on legislative developments in DC. We are a heavily regulated industry and keeping abreast of legislative and regulatory changes is a full time job. You may recall back in late 2003 and early 2004, Congress was working on the Energy Policy Act in the wake of one of the worst blackouts in New York City."

"I sure do remember that incident," Rebecca said. "We felt the effects of that all the way down in Philly."

"One of the concerns at the time was updating and refurbishing old power plants and modernizing outdated electrical distribution systems. Kane was instrumental in getting some tax credits in that legislation for independent power producers like Power Systems."

"Does Senator Kane have any day-to-day responsibilities?" she asked.

"No, not really. He comes to our monthly board meetings and then he is always available to deal with company business as the need arises. We also use his law firm to do a lot of our corporate work. For example, Kane's law firm does all of our carbon contracts, but Kane doesn't get involved in that stuff too much. His background is in criminal law."

"Let me shift gears on you, John," Rebecca said. "So, you started operations at the Tacony plant in 1998. If I understand correctly, you had some operational problems during the first year or so, correct?"

"Yes, we did. It was touch and go there for a while."

"What was the problem?" Rebecca asked.

"To be honest, Rebecca, I don't know. I'm not trying to play dumb, although I'm usually pretty good at that. Frankly, I leave that stuff up to the engineers, but I remember kicking some serious ass."

"What do you mean?"

"We had a lot of money riding on the Tacony plant by the time it was operating. Plus it was our flagstone facility. If it didn't work, there was no way we would be able to get others built elsewhere. I remember not getting definitive answers from the engineers as to the nature of the operational problem. So, I had them working around the clock for a while to fix it and get the plant back up and running. If I recall, I had Senator Kane working on it too."

"Why Senator Kane?" Rebecca pondered. "He has no engineering responsibility, right?"

"Correct, but I wanted everybody working together on a solution because of the tremendous financial investment in that plant. So, I had Senator Kane working on the EPA down in Washington and in Philly too. The engineers eventually worked out the problem and the plant was operational again."

"Any idea what they did?" Rebecca asked, shaking her head back and forth realizing in advance that Braddon's answer would be no.

"Like I said, I'm just the money guy."

"As you know, the Philadelphia prosecutor took possession of all the company's environmental files, following the murder of the company's environmental compliance manager." Braddon shifted in his seat. "In those files, I came across a copy of a memorandum from Robert Stark advising you about these mysterious shutdowns early on in the operation. Here it is. Do you recognize it?" Rebecca pushed it across the table in the direction of Braddon.

"Again, Rebecca, to be honest, I don't recall seeing it. That's not to say I didn't receive it. I'm sure if you were to look in my Power System files, you would find a copy of it. I admittedly receive those kind of documents in the normal and ordinary course of business, but I remember quite distinctly that I left the remedy of that problem to the Power System engineers at the Tacony plant. On top of that, it was an extremely crazy time. I probably wouldn't have taken the time to read a routine memorandum from Stark."

Rebecca motioned to Braddon for the memorandum back. "Here it says that a likely cause of the problem was an unexpected buildup of gases in the burning chamber. Do you see that?"

"Yes, uh hum."

"Do you recall that being the problem?" she asked.

"Well, now that you mention it, I do recall talking about that issue with one of the Tacony plant engineers. I don't recall seeing that particular memorandum, but I do recall talking with one of the engineers about the issue, yes."

"Can you tell me what the engineers advised you?"

"Well, not exactly," he answered. "But I'm sure it would have been along the lines that they had discovered what they thought was the source of the problem, at which point I would have told them to do whatever is necessary to remedy the problem."

"Do you recall ever talking with Robert Stark about the reported gas buildup in the furnace?"

"No. I had a difficult time dealing with Stark."

"What do you mean?" Rebecca asked.

"I don't mean to be disrespectful, considering that the poor guy was murdered, but Stark was on the whiny side for my taste. He was constantly agonizing over the minutest things that he should have been able to take care of on his own. Like that damn pH issue in the river. I got a fucking call once a month about the fucking pH in the Delaware."

"Okay, so you know about that issue. I was going to ask you a few questions about that. My understanding is that the company was never able to figure that one out. Is that correct?"

"Bingo. And that's why I used to tell Stark not to worry about it. We did what we were supposed to do as far as sampling the surface water. So what if the pH in the Delaware is low. The river's a cesspool anyway, right?"

"Well, I wouldn't go that far," Rebecca responded rather abruptly, obviously unhappy with Braddon's flippant attitude. "Tell me about revenues, John. How has Power Systems being doing financially?"

"We're doing exceedingly well now, but that wasn't always the case, as you can guess with the operational problem back in '98. We were at risk of losing a shit load of money. In addition to the normal losses that any start up business encounters, the shut down of the Tacony plant early on compounded that effect. Once we got it operating steadily and reliably, though, we started to see a good cash flow and surprisingly wound up making a profit that first year of operation."

"Give me some idea of actual numbers please," Rebecca asked courteously.

"I figured you would ask that question at some point today, so I made copies of some financial statements. Let's see," Braddon said as he looked at the papers now in front of him on the conference room table. "Total revenues for Power Systems in last year were just about $100 million with expenses against that in the range of $10 million."

Rebecca interrupted, "So, if I'm following you, profit last year was about $90 million?"

"That's about right," answered Braddon.

"Not bad."

Braddon answered. "In a perfect world that would be the case, yes. But, as I'm sure you are aware, Rebecca, it is dangerous to think of an investment that way. The operational problems we had in the first year with the Tacony plant are a good example. You can never rest on your laurels in a situation like this. We are constantly working on improving the business of Power Systems at every level to make sure that we stay competitive. Staying with that thinking, we haven't taken too much money out of Power Systems yet, even though the company has been good to us financially."

"How have you distributed profit?" asked Rebecca.

"Well, once we hit the black, the originator of the patent got aggressive about starting to see some money for his ingenious furnace design. So, to shut him up, we got the approval from our investors to give him a $1 million bonus. We gave Kane sizable bonuses every year of operation, and then used a several million to set up a capital reserve fund for Power Systems. The rest we returned to Alternative Energy and Environmental Investments."

"So what are the future business plans for Power Systems over the next five years?"

"Keep churning out the greenhouse gas credits. That's it. We have a lot of credits dedicated for sale through carbon futures contracts. In fact, we are booked for the next five years of operation."

"Wait a minute," Rebecca said. "Are you telling me that every ton of available credits that will be produced over the next five years are already accounted for? They are already sold?"

"That's right," Braddon answered. "I feel like the owners of Harley-Davidson."

"How's that?"

"Harley-Davidson," Braddon said again. "That company's manufacturing is booked solid for up to five years on some motorcycles. There is such a demand for Harley-Davidson motorcycles that customers get put on waiting lists that can last up to five years. Hell, I ordered a Fat Boy last year and the dealer told me he would call me in a year or two to let me know when I might expect a delivery."

"That's incredible," Rebecca commented.

"To be sure. Talk about job security, huh! Anyway, Power Systems is in a similar position, at least with respect to the projected greenhouse gas credits from the Tacony plant. This guy with The Climate Exchange is a miracle worker. He convinced a broker in Europe to enter into firm commitments to purchase all of our credits for the next five years. We can't lose."

"You mean Byron Russell with the European Union," she asked.

"Yes, I think that's who the carbon futures contracts are with. But, you see, I really don't get involved in that process. Power Systems commits to supply greenhouse gas credits to The Climate Exchange. What the Exchange decides to do with them is really of no concern to Power Systems. With that said, though, it is nice to know that you have firm commitments to purchase all of your product for a five year period. The company has leveraged those carbon futures contracts to come up with additional financing to construct other plants like the one in Tacony. To be honest with you, Rebecca, we had a gut feeling that this enterprise would eventually be successful, but we never anticipated that it would be as wildly successful as it has been, nor did we expect it to be so successful so soon. And it's all because of those carbon futures contracts."

"I am glad to hear," Rebecca said, "that the company is doing so well, and, actually, I think at this point you've answered all of my questions," Rebecca said as she began to stand up in her usual quick exiting fashion. "Thank you for your time, John."

"That was fairly painless," Braddon said jokingly. "Do you have time for lunch? There's this great French restaurant over on Forty-sixth Street."

As tempting as it sounded, Rebecca did not like to linger. "No, thanks. I've got things to do back at the office this afternoon, so I'm going to head back to Philly. Can you have your secretary call me a cab, please?"

"Sure enough," Braddon answered, after which he picked up a telephone on the conference room table and passed the instruction for a taxi on to his secretary. "Usually takes about ten minutes."

"I'll wait downstairs, then. Thanks again for taking the time to meet with me."

"We aim to please, Rebecca." Braddon joked. "Especially when it is the DOJ."

⊰ ⊰ ⊱ ⊱

Rebecca took advantage of the time she had on the train ride back to Philly to report in to Sean Murphy.

"Sean, Rebecca on the phone for you," Kate bellowed into Sean's office after she answered the phone.

"Becca. Are you in New York?"

"I'm on the train heading back."

"So, who were you meeting with again?"

"John Braddon, you stooge. You know, the president of Power Systems."

"Right, right. How'd it go?" Sean asked cavalierly.

"I thought you might like to know that the Kane of Power Systems is indeed your buddy Senator Kane."

"No shit! Well, now. It truly is a small world. This case just keeps getting more and more interesting. That it?"

"Yeah. I'll probably catch up with you later this afternoon or tomorrow morning."

"All right then, Ms. Lockhart. Thanks for the info. You should try to slip in a nap on the government's dime."

"That's the best idea you've had in a long time, Sean. I'm going to do just that."

⊰ ⊰ ⊱ ⊱

Sean Murphy couldn't wait to dig into what Senator Kane had been up to since their fateful meeting. As soon as he hung up with Rebecca, Sean surfed through the United States Senate internet website. *Let's see if I can dig up any interesting dirt on my 'bestest' friend Mr. Kane.* After a little searching, Sean hit on a current events report mentioning a group of Senators advocating mandatory cuts in greenhouse gas emissions. *Eureka! Kane is co-sponsoring the Climate Stewardship Act.* Reading on, Sean came across a number of quotes by Senator Kane in support of the proposed legislation: "the dramatic and devastating impacts wrought by climate change can be seen all around us," "experts in their respective field of climate change research have provided the Senate with scientific evidence that greenhouse gases are accumulating at a rapid rate and becoming more and more dangerous, which requires more than mere cosmetic action to reverse," and "burning of fossil fuels is the dominant cause of the ever-increasing concentrations of carbon dioxide in the atmosphere, which directly warm the planet. There is no scientific controversy about this fact. None." *No shit, pal. And with every mandatory reduction*

114

in greenhouse gas goes an increase in your Power Systems' salary. I'll bet my bottom dollar that this chucklehead didn't disclose his financial interest in Power Systems when he introduced this bill.

CHAPTER 18

Senator Oren Kane was the product of being in the right place at the right time. Though he would never admit it, convinced that a superior education and an untouchable work ethic were the cornerstone of his success, Kane nevertheless owed his good fortune to others.

He had spent the better part of his professional life working as a white collar criminal defense attorney with a large law firm in Washington, D.C. There he defended Fortune 100 corporations, and their officers and directors, against claims of securities fraud, racketeering, corruption, and anti-competitive practices. Dealing daily with the criminal mind, especially the educated and sophisticated one, gave Kane a singular and preferential insight into how the business world really worked. Scheming ruthlessness was the rule rather than the exception, Kane would learn, and he understood and appreciated the fact that it was his job to figure out how to manipulate and argue the law in a way that would transform unlawful recklessness and disregard into legitimate and productive capitalism.

After graduating from Harvard Law School, Kane spent two years with the U.S. Attorney General's office. There he "cut his teeth" on a few extraordinarily high profile corporate criminal prosecutions. Even at this early point in his career, Kane wanted the spotlight. Although he welcomed the media attention surrounding the cases he worked on while at the U.S. Attorney's office, doing the grunt work for, and being second chair to, what Kane considered to be lesser qualified lawyers set the stage for a short career in government service. The only real value of this job, in Kane's opinion, was the fact that he had a chance to meet defense attorneys who he hoped would take notice of him and make an offer to join them. It was on one particular case where he was prosecuting the client of a DC firm, which, because of that case, realized that it needed someone young and aggressive like Kane, that he had been given the opportunity to create and build a criminal defense practice.

Through no great effort or distinguished ability of his own, Kane bridged the gap from junior associate to partner of his law firm in a relatively short period. Most of his clients were handed to him by other, more senior attorneys in the firm who, for one reason or another, had some unexplainable sense of connection to, or respect for, Kane. This method of advancement was an accepted form of evolution in the practice of law, especially in large law firms like Kane's. The only difference between him and other young advancing attorneys was Kane's egotistical conclusion that he was the sole reason for his success. Indeed, Kane seemed to be the only one who didn't understand how much of his good fortune was attributable to others. The end result of this selfish style was that Kane never did for other, younger attorneys what his more gracious predecessors had done for him. Kane greedily claimed ownership of every possible client and matter, knowing that at the end of the year it would translate into more income for him.

The refusal to acknowledge that his success was in large part attributable to others also led to the incorrect assumption that he was a good attorney. However, his legal skills were mediocre at best. All things considered, the mere fact that Kane advanced so quickly in the practice of law was puzzling, but no one could deny that he had a unique ability to fake his way through things and come out glistening.

One thing was for sure: Kane's professional success wasn't due to his good looks or good nature. He was a short man. Tiny to be exact. And, just like Randy Newman was heralded for saying in his song "Short People," Kane had "stubby little hands." By the time he was about forty years old, he was already quite bald and had a button-stretching paunch. From his toes to his head, which was an unusually large one in proportion to the rest of his body, Kane looked more like a "weeble" than a human.

His actions and words were always slow and deliberate, seemingly thought out in advance and carefully orchestrated. This methodical style translated well into an air of security and confidence. However, his underlying insecurities uncharacteristically emerged in an oddly uncontrollable nervous "tick." Whenever Kane talked, he would place his chubby little hands together, as if in a prayer, and grind them back and forth. After a minute or two, he would usually separate them, but his index and middle fingers would continue the grinding motion. The second his mouth stopped moving, so too did his hands or fingers, as the case may be.

He was an irascible pain to his peers, especially women. Having no fear of or respect for anti-discrimination laws, Kane never hesitated to demean his female colleagues. His regular use of the word "bitch" was rivaled only by his favorite phrase "useless fucking whore." He considered all women inferior, particularly those who had the audacity to want a professional life. These, he thought, started with a chip on their shoulder and were perpetually unable to dislodge it. His hatred and distrust of women had no doubt sprouted at a young age because it would take many years for any person to develop and nurture that amount of emotion.

Along the way, Kane learned how to play politics, which suited him exceedingly well. Although he would never declare a party, considering that favors from both sides of the aisle helped in defending clients, especially the ones with the more difficult cases, Kane leaned to the conservative end of the political spectrum.

By the time he was in his early forties, Kane decided to run for office. He successfully procured a number of local offices, running on the republican ticket, but as with most other ventures for Kane, local politics quickly became boring and uneventful. It was with the resignation of a senior senator from Virginia, which Kane called home, that he got his big chance to engage in some real politics. A few days after Kane turned fifty, he filled the empty senatorial seat and went on for several more full terms in the United States Senate.

Environmental protection was a sexy topic when Kane took office, so he jumped at the opportunity to become a member of the Senate Committee on Environment and Public Works, which is where all federal environmental laws are considered by the Senate after introduction and, for the most part, negotiated and "hammered out" into final form ready for adoption. Additionally, almost every federal environmental law has a re-authorization clause in it. What this means is, every fifth or tenth anniversary of the adoption of an environmental law, Congress must reconsider it to determine whether the law has effectively accomplished its intended goals and objectives. Senate review of environmental legislation up for re-authorization likewise occurred in the Committee on Environment and Public Works. And Senator Kane was in the middle of it all, eventually being named chairman of the committee after serving three terms in the Senate.

⊲ ⊲ ⊳ ⊳

"Senator Kane," his secretary, Joan, said when his telephone rang. "Mr. Braddon is on line one."

"Did he say what he wants?" Oren Kane shouted back to his secretary, with the usual tone of disgust.

"No, I didn't think to ask him. I assumed you would want to talk to him."

"Just because someone like John Braddon calls doesn't necessarily mean I will automatically accept that call. Is that crystal clear?" No answer. "Is that clear, Joan?"

"Yes, Senator," *And fuck you too,* Joan thought to herself.

"John, what's goin' on up there in New York?"

"The DOJ investigator was here this morning."

"Oh, that's right. I completely forgot about that. How'd it go?"

"Relatively uneventful, as far as I could tell. This investigator asked some general background questions about Power Systems and the Tacony plant. She was also interested in how you fit into the Power Systems operations."

"Oh, it's a 'she' huh? That's wonderful," Kane said with his usual obnoxiousness. "She knew about my position with the company? She must have done her homework before meeting with you."

"My sentiments precisely. In fact, she knew about your bonus program and asked me how much you make."

"You didn't tell her, I assume, John," Kane said.

"You assume wrong. Of course I told her."

"I can't believe you fucking told her my salary, John."

118

"Don't be so cautious, Oren. She is obviously a smart girl and could have figured it out on her own with a little more research."

"What's her name?" Senator Kane asked.

"Rebecca Lockhart. She has her own financial advisory firm in Philly. I'm surprised you're that interested, Oren." Braddon observed as he heard Kane repeating Rebecca's name slowly indicating to Braddon that Kane was taking a note.

"Well, if she is so interested in me, I'm going to do a little research on her."

"Kane, don't do anything stupid. This is the Department of Justice for God's sake."

"Relax, John. You're in my world now. I eat the DOJ for breakfast."

"You know what, Oren, it's that kind of attitude that's going to get us in trouble," Braddon warned Kane. The more they talked, the more Braddon got nervous about the investigation and the more Braddon was convinced that Kane needed an appreciation of the circumstances. "Oren, we have a potential nightmare brewing here. The DOJ is knocking on my door. The EPA is sniffing around the Tacony plant. And all because of that dickhead Stark. I warned you that things would get out of hand. You need to shit can these investigations pronto. Understand?"

"All right. All right. I'll take care of it. Don't worry. Just relax."

CHAPTER 19

After he received the call from Tom Roth about the third exhaust pipe, Bob Morrone decided he would take a closer look; the easiest method was to extract information from the plant engineer. When the plant engineer arrived in Bob Morrone's office, he explained to the plant engineer that the EPA investigator had raised some questions about the exhaust system. Bob was surprised to learn that the Tacony plant had been originally constructed with two exhaust pipes, both of which were routed back into the furnace, at differing elevations. Soon after the Tacony plant began operating, the plant engineer explained, the burning chamber started to "choke" out and the whole system would shut down. The plant engineer also explained to Bob that he would open up the burning chamber to inspect it, but found no obvious problems. The furnace would restart without any difficulty after a day or two, which led the plant engineer, at least initially, to conclude either that the source of the problem had been removed or that these unexplained shutdowns were just because of the newness of the Tacony plant. After it happened a few more times, though, the plant engineer realized there was some significant underlying problem. When he reported this situation to the officers of the company, Morrone would learn, they surprisingly decided to bring in outside contractors to resolve the difficulty.

According to the plant engineer, the outside contractor attributed the periodic shutdowns to a buildup of gases in the burning chamber, which they related back to an under-sizing of the exhaust system. It was the plant engineer's understanding that the third exhaust pipe was added onto the Tacony plant to provide better and more complete re-circulation of exhaust gases as a way of resolving the problem, which it apparently did. There were no further shutdowns after that third exhaust pipe was added. When asked by Bob Morrone whether he had seen any of the construction modifications or any related documents related, the plant engineer advised Bob Morrone that all of the work had been done during a scheduled two-week shutdown of the Tacony plant during which time the plant engineer was asked to take vacation. He was never given any records of the exhaust system modifications. The plant engineer informed Bob Morrone that the officers of the company had made it readily apparent that they did not want anyone from the existing engineering or maintenance staff involved in the exhaust system expansion, almost along the lines that the company's management held them responsible for the fact that the Tacony plant had been experiencing operational problems during those first few weeks after startup. As far as the plant engineer was concerned, recalling his feelings at the time of the construction modifications, he was fine with the fact that the company was relying on an outside contractor to remedy the problem, even if some subtle finger pointing was involved, because it gave the plant engineer one less thing to worry about. Plus, the plant engineer reported, after the exhaust system was expanded, the Tacony plant operated like a charm. So, whatever the outside contractor did worked the way it was supposed to, which was all the plant engineer needed to see.

Bob Morrone decided that this additional information should be reported immediately to Tom Roth as a means of hopefully putting this issue to rest.

⊰ ⊰ ⊱ ⊱

"Hello, Roth here," Tom said as he picked up his ringing telephone.

"Hello, Tom. This is Bob Morrone from Power Systems. I'm surprised to hear you answer your own phone."

"Government work is much different than what you rich private guys are used to," Tom said as he laughed. "What can I do for you Bob?"

"I checked into that third exhaust pipe for you. Turns out that it was added during the first few weeks of operations to help alleviate a problem they were having with unexplained shutdowns of the Tacony plant soon after startup."

"Yeah, I remember seeing some passing reference to that issue in the Power Systems files," Tom acknowledged.

"I'm told by the plant engineer that the company retained an outside contractor to expand the exhaust system, which apparently took care of the problem. Seems pretty straightforward."

"Did you find any plans or reports from this outside contractor?" Tom asked.

"No, I didn't. I asked the plant engineer that same question and he said the officers of the company never gave him anything either."

"Doesn't that seem odd, Bob?"

"I'll admit that it isn't customary, but my gut sense is that, so long as the problem got solved and the plant was back up and running, nobody really gave two shits about documenting what was actually done physically to the plant."

"Well, Bob, I'm interested, and there's good reason. The time frame of the exhaust system expansion stuck in my head. I was having trouble pinpointing why. So, as I always do when I'm mentally blocked, I went back to the files. I spent hours going over the same information I had already reviewed several times before. Nothing was jumping off the page at me, until I was just about to give up and write off my concern to an early onset of senility. Low and behold, though, I found something very interesting on the monthly discharge monitoring reports for the Tacony plant. You're familiar with discharge monitoring reports, I assume?"

"Yes, absolutely. They are the monthly reports of sampling that Power Systems does for the wastewater discharge into the Delaware."

"That's correct, but they are more than that. If you look closely at the data you will see that Power Systems is required to check the water quality in the Delaware just downstream of its outfall pipe, including a test for pH. There is a time in the historical data where the pH of the river was almost neutral, and then it becomes acidic. Not only that, but the change from neutral to acidic was not a slow progressive thing. Rather, it occurred over just a couple of months. Don't you know that the time when that change in pH occurred was precisely the time when Power Systems was expanding the exhaust system."

A few seconds passed before Bob Morrone spoke up. "Are you saying the Tacony plant has something to do with the low pH condition in the Delaware?"

"I don't know what I'm saying just yet, but the timing seems to me to be more than just coincidental. I was thinking I would stop by this afternoon and you and I could have a closer look at this exhaust system."

"Unfortunately, Tom, I am unable to join you. I have a meeting with some management folks this afternoon, but I'll leave a message at the security gate that you are coming and they are to give you full access to the site. Does that work for you?"

"Sure enough."

⊰ ⊰ ⊱ ⊱

"Mr. Braddon, please," Bob Morrone said to Braddon's secretary on the other end of the telephone line.

"Yes, who's calling?"

"This is Bob Morrone, from the Tacony plant."

"Oh, hello, Mr. Morrone. Let me get Mr. Braddon for you. Here he is, Mr. Morrone."

"Hello, Bob. How are things in Philly?"

"Fine, Mr. Braddon. The plant is running top notch, but you asked that I let you know if I heard from anyone at the EPA. I just got off the phone with the EPA investigator, Tom Roth, who was out to the plant last week."

"Okay, Bob. What did he want this time?"

"Well, Mr. Braddon, he asked a number of questions about the exhaust system expansion. I couldn't tell him much because frankly I don't know much about what happened back then. I've been barely keeping my head above water with the normal day-to-day stuff."

"And you're doing a great job of it, Bob. We're all very much impressed with your abilities."

"One other thing, Mr. Braddon. Tom Roth is coming back out to the plant this afternoon. He said something about the timing of the exhaust system expansion correlating with the low pH problem in the Delaware. Are you familiar with the history of that issue?"

Braddon's face went pale and it took him a few seconds to respond to Bob Morrone. "Ah, yeah . . . yeah, Bob, I'm familiar with the pH issue." Another few seconds passed and Braddon continued. "What in the hell does Roth think is the link between the exhaust and the pH? This is bullshit. You know what, fuck this idiot. Call him back and tell him he is not welcome on the plant property any more. Tell him that if he wants to come back in and inspect, I want to see a search warrant. We've been more than accommodating to these boneheads. Enough is enough. Tell this prick Roth he needs a search warrant this time."

The aggression in Braddon's voice caught Bob Morrone off guard. "Mr. Braddon, with all due respect, sir, technically the EPA does not need a search warrant. The fact that we have a Clean Water Act permit for the Tacony plant means that the EPA can walk in here unannounced at any time they like."

"You're shittin' me, right?"

"No, sir. I am very familiar with that aspect of the Clean Water Act. Most times the EPA will bring a search warrant on their more important investigations, but they don't have to do so legally. Plus, Mr. Braddon, we have already allowed Tom Roth on the plant site once. To ask him for a warrant now would look quite suspicious."

Bob Morrone was one of those people who struggled with confrontation, so it was not unusual for him to stay away from demanding search warrants from the EPA. But, in this case, his last comment to Braddon was more for Morrone's benefit—in searching for an answer to why Braddon was suddenly becoming insistent about refusing Tom Roth access—than it was attributable to any underlying desire to avoid conflict with Tom Roth.

"You're right, Bob. I'm just getting a little frustrated with these government investigators. I don't like their smugness. Give me a call back after Roth is done, please."

"Will do, Mr. Braddon. Goodbye."

⊰ ⊰ ⊱ ⊱

By the time Tom Roth put out all the fires in other cases he was working on, it was after 4:00 PM. He left his office and headed for the elevator to the parking garage, which was a series of old converted utility sub-basements below the Arch Street building. As usual, he hadn't got to the office until late that morning, which meant he was parked on the bottom floor of the parking garage. As he exited the elevator, walking with his head down while scrambling through his briefcase for his car keys, Tom bumped into Sean Murphy, who was waiting for the elevator on his way to visit with Steve Cooperhouse. Tom let go of one of his characteristic yelps.

"Tommie, me lad. I always love to hear you scream like a girl."

"Fuck you, Murph."

"Nice language! Do you kiss your mother with that mouth? On second thought, Tommie, I don't want to know the answer to that question. It may keep me up at night. I'm going to meet Steve to talk about this Power Systems case. Want to join me?"

"Actually, that's where I'm headin' now. I already brought Steve up to speed with some of the stuff I'm finding. He can tell you all about it. No need for me to be there too."

"All work and no play, huh Tommie. That's what I love about you, buddy." Sean Murphy squeezed in the last few words just as the elevator doors closed.

Although the parking garage for the EPA employees had recently been built, its newness gave way to a lot of the unchangeable old historic features of the building, one of which was an almost complete absence of lights. Tom Roth remembered he was parked down the far end of the garage and began to walk in that direction as Sean Murphy's last words were muffled by the closing elevator doors. Immediately Tom noticed the sound of footsteps matching his as he walked. Looking around, he noticed a few other EPA employees off in the distance getting into their cars. They sped by Tom and waved on their way out of the garage. As he continued walking, Tom heard the sound of footsteps again, this time a little louder than before. Looking around again he saw no one. "Hello, who's there?" No answer. "Quit fuckin' around, Murph. I know it's you." Nothing again. Tom continued walking toward his car, this time surrounded by absolute silence. He took one last look around as he opened the car door. Tom's cautiousness was not without cause. A few years earlier, he had been robbed at gunpoint in this same garage by a junkie hopped up on crack cocaine. It was an event that was always on Tom's mind whenever the garage was empty like it was now. He wrote off the unexplainable sound of footsteps to his nervousness, got in his car and left for the Tacony plant.

⊰ ⊰ ⊱ ⊱

By the time Tom Roth made his way north through center city traffic and entered the Tacony section of Philly, it was just after 5:00 PM. The fact that a downpour had started while Tom was in transit didn't help his time. He pulled up to the security gatehouse at the Power Systems facility.

"You must be Tom Roth," the security guard said.

"That's correct. Bob Morrone said I could walk the property again." Tom handed his EPA identification badge to the security guard.

"Yeah. We've been waiting for you for a while. Bob called down earlier to let us know you were coming. Park you car in one of those spaces over there," the security guard said as he gestured toward a small parking area next to the gatehouse. "I'll drive you to wherever you want to go."

"Okay."

After Tom had been cleared by the security guard, they went to the furnace building at Tom's direction. The security guard waited in the truck while Tom looked at the massive exhaust pipes running down the side of the building. He measured off the distance between the nearest doorway and the exhaust pipe entering the ground, getting pounded now by rain. Tom disappeared into the

124

building. Once inside, Tom started looking for evidence of the third exhaust pipe inside the building.

Let's see. Seventy-five feet from the doorway to the center of the pipe. Tom measured off seventy five feet on the inside of the building and looked around. *Nothing.* Tom noticed a stairwell a few feet away from where he was now standing. He scampered down the stairs to the next level, popped his head out of the doorway and again saw no evidence of the exhaust pipe entering the building, understanding that he was now about ten feet below ground surface. One more level down was the bottom of the plant and he went through the same routine a second time. Again, he found no evidence of the third exhaust pipe re-entering the building.

When Tom reappeared outside, the security guard was still waiting in his vehicle. Tom walked over to the third exhaust pipe entering the ground and began looking around. He walked toward the river, looking at the ground. However, by this time, the combination of rain and waning daylight made it virtually impossible to see anything. Tom waved to the security guard to pull the truck over by Tom.

"Do me a favor," Tom shouted to the security guard to overcome the din of the pounding rain. "Turn your high beams on and turn the truck around toward the waterfront."

"No problem," the security guard answered.

With the trucks lights now forming a fairly straight line to the river, Tom began to walk in the illumination and check the ground. He noticed a series of small utility manhole covers stretching between the building and the waterfront. Lifting one of them up, Tom observed a concrete utility trench about four feet deep and wide, with nearly half a dozen heavily insulated pipes running through it. He could hear the sound of gas moving through the pipes. *What the hell is this? I don't recall see - ing this pipe run on any of the engineering drawings.* He walked all the way to the chain link fence along the Delaware River and peered down the bulkhead, but it was difficult to get a good look from that angle. Plus, it was too dark to see anything but the blackness of the river. All along the security guard had been inching the truck behind Tom so that it was idling pretty close by when Tom turned back.

"So, did you find anything interesting?" the security guard asked as Tom got back in the truck.

"No, not really."

"I noticed you pick up a manhole cover back there. What'd you see?"

"Just a pipe trench. I'm sure the property is loaded with them. Could you take me back to my car, please?"

"Absolutely."

❦ ❦ ❦ ❦

On a good weather day, Tom would have another hour drive to his home in Brownsburg, near Washington Crossing State Park, which is a small town in Bucks County, north of Philadelphia. Tonight, however, with the torrential rains, he expected at least a extra half hour. It gave him some time to check in with Steve Cooperhouse, even though Tom despised using his cell phone.

"Hello, Steve. It's Tom."

"Tom. Sean Murphy and I were just talking about you. He told me he gave you a good scare when you were getting off the elevator."

"Yeah, I bumped into that lunkhead on my way out."

"Where are you, Tom?" Steve asked.

"Didn't Murph tell you? I went to the Tacony plant again. Remember that issue I came across with the third exhaust pipe?"

"Yeah, sure. Has it turned into something noteworthy?" Steve asked.

"I'm not exactly sure just yet. Earlier today I was on the telephone with the new environmental compliance manager for Power Systems. He told me that the exhaust system was expanded as a means of resolving some operational problems they were experiencing at the Tacony plant. But the kicker is, nobody knows what was done because the company hired an outside contractor to do the work and it all took place during a scheduled plant shutdown when nobody was around."

"That's not unusual, though, Tom. It happens all the time. The management team loses confidence in their engineering and science staff so management brings in an outside contractor."

"Yeah, I understand that," Tom said, "but what piqued my interest was that the exhaust system expansion happened at exactly the same time the low pH problem cropped up in the Delaware. So, I went back out to the plant today to check this extra exhaust pipe. I didn't find any evidence of it in the building. Then, I found an unidentified pipe tunnel running from the building to the river, and it starts right where the third exhaust pipe enters the ground."

"So, what are you telling me, Tom?" Steve asked.

"I'm not sure just yet, but I think the company is routing the exhaust somewhere other than back into the furnace."

"What makes you say that?" Steve inquired.

"Put yourself in their shoes. They have a brand new plant that they can't keep running. I assume they are losing money hand over fist. They've got to get this thing back up and running and quickly, right? I was also told that the problem with the plant was that the burning process kept 'choking' out because of the buildup of gases. So, the easy solution is to suck off all the gases and vent them somewhere else, and if that's in fact the case, it conflicts with all of the plant design information on record."

Steve pondered Tom's theory for a time and then said, "That would be an interesting solution, considering all of their greenhouse gas credits are based on no emissions."

"Bingo," responded Tom. "If they are venting gases to the environment in some way, instead of recycling and reusing them, as the patent states, the Tacony plant becomes just another electric generating facility. No emissions reduction credits to market and no tagging the plant as environmentally friendly."

"But you couldn't confirm that the third exhaust pipe is in fact discharging to the environment?" Steve asked.

126

"No. Even if I had good weather today, I wouldn't have been able to come up with that answer. We need to rip up the ground where the third exhaust pipe enters the subsurface to confirm that it is somehow entering that tunnel leading toward the river. Plus, we need to find the actual end point of that pipe run."

"Okay Tom," Steve said, knowing Tom's dislike for cell phones. "We'll pick up with this tomorrow. Safe home, buddy."

⤴ ⤴ ⤵ ⤵

The next morning, Steve Cooperhouse's telephone was ringing as he walked in the door to his office, which was a surprise considering it was only 6:45 AM.

"Hello, Steve Cooperhouse here."

"Steve, this is Ginny Roth, Tom's wife."

"Oh yes, Ginny, it's nice to hear from you. How are you?"

"I've been much better, Steve. Tom is dead."

"What!" Steve exclaimed. "Tom is dead. I don't . . . I don't understand what you're telling me. I just talked to Tom last night in the car while he was on his way home. I can't believe this."

"I know. I'm numb. I got a call from the Pennsylvania State Police last night about 9:30 PM. They found Tom in his car just off River Road, a couple of miles from home. There is a sharp bend in the road there. The State Police think that Tom must have lost control of the car with the bad weather. They tell me he was killed on impact. There is a steep drop off of River Road . . . ," she had to stop because her sobbing prevented the words from flowing. "Excuse me. I'm sorry. At that curve, there is a steep drop from the road down to a rocky bottom. I knew something was wrong before the police arrived, though. Tom called me from the road to let me know he was on his way home. He was good that way . . . " at which point the need to cry became too much for her to hold back. Several seconds passed before she could regain her composure. "Anyway, he told me he would be home by eight or so. When he didn't show up, I felt in my heart that something was wrong, but I never expected this. He was such a careful driver, especially on that damned curve. There have been so many accidents at that spot. He would always slow down to almost a crawl when he got near that curve. It drove me fucking crazy." She broke down into a choking cry. "Apparently, some teenagers were partying down by the river and heard the car crash. They called the State Police."

"Ginny," Steve said softly. "Tell me what I can do to help. Anything. Just say the word."

"Pray for me, Steve. Please pray for me."

⤴ ⤴ ⤵ ⤵

What neither Steve Cooperhouse nor Tom Roth's wife knew was that just minutes after Tom had finished his conversation with his wife, he noticed in his rear view mirror a set of headlights approaching rapidly. River Road was characteristically empty so Tom moved over to the shoulder and slowed down to allow the vehicle behind him an opportunity to pass. Much to Tom's surprise, the vehicle did not take advantage of the opportunity. Looking ahead of him, Tom thought the driver's unwillingness to pass must be due to the upcoming sharp curve in the road, which Tom always slowed down for anyway. He moved off of the shoulder and into the main roadway, keeping his speed extra slow because of the heavy rain. Just as Tom entered the curve, the vehicle behind slammed into the rear end of Tom's car. In a panic, Tom tried to straighten out his car's front end, which was heading directly for the guardrail on the side of the road. He gained control and started to slow down. The front end of Tom's car rammed the guardrail, causing the air bag to engage. Tom let out a sigh of relief when he realized that the guardrail had done its job. His relief would last only a short time as Tom noticed in his rearview mirror the outline of a pickup truck speeding toward him. The crashing blow sent Tom's vehicle ripping through the guardrail, over the edge of a ravine, and fifty feet straight down to the rocky bottom. No air bag was available to protect Tom at that point.

⊰ ⊰ ⊱ ⊱

"Sean, Steve Cooperhouse is on the phone for you."

"Hey Steve."

"Sean, I got some bad news. Tom Roth is dead."

"What. . . . What the hell. How?"

"I know. I just got off the phone with his wife. The State Police say he lost control of his car and went through a guard rail on River Road. There's a steep drop down to the Delaware at that point on the road, so he was killed on impact."

"Steve, I'm so sorry to hear this. You knew Tom a lot better than I did. I mean, you two worked together for a long time."

"Yeah, I feel pretty horrible. Not that we were close or anything like that. But, when you work with someone that long, you get to know them pretty well."

"Sure you do," Sean said.

"Well, I thought I should let you know about this considering Tom was my main guy on the Power Systems case."

"Yeah, that's right." Sean debated whether to ask the obvious question and then went ahead with it anyway. "How are you going to handle that?"

"I think I'll just take over the case investigation from this point forward."

"Any idea of what remains to be done, Steve?" Sean asked.

"Tom told me," said Steve, "that he discovered some pipe trenches in the rear yard of the Tacony plant. I want to go out there one last time and take a look at the pipe trenches before I close up the file. It's probably nothing, but I just want to be sure."

"Wait a minute. You talked to Tom before the accident?"

"Yes, I did. He called me just after he finished up at the Tacony plant and was heading home."

"Oh, man. That's spooky," Sean observed.

"Tell me about it. That's a first for me."

"You're probably the last person Tom spoke to before he died," said Sean.

"No. Tom's wife Ginny told me that he called her to say he was on his way home. My guess is Tom talked to Ginny after me."

"Okay, Steve. I know this is probably not the best time, but I want to schedule a meeting with the officers of Power Systems, one of whom is Senator Kane."

"Senator Kane, huh?" Steve pondered. "I recognize that name. Doesn't he head up an environmental subcommittee in Congress? I seem to recall his name plastered all over a bunch of environmental legislation."

"You are indeed correct about that, my friend. He chairs the Senate Committee on Environment and Public Works. In fact, he was recently involved in sponsoring legislation seeking mandatory greenhouse gas reductions."

"How can someone who has a financial interest in a company like Power Systems, a noted greenhouse gas emissions credit holder, at the same time be sponsoring legislation regarding mandatory greenhouse gas reductions? Isn't that a conflict of interest?"

"My sentiments exactly," replied Sean. "That's why I'd like to sit down with these guys, among other reasons obviously. I'll need you there with me to cover the technical stuff. I'll take care of making the arrangements. We'll probably do it in Kane's Washington, D.C. office, okay?"

"Sure. Whatever works for you, Sean. I'll work around your schedule."

"Okay, pal, I'll be back in touch. In the meantime, pass my condolences along to Tom's wife. Talk to you soon."

CHAPTER 20

Rebecca Lockhart, Steve Cooperhouse, and Sean Murphy boarded the 8:00 AM Amtrak Metroliner for Washington D.C. from Thirtieth Street Station. It was an unusually chilly morning for the first day of autumn, and the first time since the onset of summer that the oppressively sticky humidity was being forced out of the Delaware Valley. A cold front moved into the region overnight bringing with it the first temperature inversion of the year, which offered a vibrantly crisp blue sky. As they walked outside onto the train platform, Sean breathed the chilly air into his lungs deeply and directed Rebecca's and Steve's attention to the frosty mist created by his exhale. "I love this time of year, guys. Summer's heat and humidity are my 'kryptonite.' I feel weak and sluggish from about Fourth of July on, you know what I mean?" Rebecca and Steve nodded in acknowledgment. "But, once the weather turns . . . I'm back, baby!"

"Sean, you are such a weirdo," Rebecca said.

"I'm not kiddin', man. I feel strong as an ox this morning," Sean boasted as he sucked in another chest full of air, which took what seemed an eternity.

"That's because," Steve observed, "you had three cups of coffee in the station while we were waiting for the train."

"That helps, of course," Sean admitted. "I remember when I was playing football, the triples practices would start mid-August. They killed me. There would be days where the humidity was so heavy that you couldn't find any oxygen in the air. Late afternoon was the worst. It was like running through soup and breathing in pure water. My first few games of the regular season were always slow motion. Then, once this time of year rolled around, my performance skyrocketed. My coaches could never figure out why my number of tackles went from just okay during the early part of the season to out of the roof in late September. I actually got drug tested once in high school because the coaches thought I went on a performance enhancing steroid."

"I still say it's the coffee, Sean," Steve responded.

Rebecca laughed and added, "This is my favorite time of year too, Sean. I love the change of seasons, but going from summer into fall is the best. Lots of color."

"That's right, Becca, you are the 'mum queen," Sean said.

"What are you talking about?" Steve asked.

"Becca," Sean responded, "has this beautiful house out on the Main Line with an incredibly huge porch. She smothers it with 'mums every year on the first weekend of autumn. Right Becca?"

"Mums, yes indeed. I usually have about thirty large 'mums covering the porch. But, that's not all, Sean. You know that. I put corn stalks along all of the pillars and then hay bails with gourds and pumpkins on them. It's without a doubt the prettiest time of year for the house."

Steve asked Rebecca, "Do you use just one color of 'mum?"

"No, no. I mix a whole bunch of colors together. Red, white, purple, and, of course, gold. Mix them all together for nice contrast. I place them all over the front steps to the porch and then bring them down onto the front lawn, so it has some flow."

"Quite lovely, I must say," Sean observed with a hint of sarcasm in his voice.

"It's not just that, though," Rebecca pondered. "There's something about autumn. The sun starts to set a little earlier and it cools off in the evening. I love walking around the neighborhood to see the houses all dressed up for fall. Plus, it's the first time since winter that I start to light candles again in the house again, mainly on the weekends. There's a special place in my heart for lounging around in my family room on Saturday afternoons in the autumn watching college football on the boob tube."

"That's my Becca," Sean exclaimed. "I trained her well, didn't I Steve?"

"No, Sean," she said. "I hate to disappoint you, but the college football part is a remnant of my father's habits. So, shut the hell up for once and let me finish. There's more to it. I don't know. Something about how the late afternoon sun lights up the first floor of my house. It puts this reddish tint on everything in my family room. There's this evergreen tree down the end of my street. It must be seventy or eighty feel tall. It towers over all the other trees. At dusk, all the trees in the neighborhood fall into shadow, except for the top of this one evergreen tree. It gets so red and stays lit up by the sun for about an extra ten or fifteen minutes. It is one of the most beautiful things I've ever seen. The mixture of red sunset on a background of green creates a "Christmassy" effect. You have to be careful, though, because it doesn't last long. Every once in a while I catch my neighbors looking at me trying to figure out what I'm staring at. They must think I'm freaking crazy. I don't care. It mellows me out. Plus, as it gets darker earlier, the amount of traffic on my street lightens up. All those old fogies in my neighborhood, I guess, not wanting to get caught out in their cars when it starts to get dark. So, my neighborhood gets real quiet in the afternoon on fall weekends. I can actually hear the bells from the Catholic Church about a quarter mile away. Crystal clear. Then you get the people who still burn leaves in their backyards. I love that smell. I purposely leave all the screens in the windows and the front and side doors so I can open them all up on the weekend and invite in all those smells."

"How spiritual," Sean joked in a slow and mellow voice. Seeing that Rebecca was upset by his comment, Sean continued. "Just kiddin', dear. I have to admit, Steve, it is a cool house, especially in autumn," Sean said. "I should know. I spent many a Saturday afternoon lying on Becca's family room sofa watching my Nittany Lions kick ass."

"Don't start, Sean," Rebecca warned, not liking the reference to their time together, which caused both Sean and Steve to chuckle.

Most of the seats were open and they lucked out finding two rows facing each other. Sean grabbed a window seat and Rebecca slid in beside him. Steve took the window seat facing Sean, who didn't waste any time trying to embarrass Rebecca.

"Steve, did you see that 'hottie' who just walked by in the short leather skirt?"

"Yes, Mr. Murphy, I did. I may be getting old, but I am proud to say that I still enjoy the pleasure of God's marvelous works."

"Me too, dude," Sean said, grinning back at Steve. Rebecca shook her head in disgust, which prompted Sean to continue the absurd discussion. "Steve, any girl who wears a slinky leather skirt like that must be what?"

"She must, of course, be a naughty girl, Sean."

"Exactly. And what happens to naughty girls?"

"They get a good spankin'. That's what happens to them," Steve joked, after which both he and Sean got hysterical laughing.

"That reminds me, Steve. I was just bestowed with a great honor by the Philadelphia Bar Association."

"Oh yeah, what's that?" Steve asked, knowing something good was coming.

"Well, I was just involved in a case where a homeowner's association was trying to figure out how to stop flooding in their townhouse development, which was right next to Darby Creek. Turns out that a couple of beaver are building dams on the creek and it's backing up the water flow. The townhouse development is literally under water, at least up to a couple of feet."

"I know where you're talking about," Steve said. "I read something in the newspaper over the weekend about that place."

"Right, right," Sean continued. "Anyway, the case comes to me because Darby Creek is on a list of federally protected waters and this homeowner's association wants to kill the beaver; make a stew of them or something." Rebecca listened, but held back on showing any real interest because she knew deep down that this story was going to end up sordidly. Sean continued, "In order to kill the beaver, the homeowner's association has to get a federal permit from the Department of Interior. Of course, the environmentalists get up in arms when they hear about the permit application because the beaver are just doing what their instinct tells them to do. So, I get involved and, as usual, try to come up with a solution that will make everyone happy. As it turns out, there's an option that will allow the homeowner's association to trap the beaver without killing them and release them in some other location. Happiness all around," Sean finished with a smile.

"So," Steve interjected, "what's this award the Philadelphia Bar Association gave you?"

"Well, they gave me a plaque at the annual awards dinner designating me as the foremost expert on local beaver." Steve erupted in laughter when he heard this ending.

Rebecca finally decided to bring the stupidity to an end. "All right, guys. That's enough. You two are pathetic." She knew exactly how to turn the conversation back to a worthwhile subject. "So Sean, what do you think about meeting Senator Kane again? Are you nervous?"

Sean initially looked disappointed by the topic, but dove into an answer anyway. "Ten years ago, I would have been nervous. Now, though, ain't nothin' anybody can do to me that ain't already been done. I have no fear anymore. Kane's just another person to me now." Despite Sean's flippant attitude and usually horrible grammar, Rebecca and Steve understood the profoundness of his thought. Sean Murphy had indeed suffered through his fair share of life's difficulty and pain, and it gave him a unique view on the world.

"Steve," Rebecca said, "I understand from Sean that you are a global warming guru. There's a scientific part of the equation that I think you will be more capable of answering than I can do on my own research, and I'd like to put the last piece of this puzzle together before we meet with these Power Systems folks."

"I'd be glad to help you, Rebecca," Steve answered, "assuming I can, of course. What's your question?"

"Excellent! Okay, I understand from my visit to the 'Carbon Expo' that there are these EPA reports documenting the buildup of greenhouse gases in the atmosphere. I've read them. They describe how we have some measurements showing that the average temperature around the globe is rising. What I haven't heard yet is what does one have to do with the other. In other words, I need somebody to explain to me how an increase in the amount of these gases is leading to higher temperatures."

"I can do that for you, Rebecca," Steve said with an air of arrogance aimed at tormenting Sean. "After years of research, atmospheric scientists put together data showing that the reason why the air temperature is increasing is because heat from the sun can't escape the earth's surface. Picture a pot of water that you put on the stove. If you leave the top of the pot off, it takes longer for the water to boil than if you have the top on, correct?"

"I agree with that point," Rebecca answered.

"The reason why it takes longer for the water to boil with the top off is because heat is allowed to escape to the surrounding environment. Put the top on the pot and the heat builds up inside. Well carbon dioxide and other greenhouse gases are like a top on a pot sitting on a stove."

"You need to explain that one a little more for me, Steve," Rebecca asked quietly.

"Sure. The sun is equivalent to the burner underneath the pot. What happens is the sun beats down on the earth and heats it up, just like the burner of a stove adds heat to a pot of water. Under normal circumstances, the sun's heat bounces off the earth's surface and, as in the case of a pot with no top, will escape back out of the earth's atmosphere. In that situation, there is some balance to the system. Heat in and heat out. However, as carbon dioxide builds up in the earth's atmosphere, the theory goes, it creates a blanket over the earth's surface, preventing the heat from escaping. What happens is the heat from the sun bounces off the earth's surface, rises into the atmosphere and then hits this layer of greenhouse gases, which prevent it from escaping out of the earth's atmosphere. When the heat can't escape, the air temperature begins to increase. Are you still with me?" Steve asked.

"You're making a lot of sense to me now. So, this phrase "greenhouse effect" comes from the fact that the carbon dioxide is acting like the window panes of a greenhouse. They act as a barrier to the heat from leaving the greenhouse, right?" Rebecca asked.

"That's exactly right," Steve answered. "Now the problem is that the United States has never bothered to regulate the amount of carbon dioxide going into the atmosphere from any source. A whole bunch of other things have been either eliminated or substantially reduced by the Federal Clean Air Act, but not carbon dioxide. It has never been viewed as the source of any health problems to the general public so it has never been targeted, and it is now starting to piss off other countries."

"Why should other countries give a damn about what we are doing or not doing regarding carbon dioxide?" Rebecca asked.

"Well, unlike most other forms of pollution, air contaminants do not obey geographical boundaries. So, for example, the acid rain we experience in the Northeast actually originates from sulfur dioxide and nitrogen oxide power plant emissions in the Ohio River Valley. The stacks on those power plants are specifically designed very high to prevent downwash into the local community. The end result is that the air emissions from those power plants get into the upper atmosphere and trends east on the prevailing winds. The same concept applies with other countries regarding carbon dioxide emissions, but with a slightly different twist. The countries of the European Union that have signed The Kyoto Protocol are now obligated to make mandatory reductions in carbon dioxide emissions over say the next twenty years. Because the United States did not sign that treaty, it does not have to make those same reductions, which means what?" Steve inquired of Rebecca.

"Economic advantage!" she exclaimed now that the discussion had moved more into Rebecca's area of expertise.

"That's right," Steve responded. "The members of the European Union, and others that have signed The Kyoto Protocol, are painting the United States as a two time loser. Not only is the United States an environmental monster—because it refuses to take affirmative action to address what has come to be regarded as a serious pollutant—but it is doing so purely for economic gain, they say. In other words, the United States gets to run its power plants and other manufacturing facilities unhindered while the signatories to The Kyoto Protocol have to place controls on their operations to meet the mandatory carbon dioxide reductions. Not only that, but those counties have to figure out ways of reducing carbon dioxide over the next twenty years. They can't just "hold the line" on their current productivity rates. They instead need to achieve actual measurable reductions in the amount of carbon dioxide that the particular country is emitting."

"Okay, you lost me a bit there," Rebecca chimed in. "Give me a concrete example to explain that last point," she asked.

"Fair enough. Let's say Germany generated a million tons of carbon dioxide from its power plants last year. That's not a real number. I'm just using it as an example. I'm sure Germany's carbon dioxide emissions are much greater than. . . ."

"I understand, Steve," Rebecca interrupted. "The one million number is an example only. Go ahead, I'm with you." Sean smiled sarcastically at Steve.

"Okay. As Germany's economy grows, which everyone in Germany hopes is the case, so will its need for energy. So, as the economy of grows, one would expect Germany to generate more than the million tons of carbon dioxide that it generated last year. It is a must." Rebecca's head nods seemed to show Steve that she understood the concept.

"The Kyoto Protocol says next year Germany can't generate more than a million tons of carbon dioxide, even if its economy is booming. In fact, Germany has to take measures to reduce the carbon dioxide to less than a million tons. So, even as the economy grows, the amount of carbon dioxide must go down below a baseline level."

"Stupid question," said Rebecca. "Why not stop the source of the problem?"

"What do you mean?" asked Steve.

"Well, if carbon dioxide is creating this greenhouse effect, which is leading to global warming, why not eliminate the sources of carbon dioxide?"

"Very good point, Rebecca, but like most good points, it's easier said than done. Dreams of a no carbon future are appropriate in considering a long-term approach to solving climate change. But because fossil fuel use will continue to be with us for the foreseeable future, especially when it comes to energy production, eliminating the sources of man-made carbon dioxide is premature at best."

"What do you mean by dreams of a no carbon future?" asked Rebecca.

"The backbone of fossil fuels is carbon. So, when you burn a fossil fuel, it creates carbon dioxide as a byproduct. Eliminating carbon dioxide means mainly eliminating burning fossil fuels for energy production."

Both Rebecca and Sean asked at about the same time, "What can be done to replace fossil fuels?"

"The answer to that question has resulted in dispute, even long before global warming assumed such prominence. I'm sure you've heard the advocates of alternative energy. The original arguments in favor of things like solar energy, wind, geothermal power, and, yes, even the supposed bad guy, nuclear energy, were methods of getting away from some of the more commonly acknowledged and understood problems with burning fossil fuel, like acid rain, smog, and so on. Well, those looking to fight climate change are now advancing those same alternative energy forms as a means of solving the global warming problem, with the exception of nuclear energy, of course. That topic is still a major no-no among most environmental advocates, even though it is probably the least polluting form of energy production."

"Old tricks for a new dog, huh? I assume the energy production industry continues to resist these suggested alternatives," said Rebecca.

"Yeah. The industry mantra now is a low-emissions economy, not a carbon-free economy." Both Sean and Rebecca stared at Steve blankly. "In other words, the energy producers, like the environmental protection advocates, are relying on old arguments in response to the global warming concerns: energy efficiency, conservation, and development of new technologies for fossil fuel combustion."

"What do you think about that point, Steve?" asked Rebecca.

"Well, energy conservation and the other stuff didn't work before as a means of solving air pollution problems. I don't know why it should work now, except perhaps that climate change is unmistakably an international phenomenon, which really wasn't the case with earlier air pollution situations. The only real difference now is the possibility of a hydrogen economy."

"What the hell are you talking about?" blurted Sean.

"Pure hydrogen burns just like fossil fuels, except it doesn't have any nasty byproducts like carbon dioxide. When you burn hydrogen, the end result is energy and water vapor. However, production, storage, and distribution are problems that must still be solved before we can establish a hydrogen economy. But it is a much more realistic alternative that wasn't around when this debate raged before. Nuclear energy was the only realistic option back then."

"So, the end result," Rebecca commented, "is that no matter how many scientists agree that burning fossil fuels is the main reason for the build up of carbon dioxide in the atmosphere, that activity is not going to stop in the foreseeable future?"

"Yep, that's right," Steve replied.

Sean Murphy spent a few minutes thinking and then responded to Steve's and Rebecca's exchange. "Before, Steve, you were talking about the mandatory greenhouse gas reductions under The Kyoto Protocol and how the United States is taking a beating like a red headed stepchild because it won't participate. I'm not at all surprised to hear that the United States won't participate. This country would never go for something like that, regardless of what political party is in charge. As the economy grows so must the amount of pollution we are generating as a country. No administration will bind itself to a mandatory standard where it risks negative impacts on the economy."

"Interestingly enough," Sean interrupted, "Senator Kane sponsored legislation requiring mandatory greenhouse gas reductions. He took a lot of flak from his fellow Republicans for doing it."

"That's right," Sean recalled. "He led the charge on the Climate Stewardship Act, right?"

"That's the one," Steve responded.

Rebecca started pulling files out of her briefcase, which Sam and Sean took as a clear signal that she did not want to talk any longer. They likewise decided to close the conversation. By this time, they had pulled into the Wilmington,

Delaware station, after which the steady view of concrete and mortar from Thirtieth Street Station south started to give way to more appealing landscape. The increasing prevalence of surface water forecast the fact that the train was working its way into the Chesapeake Bay area. All three of them were gazing out the window. A low lying fog on the fields was beginning to burn off as the sun rose and mustered up enough heat to challenge the chill that had settled in overnight. They noticed that the leaves on a few trees were starting to change colors, as were some of the late crops, mainly pumpkin.

⊲ ⊲ ⊳ ⊳

When Rebecca, Sean, and Steve exited Union Station, they walked out into 60 degree sunshine, a sharp difference from the chilly morning they left behind in Philadelphia. Sean headed for the taxi service just outside the train station, knowing all too well that he could not navigate the streets of Washington, D.C. He was used to the simple x/y axis of the Philadelphia street system. D.C., by comparison, seemingly had streets coming from ten different directions at once. Some were numbered, some lettered, and still others had full names. But, because of Rebecca's resolute refusal to get into a taxi on such a gorgeous day, they finally began to walk to Senator Kane's office. It was only a short distance to North Capitol Street and Q Street, which is where Senator Kane's law firm was located. The late morning air was fragrant with the smell of roses that blanketed the sides of several buildings and monuments along the way. Rebecca noticed two gentlemen walking toward them and said hello. Their response was accompanied with a wide smile. "People are so cordial and pleasant down here," she observed.

"I think, Rebecca," Sean answered, "that it has something to do with the fact that you're easy on the eyes."

"No, I can tell the difference, Sean. Plus, that woman at the taxi stand back at Union Station was very nice, too. So, it's not just the men."

"I know. I'm just kidding with you," Sean admitted. "I agree with you. There's some imaginary line in . . . Maryland, maybe Baltimore, below which there is a rule that people must be courteous. Above it, all bets are off. It's kill or be killed."

As they walked, the three of them observed that the attire of the day, for men, was a dark blue, pin-striped suit, with white collar buttoned shirts—initials on the cuff optional—and bold colored ties, mainly yellow and red. For ladies, it was simply substitute an ivory silk blouse for the white shirt and take away the tie.

They arrived fifteen minutes late for their meeting, but blamed it on the train and a fictitious inability to find an empty cab. Like many of the buildings in Washington, D.C., Senator Kane's office was located in a grayish marble one, the inside of which was outfitted entirely with beautiful, and obviously expensive, light colored wood. Sean Murphy made a mental note that the conference room where they met was close to the size of the entire DOJ office back in Philly. Centrally located was a square conference table, which had a much more modern appearance than the other features and fixtures in the office, and indeed, it was. Directly in front of each chair was a built in LCD screen that recessed into the conference

137

table when it was not being used. Underneath the table were retractable keyboards and computer mice, the combination of which provided each chair location at the conference table with a fully functional desktop computer. Also recessed into the conference table top were small speakers, networked into other speakers in the conference room walls, for a total surround sound audio capability. The final touch was an imbedded banker's lamp at each chair station providing a subtle and personal illumination for each person sitting at the table, which at the time was unnecessary because of the intense sunlight beaming in from a series of windows on the far side of the conference room.

Located along the windows was a long table set up with lunch. The bill of fare included a garden salad, prime rib of beef, whipped potatoes, and carrots, along with an assortment of juices and other soft drinks. On a separate table sat a plate of cookies, brownies, and a fruit salad. Sean had seen this kind of lunch before at many of his meetings and liked to think of it as an attempt to soften up the big, bad government attorney, but he knew better: lawyers at big firms ate like this all the time.

Senator Kane welcomed his guests and invited them to get started with lunch immediately. Sean Murphy took the lead once they began to assemble around the conference table. He instructed Rebecca and Steve to sit on the same side with him, which reflexively forced Senator Kane, John Braddon, and Harvey Morgan, one of Kane's law partners, to take an opposite side of the conference table. Senator Kane began introductions.

"Mr. Murphy," Kane said, "this is Mr. Braddon, the President of Power Systems," after which Sean nodded to Braddon, "and this other fine gentleman is a partner of mine, Harvey Morgan."

"Nice to meet you. Please call me Sean," he answered. Sean was surprised to see that Senator Kane did not seem to remember Sean, although it had been a long time since Sean had had his run-in with Kane. "I believe, Mr. Braddon, you have already met Rebecca Lockhart." They nodded to each other. "Rebecca assists the Department of Justice with certain financial issues on an independent contract basis. This likewise fine gentleman," Sean said pointing to Steve and smiling, "is Steve Cooperhouse. He is with the EPA's regional office in Philly." Sean paused for a second to two, thinking about the presence of Harvey Morgan, who, as an attorney, obviously had some reason for being at the meeting. Sean decided to probe the idea. "So, I take it that Mr. Morgan is here in a formal capacity as legal counsel to Power Systems."

Senator Kane responded. "As you can expect, the officers of Power Systems are getting concerned about these informal meetings with the DOJ and the EPA. We have no idea whether the company is the target of an investigation, criminal or otherwise, which makes us nervous about responding to your questions and allowing the EPA onto the Tacony plant property for inspections. At the same time, we want to be cooperative."

Sean responded quickly and directly. "Senator, if Power Systems has nothing to hide then it should have no reason to be concerned about the purpose of the

DOJ's and the EPA's investigation." The rash comment made Senator Kane red in the face.

"That's not fair, Mr. Murphy," the Senator quipped back at Sean. "There's a right way to do business and a wrong way to do it. The company has every right to competent representation and defense, if that is necessary. We prefer not to have an attorney here, Mr. Murphy. The only reason he is here today. . . ." Senator Kane's voice began to rise as he continued ". . . is because no one will tell us whether Power Systems or its officers and directors are the target of this investigation. You leave us no choice."

"Senator," answered Sean, "in all of our meetings so far, you're the only one who seems to be nervous about the situation. If you and the other officers have done nothing wrong, then you have no reason to worry." All of the others in the conference room began to feel uncomfortable with the tone of conversation between Senator Kane and Sean Murphy. He, however, was obviously encouraged by it, to the point where Sean leaned over his plate of food, took a bite of prime rib, and then continued. "Let's do this. Let's look at what's happened here. The environmental compliance manager for Power Systems shows up in the Delaware River with a hook buried in his back. The stiff's family reports to the Philadelphia prosecutor's office that he was planning to blow the whistle regarding some environmental violation happening at the Tacony plant. In the course of its investigation, the Philadelphia prosecutor uncovered what appears to be a draft letter authored by Mr. Stark where he mentioned on-going violations of the Clean Air Act. Finally, our review of the company's environmental files shows that there is a persistent acidic condition in the Delaware just down river of the Tacony plant's discharge. . . ." Howard Morgan interrupted Sean mid-stream.

"Yes, Mr. Murphy. You are correct about the existence of a pH condition in the Delaware, but there is also nothing to link that condition in any way to the Tacony plant's operations. As I believe you are aware, the company's monitoring data conclusively demonstrates that the discharge from the Tacony plant is fine. It complies with all applicable standards."

"To be sure, Mr. Morgan," Sean replied putting his palm up in the air to let Morgan know that Sean did not want to be interrupted again. "But, as I was about to say, that pH problem began to occur only after the plant was operational." Sean debated for a second about whether or not to tell those on the other side of the conference table about Tom Roth's recent visit to the Tacony plant and his suspicions about the expansion of the exhaust system, but decided against it. "So, to answer your question, Senator, the EPA and DOJ combined have a lot of questions about Power Systems as a company and the Tacony plant as an operation. But, Senator, I'm willing to put all my cards on the table here today, considering you were willing to meet with us without objection. We don't have any evidence right now that could reasonably target Power Systems for an environmental crime or any other kind of environmental violation for that matter. With that said, though, you have to agree with me that the circumstances surrounding the operation of the Tacony plant appear oddly suspicious."

John Braddon attempted to ratchet down the level of tension in the conversation. "I appreciate your honesty, Sean, and I assure you that all of these events are just as you describe them: odd circumstances. So, let's see if we can help you with some of those questions you have and hopefully convince you about the legitimacy of Power Systems."

"Good. Let's get started, then. I want to understand better the senator's involvement with the Climate Stewardship Act."

"I know what you're going to ask," Kane responded anxiously. "How can I be sponsoring a bill like the Climate Stewardship Act when I have a financial interest in Power Systems. Am I right?" the senator blurted.

"Exactly," Sean responded bluntly.

"The answer is an easy one. I disclosed my financial interest in the company to the president, the senate, and the attorney general's office before sponsoring the legislation. I have a written opinion from the attorney general that it would be okay for me to advance the Climate Stewardship Act and so I did. As you know, the United States has been taking a lot of heat from the European Union about the fact that we have not joined in on The Kyoto Protocol. It is against that backdrop that the president came to me in my capacity as the Chairman of the Senate Environment and Public Works Committee to author legislation that would encourage voluntary reductions of greenhouse gases in the United States, while at the same time allowing the economy to expand."

"I haven't had the benefit of reading the entire Climate Stewardship Act," Sean admitted and then asked, "how do you go about accomplishing the president's mission?"

"The easy part," the Senator said, "was deciding to regulate carbon dioxide and other greenhouse gases. It had never been done before so it wasn't like we were cleaning up a mistake or troublesome difficulty from existing legislation."

"How so?" Sean asked.

"Well, many times I am asked to modify or amend one of the fifty or so federal environmental laws that Congress has on its books. That process requires a lot of committee hearings and public debate, principally on issues of complex environmental science underlying the law. In this case, though, I was given a very simple instruction: come up with a scheme to control greenhouse gases and preserve economic flexibility and versatility. We didn't have any resistance from the public. Everyone was behind the concept. We didn't get into the debate about the science of whether global warming is occurring. We accepted that as a fact in support of the legislation. The only question to answer, then, was how to save face with the European Union and other signatories to The Kyoto Protocol without jeopardizing the economy. It was this last part that was the difficult thing to handle."

"So, how'd you do it?" asked Sean again.

"Greenhouse Gas Intensity Target," the senator answered proudly, making it clear to the group that the concept was in large measure the senator's brainchild. Rebecca immediately jumped into the conversation, aware of the scheme behind this legislative construct based on some research materials she had picked up during the "Carbon Expo" in Sydney, Australia, and it was fresh in her mind. Rebecca pointed out that the White House, in response to increasing public pressure about global warming, had announced its commitment to implementing measures aimed at controlling greenhouse gas emissions. The principal thrust of the initiative was a concept known as a Greenhouse Gas Intensity Target. To an untrained eye, Rebecca explained, it would appear that at least the United States was proposing to do something, instead of continuing its skepticism about whether global warming was indeed a real or simply perceived phenomenon. However, she explained that this approach is fundamentally flawed, especially when comparing it to the mandates of The Kyoto Protocol. "That treaty seeks to reduce greenhouse gas emissions by 5.2 percent compared to 1990 levels no later than 2012." This method, Rebecca explained, is easily measurable and achieves an absolute reduction. "The math is simple. If you had 100 units of greenhouse gases emitted in 1990, then you are supposed to emit by 2012 no more than 94.8 units of greenhouse gases. This is not how the Greenhouse Gas Intensity Target works. In fact, people are surprised to hear that the use of the Greenhouse Gas Intensity Target will probably result in increases in greenhouse gas emissions over time as opposed to reductions, as contemplated by The Kyoto Protocol. The Greenhouse Gas Intensity Target is designed to reduce the ratio of greenhouse gas emissions to U.S. gross domestic product. This standard dupes the American public. When they see the word 'reduce' in the Climate Stewardship Act, the American public assumes that this means an actual reduction in the amount of greenhouse gases being emitted by U.S. sources. But that is not the case. As the U.S. gross domestic product increases, which it does every year, the amount of allowable greenhouse gas emissions also increases. So, the proposed 18 percent decrease in the greenhouse gas intensity by 2012 would actually result in a net increase of 12 percent in emissions because the U.S. economy is continually growing. You see, a ratio is a percentage. It's kinda like when food manufacturers advertise something as 85 percent fat free. What you should be asking yourself is 85 percent of how much fat initially. Although an 85 percent reduction appears to be a lot, if the starting amount is a big number that means the remaining 15 percent will still be a big number. It's the same thing with the Greenhouse Gas Intensity Target. If the U.S. economy is humming away, the 18 percent so-called reduction in the ratio will actually be an increase in the tonnage of greenhouse gases being emitted by the U.S. The end result of using the Greenhouse Gas Intensity Target is that the U.S. will continue to emit greater and greater amounts of greenhouse gases every year, but just at a lesser rate than would be the case without the intensity target."

Senator Kane was red in the face by the time Rebecca finished her oratory, a sight that brought a mildly noticeable smile to Sean's face. "I guess the question then, Senator," Sean said, "is whether this ruse has worked with the European Union."

"Despite what you skeptics think, what matters is that the president has taken steps to control greenhouse gases, and that is better than doing nothing. The European Union is fine with our approach."

It was at this point Braddon stepped back into the exchange. "I understand your skepticism, but the reality is that the legislation is working. Power Systems has a patented system to prevent the emissions of any gases and it was the prospect of greenhouse gas reductions that led to the technology. There are a bunch of other companies doing voluntary reductions, just like Power Systems."

"Well, Senator," Sean prodded, "with all due respect, the members of Trust to Save the Environment obviously weren't too happy with the legislation."

"A bunch of fruits and nuts!" decried Senator Kane. "Who cares about those assholes? Bunch of fucking tree-hugging terrorists. They got what they deserved." The senator's last comment sickened everyone in the room because they all knew that Senator Kane truly believed in his heart that burning to death was an appropriate form of punishment for such an outrage. The senator's comment led to an uncomfortable silence for a few seconds, which would have continued but for Rebecca's inability to cope with it. She decided to break it.

"Mr. Braddon, I am interested in some additional background information on the company, if you would be good enough."

"Sure, anything you need," Braddon answered, at which point Sean Murphy's cellular phone rang. He excused himself to take the call.

❧ ❧ ❧ ❧

"Hello, you got Murph," he answered as he walked toward a window in the conference room. As he looked back, he noticed Rebecca asking Braddon some questions.

"Murph, it's Charles Sands. I just called your office and your secretary told me you were meeting with the Power Systems folks today. Are you there yet or still on the train?"

"Meeting is underway as we speak."

"Damn, I was hoping to get to you before the meeting started."

"Why?" Sean asked. "Do you have some information regarding the company?"

"You sure you want to do this now? I don't want to interrupt your meeting. This can wait until you get back to Philly."

"No, go ahead. One of my investigators is covering some company background stuff. I don't really need to hear it."

"All right. Well, one of my buddies is the prosecutor for Bucks County. His name is John Blazen. I don't know if I ever mentioned him to you before. Anyway, I was over his house this past weekend and he told me about this guy Tom Roth who ran off River Road a few days ago. I thought I recognized the name and then my buddy told me he was an EPA investigator. That's when I remembered you told me about this guy Roth working with you on the Power Systems case."

"Yeah, that's right," Sean answered. "Is the Bucks County Prosecutor's Office looking into Tom's death?" Sean asked in a very low tone with his back toward the rest of the group in the meeting so as to avoid their overhearing him.

"Well, I don't really know for sure. All I know is that John was advised by either the local police or the state police that there was some unusual and unexplainable damage to the back of Roth's car. You see, the car supposedly crashed front end first through the guard rail and then hit the river bank below in the same

142

way, front end first. When the police investigated the car the next day, they noticed a lot of damage to the back end of the car."

Sean decided that the conversation was going in a direction that warranted his leaving the conference room. He made a gesture to the group, as he exited the conference room, that he would only be a minute or two longer. After he closed the door behind him, Sean found an empty conference room and continued his conversation with Sands. "Yeah, but it was like a fifty foot drop at that point, right. I'm sure the car was banged to shit. Maybe it even flipped. I mean, maybe the car hit the ground and bounced, damaging both the front and rear ends."

"You're absolutely right, Sean. But, according to John Blazen, the back part of the car had a bunch of light blue paint streaks that don't correlate to any structure that Roth's car would have encountered during the accident. He ran through a silver painted guard rail and then hit a bunch of brick and concrete at the bottom of the fall."

"So, the Bucks County prosecutor thinks Roth was murdered. Is that what you're saying?" Sean asked.

"Sean, I really don't know. I didn't push it too much with John when we were talking about it over the weekend because I hadn't yet made the connection between Roth and your investigation of Power Systems. Then, I started to think about it some more when I got home and started to put the pieces of the puzzle together. The only reason I thought to call you today was because of the fact that we already have one murder where the name Power Systems comes up. Remember, the stiff who came up floating in the Delaware a few weeks back?"

"Yep, I sure do," said Sean. "Well, I'm glad you called, Charles. Let me get back to my meeting. Do me a favor in the meantime, would you?"

"Sure, what do you need?"

"Check back in with this friend of yours at the Bucks County Prosecutor's Office and see if he has any new information on the investigation of Roth's death."

"No problem. I'll do it as soon as we hang up. Do you want me to call you back on the cell?"

"No, that's okay," Sean said. "I'll check back in with you later."

⊲ ⊲ ⊳ ⊳

When Sean reentered the conference room, Rebecca was in the middle of asking a question. "Here is another thing I'm interested in learning more about, Mr. Braddon. The only market I can find out there for greenhouse gases in the United States is this Climate Exchange, and it looks like the bulk of the emissions reductions credits in the Exchange belong to Power Systems. Why aren't other folks out there in the manufacturing or electric generating industry trying to come up with emissions reductions and market them like Power Systems? It seems to me that the cost of a credit would be much lower if there was some competition in the marketplace."

Braddon replied, "The answer is pretty simple. Banks are generally unwilling to recognize expected revenue from emissions reduction projects, making such projects ineligible for conventional loans. You don't want to be the person explaining something as complex as the Kyoto Protocol to people used to looking at simple business loans. So, banks just aren't looking at it. Until the World Bank or some similar financing institution gets into the market, Power Systems is going to be the primary provider of credits. And, you know as well as I do, for that to happen, the emission trading markets need to become much bigger before international financial institutions become involved in carbon financing. The only way that is going to happen is if the Kyoto Protocol takes effect. The protocol will drive the supply side of the market. The demand is there and is increasing."

"Senator Kane," Sean asked, "were you aware the former environmental compliance manager for Power Systems was planning to blow the whistle on the company regarding something he had discovered at the Tacony plant?"

"You mentioned it earlier in the meeting." Kane responded. "That's the first time I heard anything about it. What could he possibly have come across that would warrant the need to blow the whistle on the company?"

"We don't know," Sean answered. "All we have is a copy of a letter on Robert Stark's personal computer that was found in his apartment. The letter was addressed to the EPA in Philly, but we don't think it ever got sent. We have no record of it in EPA's files."

"There were always operational issues," Kane answered, "that would come up and we would work them out."

"No matter what the cost, Senator?" Sean asked.

"Now what the fuck is that supposed to mean?" Senator Kane shouted. "Do you believe this bullshit?" Kane yelled as he looked toward Braddon and Morgan. "Do you have something specific or don't you?" Kane demanded looking directly at Sean Murphy, who continued to let Kane vent his anger. "We had regular meetings with Robert Stark to discuss the operation of all aspects of the Tacony plant. The company had over $1 million in last year's budget for Robert Stark's environmental compliance needs, and my recollection is he used either most or all of it to make sure the company complied with all environmental regulations. He never brought to our attention any environmental problem at the Tacony plant that he couldn't handle within that budget, and if he had, we would have given him whatever he needed."

"What are you saying, Mr. Murphy?" Braddon asked. "Robert Stark's murder was tied to this supposed plan to blow the whistle about something that was happening at the Tacony plant?"

Sean replied matter of factly. "I'm not saying anything just yet, Mr. Braddon. I'm searching for facts, that's all. Who did Robert Stark report to?"

"He reported to me," Senator Kane replied. "And like I said, he never brought to my attention any problem at the Tacony plant. Plus, Mr. Murphy, our industry is so highly regulated that if there were a problem at the Tacony plant, the EPA would probably know about it before we would. Almost everything we do gets reported to the EPA on a regular basis."

"I agree with you, Senator," said Steve Cooperhouse, who had been quiet up until this time. "But how about Robert Stark came across something unusual that he wouldn't normally report to you?"

The senator was visibly irritated. "What do you mean? Power Systems was intentionally withholding information and Robert Stark stumbled across it?"

Steve answered quietly. "Senator, I didn't say anything like that. We are just trying to piece together the puzzle."

Then, Sean Murphy addressed Kane. "Senator, first of all, your getting loud and excited isn't going to help this process. Second of all, your theory isn't all that far fetched, if you think about it. And, yes, to be honest with you, the thought of a corporate cover up did indeed cross my mind."

"Oh, I fucking knew it!" yelled the senator. "Do you believe this horseshit? Tell me, counselor," Senator Kane asked, staring at Sean Murphy across the table, "since when is the Department of Justice Natural Resources Division engaged in murder investigations?"

"You're absolutely right, Senator. That will be for my friends at the Philly prosecutor's office to deal with."

"Look," said the senator. "We run a clean organization. Oh, and by the way, we're not in the business of contract killing. As far as I'm concerned, if you think you have something against the company, then prove it."

"That's fair enough, Senator," replied Sean, "I have a lot of resources at my disposal. It's just a matter of time as far as I'm concerned."

"Mr. Murphy, we can joust all day like this if that's what you want to do," Kane responded. "I enjoy jousting as much as the next guy."

"Jousting!" exclaimed Sean. "Is that what you think this is, Senator?" Sean waited a second or two to see if Kane wanted to say something. After a few seconds of glaring at one another, Sean broke the silence, "So you consider this jousting, huh? You're sorely mistaken Senator, and I'll tell you why. When knights jousted, they risked serious injury or even death. Jousting required courage and bravery because of the personal sacrifice involved. That's jousting, Senator." Rebecca glanced over at Steve with that, "Here we go again, Murphy's on a crusade" look. Sean continued, "You're simply one of the pathetic acquaintances of royalty sitting in the stadium criticizing those who are truly brave and courageous and then handing them some kind of plaque or medal when they win. No, Senator, you're one of the insecure bunch who never could muster up the guts even to mount a horse, no less actually joust."

"Gentlemen, please." pleaded Braddon, "We're all here in good faith. There's no need for this meeting to become adversarial. Mr. Murphy, we want to be as helpful as possible. If you would let us know what it is you are trying to accomplish with your investigation, we will assist to the greatest degree possible. With respect to Mr. Stark's unfortunate murder, we have cooperated to the fullest extent with the Philadelphia prosecutor's office. As far as we can tell, Mr. Stark was robbed while on his way home from work. We know nothing about any plan of his to blow the whistle on Power Systems. And, as the Senator has indicated already, we are unaware of anything whatsoever at the Tacony plant of such a magnitude that would warrant Mr. Stark wanting or needing to blow the whistle on the company."

"I appreciate that fact, Mr. Braddon.," Sean replied. "And, along those lines, we want to do a detailed inspection of the Tacony plant."

"You've got to be fucking kiddin' me!" exclaimed Senator Kane, not having shown any interest in calming down despite Braddon's attempt to do so. "This investigation is getting to the point of becoming more than just an inconvenience. It is going to upset the smooth operation of the plant. We have had to set aside plans twice now for an EPA investigator to inspect the plant. If you haven't found anything yet, you're never going to." Senator Kane paused for a second, obviously pondering whether to introduce what he thought might be an unwelcome topic. "You know what this is all about," Senator Kane said to the entire group. "Mr. Murphy here is lashing out against the company for personal reasons."

"Oren, what the hell are you talking about?" Braddon interjected.

"That's right. Many years back, Sean Murphy worked for the Senate Committee on Environment and Public Works. I felt he was not qualified for the job, so I had him replaced. We are paying a price now simply because Mr. Murphy is in a revenge mode for what happened back then. Isn't that right, Mr. Murphy?" Senator Kane gave Sean Murphy a solid glare. Sean's initial uncertainty about whether Senator Kane remembered Sean was quickly dispelled.

"As much as you might like to think that event had some significance to me or meaning in my life, Senator," Sean answered, "I'm just focused on finding out whether there are any environmental violations at the Tacony plant. The fact that you happen to be involved in the case has nothing to do with my actions. Sorry to disappoint you, sir."

Braddon responded. "Oren, regardless of what happened between you and Mr. Murphy years ago, I am sure the DOJ and EPA have nothing but the most professional of intentions in this case. So, let's try to move on if we can."

"Thank you, Mr. Braddon," answered Sean. "What we want to do is complete what Tom Roth started."

"I thought Mr. Roth finished his investigation," Braddon mentioned, with an air of uncertainty in his voice. "By the way, Sean, I was sorry to hear about Mr. Roth's accident. From what Bob Morrone mentioned to me, Mr. Roth seemed like a very nice man."

"Thank you for your concern. Yes, Tom was a good man, and a thorough investigator. Steve spoke with Tom after his last inspection at the Tacony plant. There were a few things Tom mentioned that we think require some additional investigation."

"And what might those 'few things' be?" Senator Kane asked smugly, showing absolutely no emotion about the death of Tom Roth.

"I'm not prepared to share that information with you just yet, Senator," replied Sean, which not so surprisingly brought a bright red color back to Kane's face.

"Well, Mr. Murphy," Braddon said, "we would like to wrap this investigation up as quickly as possible so we can get back to business as usual at the Tacony plant. Hopefully, you can appreciate that goal."

"I am mindful of that fact, Mr. Braddon. We will be in touch in the next day or two as to when we will need access again to the Tacony plant and what our plans will be in terms of additional investigation." Sean paused for a few seconds and looked around the conference table, catching a satisfying look at Senator Kane's reddened cheeks, and mutely inviting any other questions. "Well, then, unless any-one else has any questions, I suppose we are finished for today. Thank you for your time gentlemen."

Braddon showed Rebecca, Sean, and Steve to the building exit, after which he returned to the conference room, where Senator Kane was sitting in one of the chairs talking on the telephone. Harvey Morgan had left the room. Braddon paced restlessly around the conference room waiting for Senator Kane to finish up the call. When he was done, Braddon wasted no time.

"I thought I told you to take care of this, Oren. They are getting too cl. . . ." Braddon was midstream in his statement when Senator Kane interrupted him.

"It's done."

"What do you mean it's done, Oren?"

"I was just on the phone with the Attorney General here in Washington. I told him to bring this investigation to a close immediately or else."

"Or else what? That kind of shit is how we got to this point in the first place."

"Not to worry," Kane said reassuringly. "This guy owes me many, many favors, not the least of which is his position."

"You know, Oren, the only reason we brought you on at Power Systems was because of your supposed political connections. I haven't seen a convincing demonstration of that yet."

"I'm sick and tired of hearing that bullshit," Kane yelled back at Braddon. "I have done more for this company than. . . . All of your money would be nothing if it wasn't for what I have been able to accomplish here in Washington. It was my efforts and my connections that got this technology patented so quickly and the Tacony plant up and running in record time. So, enough with the story about how I haven't contributed anything to the success of Power Systems."

"Well, all of your reportedly wonderful contribution is going to mean nothing if you don't get the EPA and the DOJ to back off immediately. Understand?"

"I understand. Let me worry about these jerk offs from Philly."

"What do we know about Tom Roth's last visit to the Tacony plant?" asked Braddon.

"I'm not sure. I told Bob Morrone to call me after the inspection, which he did. With everything else happening, I just haven't had the chance to call him back."

"Let's do it now," demanded Braddon, after which Senator Kane dialed the phone on the conference room table.

"Morrone here."

"Bob, it's Oren Kane and John Braddon."

"Hello fellas, what can I do for you?"

Braddon took the lead. "Bob, we understand Tom Roth visited the Tacony plant a few days back. Tell us about what he inspected and what he came up with."

"Well, I can't tell you first hand. We were having some operational problems at the plant, and I was working with the engineer to resolve them at the time. But I had our security guard stay with Tom the entire time. He told me Tom did some checking around the exhaust pipes on the outside of the building. He then went into the maintenance door next to the exhaust pipes for a few minutes. After that, he walked the back lot toward the river. The guard told me that while Tom was walking he picked up a manhole cover. Are you guys aware of why we would have a manhole between the plant and the river? I just haven't had the time to check it out."

"No, I'm not sure what that is, Bob," Braddon answered. "My guess is that the manhole, or whatever it might be, is a remnant from the past industrial use of the property. Remember, the Tacony site was used since the mid 1800s for a host of industrial activities. When we decided to rehabilitate the site, we made a decision that it would be much too expensive to identify and remove every last trace of prior infrastructure from the property. Anyway, don't worry about it. We know how busy you are. I'm sure it's nothing. Also, you shouldn't be bothered anymore by the EPA. If you do get a call from them, in particular a guy named Steve Cooperhouse, give me a call. Thanks for your time, Bob."

"Okay guys. Talk to you soon." Oren Kane and John Braddon waited to hear the click of Bob Morrone's telephone indicating that he was no longer on the line, before they started to talk again.

"I hope to God this so-called favor you're owed works out."

"It will, I assure you. It will."

⊰ ⊰ ⊱ ⊱

On the train ride home, Sean's cell phone rang again. Assuming it was Charles Sands with an update about the investigation of the Bucks County Prosecutor's Office into Tom Roth's accident, he answered without the usual formality.

"Sands, I told you no need to call me back today. What did you find out about Roth?"

"Hello, is this Sean Murphy?" said the unrecognizable voice on the other end of the cell phone.

"Yes," Sean replied, embarrassed by his incorrect assumption. "I'm sorry I was expecting a call from someone else. Yes, this is Sean Murphy. And who is this?"

"Sean, this is Calvin Blake, I need to talk with you about one of your investigations."

Son of a bitch, Sean thought to himself. *What the hell could the United States attorney general want to talk with me about?* Sean glanced over at Rebecca, who noticed the concern in his eyes. *This guy has never bothered me before about one of my cases.*

"Yes, Mr. Blake, how can I help you?"

"Sean, it has come to my attention that your division has been spending a tremendous amount of resources on this company known as Power Systems. I assume you have something concrete that justifies you spending so much time and effort on this case. So, what is it? What do you have?"

148

"To be honest, Mr. Blake, we are still piecing things together."

"I understand, Sean, but exactly what is it that you think warrants the dvision's attention? I assume there is some imminent environmental threat or public health hazard with this plant in Philadelphia."

"No, sir. Not necessarily." Sean could feel the tension growing on the other end of the call.

"What do you mean, not necessarily? You must have something."

"Actually, Mr. Blake, I'm just acting on...ing on a hunch in this instance."

"Not on the taxpayer's dime, you're not. Bring this investigation to a close immediately, Sean. Are we clear on that point?"

"Yes, sir. Crystal clear."

Sean turned off his cell phone and looked over at Steve and Rebecca.

"What the hell was that all about?" she asked.

"Senator Kane must have gotten to the attorney general. I've been directed to cease and desist on the Power Systems investigation."

"What? You mean we are expected to drop the investigation of Power Systems?" Steve asked.

"That's right," Sean answered reluctantly.

"And you think Senator Kane is behind it?" Steve asked.

"What do you think?" Sean replied rhetorically. "C'mon, we're barely out of the senator's office an hour and I get a call from the head of the DOJ, who, by the way, has never complained to me about any of my cases before."

"Yeah, I see what you're saying," said Rebecca. "So what are you goin' to do?"

Sean pondered Rebecca's question for only a second or two. "Screw 'em. I'm going to keep pushing. Kane's a crook. I can smell one a mile away, and Kane stinks like the worst of them. I'm going to keep digging until I find something. What was it, Steve, that Tom mentioned about the Tacony plant?

"Sean," Steve started responding, "I don't think you should be pissing off the attorney general. This isn't a good idea. If anybody knows you and your tendencies, it's me, Sean. I've seen you do this kind of thing before and get yourself into trouble. I say give it up."

"Steve, don't puss out on me now."

"Sean, you may not give a shit about getting fired, but I do."

"You know, Sean," Rebecca added, "I think Steve is correct here. I don't see any reason to push this one. We really don't have anything damaging against Power Systems at this point. Why are you pushing so hard? Is it because of Kane?"

"In part, I guess," Sean answered.

"Sean, quit dickering around," Steve said frustratingly. "What the hell do you mean by 'in part'?"

"That call I got in the meeting. It was from Charles Sands. You know, the Philly prosecutor. He told me in not so many words that the Bucks County Prosecutor's Office is looking into Tom's death as a possible homicide."

Both Rebecca and Steve looked stunned. Sean sensed that they did not know what to say so he filled in the blank. "I know. I know. It sounds almost 'twilight zoneish.'"

Rebecca finally gathered herself and asked, "Why in the world would the police suspect murder?"

"All I know," answered Sean, "is that the rear end of Tom's car had some unusual damage, perhaps indicative of someone intentionally running him off the road."

"Sorry, Sean," said Steve. "But I have a difficult time seeing anything suspicious about Tom's death. It was bad weather and everyone knows about how treacherous that curve is where Tom slammed through the guardrail. No, I just can't accept that we're in some kind of murder scenario here. And, even if he was killed, what makes you think it has something to do with our investigation of Power Systems?"

"If you remember, the whole reason this investigation got started was because the former environmental compliance manager for Power Systems showed up face down in the Delaware River."

"Sean, I have to agree with Steve," Rebecca insisted. "I find it hard to believe that Tom was murdered because of something he learned about Power Systems. Like I said before, all of my research shows that Power Systems is on the up-and-up."

"Steve, you know Tom was on to something during that last visit. He must have been. Why else would Senator Kane go to the extent of calling on the Attorney General as a way of forcing me to stop the investigation?"

"I'm still not convinced, Sean," Steve said reluctantly.

"Steve, I need your help here," Sean pleaded. "I can't tell the difference between my ass and an exhaust system. I want you to walk me around the Tacony plant and explain things to me."

"Okay," Steve replied.

"All right, then. What was it Tom mentioned he found during his last inspection?"

"He mentioned something about pipe trenches in the rear yard of the Tacony plant. That's it. The property is probably full of them, Sean."

"I know. I know. Here's what I want you to do. Don't go back to the office today. I'm sure there will be a message waiting for you just like the one I got from the Attorney General. I'm sure Kane got to the EPA Administrator and you're being put under a gag order too. So, go directly to the Tacony plant tomorrow morning and I'll meet you there. I want to find out what is going on with these pipe trenches."

CHAPTER 21

Sean Murphy and Steve Cooperhouse arrived unannounced at the Tacony plant, much to Bob Morrone's surprise and chagrin.

"I don't think we've ever met, Mr. Murphy and Mr. Cooperhouse. Although, I've heard your names before. I was used to corresponding with Mr. Roth on this matter, and he usually called in advance to let me know he was coming."

"Tom Roth is dead," Sean said bluntly. "He was killed in a car accident on his way home from his last visit here."

"Oh my God! That's horrible. I remember the weather being quite bad that night. Come to think of it, I didn't get a chance to say goodbye to Tom. I was so busy with other things. The security guard let me know later that evening that Tom had finished up and left immediately after he was done. My God, I can't believe Tom is dead."

"Yeah, we were all quite shocked too," Sean said. "You always expect the whole world to come to a screeching halt when someone close to you dies, but, it doesn't. Anyway, Mr. Morrone, Steve and I'll be picking up with the investigation."

"I assumed Tom's last visit would have been the end of it," Morrone commented.

"Actually, Mr. Morrone," Sean said, "I don't think this is going to take long. Tom Roth came across a pipe trench in the rear yard area of the plant when he was out here last time. My guess is it's nothing, but we just want to check and be sure."

"Okay, Mr. Murphy, whatever you want, but first I have to call my boss, Mr. Kane, and let him know you are here. He and Mr. Braddon made it clear that if anyone from the government showed up, I was to let them know."

Sean smiled at Steve, knowing for sure after Morrone's comment that Kane was the mastermind behind the order to terminate the investigation, just as Sean had suspected. Realizing that the utmost confidentiality was now essential to buying time for the investigation, Sean instructed Morrone accordingly. "I'm sorry,

Mr. Morrone, but we don't have time for that. I need your assistance now, which doesn't leave time for any phone calls."

"But, Mr. Murphy, please. I could get fired for not following Mr. Kane's instructions."

"You let me worry about that Mr. Morrone. Now, please show me to the rear yard, and I want you to stay with me the entire time I'm here."

"Okay, sir, whatever you say." Bob Morrone had been in the environmental business long enough to know that the government had the right to make unannounced inspections and that, if you resisted in any way, you might wind up in jail for a few days. That knowledge, together with the fact that the federal government was obviously taking a keen interest in the Tacony plant, easily shifted Morrone's priority from one of worrying about his position with the company to one of making sure that Sean Murphy had whatever he needed.

The three of them walked to the back of the plant. When they reached the middle of the rear yard area, Sean stopped to look around. "All right, Mr. Morrone, Tom Roth said he found something out here. Something about a pipe trench." Morrone joined Sean in looking around the plant rear yard area.

"I don't see anything here, Mr. Murphy."

"C'mon, Bob," Sean demanded. "What was it Tom was concerned about? I mean, why did he come back out here for that second visit?"

"Mr. Murphy, all I can tell you is that Tom Roth called me with questions about the modification to the exhaust system. The company added a third exhaust pipe and Mr. Roth wanted to look at that system."

"Okay, now we're getting somewhere," said Sean. "Show me this third exhaust pipe, please."

"Sure, follow me. It's over here," answered Morrone.

When they arrived at the side of the building, Sean stopped to look at the three exhaust pipes running down the side of the building. "Which of these three pipes is the one that the company added?"

"This one here," Morrone said, pointing to the exhaust pipe entering the ground.

"Where does it go?" Sean asked.

"I'm pretty sure it recycles back into the plant," Morrone answered. "At least that's what I'm told by the plant engineer."

"Show me," Sean demanded.

They entered the plant through the same door that Tom Roth had. Morrone was surprised by the absence of any physical sign of the exhaust pipe entering the building when they descended the stairs to the lowest level of the building. When they re-entered the rear yard area, Sean looked at Steve Cooperhouse for an idea of what to do next.

"I don't know, Sean. I'm lost because I never had the chance to review the engineering plans for the plant. Tom Roth pored over those documents in his usual exhaustive style. I'm sure he had an idea of what he was looking for when he came out for his inspection."

"All right. Let's do this," Sean said, trying to bring some vision and sense to the process, realizing that he had to come up with something during this visit and do it quickly. "Roth said something about a pipe trench. Let's figure out where that pipe trench is." Sean stood next to the exhaust pipe entering the ground. He started walking arcs in intervals of several feet from the exhaust pipe. Sean instructed Morrone and Steve Cooperhouse to do likewise. The three of them wandered around the rear yard with their heads down, appearing like inmates at a state mental institution. Before long, Sean stumbled across a manhole.

"Help me with this," Sean demanded as he bent down to lift a steel cover from the manhole.

"Surely," Morrone responded as he likewise bent down to assist Sean. As they peeled the cover off, the three of them looked into the same pipe tunnel that Tom had seen a few days earlier.

"Mr. Morrone, what are all these pipes?"

"Honestly, Mr. Murphy, I have no idea. I just haven't had the time yet to learn every aspect of this operation. The day-to-day stuff is keeping me so busy that I'm pretty much learning as I go. I only would have learned about these pipes if we had a problem out here and we had to come out to fix them."

"Okay, here's what we're going to do. I see you have a backhoe over by the coal piles. Do you have a trained operator on-site?"

"Yes, we do."

"Good. Get the operator and a couple of laborers with some shovels. Bring them to the location where that exhaust pipe first enters the ground, okay?"

"You got it," Morrone assured Sean as he grabbed the walkie-talkie off of his belt and called for assistance. They walked back toward the building as Morrone dispatched the help Sean wanted. When he was finished, he asked Sean, "What do you have in mind?"

"We're going to dig us a hole, Mr. Morrone. I want to see where that third exhaust pipe goes."

"Mr. Murphy, that's a dangerous proposition. Those exhaust pipes are carrying superheated flue gases. If we puncture a line, someone could get seriously hurt."

"Yeah, Sean," Steve confirmed. "We don't want to be responsible for any damage to this plant, Sean. We're on thin ice as it is."

"What do you mean you're on thin ice, Mr. Cooperhouse?" Morrone asked.

"Don't worry about that," Sean said to Morrone. "Steve gets persnickety about these kinds of things. Just carry on please, Mr. Morrone."

"Okay, we'll just be very careful when we dig," answered Morrone.

"I'd expect nothing less," replied Sean. By the time they made it back to the building several workers were already waiting for them, at which point they all heard the ignition of the backhoe. It rolled slowly toward them. Bob Morrone yelled out the instructions to the laborers and the backhoe operator over the deafening sound of the gases rushing through the exhaust pipes. The backhoe ripped a hole in the ground, about three feet deep, directly next to the gigantic exhaust pipe. Sean and Steve moved closer to have a look down into the pit. The backhoe operator dropped the bucket into the hole for a second scoop. He tore out another foot and a half of soil and stone. Bob Morrone instructed the laborers to get into the pit and start digging by hand.

"Mr. Murphy," Morrone said, "if I had some idea what you are looking for, I might be better able to instruct the workers."

"I'm not exactly sure yet," Sean replied, giving rise to a stunned look on Bob Morrone's face. Just as Morrone was about to probe Sean further on the purpose of the investigation, one of the workers yelled to the three of them. They couldn't hear him the first time, so the worker shouted again.

"The ground is hot as hell right here," the worker said pointing to his feet. "Gotta be somethin' underneath here." Bob Morrone instructed them to use their shovels, but to proceed slowly and carefully. After removing another six inches or so of soil, the worker moved to the side to make room for the three of them to see into the pit. He yelled to them as he stepped aside, "Definitely some pipe down here. Look's like that exhaust pipe. It's definitely carrying something warm." The worker then leaned down and put his ear toward the ground. "Yep, sounds like gas flowing through it."

Sean looked at Bob Morrone and asked, "Why is an exhaust pipe heading east toward the river when it should be going back into the plant?"

Bob Morrone had a look of shock and panic on his face. "I have no idea! I was told this plant recycles all of its exhaust gas. There should be no discharge whatsoever."

"I want this pipe tunnel traced until we find the end point," Sean demanded. Bob Morrone, in an obvious state of distress, gathered the workers together and explained what he wanted. An hour later, Sean, Steve and Bob were watching as the backhoe and the workers were digging about ten feet away from the bulkhead, at which point the pipe made a ninety degree downward turn. The workers looked up to for instruction. "Keep chasing it," yelled Sean, "I want to see where it goes."

As the laborers continued with their work, Sean pulled Steve aside to reflect on the conversations they had with Tom Roth, especially the results of sampling data in the Delaware River.

"Steve, what was it Roth found in the river?"

"A low pH," he answered.

"No shit, Sherlock. I mean what did Roth find out from the EPA lab? What is the source of the low pH."

"Carbonic acid."

"Right, that's it. Take me back to our environmental chemistry course at Penn State. What was that chemical cycle we learned about? You know, the one that involved carbonic acid?"

"The bicarbonate cycle. Is that the one you mean?"

"Yeah," Sean responded. "How does that work again?"

"What do you mean, Sean, how does it work? I'm not sure what you're looking for."

"Explain the chemical process, Steve."

"I don't know if I can remember it off the top of my head, Sean. It's been over twenty years since I worked on that subject matter."

"Give me a break, Steve. Try! Work it out."

Steve Cooperhouse pulled out a small notepad he had in his pocket. Putting pencil to paper, he started to work out the chemical equation. When he was done, he showed Sean what he had worked out."

"Okay, now what is this telling me, Steve?" Sean asked.

"Well, it tells us that water is a sink for carbon dioxide. What I mean is carbon dioxide dissolves into water and chemically reacts with it. Remember, the concept of carbon sources and sinks, Sean?"

"Not really. Enlighten me," he said.

"Carbon sources include certain naturally occurring events, like volcanoes, and all of the man-made stuff, especially energy production. Carbon sinks are activities or locations where carbon is used up. The world's oceans and other large surface waters are the biggest sinks for carbon dioxide. It actually dissolves into the water forming carbonic acid, among other things of course."

"That's what I thought."

"What?" Steve asked.

"That's what Power Systems has been doing at the Tacony plant. I'm sure of it."

"What do you mean?" Steve asked.

"They are bubbling the exhaust from the furnace into the Delaware River, and it's forming carbonic acid. Tom Roth told us that the pH problem started right after Power Systems retooled the Tacony plant to take care of the shutdown problem they were having early on when the plant was first operating. All they did was pipe the exhaust to the river, and they used an outside contractor to do the work as a way of making sure nobody from the plant figured out what was going on. Remember the plant was totally shut down for a period of time and that's when they brought the contractor in to do the work. Once they turned the switch back on, the carbon dioxide entering the river depressed the pH level. My guess is that Robert Stark figured it out somehow. That's why he was going to blow the whistle on Power Systems."

"You keep using the word 'they.' Who is 'they' Sean?"

"My guess is it's that prick Senator Kane. He's a murderer. I'll bet my bottom dollar on it, Steve. Answer me one question."

"What's that Sean?" Steve asked.

"Can you say with a reasonable degree of scientific certainty that Power Systems is discharging more than just carbon dioxide? We've talked many times about the fact that carbon dioxide is not regulated by any federal environmental law. So, if Power Systems is simply diverting carbon dioxide then there is no violation of the Federal Clean Air Act. But, if Power Systems is emitting a regulated pollutant, then we have a case."

"I don't know, Sean. I'd have to take a close look at the engineering drawings and figure out exactly what else might be in the exhaust gases."

"Steve, I don't have time for this bullshit. Kane and Braddon are going to know in the next few hours that I circumvented the Attorney General's order. All hell is about to break loose. So, I really don't have time for you to get comfortable with the entire situation."

"All right," Steve said. "I suppose there is no way Power Systems can be polishing out all the other pollutants that typically go up the stack of an electric power plant, but what do you mean when you say 'we have a case,'" asked Steve tentatively.

"All right, Steve. You convinced me. Shut them down."

"What?"

"You heard me," Sean said convincingly, "Shut . . . them . . . down."

"I can't do that," Steve responded meekly.

"Steve, c'mon. Now's not the time to turn into a pansy on me. If I could do it myself, I would, but the Department of Justice can't issue a field directive to cease operating. However, the EPA, and you in particular Steve, have the authority to issue that kind of an order. I'm telling you, as your legal advisor, you have the authority to shut them down. Don't worry about anything. I got your back. Shut them down and do it now."

"Okay, here goes nothing."

Steve Cooperhouse moved over toward Bob Morrone. "Mr. Morrone, Mr. Murphy and I've seen enough to convince us that Power Systems is not recirculating this exhaust gas. Do you have any reason to disagree with me?"

"None whatsoever," Morrone responded nervously.

"Fine. I'm ordering you to shut down the plant immediately."

"Shut down the plant! Mr. Cooperhouse, I don't have that authority. I have to speak with Mr. Kane or Mr. Braddon in order to do something like that. Power Systems has contractual commitments to deliver electricity to Philadelphia Electric Company on a continuous and uninterrupted basis. If we shut down without notice, we will be in breach of contract with Philadelphia Electric and probably ten other parties. We'll be facing lawsuits for the next ten years."

"Sorry Mr. Morrone, but I don't have time to wait for you to call anyone. Plus, trust me when I tell you any kind of lawsuit you can imagine is the least of this company's worries right now. So, shut it down and do it now."

"Okay, Mr. Cooperhouse. Whatever you say." Bob Morrone called the plant manager on his walkie-talkie. After some arguing, the hum from the Tacony plant turbines went silent.

CHAPTER 22

As soon as Sean Murphy returned to his office, his mental wheels started turning about what should be the next step. He had seen too many cases botched because of a lack of attention to procedural detail early on. He wasn't about to let this action against Power Systems, Inc. go sour, especially considering it might turn up something against Senator Kane.

Sean began pacing tigerishly around his office, which was a guaranteed method of generating the speedy mental productivity he needed in a circumstance like this one. The fact that Senator Kane and John Braddon would know within a half hour or so that the EPA, and Steve Cooperhouse in particular, had ordered the Tacony plant shut down made time of the essence. *Okay, Sean,* he thought as he paced, *what's first on the enforcement agenda? Procedural issues first. This will be a sit - uation most likely involving both civil and criminal enforcement.* Sean had been through this procedural thought process countless times before: which comes first, a criminal action or a civil action? Sean knew all too well that if the criminal action proceeded first, it allowed the witnesses to "dummy up" under the Fifth Amendment's right against self-incrimination. Plus, the standard of proof that the government had to meet in an environmental criminal action was much more difficult than a civil penalty action. But, Sean was quick to remember that proof of an environmental crime was not as stringent as other intentional criminal actions, like murder and so on, where the government has to show beyond a reasonable doubt that the person knowingly and willfully acts in violation of some code of conduct. To prevail on an environmental crime, all Sean Murphy would need to demonstrate was simply that Power Systems, Inc., through one of its employees, knowingly performed some act that violated a federal environmental law, most likely the Clean Air Act in this case. Sean continued to think through his strategy. *If I go with the criminal action, all I need to show is an intent to perform the act. I won't have to show that Power Systems or the responsible individuals intended to commit an environmental crime. Just an intent to perform the act. Let's see. What is that going to be here? C'mon, Sean, think boy, think. All I need to demonstrate is that the company intended to divert the exhaust pipe to the Delaware. That's it. Easy enough. Simple actually.*

It always dumbfounded Sean how easy it was for the government to prove an environmental crime, compared to the more common everyday crimes, yet how few environmental criminal actions were initiated by the federal government. For some unexplainable reason, both federal and state environmental enforcement agencies more often opted for the less compelling action of seeking civil penalties from companies that violated environmental laws. *If I go with the civil penalty action first, I don't have to worry about the Fifth Amendment. Kane and Braddon have to answer all my questions. They will have no right against self-incrimination.* Sean continued to push his brain at light speed. *Plus, I have a much easier burden of proof in a civil penalty situation. If I lose the civil claim, though, I'll never be able to prevail on a later criminal action.* Sean's last thought was a conundrum that plagued all prosecutors. Because a civil action has a lesser burden of proof than a criminal action, if a government attorney could not win the civil claim, there was no way he or she would be able subsequently to meet the more stringent, and therefore tougher, criminal burden of proof. Sean then took stock of the fact that all of his thoughts were geared toward proofs. He decided to call Steve Cooperhouse back, considering he would be the government's lead fact witness to testify about issues of intent and the nature of the environmental violations at the Tacony plant.

"Steve, it's Murph," Sean said when Steve Cooperhouse picked up his telephone. "Listen, I'm struggling with how to proceed in a case against Power Systems. As usual, you will be my best evidence against the company. What if I decide to proceed criminally? What can you say based on what we know right now?"

"I figured you would be calling me about this. Kane is responsible for an environmental violation at the plant."

"Wait a minute," Sean responded. "You're getting ahead of me there, buddy. What I'm looking for is the technical factual detail of your testimony."

"My testimony would be that Power Systems, and one or more of its key employees, diverted the Tacony plant exhaust gases to the Delaware River without the proper environmental permits from the EPA."

"Okay, that's what I needed to hear."

Sean decided his procedural course immediately after hanging up with Steve. He was going to charge Power Systems, Inc. criminally and, depending on how the evidence panned out, maybe even one or more of the company's principals. Civil penalties would come later. The next thing for Sean to consider was how to set up the criminal case. He fell back on the time honored and proven rule that a written confession was the easiest and cleanest way to go with any crime. Sean knew exactly what to do. He went to his computer and hit the Microsoft Outlook icon. Next, he clicked on the new e-mail prompt. A blank screen popped up and Sean started typing quickly:

braddon@eeil.com
Subject: Tacony Plant
Dear Mr. Braddon,

I am writing to notify you that U.S Environmental Protection Agency, on my advice and consent, ordered the immediate cessation of operations at the Power Systems Tacony plant this morning on the basis of an imminent and substantial threat to public health and the environment. It has come to our attention that Power Systems is engaged in the unlawful discharge of air pollutants to the environment. Moreover, we have reason to believe the company and its officers intentionally, and without proper governmental authorization, violated the federal Clean Air Act and Clean Water Act for the sole purpose of financial gain. Be advised that, as of this morning, the Department of Justice commenced an investigation into the possibility of criminal activity at the Tacony plant. Be further advised that, as the president of Power Systems, Inc., you are a principal target of this criminal investigation.

I am willing to meet with you to discuss your participation, if any, in the construction of an unauthorized exhaust system at the Tacony plant. The Department of Justice has the authority to offer you transactional immunity in exchange for testimony leading to the successful criminal prosecution of the violator. What this means is that we can agree not to prosecute you criminally for any environmental violations at the Tacony plant so long as you confess to knowledge of the unlawful conduct and so long as the factual testimony you provide is sufficient to gain an indictment of, or written confession from, the responsible party.

This offer of transactional immunity will remain valid until the close of business today. If you are interested in accepting this offer, call me on my direct dial: 215-555-4035.

Sincerely,
Sean Murphy

Sean clicked on the send button and waited. Between John Braddon and Senator Kane, Braddon seemingly was the more pliable. Sean noticed during their meeting that Braddon was the one trying to "keep the peace." Braddon, in Sean's opinion, was the one more likely to break under pressure. He was the one more likely to 'rat out' the other guy in order to save his own ass. Plus, while Braddon had access to a bottomless pit of money, he did not have the political influence of Senator Kane, which had already reared its ugly head and would no doubt be the first line of defense that Kane would look to in the event of a prosecution. Braddon would thus be less able, in Sean's opinion, to manipulate the criminal judicial process. All these things considered led Sean to conclude that Braddon would hand over Senator Kane, who Sean believed in his heart was the mastermind behind this scheme. A minute or two after he sent the e-mail, Sean's telephone rang.

"Sean Murphy, here."

"Sean, it's John Braddon. I want to talk."

"Mr. Braddon," Sean replied, "I have not sought an arrest warrant for you yet, so you do not have the benefit and protection of Miranda warnings. That said, though, I want to remind you that you have a right to be represented by an attorney in any discussions or meetings you have with me."

"That's unnecessary. I trust you, Sean. If I understand your offer of immunity, you will not target me for any environmental crime that may have taken place at the Tacony plant. Is that correct?" Braddon asked directly.

"Yes, that's correct."

"Okay, then, Sean. I suggest we do this face-to-face. Where would you like to meet?"

"I'll come to your office. I can be there first thing tomorrow morning."

"Fine. I usually get in by nine. Any time after that is okay with me."

"All right, I'll see you then. Oh, and Mr. Braddon, don't speak with any other officer or director of Power Systems about my offer."

"I won't."

CHAPTER 23

Braddon was notably distressed. His distinctively calm and confident style during the meeting at Senator Kane's office was now undermined by a nervousness that Sean first recognized by Braddon's sweaty palm when they shook hands.

"Well, Sean, you're more familiar with this process than I am. Where do we begin?"

"At the beginning, Mr. Braddon, at the beginning. First of all, do you understand what I meant in my e-mail when I offered you transactional immunity?"

"Only what I read in the newspapers, Sean."

"Okay, that's a start. What I am offering you is complete protection from any criminal prosecution for actions or events in which you may have had some involvement that rise to the level of an environmental violation at the Tacony plant. So, it doesn't protect you from civil penalties, like fines, which could be substantial in this case. The most important part of my offer, though, is that I have the discretion to back out of the deal if the information you supply does not lead to the successful criminal prosecution of another person. Do you understand?"

"Yes, I understand."

"And you would like to proceed with this meeting, understanding those limitations?"

"Yes, I do."

"All right then. Tell me what you know about the exhaust system at the Tacony plant."

"Okay," Braddon paused for a minute, trying to find the words. He and Sean knew that this point in time was the moment of truth, not only for Braddon but for Power Systems and its many investors. If what Braddon was about to tell Sean resulted in the collapse of Power Systems, the immunity Sean was offering Braddon might turn out to protect him from only the "tip of the iceberg," considering that Braddon's testimony could implicate federal securities laws and other similar issues. "I believe you are aware of the operational problems we were experiencing at the Tacony plant early on."

"Yes, I am aware of that problem."

"Well, although the underlying theory and patent for the furnace was developed by one of our own engineers, we relied on an outside furnace manufacturer to build the Tacony plant. The company name was. . . . " Braddon thought about it for a few seconds, "Electric Refractories or something along those lines. Anyway, after we started experiencing the shutdown problem, we brought the manufacturer back in to diagnose the problem. They concluded that a buildup of gases, mainly carbon dioxide, in the main burning chamber was essentially 'choking' out the flame. The way it was explained to me was that the burning chamber wasn't getting enough oxygen to support the combustion process. So, we initially tried adding another exhaust pipe and injecting it into the burning chamber at a different location, combined with increasing the amount of fresh air intake. It didn't work. In fact, that fix just seemed to make the problem worse. The manufacturer then concluded that we had to vent at least some of the exhaust, with a main focus on getting rid of carbon dioxide."

"You mean the plant couldn't remain a 'zero emissions' system?" asked Sean.

"Yes, that's correct. But, the idea was that we could still operate the plant by getting a permit to emit a certain amount of pollutants to the atmosphere. Because carbon dioxide is not regulated by the Clean Air Act, we could get rid of as much of it as we needed without a permit. The tradeoff, though, was that we would not get the amount of greenhouse gas credits as we originally calculated. All that meant was that the Tacony plant wouldn't be as profitable as we originally projected, which frankly wasn't that big of a deal. This kind of thing always happens with innovative technology investments. Because any new and unproven technology has to be tweaked and adjusted to meet government standards, the projected profits are many times lower than analysts originally predict. So, the loss of greenhouse gas credits didn't concern me too much. I felt fairly confident that I would be able to deal with investor confidence as long as we were showing some financial return."

"So what happened?" Sean asked, realizing that Braddon was getting a bit off track.

"Well, considering this problem was turning out to be a regulatory issue, I put it in Oren Kane's hands to handle. If Power Systems was going to need an air emissions permit to get the Tacony plant back up and running, Kane was the guy with the contacts to make sure that we got the environmental permit quickly. All I wanted to know was how much in the way of greenhouse gas credits would we have to forfeit because of the fix we were planning for the Tacony plant. A couple of weeks after I tasked Oren to resolve the problem, I got a call from him that both the EPA and the Pennsylvania Department of Environmental Protection had agreed to a creative solution to our problem. I don't know how much you understand the concept of carbon sequestration, but one accepted form of developing carbon dioxide credits is to sequester it in a body of water. Well, Oren told me that he had worked out a deal with the governmental authorities that Power Systems could, at least on a trial basis, dissolve carbon dioxide in the exhaust from the Tacony plant into the Delaware River."

"Did you see any documentation confirming this so-called deal?" inquired Sean suspiciously.

"No, Oren told me that because Power Systems was still not going to be emitting anything to the atmosphere, we did not need an air emissions permit or any other form of document for that matter. According to Oren, all the government wanted Power Systems to do was to check the water quality just downstream of the exhaust gas injection point, which we were already doing for the wastewater discharge anyway. So, we scheduled a two week plant shutdown and brought in an outside contractor to re-route the exhaust to the river. The Tacony plant re-started and operated problem free."

Sean pondered for a few seconds the story that Braddon was feeding him. He then asked, "I assume, at some point Mr. Braddon, you realized Oren's strategy was illegal. Otherwise, you and I wouldn't be sitting here talking together."

"Yes. Well, let me put it this way," Braddon backtracked. "Let's say I started to have my suspicions that Oren had not been forthright with me."

"Tell me about how you came to that conclusion, please."

"One day I got a call from Robert Stark, who I think you know was the environmental compliance manager at the Tacony plant. He called me in a state of panic telling me that the Tacony plant was violating environmental laws and that he was going to blow the whistle. I calmed him down so I could understand what he was trying to say, which wasn't easy. All I really got out of him was that there was a problem with the exhaust system, that it wasn't recycling as originally planned. You see, the difficulty in putting two and two together here was that, even though we modified the exhaust system, the way Oren explained it to me, there was still some level of recycling of the exhaust gases going on. According to Oren, we were pulling off and diverting to the Delaware only that amount of carbon dioxide needed to keep the plant operational. Kane told me that, with the furnace technology we were using, we had the ability to strip off the carbon dioxide only and return the remaining exhaust gases to the plant for recycling in the burning chamber. So, when Robert Stark called me that day, I assumed he was talking about some problem with the amount of exhaust gas we were still supposed to be recycling."

"So, what did you do?" Sean asked.

"I told Stark that the only way we could make sense of this reported problem would be for him to bring the plans and specifications of the exhaust system to my office the next day and we would sit down and figure things out. I pretty much begged him not to call any environmental authorities until we met, on the assurance that I would take whatever steps necessary to resolve any problems or violations we discovered during our meeting."

"So, Stark comes to your office the next morning and what happens then?"

"He never showed. Not only that, he never showed up at work the next day. When he didn't make it here for our meeting the next morning, I called the plant and they told me he never arrived for work. I just assumed he decided to blow me off and went straight to the governmental authorities."

"What happened to him?"

"Well, I can't be sure, but I assume it was sometime between our telephone conversation and the next day that he met someone with a cargo hook."

"You mean Stark was probably murdered that same day he talked to you?" Sean asked with a look of total shock on his face.

"I assume that's the case," Braddon answered.

"Why?"

"Well, if he had gone to the governmental authorities instead of coming to see me, I assume I would have received a call within the next day or so from the EPA, but I didn't hear anything. Stark didn't show up for work any day thereafter. The next thing I heard, he was fished out of the Delaware River."

"So, what happened next?"

"Well, even though Stark didn't show up for our meeting, Oren made it. So, I asked him if he had any idea what Stark was so excited about regarding the Tacony plant."

"Wait a minute," Sean interrupted. "Did you say Senator Kane was at your office the morning Stark was supposed to be there?"

"Yes. After I hung up with Stark when he first called about this supposed exhaust system violation, I realized that Oren was the one who knew most about the modifications. I figured the only way we would get anything done was if Oren was at the meeting with me and Stark. So, I called Oren after I hung up with Stark and asked Oren to be at my office first thing the next morning."

"Mr. Braddon, exactly what did you say to Senator Kane?" Sean asked.

"Well, I described for him the telephone call I had with Stark and that I wanted to figure out if a problem existed with the exhaust system at the Tacony plant. Why do you ask, Sean?"

"No reason in particular," Sean answered slowly.

"Wait a minute," Braddon said in a moment of revelation. "Do you think Oren Kane had something to do with Stark's murder?"

"I guess that depends on what you tell me next, but the timing seems to be a bit more than just coincidence. So, you were saying that the first notice you had of a problem with the exhaust system was this panicked call from Stark. I assume at some point Senator Kane spilled the beans, right?"

"Yes, he did. Believe me, it wasn't a good day for me. A few days after Stark's body was discovered, the Philadelphia prosecutor showed up at the Tacony plant and took all of the company's environmental files. Then, soon after that event, the EPA started its investigation. You don't have to be in this business too long to realize that something is amiss. So, I called Oren Kane and asked for an explanation. That's when Oren told me his story about the government approving an innovative remedy for the exhaust problem at the Tacony plant was just that, a story. That son of a bitch! I was ready to kill him. I remember screaming over the phone to him that we had broken about a hundred separate laws."

"What was Senator Kane's answer?" asked Sean anxiously.

"He told me I was in this mess as deeply as he was. That smug fuck!" Frustration showed glaringly on Braddon's face.

164

"Why didn't you report the situation to the appropriate authorities?"

"Because I'm a stupid shit. Oren persuaded me that there was no way the authorities would ever find out about the situation at the Tacony plant. First of all, he reminded me of the fact that the plant had been operating for years by that time without anyone ever taking an interest in the exhaust system. Although I was quite uncomfortable with that limited assurance, he was right. We never had a single inspection by a governmental authority at the plant the entire time the facility was operating. In hindsight, I realize the reason for the lack of interest was because Power Systems was not in any environmental database regarding air emissions. It wasn't an air permitted facility because of its 'zero emissions' status. We had a number of disputes with the EPA and the Pennsylvania Department of Environmental Protection on the wastewater discharge because of the acidity condition in the river, but nothing ever came of that. No one could ever pin responsibility on Power Systems for that condition. Then, Oren did a good job of scaring me about the financial consequences if I reported the situation to the authorities. We would lose all of the greenhouse gas credits, including those that we had already sold through The Climate Exchange. We were facing a breach of carbon futures contracts that ensured the continued profitability of the Tacony plant for years. That kind of an upset would put the already tenuous carbon market in a complete tailspin."

"How so?" Sean inquired, showing his inability to grasp the financial part of the case.

"Nearly fifty companies have been buying Power Systems greenhouse gas credits since late 2003. Those companies rely on those Power Systems' credits to meet greenhouse gas reduction benchmarks at the end of each calendar year. If the Power Systems credits turn out to be fabricated, then all of those companies that relied on the credits are in violation of the Exchange's binding reduction goals. Plus, those companies participating in the Exchange have probably been marketing their products on the basis of being environmental friendly and so on. Once the public gets a hold of the fact that the Power Systems credits are worthless, corporate scandal is plastered all over the newspapers."

"So, you allowed the cover up to continue," Sean prompted Braddon.

"Bad choice, I know," Braddon admitted. "It's been eating away at me ever since I decided to go along with Oren."

"Extremely bad choice, Mr. Braddon."

"So, what do we do now, Sean?"

"Other than your discussion with Senator Kane, is there anything else we can use to show that he was the moving force behind this unauthorized exhaust system modification?"

"As I said, I pretty much let Oren run with it on the belief that it was a legitimate project. Let me think." Braddon stared off into space thinking for a minute or two. "You know, if we could track down the contractor that did the work, I assume Oren's signature will be all over the invoices."

"Good idea. Check the company's accounting records to see if you can find any record of that work. Otherwise, Mr. Braddon, it's going to be your word against Senator Kane's. He is a very powerful man. Plus, I've seen him work. I guarantee you he'll testify that you told him to do the work and he'll put together a story to support it. Along those lines, is there anything you can think of today that Senator Kane could use to defend a criminal action?" Sean was obviously very nervous about putting together the strongest case against Senator Kane, which meant leaving no stone unturned.

"Nothing I can think of right now," responded Braddon.

"Well, noodle it further so we don't forget anything."

"Sean, may I make a suggestion?"

"Sure."

"As far as I know, Oren is unaware of the shutdown at Tacony. I'm sure he'll find out about it soon, though. I suggest, if you want to keep Oren Kane fat, happy, and oblivious to what we are doing, you get the plant back up and running. Business as usual, if you know what I mean."

"Excellent idea. I'll take care of that on the train ride home." Sean stood up from the conference table and began collecting his notes. As he was placing them in his briefcase, he said, "Okay, remember to make yourself sparse the next few days and avoid any contact with Senator Kane."

"Actually, I was planning on taking a vacation at my house in the Hamptons over the next few days. Everybody knows about my rule that I am unreachable when I am there."

"Excellent. Give me your phone number and . . . let's see. . . . Do you have a personal e-mail address I can use to reach you in the Hamptons?" Sean asked.

"Yes, absolutely. Here is the contact information." Braddon wrote a telephone number and AOL account name on a slip of paper and handed it to Sean. As they shook hands goodbye, Sean noticed that Braddon's hand was no longer hot and sweaty.

⋅⋅ ⋅⋅ ⋅⋅ ⋅⋅

Sean bolted across Twenty-second Street to Penn Station to catch the next train back to Philly. As soon as he was on board, he called Steve Cooperhouse on his office phone. No answer. Sean then dialed his cell number.

"Hello, Cooperhouse here," Steve answered customarily.

"Steve, it's Murph. I just had an interesting meeting with John Braddon."

"Where are you Sean?" asked Steve.

"I'm on the Metroliner heading back from Manhattan. I spent the last hour or so with Braddon at his office. He spilled the beans, my man."

"What are you talkin' about?" Steve asked.

"Well, we've both had suspicions that Senator Kane was up to no good here. So, I sent Braddon an e-mail yesterday offering him immunity from criminal prosecution if Braddon offered me some useful testimony. My gut was right. He dumped all over Kane," Sean boasted.

"What did Braddon have to say about Senator Kane?" Steve asked.

"I'll tell you about that later," Sean responded cautiously. "I don't want to get into too much detail over the phone."

"I understand. So, I assume you're looking for something from me, right?" Steve observed astutely.

"Yep. Braddon made a good point just as we were finishing up with our meeting. If our strategy is going to work, we need to buy a little time. The only way we can make that happen is if Kane has no idea what is going on. Otherwise, we're going to have the entire federal government coming down on us. Kane wields a heavy hand."

"I agree with that. So what does that have to do with me, Sean?"

"Well, you know how I told you to shut down the Tacony plant yesterday?" Sean said with a note of sarcasm in his voice.

"Yeee . . . sss?" Steve could feel something absurd coming.

"Open her back up," Sean instructed.

"You gotta be fuckin' kiddin' me! How am I supposed to do that? We're going to look like total idiots here, Sean, wavering back and forth."

"Relax, Steve, relax. Call Bob Morrone and let him know that we have the information we need from our investigation. Tell him the company can restart the plant. I don't want Kane hearing that the plant was shut down. As far as he is concerned, you and I were never there," Sean observed.

"What do you mean?"

"Remember the call I got on the train ride back from D.C. the other day? Kane is under the impression that our investigation came to a screeching halt that afternoon. Kane doesn't know that you and I were at the plant yesterday, and he doesn't know you issued the verbal shut down order. Most importantly, he doesn't know that I met with Braddon today."

"How can you be so sure?" Steve inquired.

"Because Kane is an arrogant fuck. He would never think to check on whether his directive to the Attorney General worked. Kane just assumes that his influence worked."

"All right, I'll call Bob Morrone as soon as we hang up, but, my guess is somebody at the plant is going to report the situation to Senator Kane," Steve observed.

"I'm not so sure about that, Steve. I think the folks at the Tacony plant, especially Bob Morrone, are scared to death about what's going on. The last thing they want to do is be the one to initiate a call to a bonehead like Kane. They know he would go berserk."

"If you say so, Sean."

❧ ❧ ❧ ❧

While Sean was talking to Steve Cooperhouse, John Braddon was on his cell phone from his car, which was tearing along the Long Island Expressway toward the Hamptons. Bob Morrone's cell phone began to ring.

"Hello," Bob answered.

"Bob, this is John Braddon."

"Mr. Braddon, hello," Morrone said nervously, not having called anyone yet to report the shut down of the Tacony plant. "Mr. Braddon, I'm afraid I have some bad news."

"I already know, Bob. The EPA ordered you to shut down the Tacony plant. Something to do with the exhaust system, right?"

"Yes, sir. How did you know?" asked Morrone.

"An attorney for the Department of Justice paid me a visit today and we talked things through. Everything is fine. Don't worry."

"Steve Cooperhouse, you know the EPA guy, believes that the exhaust system from the plant is illegally being piped to the Delaware River, Mr. Braddon. And I got to tell you, from what I can see, that seems to be the case."

"I know, Bob. What you aren't aware of is that we had the government's approval to do the exhaust system modification shortly after we started the plant up. Steve Cooperhouse and this DOJ attorney just weren't aware of it," Braddon said to Morrone, trying to keep him calm so he would not be surprised by the next thing Braddon had to say. "In fact, the EPA will most likely call you soon to tell you to get the plant back up and running."

"I don't understand, Mr. Braddon. This is like nothing I've ever seen before. I've got to be honest. I'm scared to death. Why didn't somebody tell me about this exhaust system modification? We could have avoided a lot of headaches."

"I know, Bob. My mistake. The plant had been operating so nicely for the past few years that the exhaust system modification just became an unimportant historical artifact. Admittedly, not the best way to do business and I apologize." Bob Morrone was quite surprised to hear Braddon talking this way. What Morrone didn't know was that Braddon had an agenda behind this discussion: to ensure that Morrone would not call Senator Kane and tip him off as to the events of the past few days. It was almost as if Braddon and Sean Murphy were on some common mental wavelength. "Bob, one question. Did you mention the plant shut down to anyone else?"

"Mr. Braddon, I have been so scared all day today that I stayed away from the telephone. I just couldn't take the pressure of having to explain to you or Senator Kane what happened."

"No problem, Bob. In fact, I think it's for the better. In case you haven't figured it out yet, Senator Kane can be a bit of a hothead. So, I suggest we keep this incident as low key as possible. No harm, no foul, if you know what I mean."

Morrone was still unnerved about the whole situation and Braddon's last comment. "Mr. Braddon, you know as well as I do that Senator Kane will see that we had an unscheduled one day shut down when he gets the monthly operational reports."

"I understand, Bob. Let me take care of informing Senator Kane. The best way you can help me to do that is to get the plant up and running again once the EPA gives you the okay. Agreed?"

"Yes, sir. Well, at least I'll be able to sleep tonight," Bob said with an obvious tone of relief.

When Braddon got to his vacation home in Noyack, he understandably broke his tradition of going out onto the deck overlooking the Noyack Bay. His custom of sucking the salty air into his lungs, almost as a ritual cleansing, had to wait for more urgent business. Braddon immediately went to his computer and booted it up. After a few minutes of mandatory debugging, the large screen went from black to a multi-colored image of tropical fish, followed slowly by almost a full page of icons for the voluminous operational programs. He clicked on the Microsoft Outlook icon and waited a few seconds for his e-mail messages to download. Nothing from Sean Murphy yet. Next, he began to write a new message to his secretary. His first purpose was to remind her that he was not to be bothered for the next few days, but more importantly, he wanted to start a process of collecting data about the exhaust system modification. The trick was how to collect that information without tipping Kane off to the fact that Sean Murphy was still on his tracks. *I have to make this look innocuous,* Braddon thought to himself, as he authored the message. *Kane is impatient. So, if I bury the request in some broader purpose, Kane will miss it. Guaranteed.* With that thought, Braddon wrote:

> *Dana,*
> *I'm just writing to remind you that I'll be at the beach house for the next week or so. Remember, no calls, unless it is Jesus of Nazareth himself, or some higher authority, of course. In the meantime, I have a project for you. We are being asked to produce for tax purposes any and all documents in our possession, custody, or control related to the capital costs for the con - struction and maintenance of the Tacony plant. My recollection is that Oren Kane's office would be the principal location where the files with this information are located. Accordingly, please do a memorandum to Mr. Kane, under my signature, asking for those records. Be sure to put in the memorandum that the failure to include cost records would work to the company's harm. So, Mr. Kane's office should err on the side of being overly inclusive of documents rather than restrictive and let the company's accountants decide what should be included in the final report.*
> *Thank you.*

That should do it, Braddon concluded after proof-reading the e-mail message. So, he hit the send button and walked out the deck.

It had been a day of dramatically mixed emotions for John Braddon. On one level, he was scared by what had happened with Sean Murphy. After all, it's not every day that someone threatened him with jail time. In fact, although John Braddon and many of his colleagues flirted with the prospect of criminal activity pretty much every day of their business lives, he had never been the target of an investigation before. Neither had any of the companies which he either owned or invested in financially. On another level, admitting to his stupidity of following Kane's plan had been personally liberating. Braddon's decision to do so had truly haunted him to such a degree that Braddon had had an uncanny feeling ever since making that decision that someone would discover the fraud. Aiding his sense of freedom was the fact that Braddon, for some unexplainable reason, trusted Sean Murphy implicitly. He knew in his heart that Sean would honor his deal of immunity. Braddon had nothing against Oren Kane, even though his purported political contacts never seemed to turn out to be as strong as represented. On balance then, "diming" out Kane was a much better alternative than a visit to a federal penitentiary. Braddon knew that the board of directors of Environmental & Energy Investments would ask for his resignation. Even that, though, was not a difficult pill for Braddon to swallow. He was nearly seventy years old and it was time to simplify. Standing on the deck of his beach house, finally breathing easier than when he had first arrived, Braddon accepted what he had to do now and welcomed the opportunity to move permanently to his beach house and do some fishing.

CHAPTER 24

With the Tacony plant back up and running, and John Braddon tucked safely away, Sean Murphy debated his next move. He knew that Braddon's testimony alone would not make a strong case against Senator Kane, especially for purposes of a criminal conviction. Although Braddon was unaware of Senator Kane's unlawful actions at the time he was modifying the exhaust system, and although Braddon didn't learn about them until Robert Stark brought them to Braddon's attention, he nonetheless perpetuated the fraud that Senator Kane orchestrated. Regardless of the fact that Braddon had decided to come forward and admit the truth, any reasonably competent criminal defense attorney would be able to impeach Braddon in front of a jury.

Sean also knew that he had to move quickly, not only because of the possibility that Kane would learn of the plan and report it to Sean's superiors in Washington D.C., but also because operating the Tacony plant with the modified exhaust system was a continuing violation of several environmental laws. It was a difficult moral dilemma that Sean had to reconcile in this case. In order to have any chance of winning a criminal conviction against Senator Kane, Sean had to order the continued operation of a facility that he knew was polluting the Delaware River, a natural resource that Sean had spent the better part of his adult life protecting. Sean spent the entire train ride back from Manhattan debating the order he had given to Steve Cooperhouse. By authorizing the Tacony plant to restart, Sean was arguably engaged in a scheme of knowingly polluting the Delaware River. However, Sean's best guess about the nature and extent of the pollution that would occur was merely a continuation of what had been going on for several years now. Plus, if he acted quickly to make his case against Senator Kane, he would be able to order the shutdown of the Tacony plant in short order, which meant that not much additional harm would be done to the river.

In exchange for allowing this continuing pollution, Sean was hoping to be able to make a compelling criminal case against the one person who was perhaps the single most powerful lawmaker in the field of environmental protection. Kane's demise was vital, according to Sean's way of thinking, to the preservation of the fabric of the environmental regulatory system in the United States. If at the helm of the our national environmental lawmaking body was a person who was knowingly willing to pollute the Delaware River in exchange for financial gain, then what prevented that person from allowing that same self-interest from affecting his future actions in making environmental protection policy? In the final analysis, Sean felt the more important way to balance this equation was to divulge to the world the fact that Senator Kane was a criminal. In the long run, Sean thought, protection of the environment and natural resources would be better served by achieving that end. Sean fully appreciated the fact that his decision was going to be subject to criticism, especially in light of Sean's history with Senator Kane. Some would undoubtedly say that Sean's actions were motivated by revenge alone. He would simply have to deal with that challenge if and when it came.

Sean likewise agonized over the fact that Steve Cooperhouse was involved in the act of restarting the Tacony plant, but after thinking about Steve's situation briefly, Sean recognized that Steve was not in the same situation as Sean. Steve was merely reacting to Sean's counseling and advice. If anyone ever challenged Steve on the issue, he had the benefit of saying he relied on the advice of counsel, which was exactly the way Sean wanted it.

Sean decided that the first thing he would need to do was to present to a federal grand jury John Braddon's and Steve Cooperhouse's testimony. Sean had no doubt he would get an indictment based on what he knew would be a compelling story.

❦ ❦ ❦ ❦

Steve Cooperhouse had testified before a federal grand jury many times before. Sean felt confident that Steve would know exactly what to say. Braddon, however, would require some preparation. Sean decided to call him the next morning at his beach house.

"Good morning," Braddon said sprightly, much to Sean's surprise.

"Good morning to you, Mr. Braddon. It's Sean Murphy. I'm glad to see you are in such high spirits."

"You know, Sean, I was very scared when you e-mailed me yesterday and rightly so. But, after you and I talked, and I had a chance to ventilate on my drive out to my beach house, I actually felt a lot better. I guess it's pathetically axiomatic that 'the truth will set you free,' but, to be honest, that is exactly what happened to me yesterday. I felt horrible about falling into Kane's trap, but, believe it or not, today I don't feel that same burden. Don't get me wrong, Sean. I'm still anxious about how this is all going to play out and the fact that my reputation will take a beating. No doubt I'll never work in the financial world again. But, interestingly, the anxiety of those things pales in comparison to the burden I was carrying around for the past month or so being part of Kane's conspiracy. The end result is I can deal with the

172

anxiety. I've been dealing with it for years, just in different circumstances. I know that in a year or so, everything will quiet down and people will forget about me."

"I'm glad for you, Mr. Braddon. Actually, the reason for my call is to pick up on a comment you made about 'how this is all going to play out.' As you suggested, the Tacony plant is back up and running, so, I don't think Senator Kane got wind of the trouble. What I want to do next is have you testify before a federal grand jury so I can get an indictment issued. Federal grand juries are convened for periods at a time and there is one sitting right now in Philly. I think I can get some time tomorrow. Can you be down here, say around noon?"

"Yes. I don't have anything else to do, right?"

"Understood," Sean answered.

"But, Sean, what about my immunity? How does that work?"

"Come to my office, and I'll have papers for you to sign along the lines we already discussed. Obviously, you should feel free to bring an attorney with you to make sure I'm holding up my end of the bargain."

"Not necessary. I trust you, Sean. What about the grand jury? How does that work?"

"Good point. That's actually the reason for my call. Considering the question, I assume you've never testified before a grand jury before."

"That's right," answered Braddon.

"Well, a grand jury hears preliminary evidence of a crime. We don't have to put on a full case. So, all I plan to do is call you to describe the conversation we had yesterday. Very simple and straightforward, you know what I mean. If I think you've forgotten anything, I will prompt you with specific questions. Just tell the grand jury what you told me about Senator Kane's unauthorized modification to the exhaust system. Any questions?"

"Well, it sounds simple enough. What if someone on the grand jury asks about my involvement with the violations at the Tacony plant?"

"Good point," Sean acknowledged. "I'll explain to the grand jury in advance that you have been given immunity from prosecution. Not only that, but I plan to paint a picture that you were sort of duped by Senator Kane. So, let me take care of that one."

"Very good then," Braddon responded calmly.

"One other thing your question reminded me about, though, Mr. Braddon. My order to restart the Tacony plant creates a continuing environmental violation condition. I plan to avoid that issue like the plague. I don't think anyone on the grand jury will be smart enough to pick up on the nuance. But, in case you hear any question about the current operational status of the Tacony plant, I don't want you to lie or be evasive. Just tell them that, as far as you know, the Tacony plant is continuing to operate, which is in fact the truth. I'll take the flak in the event the grand jury gets concerned or argumentative on that point. Again, though, I don't think it will come up. Any other questions, Mr. Braddon?" Sean asked with a clear indication in his voice that he wanted to finish the conversation.

"No, that should just about do it."

"All right, then. Try to relax today and I'll see you tomorrow at noon."

Everything went as expected with the grand jury. Steve Cooperhouse was a spectacular witness, as usual. And, even more importantly, with Braddon's testimony, the grand jury was righteously indignant with the reckless acts of Power Systems, Inc. and its principal, Oren Kane. Sean Murphy's guess was that no one on the grand jury knew that Kane was also a United States senator. Sean was also pleased that no one was astute enough to pick up on the fact that the Tacony plant was still operating. In fact, nobody even asked the question. Immediately after receiving the indictment, he told John Braddon to shut the plant down again.

As soon as Sean got back to his office, he began dictating a press release to his secretary. "Start with the usual introductory material, on the Department of Justice letterhead, of course. Then let's have something like . . . 'Power Systems, Inc. and its officer, Oren Kane, have been indicted for criminal violations of the federal Clean Air Act. The company, which owns and operates an electric power plant in the Tacony section of the City, has been knowingly discharging pollutants to the Delaware River without the proper authorization and permits. According to the indictment issued today, Oren Kane, who is also a United States senator for the Commonwealth of Virginia, intentionally modified the facility's exhaust system without prior notice to, or approval from, the United States Environmental Protection Agency in an effort to circumvent federal statutory and regulatory legal requirements. Evidence indicates that this illegal conduct has caused pollution of the Delaware River in and around the vicinity of the Tacony plant. Additionally, the violations jeopardize greenhouse gas emissions reductions credits that the company has been marketing on The Climate Exchange, which is located in Chicago, Illinois. The Department of Justice will be seeking maximum criminal sanctions against both the company and Senator Kane. By order of the United States Environmental Protection Agency, all business activity at the Tacony plant has been suspended indefinitely.' . . . What do you think, Kate?" Sean asked his secretary. "That should give Kane a scare, huh?"

"I believe it will," she answered.

"As soon as you are done typing it up," Sean instructed, "fax and e-mail a copy to The Philadelphia Inquirer and . . . let's see . . . what the hell, let's send a copy to The Washington Post. What do we have to lose."

"Yes, Sean. Anything else?"

Sean stared off into space for a few seconds and then responded with a question. "Do you think I should fax a copy to Senator Kane?" Before his secretary had a chance to answer, Sean was already settled on the issue. "No. The hell with Kane. Let him find out through the newspapers. That should just about do it. Let's see what happens."

⊰ ⊰ ⊱ ⊱

The next morning, the front page headline in The Philadelphia Inquirer read: "Tacony Power Plant Ordered Closed By EPA," and a subheading read "company and its officer to be prosecuted criminally." The article opened up with a nearly word-for-word presentation of Sean Murphy's press release, followed by an historical account of the plant's construction and its fanfare opening along with an incredibly detailed corporate description of Power Systems, Inc. A similar article appeared in *The Washington Post*, but it was buried quite deep in the business news section.

One of Oren Kane's female law partners, Karen Wood, tripped across the article in *The Washington Post* on her train ride to the office. Considering she had for many years been the target of Kane's mysogenistic tendencies, she was more than happy to stop by his office and break the wonderful news. Unfortunately, Kane was not in yet when she arrived. However, she was good enough to leave the article on his seat with a note reading, "Thought you might be interested," and she simply spelled out at the bottom of the note, "Karen." As Karen walked away from Kane's office toward her own, which was just down the hallway, Karen felt momentarily sympathetic toward Kane's plight, which was odd considering he had been the only one in the firm to oppose Karen's nomination for partnership. Not only that, but in Kane's inimitable style, he let Karen know about his planned opposition before going into the partner's meeting when Karen was up for a vote. His words were forever carved deeply in her mind: "I just want you to be aware that I am not voting in favor of your being admitted to the partnership. You're exactly the reason why this firm has financial troubles, attorneys demanding a partner's salary without having a book of business." Kane knew how to play on a person's insecurities, and that was one Karen had struggled with for many years. She was an excellent attorney, but she did not have any of her own clients. She was worried that the lack of business might prevent her from making partner at a large law firm. Kane's comment had been only one in a long line of miserably hurtful things Kane had said to Karen, even though everybody else in the firm loved her. As she sat down in her seat, Karen thought that the better thing to do would be to go back to Kane's office and pick up the article. The thought didn't last long, though. Instead, all Karen could come up with was the mental note she had always recorded about Kane whenever he mistreated her: *WHAT . . . A . . . DICK!*

᚛ ᚛ ᚜ ᚜

"Son of a bitch!" bellowed Kane from his office. Karen heard it and knew he had just read the article. "It's that bastard Sean Murphy." For a moment, Karen worried that Kane would arrive at her office and take out his frustration on her, considering she had left the article on his seat. On second thought, though, Karen realized that Kane was too proud to let Karen know that her stunt had gotten to him. She was right. He never showed. The only thing she noticed was the sound of his door slamming and, although there was steady flow throughout the day of the firm's senior partners visiting Kane's office, the door remained closed all day. It was still closed when Karen walked past that evening about 7:30 P.M. She heard Kane's bellowing voice, obviously barking at someone on the telephone. As Karen exited the building that night, she wondered what life at the firm would be like without Kane. He and his crass nature were fixtures at the firm. In fact, despite all the abuse she had taken from Kane over the years, she had become accustomed to him. Kane had likewise learned to live with Karen, and all of the other woman partners in the firm, mainly because he had no choice. Although Kane wielded tremendous power at the firm, his was only one vote. No matter how much he disliked the idea of woman partners, his "no" vote always lost out to those of the more reasonable partners in the firm. After some point, he had simply given up on his quest of an all male business society. Once he had reached that point, Karen sensed that professional life with Kane had become at least bearable. There was, however, a distinct possibility that he would be asked to leave the firm.

The day's events were indeed one of a kind for Senator Oren Kane: receiving end instead of delivering. The report of the indictment sent Kane into a rage. After reading the article and slamming his door, Kane went immediately to work on the telephone. His first call was to U.S. Attorney General, Gary Pierson, who was the head of the Department of Justice.

"Good morning, Mr. Pierson's office."

"This is Senator Kane calling. Tell Gary I need to speak with him immediately," demanded Kane.

"Yes, sir. Hold on a second please." Only a second or two passed by before Pierson picked up the line. "Well, Oren, I would say good morning, but I don't think that's the case."

"So you saw the article?" Kane asked.

"No, but one of my deputy AG's called me to let me know about it."

"What the fuck is going on here, Gary? I thought when we talked the other day you promised this bullshit would end."

"I thought so too, Oren. I already have a call in to the assistant attorney general who heads up the Environment and Natural Resources Division to find out what happened. This guy who runs the Division office in Philly obviously is a bit of a rogue."

Kane was not satisfied with the explanation. "A bit of a rogue. That's a fucking understatement. This guy Sean Murphy thinks he's the second coming of Christ. I want to know what we do now, Gary."

"The answer is not an easy one, Oren. The indictment is out and it's public. It's hard for us to take any action that would have the appearance of interfering with the legal process. This guy Sean Murphy knows what he is doing, to be sure."

"That's not what I wanted to hear, Gary. I need your help here. I hate to say I'm calling in a favor, but you need to remember, Gary, about how much help I was to you in getting the Attorney General position."

"I know, Oren, and I will do what I can. But, for both our sake, I need to be careful about how we handle this one. I'll get back to you as soon as I hear from my assistant AG, okay?"

"Don't leave me hanging, Gary," demanded Kane nervously.

By the time Senator Kane was hanging up with the U.S. attorney general, three senior partners were breaching the closed door into Kane's office.

"Oren, what the hell is going on?" one of them demanded.

"Just calm down," Kane responded. "It's all a mistake. I just finished up a call with Gary Pierson. He assured me he would derail this before it even gets started." Kane reassured his partners with an outright lie.

"Before it gets started!" another of Kane's partners exclaimed. "Oren, in case you haven't had your coffee yet this morning, wake up and smell it. There is a federal criminal indictment in the papers naming you personally. You know as well as I do that tomorrow's paper will mention your connection with this firm. Clients are going to panic and start running."

Senator Kane's face was beet red with his partner's comments, but Kane also knew he was backed into a corner. Although he rarely honored it, he was cognizant of the rule that "discretion is the better part of valor." It definitely applied to Kane's current situation, and it governed his cautionary response to his partner. "I understand. We will have a lot of damage control to do here. But, let me get past the first step, which is to make sure that the AG gets this mess cleaned up quickly."

One of Kane's partners sensed that the discussion was going nowhere and decided it would be better to leave Kane alone to work the telephone. "All right, Oren. I'm sure we're going to be getting calls from the media all day today, so keep us posted on your progress. Hourly reports, okay? In the meantime, I'm going to get an e-mail out to all of the attorneys in the firm that we are in a 'no comment' mode right now. Agreed?"

They all looked at one another and acknowledged with a nod of their heads that silence was best. As they exited Kane's office, he was again reaching for the telephone.

"Mr. Braddon's office."

"Dana, Senator Kane here. I need to speak with John immediately."

"I'm sorry Mr. Kane, but John is taking a few days vacation at his beach house. I e-mailed you a memorandum yesterday. You know the rule: no business calls while he is at the beach."

"I don't give a shit about his rule!" shouted Kane, startling Dana on the other end of the line. She had become accustomed to Kane's brashness over the years, but today was exceptionally painful.

"Mr. Kane, I can't give you his telephone number. The best I can do is offer to call him for you and let him know there is something urgent that you need to speak with him about. Okay?"

"Urgent is an understatement, dear. In case you haven't heard, the company that you and I work for has been charged with a crime. I think that qualifies as urgent. Tell John to cut his vacation short and call me back immediately. I'll be standing by the phone." Kane slammed down the phone and logged onto his e-mail to check the memorandum that Braddon had reportedly sent. As Kane read, he thought to himself, *why would Braddon be looking for capital costs for the construction and maintenance of the Tacony plant? Tax purposes. Bullshit! I smell a rat. I bet Murphy got to Braddon. Probably scared the shit out of him.* Oren Kane leaned back in his chair, folded his hands and began to rub them together. After a few minutes of staring out the window and thinking about Braddon's memorandum, he picked up the telephone and his secretary immediately answered.

"Yes, Mr. Kane?" she asked

"Bring me the Power Systems file," he demanded and again slammed the phone onto the receiver. He pondered Braddon's document request again. *There's gotta be something in that file Sean Murphy wants to get his hands on. I just know it.* Senator Kane's secretary walked into his office and said to Kane as she handed him the Power Systems file, "Sir, you have about fifteen calls already this morning from several members of Congress and one also from the White House."

"Who at the White House?" he inquired.

"The gentleman . . . " she couldn't remember his name given the flood of calls, " . . . I have his name out on a note pad . . . he described himself as an aide to the President. Actually, this President's aide has called twice already and sounded very anxious about talking to you."

"All right, I'll return the call in a few minutes. I just need a little time to review this file." Kane immediately began to turn the pages of documents in the file, hastily trying to understand the purpose and meaning of each one. His frustration became obvious with each passing page, not seeing anything that might be troublesome in the context of the federal indictment. Then, he hit it: a sub-file titled exhaust system invoices and he knew at once that these documents were the "smoking gun" that Sean Murphy was seeking. *God damn it!*, Kane screamed in his head. *My signature is all over these documents. I'll bet Braddon tipped Murphy off about these. They are the only things that link me to the exhaust sys - tem modification.* Kane called his secretary back into his office and handed her the sub-file. "Shred all of the documents in this file. Shred the file jacket too." Kane's secretary was used to this routine. They did it regularly. So, she exited Kane's office and shredded the materials without question.

After his secretary left the office, Senator Kane gave the Power Systems file one more sanitizing review. Nothing. Kane's many years of criminal defense experience came in quite handy. It was that experience which led Kane calmly to the correct conclusion: *The only thing Murphy can possibly have in his pocket now is Braddon.*

CHAPTER 25

John Braddon felt good about his testimony before the federal grand jury. Sean Murphy had walked Braddon through the process, just as Sean had promised to do. Much to Braddon's surprise, no one on the grand jury seemed upset by the fact that Braddon had failed to remedy the environmental violations at the Tacony plant once he learned about them. However, Braddon also got the sense that testimony like his was a fairly common thing being heard by this federal grand jury. By the time he got back to his beach house, although he didn't feel completely redeemed by his testimony, it certainly helped him achieve a certain peace of mind. He slept soundly for the first time in over a month.

When he logged onto the Internet the next day, he did a "Google" search on Power Systems. He wasn't surprised or upset to see the Associated Press report about the indictment. He also wasn't surprised to see his Microsoft Outlook mailbox had filled up with e-mails over the course of the day, including several from his secretary. The number of e-mails from her was equaled by the number of voice mail messages she left for Braddon at his beach house, several of which were anxious pleas that he call Mr. Kane at his Washington, D.C. office. He was surprised to learn, though, that he had not received either an e-mail or a voice mail from Sean Murphy. Although Sean had mentioned to Braddon that when they were finished with the grand jury, Sean probably wouldn't need Braddon for any reason for at least a couple of days.

Braddon thought that, rather than reading and agonizing over the e-mails and other messages all day, the better thing to do was to go out fishing. The early morning sun was gleaming on the Noyack Bay where Braddon's boat was docked, resting at the end of a deck that was as big as Braddon's entire beach house. As he walked down the deck stairs toward the bay, he sucked in a good measure of salt air. No one was on the water, which was not unusual for the second week of October, and it was exactly how Braddon liked it. He could already sense the rush of an unhampered speedy cruise out to his favorite fishing hole. As he was getting ready to cast off, Braddon noticed his cell phone in his pocket. For perhaps the first time in his life, Braddon tossed the cell phone onto to the dock and watched it bounce a few times before coming to rest. He started the boat and let it idle for a half minute or so. He unhooked the lines from the cleats and pushed off the dock. The slow movement of the boat through the water after he shifted it in to gear quieted Braddon's nerves and restored his soul, just as it always did. He was anchored at his favorite fishing spot fifteen minutes later and casting for his first catch of the day, which, to his surprise, likewise brought a characteristic smile to his face, despite the fact that the world around him was crashing down.

John Braddon did just as he planned. He spent the entire day on the water, taking a break only to dock at a restaurant for lunch. Other than the cook who prepared a cheeseburger for Braddon, he had not seen another person the entire day. The sun was getting ready to set, which was an indication to Braddon that it was time to pack up. He feared operating the boat in the dark. So, he started the engine and let it warm up, which gave him time to reel in his fishing line and stow away his supplies for the ride back home. By the time he was underway, the last sliver of sun dipped below the marsh, leaving trails of pink and red across the few high thin wisps of clouds in an otherwise light pastel blue sky: Braddon's favorite time of day. He was already savoring the taste of a sizable gin and tonic. However, the closer he got to the dock, the more anxious Braddon became about the day's events and what messages might be waiting for him upon his return. Braddon did his best to prevent his mind and emotions from falling into a tailspin.

As he pulled up to the dock, the motion activated spot lights on the back of the house popped on illuminating the water as though it were mid-day. Braddon went through the normal routine of docking and powering down the boat. Peeking into the cooler, he smiled to see that he had caught five good sized flounder. He would eat well tonight. Ten minutes or so later, he walked up the deck stairs, placed the cooler on the deck and opened the back door of his house. The spot lights had temporarily restricted his ability to see in the blackness of the house. Continuing his routine, he looked back out over the dock to make sure the boat was securely in place. *Everything snug*, he thought. What Braddon failed to notice was that the cell phone he had tossed on the dock earlier in the morning was no longer there.

He turned off the spot lights and turned back into the blackness of the house. He reminded himself, as he always did, to move the switch for the house lights over to the rear wall so he would not have to stumble across a dark family room after a day of boating. Braddon reached out for the back of the sofa, but his hand hit something warm and fleshy first, followed by a surprising and unexpected rush of pain across his head. Braddon never saw the crowbar coming.

CHAPTER 26

Sean Murphy was barraged by telephone calls the day the press release hit the newspapers, one of which from his boss in Washington, D.C., the assistant attorney general for the Environment and Natural Resources Division. Sean admitted to his boss's charges that Sean had disobeyed a direct order to terminate the Power Systems investigation. Sean easily responded to threats of "there is going to be hell to pay" and "this will be the end of your life at the DOJ" with the fact that the indictment was supported with first-hand testimony from the company's president. Not only that, but, as Sean also explained to his boss, he was expecting documents to be produced by the company that would directly implicate Senator Kane in an intentional violation of the federal Clean Air Act. When his boss asked Sean why he didn't seek approval to continue the Power Systems investigation, Sean simply responded that things were moving too fast and he was concerned about the possibility of imminent endangerment to the public health and environment. Nice and snug. No room for challenge. And, indeed, Sean's boss didn't push the issue too far. The last thing the U.S. attorney general wanted to see was a newspaper article about an attempted Department of Justice coverup. After about fifteen minutes of back and forth with his boss, Sean hung up the telephone feeling fairly confident that he would get no further interference from the guys in Washington, D.C.

His confidence was abruptly cut at the knees, however, when he got a call from John Braddon's office the next morning.

"Sean," his secretary called, "Mr. Braddon's secretary is on the line."

"Okay, Kate. I got it." Sean picked up the telephone expecting to hear that John Braddon wanted to speak with Sean about the press release and how things were going so far. "Mr. Murphy, I'm afraid I have some bad news."

"What's wrong?" he asked.

"It seems there's been an accident at Mr. Braddon's beach house."

"Accident? Is John okay?"

"Actually, no he isn't. The local marine police were supposedly passing by Mr. Braddon's beach house this morning and they noticed a dog on his deck barking next to Mr. Braddon's boat. When the marine police pulled closer, they found Mr. Braddon in the water. He's dead, Mr. Murphy. I can't believe this has happened."

"What the hell . . . what happened? Did you get a report from the local police?" Sean asked.

"Yes, I did," she answered. "The police think Mr. Braddon had been out on the boat last night and had been drinking. They believe he became intoxicated and fell. I was very surprised to hear the police say that thing about Mr. Braddon being out at night on his boat."

"What do you mean?"

Sean could hear Braddon's secretary choking up as she tried to answer his question. "Well, I know for a fact that Mr. Braddon did not like operating his boat in the dark. I have been to his beach house many times and went out with him on his boat. It was almost gospel to Mr. Braddon that the boat be docked before nightfall. Plus, he never drank when he was out on his boat. His first drink would be after the boat was safely secured to the dock."

"Tell me," Sean said, "how did the police come to the conclusion that Mr. Braddon fell?"

"Apparently, he tripped getting off of the boat and hit his head on the side of the dock. The police found blood on the edge of the dock right next to where they found his body in the water. Plus, Mr. Braddon's forehead had marks indicating that he hit the dock pretty hard. The police think that Mr. Braddon must have knocked himself unconscious, fell into the water, and drowned."

"This is fucking wonderful! Just fucking great!" Sean shouted, then a few seconds passed before he said anything. "Excuse my language. I'm sorry. I don't mean to sound so crass. I know this must be a great loss to you. But, in case you haven't heard, Mr. Braddon was my lead witness in a criminal action against Power Systems and Senator Kane."

"I knew something was going on. I got a call from Senator Kane yesterday demanding to speak to Mr. Braddon immediately, at which point he told me about the criminal charges against Power Systems. I wasn't aware that Senator Kane was also charged. I tried several times to reach Mr. Braddon at his beach house yesterday, but he never called me back. That is his style, though."

"How's that?" inquired Sean.

"When he vacations at his beach house, he has a rule of no business related disturbances."

Sean then asked, "Do you know if Mr. Braddon ever spoke with Senator Kane?"

"I'm not sure. I never got a call back from Senator Kane saying that he was still waiting to hear from Mr. Braddon. I didn't take the initiative to call Senator Kane because he was so obnoxious on the phone with me in the morning."

"Trust me," Sean said reassuringly, "I know what you mean about that. One other thing. Did Mr. Braddon ask for any documents from Senator Kane?"

"Yes, he did, Mr. Murphy. He asked me to do a memorandum to the Senator asking for documents related to capital costs for the Tacony plant. Why do you ask?"

"Nothing really. Do me a favor, though, if Senator Kane sends any documents, let me know when they come in?"

"Surely, I'd be glad to do that for you, Mr. Murphy."

"I'm sorry for your loss," Sean said. "I know you and Mr. Braddon worked together for many years. I'll pray for both him and you."

"Thank you, Mr. Murphy."

❬ ❬ ❭ ❭

Without John Braddon's testimony, Sean had nothing. Even if he was fortunate enough to come up with some documents or other evidence that Senator Kane authorized the modification to the Tacony plant exhaust system, he would need someone to testify as to the meaning of the documents and to authenticate Kane's signature. No way was Kane going to offer up that kind of information. He could probably get someone other than Braddon who was familiar with Kane's signature to testify about it, but no one other than Braddon would understand the meaning and purpose of the documents. Plus, Sean was not holding out a lot of hope that Senator Kane would volunteer the documents anyway.

Sean realized his dream of seeing Senator Kane in handcuffs was dismally and quickly fading away. He decided to break the bad news to Steve Cooperhouse. Sean reached for the telephone and, as he was about to dial, decided instead that the short walk through Center City to Steve's office would help Sean clear his mind and give him some clarity about what to do next.

Sean always enjoyed the walk north on Market Street toward City Hall, no matter what kind of problem was bothering him. The chance to "people watch" was cathartic. Although Sean would comment that his main interest was observing the spectrum of people generally, anyone who truly knew Sean understood it was the women he loved the most. There was just something unique about them. And anyone familiar with Philly demographics could immediately distinguish their point of origin. The South Philly girls were normally the tough rocker types: tight clothes, big hair, and a lot of makeup, the classic Irish looking girls hailed mainly from the Northeast section of the City, and anyone with a remotely preppie look came from The Main Line. Every once in a while, if you were lucky, there would be a "Jersey Girl" sighting. She was a sort of wonderful mix of all the other types, but always looking hazily lost in the big city. Sean loved them all, and ever since his wife had passed away Sean tried to do just that at every possible opportunity.

The walk along Market Street also gave him the chance to pop into the Reading Terminal Market, which, although many debated Sean about this, was the best place in the continental United States for sandwiches, especially the roast pork and roast beef. Sean's timing on this particular day was perfect. He arrived at noon. Sean took his usual one pass around the market to figure out exactly what would hit the spot. Walking past the Pennsylvania Dutch outlets, his mouth began to water for a funnel cake, but he decided instead to start with a roast beef sandwich. As usual, Sean smothered the beef with horseradish. As he bit into it, the piercingly hot horseradish caused Sean's nasal passages to expand involuntarily, filling them with an acrid mist, which inevitably caused Sean's eyes to tear. Tastes and smells were Sean's main memory triggers.

⮜ ⮜ ⮞ ⮞

Outside of football season, Saturday mornings were a time for Sean to help his father with one of his part-time jobs: selling fish in the South Philly bars. The day started at 6:30 A.M. with making fresh horseradish sauce. Pop Murphy would explain to Sean that horseradish was a plant of the mustard family, grown for its pungent, white, fleshy root. While Pop Murphy was loading the car with smoked whiting, jarred oysters, and other sundries that went well with beer, Sean had the job of placing dozens of horseradishes in a large stainless steel vat. When Sean first started helping his father, he could not see into the top of the horseradish grinding vat, which could hold several hundred gallons of product. Pop Murphy built a sturdy step stool that allowed Sean to lean the crates of horseradishes on the lip of the vat and slightly tip them over, releasing the contents. After the first few crates, Pop Murphy would come back in to flip the switch on the grinder, which was located at the bottom of the vat. Once the grinder was operating the heavy fish smell in the room immediately gave way to a pungent odor that would start Sean's eyes tearing within seconds, followed soon thereafter with a running nose. Pop Murphy explained to Sean on his first time through that process that if Sean gave it a few minutes, his eyes would adjust and the tears would stop. They did. For all of Pop Murphy's time lost to drunkenness, he knew a lot about the small stuff of life, much to Sean's surprise.

Sean would continue to load a few more crates of horseradishes into the vat and then turn his attention to spooning the product, which would collect in a basin at the bottom, into mason jars, typically about fifty for the day. All in all, the process took about a half hour, at which point Pop Murphy would arrive, having loaded the car with the merchandise for the day, and turn off the grinder. Because Sean was too small to see over the vat lip when he first started helping Pop Murphy, Sean would clean the machinery, which was no more complex than hosing it down with fresh tap water. By the time Sean was a freshman in high school, he was tall enough to do away with the step stool and sophisticated enough to run the machinery by himself, including hosing it down at the end. Sean came to appreciate the fact that the acridness of the air in that small room where he made the horseradish sauce on Saturday mornings not only cleared his sinuses, but it cleared his mind too. In his last few years before leaving for Penn State, when Pop Murphy's drinking had gotten infamously heavy, Sean needed those Saturday mornings in that small room with the acrid odor. In hindsight, Sean realized that the process of making horseradish gave him a chance, even if for only a half hour, to engage his attention totally on one subject and one result, which somehow opened up a floodgate to release the pressures from the week.

184

It took him about only ten minutes to make his way through the meal, stopping periodically to stem the flow of horseradish induced tears, so as to make room for another bite. It was a ritual that most people couldn't understand. In fact, even Sean didn't have a good explanation for the need to endure such pain while at the same time trying to fill his belly. He grabbed a funnel cake on the way out of the Reading Terminal Market.

A few minutes later, Sean was at Steve Cooperhouse's doorway. "Hey buddy. Thought I'd drop by to give you the latest," Sean said.

"Sean. How's it goin? I haven't heard from you in a few days. Got a little powdered sugar there on your face, big guy." Sean wiped his face and then looked down his suit jacket to make sure there was no other residue. "What's happening with Power Systems? I saw the article in the *Philadelphia Inquirer* and figured by now the shit must have hit the fan."

Sean smiled and said, "Steve, you have no idea. Braddon's office called me this morning. He's dead."

"What . . . how?"

"He went back to his beach house after the grand jury. I told him to relax and I would call him as soon as I needed him back. Anyway, I got a call from his secretary this morning. The police at his beach house found him floating in the bay next to his boat. The report I am getting is that he went fishing, probably had too much to drink, fell off the boat and drowned. You know, Steve, dead people seem to be in ample supply in this case."

"Wait a minute," Steve said abruptly. "Are you implying that Braddon's death is somehow related to the Power Systems' indictment? C'mon Sean, boating accidents are the rule rather than the exception. It's a dangerous pastime. And if you aren't paying attention, or if you're drinking alcohol, chances are you're goin' to screw up and get hurt, sometimes dead even."

"I don't know, Steve." Sean said. "First, the Power Systems employee, then Tom Roth, and now Braddon. Seems like more than just coincidence."

"Sean, the Bucks County Prosecutor never came up with anything about Roth. It was just a theory then and it still is today," said Steve.

"I know. It's just one of those things. Kane is a bad man."

"Yeah, he's a bad man," Steve acknowledged. "He is a corporate scumbag with no conscience, and he's willing to break environmental laws for financial gain. But, that doesn't make him a murderer, Sean."

"I know. I know. No need for the lecture, Mr. Cooperhouse," responded Sean jokingly.

"If I'm not mistaken, Sean, Braddon's testimony was the meat of your case against Senator Kane."

"Yep."

"So, what do we do now?" asked Steve.

"Actually, I was hoping you might have some ideas, pal."

"No such luck, pal," Steve responded with the same tone.

"I never should have issued that press release, Steve. I got too pumped up about going after Senator Kane that I never stopped to think about the strength of my case first. All I had was Braddon's testimony, which wasn't the best evidence to begin with. Plus, I know for a fact that Senator Kane is down in D.C. pressuring the attorney general to prevent me from investigating Power Systems. When he hears that my case was all based on one witness' testimony only, and I didn't take proper precautions to keep Braddon from danger, even his own stupidity if that's what it was, I'm a dead man. Senator Kane is going to have a field day with this. SHIT! I can't believe this. I had my hands around that scumbag's throat and he slipped right through."

"So, what happens next?" asked Steve.

"Well, I at least have a little time to think about whether there's some other way to go after Senator Kane criminally. I suppose we could do it on your testimony alone. That's the interesting thing about criminal sanctions in federal environmental laws. I can make a case that Senator Kane is criminally responsible for the problems at the Tacony plant merely because of his capacity as an officer of the company, but it's not a strong case. Plus, even if I could prevail on that kind of an argument, the most that would happen to Kane is paying some kind of a fine. Oh well, maybe I'll come up with something on the walk back to the office."

"Ah, so you walked over. Babe watching, huh?" Steve knew Sean's every move and desire.

"Who me?" Sean responded spiritedly. "I'm just a simple man, Mr. Cooperhouse, trying to solve a complex case. I needed time and space to think. That's all."

"Yeah right. Time, space, and something else."

"Oh yeah. I almost forgot. Now that the press release is out, I need the EPA to start a process of notifying The Climate Exchange about the problem at the Tacony plant. Remember, the certification of greenhouse gas emissions credits is an entirely private affair. The federal government has nothing to do with it. The environmental violations at the Tacony plant are related to the discharge of regulated pollutants without a permit, not carbon dioxide. Understand?"

"Yeah, I think so. In terms of continuing the criminal action, I assume we are going to focus on the pH impacts of the discharge and some other things in the emissions, like nitrogen oxides and sulfur oxides."

"That's right. We'll make an argument that the company was emitting those regulated air pollutants without a permit. We don't care about carbon dioxide because we don't have the authority under the laws to worry about it. The fact that The Climate Exchange decided to certify the Tacony plant as a source of carbon dioxide emissions reductions has nothing to do with us. That said, though, I don't see any problem with our sharing the results of the investigation with The Climate Exchange. Work with Rebecca on this one. She understands all that carbon market stuff. I'll give her a call and let her know you'll be getting her involved."

"Okay, Sean. Enjoy your walk back."

◁ ◁ ▷ ▷

When Sean got back to his office, he noticed his secretary Kate was not at her desk. Walking by her workspace and into his office, he noticed something resting on his seat. As he walked closer, he saw it was a telefax of a couple of pages. At the top of the cover page was the title block for Senator Kane's law firm. Sean picked it up, flopped into his seat and let go a big sigh. Flipping past the cover page with its typical confidentiality notice, he began to read:

Sean Murphy, Esq.
Deputy Attorney General
Department of Justice
401 Market Street
Philadelphia, Pennsylvania 19107

Re: Announcement of Criminal Charges

Dear Mr. Murphy:
We were shocked and appalled to read the articles the other day, which we believe you authored, regarding the indictment of Power Systems, Inc. and Oren Kane, Esq. for alleged environmental criminal activity at the compa-ny's electric power generating facility in the Tacony section of Philadelphia. Oren Kane, Esq. is a partner of this law firm and a respected member of the United States senate. He has practiced law for over forty years and rep-resented the interests of his state and community in congress for an equal-ly long time. In both capacities, his reputation for integrity, honesty, and forthrightness is impeccable.
The Department of Justice's reckless public announcement of its intent to prosecute Mr. Kane personally for environmental crimes is scurrilous and risks ruining Mr. Kane's reputation both as an attorney and a legisla-tor. After diligent inquiry, we are unaware of any involvement by Mr. Kane in any alleged wrongdoing at the Power Systems, Inc. Tacony plant. In light of this conclusion, we demand an immediate retraction of the Department of Justice's pronouncement of alleged criminal conduct on the part of Mr. Kane. Otherwise, we will retain counsel to file a complaint against both the Department of Justice and you personally for a civil rights violation, among other things.
We expect your immediate compliance with this demand. Advise us immediately upon the issuance of the retraction and to what newspaper or other media sources you have distributed the retraction.

Sincerely,
For the Firm
Harvey Morgan

Fuck me!, Sean agonized to himself. *I knew it. I'm in a dog fight now. What the hell am I gonna do? Without Braddon, I'm dead in the water.* Sean began pacing around his office. Kate popped her head into Sean's office.

"Did you get that fax I left on your seat?" she asked. Sean kept pacing as though he hadn't heard Kate's question. "Sean . . . did you get the fax?" she tried again.

"Yeah, I got it. Kate, shut my door. No calls. I don't want to be bothered for a while. Got it?" he said gruffly.

"Everything okay, Sean?" she asked.

"Yeah . . . everything's fine. I just need a little time to think something through, okay?"

"Anything I can do to help, Sean?" Kate asked with a genuine heart, seeing the panic in Sean's face.

"Shit, Kate, I said I want to be left alone. No, for suffering Christ's sake, there is nothing you can do to help!"

"Okay, then, I'll leave you alone," Kate said sheepishly as she closed Sean's door. He immediately realized that he had snapped at her and ran for the door.

"Kate, I'm sorry. I didn't mean to jump on you like that. I'm sure I will need your help in just a few minutes. The biggest help you can be to me right now is to make sure I get some quiet time by making sure no one comes in to my office and by screening my phone calls. Sound good?"

"I'm glad to do that for you, Sean." she responded. As the door closed, Sean began pacing again across his office.

God tests most zealously those with the strongest will, thought Sean. *I'm being tested here. That's all.* It never failed. Whenever Sean was faced with a tense or difficult situation, he opened his thought process with a spiritual gauging. It was an admittedly unusual tactic and not one that most of the attorneys in the Department of Justice employed, but it had served Sean pretty well over the years. *What does your heart tell you to do here Sean? Fear about human consequences is just your head talking to you, not your heart. What does your heart say? Stay with it, Sean, stay with it.*

CHAPTER 27

Steve Cooperhouse and Rebecca Lockhart decided to script their presentation to the chief executive officer of The Climate Exchange before calling him with the bad news.

"So, Rebecca, what do you think we say to Brendan Frisk?" Steve asked.

"I suggest we make it simple and brief. Tell him what we found at the Tacony plant and the fact that EPA ordered it closed. Most importantly, he needs to understand that the Tacony plant is not a 'zero emissions' facility and never has been."

"Why do you say that?" Steve asked.

"The fifty or so participants in The Climate Exchange have an obligation to meet a reduction in greenhouse gas emissions at the end of each calendar year. A good deal of those participants have been meeting that obligation by purchasing emissions reductions credits supplied by Power Systems, Inc. from the Tacony plant. If the Power Systems credits have been based on a lie, that means none of the participating company's have ever actually met their greenhouse gas reduction obligation pretty much since trading on the market commenced. So, the reason why I say he needs to hear that kind of detail is because the environmental groups are going to go nuts when they hear about this situation. Brendan Frisk will need to understand the problem fully to see if he can do some kind of damage control."

"What could he possibly do?" Steve asked.

"Well, if I were the CEO of The Climate Exchange, I would try to figure out how to get financial restitution for those companies that historically purchased emissions reduction credits from Power Systems. Although I can't be sure how the carbon contracts read, I'm sure The Climate Exchange has the ability to bring a lawsuit against Power Systems for something like fraud and breach of contract."

"What do you mean by carbon contracts?" Steve asked.

"Trading carbon dioxide is like trading any other commodity. There is a written contract to evidence the trade, with terms regarding price per ton and so on. If it is like other commodity contracts, it will have a section where Power Systems made representations and warranties about the legitimacy of its credits. If I were in Brendan Frisk's shoes, I would want to know everything I can about how and where Power Systems went wrong so I could assure the companies participating in the Exchange that it was going to take appropriate legal action to get their money returned. Assuming he can do that, or at least get back the bulk of the money, he can just establish a new starting date for the Exchange's obligations."

"Slow down a second, Rebecca. You're losing me here. What do you mean by establishing a new starting date? How can he just 'willy-nilly' do something like that?"

"The Exchange can do that because it is not regulated by anyone," answered Rebecca. "Remember, it's a voluntary program. The participants are members because they believe it is the right thing to do environmentally. No governmental body in the United States is ordering companies to reduce greenhouse gases. So, the Exchange can do whatever it wants with its goals and standards, so long as the participants agree."

"Okay," acknowledged Steve, more in an effort to slow Rebecca down than to join in the conversation. "I think I'm following you, but I just want to be sure. Brendan Frisk is going to learn today of this problem with the Power Systems greenhouse gas emissions credits, which really is that the credits never existed in the first place. I guess he will make an announcement to the participants in the Exchange. Based on what you're telling me, in order to quell any fear by the participating members, Frisk will probably tell the participants that he is essentially going to start from scratch, start over that is. Any participant that took some efforts to make actual reductions, they will get credit towards compliance with the new deadlines for emissions reductions. For those that have been 'schnuckered' by Power Systems, the Exchange will seek to recover the money from Power Systems and return it to the rightful owner."

"You got it, Steve. I'm impressed," lauded Rebecca.

"I don't buy it. It's too pie in the sky. I think the more likely thing to happen will be that the participants in the Exchange will see it as a farce and try to cut their losses by getting out of the Exchange as quickly as possible. That's what I would do if I were an investor."

"It's certainly possible that will happen. The carbon market is just getting started. I don't know if it can withstand this kind of a blow. It will depend on the willpower and business savvy of this guy Brendan Frisk and his financial wherewithal to prosecute a cost recovery claim against Power Systems."

"All right, then," Steve said as Rebecca finished up, "we need to give this guy the bad news and then try to help him out with the background facts he will need to report out to the participants of the Exchange about the existence of the problem and then the information he will need to sue Power Systems. Is that correct?"

"Yes. Sounds easy enough, huh?"

"Well, Rebecca, you're the one who knows all this market stuff. So, I'm going to let you take the lead on this one."

⊴ ⊴ ⊵ ⊵

"Good morning, The Climate Exchange," answered the receptionist. "How may I help you?"

"Good morning, is Mr. Frisk there?" Rebecca asked.

"I don't think he is in just now. Who's calling?" It was the receptionist's standard response, which was designed to screen out the less important calls for Brendan Frisk, who was an extremely busy person.

Steve jumped in and said, "Please tell Mr. Frisk it is the director of the EPA's Office of Air and Radiation in Philadelphia. We need to speak with him about Power Systems, Inc."

It took only a few seconds before Brendan Frisk picked up the line. "Hello, this is Frisk."

"Good morning, Mr. Frisk, this is Steve Cooperhouse of the EPA, and I have here with me Rebecca Lockhart, who is a special financial consultant to the EPA."

"How can I help you folks?" asked Frisk.

Steve looked over to Rebecca as a signal that he wanted her to pick up with the discussion, which she did. "Mr. Frisk, we have been led to believe that Power Systems, Inc. is a principal supplier of greenhouse gas emission reduction credits to the Exchange. Is that correct?"

"I suppose you could say that. Yes, it's accurate, but that characteristic has been changing. Our first year of operation Power Systems and the country of Brazil were supplying the bulk of marketable credits. However, over the past few years, we have had more industries making actual reductions in greenhouse gas emissions, mainly carbon dioxide. Plus, we have welcomed a bunch of solid waste landfills that have installed methane gas controls. Added to this are a number of sequestration activities throughout Canada and some other forested countries. All of these are now contributing collectively to the marketable greenhouse gas credits on the Exchange. Tell me, why is the EPA interested in Power Systems' contribution to the Exchange?" asked Frisk.

"I suppose the last few days events haven't hit your local newspapers yet. The EPA ordered Power Systems' Tacony plant shut down because of violations of the federal Clean Air Act. The Department of Justice is considering a criminal prosecution against the company and perhaps one of its officers."

"I thought something was wrong," said Frisk.

Rebecca and Steve looked at one another with an air of surprise. They couldn't figure out how Brendan Frisk, if he had not read about the Tacony plant shutdown in the newspaper, would suspect a problem. Rebecca accordingly asked, "Mr. Frisk, if you don't mind me asking, why do you say that you thought something was wrong at the Tacony plant?"

"It's pretty simple. My CEM printout straight-lined for nearly a full day back about a week ago and then it did the same thing again just recently. This time, though, it didn't recover like it did a week ago."

Both Rebecca and Steve were stumped. He took the lead this time. "Mr. Frisk, what do you mean by 'CEM printout'?"

"Continuous emission monitor. The Exchange paid for and installed a continuous emission monitor on the Tacony plant back when it was beginning operations."

"Mr. Frisk, I hate to be a bore about this, but can you explain to us how this CEM system works and why the Exchange installed one at the Tacony plant?" asked Rebecca, considering she was the financial one with no technical background in air pollution control, though Steve Cooperhouse seemed equally in the dark on this one.

"No problem," Frisk answered. "The CEM tells me by way of a constant printout on my computer screen how much carbon dioxide Power Systems is sequestering in the Delaware River. By some very simple calculations, I can then determine how many tons per day of carbon dioxide Power Systems has avoided putting into the atmosphere."

The look of shock on both Steve's and Rebecca's faces was undeniable. Rebecca continued to ask the questions. "Mr. Frisk, what do you mean when you say Power Systems was sequestering carbon dioxide in the Delaware River?"

"Ask your colleague Steve there. His office is the one that issued the approval for Power Systems to bubble exhaust gases from the Tacony plant into the Delaware."

The look of shock intensified. Steve asked, "Mr. Frisk, I apologize for not being fully aware of what my staff here may have done regarding environmental permits or approvals for the Tacony plant, but I just haven't had the chance to get up to speed with the events of the past few days. I trust you understand. Can you be so good as to explain to me what approval you are talking about?"

"Sure. When Power Systems approached me with the proposal of supplying greenhouse gas emission reduction credits to the Exchange, the company told me that it was operating a 'zero emissions' electric power plant. I gotta tell you. I was suspicious. In all the years I have been in the pollutant trading business, I had never heard of a 'zero emissions' technology. So, I thought I should be extra careful with how I verified the credits for the Tacony plant. There is nothing so vital to the pollutant trading market as being able to demonstrate by some independent and verifiable means that the amount of credits being claimed by a supplier are accurate. Anyway, right at the time the company approached me to become a member of the Exchange, the Tacony plant started to have some operational problems. If I recall correctly, it was something like the plant kept shutting down as though someone came along and blew out the flame in the furnace. A few days later, I got a call from someone in the company that he had worked out a deal with the EPA on how to resolve the operational problems. My memory tells me this guy was a politician in D.C."

Steve's jaw just about hit the ground and Rebecca nearly fell out of her seat. "Does the name Senator Kane ring a bell, Mr. Frisk?" asked Rebecca.

"Sounds familiar, but it's been a while, if you know what I mean. I can check my file. I'm sure his name is in there."

"You have a file?" Steve responded quickly. "A file on Power Systems?"

"Bet your ass, I do. When I first started the Exchange, Power Systems was my main source of credits. I had to be very careful in that kind of situation. Actually, I keep a file on every one of my credit suppliers and buyers. Although, my Power Systems file is much thicker and heavier than the others."

"Mr. Frisk," asked Rebecca, "what kind of information do you have in the Power Systems file?"

"Mainly carbon contracts," replied Frisk. "But, I also recall keeping copies of all the communications from the company on this change in operational strategy to resolve the early operational problems."

"What do you mean by change in operational strategy?"

"Well, as far as I was concerned, the 'zero emission' concept failed miserably, as I originally suspected it would. There's no such thing and never will be. So, as it was explained to me, in order to get the Tacony plant back up and running, the company negotiated with the EPA this alternate approach of bubbling the emissions into the Delaware River."

Steve inquired, "Do you have a document to that effect?"

"Yeah, it's a Consent Agreement between the EPA and Power Systems. I remember it well. I was surprised to see the EPA agreeing to allow untreated power plant exhaust to be discharged like that into the Delaware River. There's a whole bunch of nasty stuff in untreated power plant exhaust, but all I was concerned about was the carbon dioxide portion of the exhaust. And, sequestration into water bodies is an accepted method of eliminating carbon dioxide from the atmosphere. So, as far as I was concerned, it didn't matter whether the Tacony plant was 'zero emissions' or was sequestering its carbon dioxide emissions in the Delaware River. All I needed to know was that no carbon dioxide was escaping the Tacony plant into the atmosphere."

"Mr. Frisk," Rebecca said, "if you have time, I would like to get on the phone the assistant attorney general working on this case. His name is Sean Murphy. Can we conference him in?"

"Yes, but I have about only a half hour or so and then I have to run out for a meeting."

☙ ☙ ❧ ❧

"Sean," yelled Kate, "Steve Cooperhouse and Rebecca Lockhart are on the telephone. They say its very important."

Sean picked up the football. "Steve and Becca, this better be a matter of life or death."

"Fantasy football?" asked Steve.

"Bingo."

"Well, pal, I think you need to hear this. Rebecca and I are on the line with the CEO of The Climate Exchange. He told us. . . . You know what, I want you

193

to hear this first-hand." Steve clicked the conference pad on his telephone and joined Sean into the call. "Sean, say hello to Mr. Frisk," said Steve.

"Mr. Frisk, nice to meet you. Steve and Rebecca tell me you have some news for me."

"I'm not really sure what you need to know," answered Frisk, at which point Steve decided to orchestrate the discussion.

"Mr. Frisk, please tell Sean about the Power Systems file." When Sean heard the reference to a Power Systems file, he jumped out of his seat.

"Steve, did you say Power Systems file?"

"Yep, you heard it right, Mr. Murphy. And it gets better. Go ahead, Mr. Frisk, tell Sean about the Consent Agreement." Brendan Frisk rehashed the same story with Sean Murphy. When Frisk was done, the line was deathly quiet. Finally, Sean collected his thoughts and began asking questions.

"Mr. Frisk, you should know the EPA has no record of this Consent Agreement you mentioned. Neither does the company have any record. Believe me, if it were in any of the government or company files, I would have seen it."

"What are you saying, Mr. Murphy?" asked Frisk.

"I'm not sure what I'm saying just yet, but what I'm thinking is this Consent Agreement may have been fabricated as a means of getting you to certify Power Systems' emissions reductions credits."

"Fabricated by whom?" asked Frisk.

"We know from one of the company's former officers that Senator Oren Kane unlawfully modified the exhaust system at the Tacony plant. He secretly contracted to have the exhaust from the plant rerouted to the Delaware River. My guess is that Mr. Kane fabricated that Consent Agreement to convince you to accept the company's equally fallacious greenhouse gas credits. Mr. Frisk, can you recall anything about the events surrounding that Consent Agreement?"

"All I can remember is that a company representative told me he had worked out a deal with the EPA to get the plant back up and running. I agreed to consider the paperwork, but demanded that I have a continuous emissions monitor installed to verify the carbon dioxide emission rates. A couple of weeks later, he gave me the Consent Agreement. I gotta tell you, it looked official. I have been in the business a pretty long time and have seen my fair share of official EPA documents. This definitely didn't come across as being fabricated or falsified."

"Mr. Frisk, I understand. I'm not trying to say you are at fault," Sean said reassuringly. "Tell me, do you recall anything about this company representative you were working with?"

"Oh yeah. He was a pushy bastard. Short one too. I think he was five foot six, if that. And he had the attitude to go with it, if you know what I mean."

Sean interrupted him. "That's Senator Kane, to be sure," making the comment more for Steve and Rebecca's sake then Frisk's. "So, Mr. Frisk, if I understand what you're saying, once Power Systems produced the Consent Agreement, and you had a continuous emissions monitor installed, you started certifying credits for the company."

"That's absolutely correct. I had everything I needed to start trading. Mr. Murphy, I understand you targeted the company and one of its officers for criminal prosecution. I assume the officer is this Senator Kane and that Consent Agreement could be very helpful in that case," commented Frisk.

"You are correct in a big way on both accounts, Mr. Frisk. How do I get that file?" asked Sean.

"I'll mail it to you."

"I don't mean to push, but could you Fed Ex it to me today?"

"Not a problem. You'll have it tomorrow." said Frisk.

"One other thing, Mr. Frisk," Sean said, "I may need to subpoena you to testify about the file you're sending me and your recollection of the events back when Senator Kane produced the Consent Agreement."

"I'll be glad to help in any way I can."

Rebecca broached with Mr. Frisk the point that all of them had seemed to sidestep during the conference call. "Mr. Frisk, what happens to the Exchange now that we have raised this issue about violations at the Tacony plant going all the way back to the date of commencement of operations?"

"I'm not concerned," answered Frisk, much to their surprise.

"We've been operating under the assumption that this event would spell disaster for the Exchange."

"No, I don't think so," answered Frisk. "Sure some members will be concerned initially, but I protected the Exchange precisely against this kind of an issue."

"How so?" Rebecca asked.

"Well, the CEM first of all. That system tells me continuously whether the Power Systems Tacony plant is operating and how much carbon dioxide is being generated."

"Yes, I understand that, Mr. Frisk," Rebecca said. "But, now that you know the company has been violating the federal Clean Air Act and that the Consent Agreement you're sending us may be a fraudulent document, won't the Exchange crumble?"

"No. No. You're missing a subtle but very important point. The Consent Agreement was something to confirm for me that the Tacony plant was back up and running. I didn't care whether or not the facility was operated lawfully. Again, you need to remember that all I care about is whether the Tacony plant was capturing carbon dioxide that would have otherwise gone up the stack. It was. Even though it may have been illegal to do so, the carbon dioxide from the Tacony plant was being successfully sequestered into the Delaware River. As long as it wasn't going into the atmosphere, Power Systems was entitled to receive credits on the Exchange. Protection against global warming was achieved by Power Systems, even though it may have been violating the federal Clean Air Act to accomplish that goal."

"So, if I understand you, Mr. Frisk", Steve said, "you don't expect any repercussion from this situation?"

"Well, I don't know if it's going to be that easy. I'm sure we will encounter some public relations issues. The environmental groups will probably be all over the Exchange for purchasing credits from Power Systems over the past few years. You know, stuff like conspiring with a criminal company. It will pass, though. I will issue a press release sometime in the next day or two explaining the situation with an eye toward heading off that kind of criticism. The carbon market is in a state of flux right now. With all of the other problems we are encountering, I don't think this issue will become a priority."

Sean concluded by saying, "Mr. Frisk, anything we can do to help you, let us know. We obviously are not out to harm the Exchange you created. It is doing good and environmentally beneficial work."

"Thank you for the offer," Frisk responded. "I'm sure I'll take you up on it. What I might do is offer to have a meeting of the members of the Exchange and have you folks in to speak to them about what happened. It's interesting that you called today. I'm testifying for a second time before the Senate Committee on Public Works and the Environmental next week on the Climate Stewardship Act. Greenhouse gases will definitely be on the agenda."

CHAPTER 28

Sean Murphy's anticipation about the contents of Brendan Frisk's file on Power Systems was overwhelming, to the point of being full blown anxiety. He was guardedly optimistic that Senator Kane was the brains behind this Consent Agreement but, in light of the events of the past few days, worried that there wouldn't be anything specifically pointing to Kane or, even more likely, that the file wouldn't show up. After he hung up the phone with Frisk, Sean spent the better part of the next four hours pacing around his office agonizing over how he could use the contents of the file against Kane, assuming there was some worthwhile evidence in it. He couldn't concentrate on anything else, especially the other case files that were calling for his attention. *What time is it,* Sean thought to himself. *Seven thirty. Time for a drink. Hard Rock Café here I come.* Sean grabbed his suit jacket and headed for the door. As he opened it, he slammed into Rebecca, almost knocking her down.

"Oh shit, I'm sorry, Becca." Sean grabbed Rebecca on the arm to help her regain balance. "C'mon, I'm heading to the Hard Rock. Join me for a drink."

"Sean, I was just dropping by on my way home to see what you thought about our chat with Brendan Frisk this afternoon. I'm in no mood for a drink. I'm tired." Sean was still holding onto Rebecca's arm, not willing to give up on his demand that she join in the celebration. He didn't say anything, but kept hold of her arm and continued to stare. "Sean, you know me and Thursday nights. I just like to go home, put on my sweat pants, and lounge around in front of the TV." Sean would not relent. "I don't feel like going out," she said with a hint of a whine in her voice. "You go and have fun. I'll catch up with you tomorrow."

"Pipe down," Sean demanded. "Another hour or so won't kill you. Plus, if you don't come with me I'll wind up drinking by myself. Not a good sign, you know?"

"All right," Rebecca relented, "but just one or two drinks, that's it. Right?"

"Deal!"

When they walked through the front door of the Hard Rock Café on Market Street, the guitar riffs in Jimi Hendrix' "Voodoo Child" were blaring so loudly that

Sean could feel the sound pounding against the thickness of his chest. It was almost as if the sound had substance, like an ocean wave rushing into the shore and beating on you as it breaks. He could tell from the look on Rebecca's face that she sensed the same thing. As they neared the bar, the sound of voices added to, and slightly diluted, the guitar racket. Sean's popularity at the bar was a clear signal of the regularity of his visits, which on some weeks, especially the tough ones, was almost daily.

"Hey Murph," welcomed the bartender, "who's the lovely lady?" Others around the bar gave a nod of their head to Sean as a way of saying hello to a kindred spirit.

"This is the wonderful Ms. Rebecca Lockhart."

"What can I get for you Ms. Lockhart?" asked the bartender.

"May I have a glass of red wine, please?"

"Sure," answered the bartender. "The usual for you Murph?"

"Yeah, Jack. Run a tab for me, please." Rebecca gave Sean a glare because she knew that he intended more than just a drink or two when he ran a tab. "What? What did I do?" Sean said in response to Rebecca's glare. "Set up the boys with a round on me." The regulars raised their glasses overhearing Sean's instruction to the bartender, indicating their thanks.

"Will do," answered the bartender as he went to work on the drinks for Sean and Rebecca.

"So," Rebecca said, "what do you think about this file at The Climate Exchange?"

"I think it's a miracle," Sean answered with a smile on his face, "assuming there's something in the file we can use against Senator Kane. Something's got to save my ass here."

"Don't start that shit, Sean. Every time something good happens you immediately revert to divine intervention."

"Tell me I'm wrong. My only witness against Senator Kane shows up face fishing on the heels of which I get a threatening letter from Kane's law firm that they are going to sue me for a civil rights violation if I push the indictment. Then, out of nowhere comes this pack rat CEO of some esoteric environmental trading market and he has what appears to be a fraudulent Consent Agreement that may—*may* I remind you—point the finger at Kane. That's not coincidence, dear."

"I know, Sean, it's God telling you that Senator Kane needs to be taken down and you are His Holiness' divine instrument with the appointed mission of accomplishing that goal."

"Couldn't have said it better myself."

"You are such a goofy bastard, Sean Murphy, you know that?" All of the people around the bar overheard Rebecca's comment and started laughing. By this time, the bartender, who was also laughing, delivered Rebecca's red wine and Sean's glass of Jamieson's.

"Wipe that smile off your face, Jack, or I'll have no choice but to kick your ass." Everyone at the bar again broke out in laughter. "Becca, don't ruin my tiny miracles. That's all I have. A whole bunch of the tiny ones can add up to something pretty incredible." Sean raised his glass toward Rebecca, to which she responded with her glass. "Here's to rock-n-roll and alcohol," Sean said. "The perfect combination."

⋖ ⋖ ⋗ ⋗

More than the allotted few hours passed as did more than Rebecca's suggested "just a drink or two." By this time, the bar at the Hard Rock Café was standing room only and, aside from the throbbing music, Sean was the main event. No matter how packed any bar ever got, Sean always stood out because of his awesome physical size, which was equally matched by his bellowing voice. The regulars loved to hear Sean's stories about playing linebacker at Penn State, which also captured the attention of anyone else nearby, causing them to stop and listen to Sean. Philadelphia sports fans were infamous for their love of football and Sean was a local legend when it came to the subject.

By about eleven o'clock, Sean noticed that Rebecca, while having a pleasant enough evening, probably was on the way to having a little too much to drink. The fact that they hadn't eaten dinner probably added to Rebecca's lack of resistance to the alcohol.

"C'mon, dear. Let's get you home," Sean said to Rebecca.

"Are you sure, Sean? I know you're having a great time. I don't want you to have to leave on my account."

"You kiddin' me? I can't stand these people. I wanted to leave hours ago, but I thought you wanted to stay." Everyone listening bursted out laughing, which wasn't hard to achieve at this point given the fact that most of the people there were stupid drunk. Sean paid the bill, and they said goodbye to everyone at the bar.

"My car is in the garage on Eighth Street," Rebecca informed Sean.

"You're jokin', right? You're in no shape to drive. I'll take you home. We can get your car tomorrow."

"I'm just tired, Sean. I'll be okay."

"No way. It's not happening. So just give it up." Rebecca didn't fight it. They walked together quietly for a minute or two. Rebecca slipped her arm through the tight space between Sean's arm and side, created as a result of Sean's walking with his hand in his pants pocket. Rebecca leaned her body into Sean's arm and brought her other hand over to rest as well. Sean took a deep breath and captured Rebecca's smell: a beautiful blend of subtle rosy perfume and light perspiration caused by the heat of the bar. As Rebecca pressed up against Sean, he reached over with his free hand and began to gently scratch hers, which was something that Sean seemingly did instinctively in this kind of situation. He never feared intimate contact.

Rebecca was the first one to talk. "Sean, do you miss Mary? I'm sorry. That's a stupid question. Of course you miss her. It's just that when you and I were together, it was so soon after she died. I could tell you were suffering, but I never could ask you any questions about either Mary or your daughter. I thought it might be too painful for you."

"I understand, and you're right," Sean responded. "It probably would have been too painful for me to talk about it at that time." Sean was quiet for a few seconds, obviously going back mentally to a place where he hadn't been in a while. Then, he spoke up again. "I miss both of them horribly. Actually, it's not exactly missing them that I feel, you know, like when someone you are close to has to move away. What I feel every day is deeper than just a sense of missing someone. It's a kind of pain that I just can't describe. Losing Kristin and Mary was without a doubt the worst point in my life. I loved them both so much. They were everything to me. I guess it just wasn't in the cards."

"What do you mean?" Rebecca asked, wiping a few unnoticeable tears from her cheeks.

"You know, wife and kids. I suppose God just has other plans for me."

"How do you do that, Sean?"

"What?"

"You turn perhaps the single most difficult life experience for any person on the face of the planet into the simplest spiritual equation. If God didn't want or intend something for your life, then, no matter how much it means to you, it's not going to happen. How can you settle for that kind of answer?"

"I can't explain that to you, Becca. It's just something that I know and accept in my heart. You can't put something like that into words. Frankly, any other answer is suicide anyway. If I had to think about it much differently than the way I do, I'm pretty sure I would have eaten a bullet."

"I just hope I was of some help to you in a time of need," Rebecca said quietly.

"Becca. C'mon now, don't say that. You know how much you mean to me. You are much more than just somebody who helped me through a rough personal ride."

She shrugged off Sean's comment and continued talking. "Are you better now? I mean do you still suffer the way you did after your wife died?"

"I have my days, but they are fewer."

"I wish I had known your wife and daughter, Sean. They must have been pretty spectacular. And, I know from talking with Steve that you were an incredible dad."

"Yeah, well. So much for that fucking job, right?" Sean started to choke up.

Rebecca realized immediately that her comment about Sean's daughter had touched a dark point in his heart, which was still there no matter how much he claimed to be better, and Rebecca felt badly for having said anything. Rebecca spun her body in front of Sean's to stop his walking. She leaned her body into Sean's, her head coming to rest directly under Sean's chin. She reached her arms around Sean, her hands barely coming together in the middle of Sean's back because of his massive size, and squeezed with what little energy she had left from the long day. "Stop talking like that Sean. It hurts me to hear you say those things. You make it sound like your life is over, but it's not. It's okay for you to be happy. It's okay for you to be at peace. It's okay for you to love again and even have another child." Rebecca stopped talking and started sobbing. Sean reached his monstrous arms around her, and Rebecca was safely hidden away from the whole world. He leaned back, which forced Rebecca's beautiful face to come into Sean's view. He kissed her gently on the forehead and left his lips there for what seemed an eternity to Rebecca.

When he lifted his lips, Sean said, "Becca, look at me. What's wrong, sweetheart? Why are you so sad all of the sudden? You shouldn't feel sorry for me. I have a great life."

"I'm not crying for you alone, Sean." Rebecca could not look Sean in his eyes so she forced her head back under Sean's chin and into his chest again. Sean could feel the warm dampness of Rebecca's tears on his neck.

"What do you mean?" he asked.

"These are selfish tears, Sean."

"Becca, I want to know what's wrong. Tell me."

"Talking about Mary and your daughter weren't the only taboo subjects I decided to hold back on when we were together."

"All right then. I'm telling you there is no reason for you to hold back any longer," Sean said demandingly.

"Oh shit . . . here goes nothing." Rebecca paused for a second or two, squeezing again to pull Sean even closer, and then said, "I love you, Sean Murphy. I have from the first day we met. You stole my heart instantly, Sean, and you still have it."

"Becca . . . sweet Mother of Christ! Why didn't . . . why didn't you say something? You mean to tell me you've been carrying around these feelings for me for over a year now? You should have said something."

"Sean, when we met, you were out of control and showed no signs of calming down. If you recall correctly, you were with a different woman every night. Anyone who knew you thought you would be dead soon. It was like you had some kind of death wish, Sean. Between that and your loss, there was no way I could intrude with a selfish comment like 'I love you.' Not to mention the fact it would have been presumptuous of me to think that you could ever love someone like me."

"It wouldn't have been selfish, Becca. No one should bear that kind of burden. And what do you mean about not being able to love someone like you?"

"Sean," Rebecca said in a languished tone, "I have seen pictures of Mary in your office. She had untouchable beauty. I'm not even in that league."

"What the hell are you talking about, Becca? Look at yourself," Sean demanded, turning her head toward their reflection in one of the store front windows. "You are incredible, make no mistake about it."

"I don't see the same thing you do when I look in the mirror, Sean. Love makes you meek," Rebecca said, barely able to get out the words before her tears arrived again.

Sean released his arms from their clutch on Rebecca's body and moved his hands up to surround Rebecca's throat. With his thumbs under her chin, Sean lifted Rebecca's head up and back so they were face to face. She would not open her eyes. "My God, I never realized how incredibly beautiful you are, Becca. Look at me, sweetheart." Rebecca would not comply. "Open your eyes, Becca. I want you to look me in my eyes when I say what I'm about to say." Rebecca relented and slowly opened her eyes, their roundness and clarity now pronounced by the moisture from her tears. After a few seconds of staring deeply at one another, Sean said, "I love you too, Becca."

Rebecca tried to pull away, but Sean subdued her. "Don't pity me, Sean. You're just saying that to return the fucking favor," she shouted at him, still trying to pry her way out of Sean's gripping hold.

"Becca, wait a minute. Listen to me. There's something you need to hear." Sean pulled Rebecca close again, despite her feeble attempts to get lose. Finally, she submitted and came to rest back in Sean's chest. "That night we first met, you came back to my house, remember? You had too much to drink at that party at Rachel's house."

"Well, Sean, I was trying to carry on a conversation with you. It seemed like every five minutes you were getting another drink."

"Yeah, I was out of control wasn't I?" Sean reminisced for a few seconds and smiled. "Anyway, that night I told Rachel that I would drive you home. When we walked outside, I put my arm around you to steady you. We walked together to my car, not really saying much. When we got in, you asked if you could spend the night at my house."

"God, you must have thought I was such a slut," Rebecca interrupted.

"Becca, I'm trying to be serious here, so don't hand me an opportunity like that." They both laughed and hugged tightly. "That night you took a shower, put on my sweat clothes, and fell asleep in my bed." Sean paused to take a deep breath. "I didn't sleep that night, Becca."

"What are you talking about? Of course you did. I remember waking up in your arms the next morning."

"I'm telling you, I didn't go to sleep. I spent a few hours walking around my house looking at pictures of Mary and my daughter. I kissed every one of those pictures, which is something I had never done before, certainly not when they were alive. I don't know for sure that I was aware that night of what I was doing, but it's clear to me now that I was saying goodbye to them. Then, I came into the bedroom and watched you sleep. The look of peace on your face was overwhelming. I've never known that kind of peace, Becca. Other than reading about it and hearing people talk about it, I didn't really know the meaning of peace. Until that night, anyway. It captivated me to see it. You were laying on your back and your long blond hair was all around you. You were breathing so deeply that just listening to you calmed me down. When the sun rose, the light coming through the bedroom window fell right on your face, turning your blond hair bright red. I thought I was looking at a painting, for Christ's sake. I couldn't help myself. I walked over to the bed and kissed you right on the lips."

"No, you didn't. We didn't kiss for the first time until I woke up and brushed my teeth."

"I'm telling you, Becca, I kissed you . . . and for a long time. Even though you were asleep, you kissed me back, at least a little bit anyway. Then I whispered into your ear 'I'm falling in love with you Rebecca Lockhart.' After that, I cried . . . like a freaking baby." Rebecca was stunned to hear Sean say that. She had never seen him cry and frankly didn't think it was possible. "Becca, it was the first time I cried since Mary's death. I spent a half hour with my head on your stomach crying like never before. The more the sun filled the room, the harder I cried. After that I hopped into bed with you. I remember this feeling of total exhaustion, but I couldn't sleep. By that time, the sun was so bright that closing my eyes didn't keep out the light, but I didn't want to close it out. It was the first time in over a year that I even noticed the sunrise. Just before you woke up, I prayed."

By this time, Rebecca had tears welling up in her eyes again. She asked, "What did you pray for, Sean?"

"I begged God not to take you away from me, like he'd done with others in my life. I begged God that you would teach me the kind of peace that shone in your face while you were laying there next to me. I begged God that you would show me some kind of love back, even in the smallest amount, so I could start to be happy again. I begged God to tell me in some way, however small or insignificant, that you were his angel sent to deliver me from my pain."

"Oh my God, Sean!" Rebecca said quietly as she cried and grabbed at him. She gently pushed Sean up against the window of the nearby store and kissed him on his neck as she cried uncontrollably. She felt Sean's tears dropping down onto her face and running down over her lips, leaving the faintest taste of salt in her mouth. Then Rebecca looked up at Sean and said, "I promise I'll never leave you or be without you again. I promise to help you find peace and happiness. And, I promise I'll love you with all my heart . . . always, Sean, always."

CHAPTER 29

Sean woke up early and made breakfast, for two. It had been a long night, and he was feeling the sting from the steady flow of drinks at the Hard Rock Café. His soul searching with Rebecca had left him a little dizzy, too. A cup of hot coffee was the first order of business. It burned his lips as Sean took his first sip. Rebecca woke up about an hour after Sean and appeared in the kitchen as Sean was reading the newspaper, already dressed for work.

"Good morning, dear," said Sean in a warm welcoming voice.

"Hey. Something smells good. Whatcha' got cookin'?" she asked.

"Scrambled eggs and scrapple."

"Scrapple! Sean, do you really eat that stuff? Do you have any clue what it is?"

"Of course I do, and I'm proud to say I still eat it. It's boiled, ground leftover pig scraps with cornmeal and spices thrown in. Pork mush for the more culinary inclined. Hell, I grew up on Philadelphia scrapple, baby. It's as addictive as heroin. A nice inch thick slice, fried up with two eggs. Ahh! Nothing like it."

"I'm sure your heart agrees when that huge mass of pork fat makes its way through the aortic valve. Why don't you just throw a cigarette in while you're at it?" Sean laughed hysterically. "If it's all the same to you, I'll stick with the scrambled eggs."

"No problem. I'll get some for you. How about some toast and coffee, too?"

"Perfect." As Sean was putting together a plate for Rebecca, she started to think about their conference call with Brendan Frisk the day before. "Sean, what do you expect to see in this file from Frisk?" she asked.

"My guess is this Consent Agreement is the handiwork of Senator Kane. In his capacity as chair of the Senate Environment and Public Works Committee, I'm sure he has seen that kind of document many times before."

"What is a Consent Agreement, by the way?" Rebecca asked.

"Almost every federal environmental law has a provision that allows the EPA to enter into agreements for a variety of reasons, like settling lawsuits or waiving certain regulatory requirements. The EPA does it all the time under the federal Clean Air Act. For example, most recently, the EPA used Consent Agreements to allow electric power plants to continue operating without required air emissions permits in the interest of preventing brownouts and blackouts, especially in the Northeast."

"I assume," Rebecca observed, "that a Consent Agreement requires the regulated party to give something back to the EPA in exchange for leniency of that kind."

"That's correct. Using that same example of the electric power plants, the EPA normally requires some kind of commitment to a time schedule for the plant to come into full compliance with the Clean Air Act and then what are known as stipulated penalties if they don't comply."

"Explain what you mean by stipulated penalties," Rebecca commented.

"That just means that the parties agree to a penalty schedule, such as $500 or $1,000 a day if the plant fails to meet a deadline in the Consent Agreement. The word stipulated in that context means nothing more than that the parties have agreed to the amount of the penalty."

"So," Rebecca started, "our guess is Senator Kane crafted this Consent Agreement as a way of persuading Brendan Frisk to start marketing Power Systems greenhouse gas emission credits, right?"

"Yeah, I feel pretty confident that's what we are going to see," responded Sean.

"Assuming that's what you get, how does that come into play in terms of your case against Kane?"

"I was spinning my mental wheels about that yesterday before we went out for drinks. I didn't want to get too carried away about the prospects of this file having anything tremendously helpful. Frankly, at this point, I'm just looking for something to backstop my actions here."

"What do you mean?" Rebecca asked.

"I got a letter from Kane's law firm threatening me with a civil rights claim if I didn't back off. Trust me, with Braddon gone, that kind of threat scares hell out of me."

"Sean, nothing scares you. Plus, you've dealt with that kind of threat at least a hundred times in your career. Am I correct?"

"Yeah, but never from anyone of Kane's caliber. This guy is an extremely powerful and intelligent man, Becca. As much as I hate to admit it, I'm not in his league. All I'm hoping for at this point is something to deflect Kane's threats."

"You mean to tell me that you don't plan to go after Kane criminally?" Rebecca asked, looking stunned.

"I honestly don't know what I'm going to do. It's premature to be making any judgments anyway. I need to see what comes up in this file, which is where I'm going now. I'm heading into the office. Do you want to come with me so you can get your car?"

"If it's okay with you, Sean, I'm going to hang out here. I'm feeling a little funky from what was supposed to be a one or two drink visit to the Hard Rock. What is it about you and bars, Sean Murphy?" Rebecca said, poking fun at Sean's drinking habit.

"Like eating a Lay's potato chip. Can't have just one. Make yourself at home." Sean got up from the kitchen table, walked over to Rebecca and kissed her on the head. He started to walk toward the front door, paused and then looked back at her. "And, Becca, I wouldn't mind very much if you were still here when I get home tonight." She smiled at Sean and waved goodbye to him, never saying a word.

❧ ❧ ❧ ❧

On his ride into Center City, Sean called Steve Cooperhouse from his cell phone.

"Good morning, Steve Cooperhouse here."

"Dick head, it's me," Sean said rapidly as he dodged cars on Route Ninety-five.

"Hello to you too, Sean. What's up?"

"I'm on my way in to the office, about fifteen minutes out. How about you stop by and we look at this Climate Exchange file together?" Sean suggested.

"Sounds good. I'll be at your office in half an hour."

"Oh, Steve, do me a favor, hold on. . . ." Sean clicked the end button on his cell phone, and Steve heard a dial tone. Steve smiled and thought to himself, *What a bonehead!* It was an on-going joke he and Sean starting playing on one another back in college. The trick was to lure the other party into a sense of security that you were having a serious talk and then hang up on him out of the blue. Steve's wife could never find the humor in it. Nor could Sean's when she was alive. It didn't matter to Sean and Steve, though, that others didn't appreciate the pleasure in the process. It was a scorecard kind of thing that kept them motivated. Unfortunately for Steve, Sean was much better at it and normally had bragging rights at the end of the day.

❧ ❧ ❧ ❧

"Sean," Kate shouted from the copying machine as he walked through the door. "Fed Ex package on your seat. It says 'Urgent' on the receipt."

"Thank you, dear. Steve Cooperhouse should be here any minute. Let me know when he arrives, please."

Sean settled in to his desk, following the same routine he did every morning: log onto the computer, check e-mail messages, and then check voice mail messages. The last of these actions produced an interesting result. It was Harvey Morgan, law partner to Senator Kane. Sean was listening to the voice mail as Steve walked into his office. Sean handed Steve the Federal Express package and gestured for him to open it up. He smiled and pointed to the telephone to indicate to Steve that this was something he would want to hear. Sean then hit the "hands-free" button on his telephone control pad, which caused the voice to pop up on speaker phone, making it audible to Steve: " . . . I'm calling on behalf of Senator Kane to find out whether you intend to comply with our demand for a retraction of the press release about alleged criminal activity on the part of the Senator." Sean gestured toward the telephone with his middle finger as the voice mail message continued to flow. "I'm in all day today. The Senator would like some response from your office today."

Sean looked over at Steve as he hung up the telephone. "Are all attorneys such dicks, Steve?"

"Of course they are, Sean, and you're one of the biggest of them."

"I'll take that, my friend, as an implicit compliment. Let's see what's in that file, Mr. Cooperhouse." Steve handed about half the documents to Sean and kept the remainder for himself. They both starting flipping carefully through them. Several minutes passed before Sean spoke first.

"Here we go. It's a Consent Agreement All right. Just like Frisk said." Steve stopped his review to listen to Sean. "Looks official, too. 'In the Matter of Power Systems, Inc.,'" Sean said as he read from the document. "Let's see here. Okay, got it. 'The United State Environmental Protection Agency hereby consents to Power Systems Inc.'s continued operation of its 300 megawatt electric power generating facility. . . .'" Sean read to himself for a few seconds and then went back into a presentation of the wording to Steve. "Ah, I think this is it . . . 'Power Systems, Inc. is hereby authorized to vent, emit, and discharge to the Delaware River any and all exhaust gases generated by the combustion furnaces at the Tacony facility.' That's interesting."

"What's that, Sean?" asked Steve.

"The document is signed by the director of the Office of Air and Radiation," answered Sean.

"Sean, that's me. I'm the director of that office."

"No shit. That's why I mention it."

"Well, is it my signature? Here let me see it," demanded Steve. Sean handed the Consent Agreement to Steve, pointing to the signature block on the last page. "That's my signature, All right. No question about it."

"How'd it get there?" Sean asked.

"I have no idea. Believe me, if my office was negotiating a Consent Agreement with Power Systems, I would have known about it, especially something of this magnitude." Steve continued looking at the signature page. After a few minutes, something unusual caught his eye. "Sean, take a look at this. The signature page has no number. The page before it is numbered thirty one, but the signature page is unnumbered. See that," Steve asked as he handed the document back to Sean.

"Yeah, you're right." Sean studied the signature page more closely. "Well, is it unusual for a signature page to be without a number?" Sean asked as he continued studying the document.

Steve replied quickly and assertively. "Absolutely. Page numbering is built into our word processing system. The computer does it automatically. In fact, it is so standardized now that we don't even think about it anymore."

"That's good to know. C'mon what else ?" asked Sean, gesturing to Steve to look at the document with him. "You know, if we had Tom Roth looking at this thing he would have come up with about a hundred different problems, including spelling errors." Steve chuckled. "Do you see anything else on the signature page that doesn't look kosher?" Sean asked.

"Let me see," Steve said while leaning over the front of Sean's desk. Again, almost immediately, he noticed something amiss. "Look here, at the top." Steve pointed to some markings on the top tenth inch or so of the Consent Agreement signature page.

"What the hell you looking at, Steve?" Sean asked confusedly.

"Right here. This confirms that the document is a fraud."

CHAPTER 30

The nineteen members of the Senate Environment and Public Works Committee were gathered for a series of hearings on the Climate Stewardship Act. Chairman Senator Kane, who was the principal author of the law, sat at the center of the dais. Despite the press release about Senator Kane's alleged criminal activity in connection with his business interests in Power Systems, Inc., no one challenged his ability to serve in the capacity of chairman of the committee, which was a singular testament to his political power, especially his strength on the committee. First on the witness list was Brendan Frisk of The Climate Exchange.

"Good morning, Mr. Frisk," Senator Kane started, "and thank you for agreeing to testify today. We have a lot of ground to cover. You've been through the process before a few weeks ago. So, I assume you recall the ground rules and understand that you are still under oath."

"Yes, sir." answered Frisk.

"If it's okay with you, then, I'd like to get underway."

"Yes, Mr. Chairman, that's fine with me," Frisk said.

"Mr. Frisk, let me get a bit of housekeeping out of the way before we get started. I just want the members of the Committee and the public to understand that you and I have a business affiliation, correct?"

"Yes, that's correct," Frisk responded.

"Could you describe for the committee members what that relationship is?"

"Well," Frisk started, "I assume you're talking about the sale of Power Systems, Inc.'s greenhouse gas credits on The Climate Exchange."

"Right," answered Kane. "And do you see any reason why that business relationship would affect your ability to answer the Committee's questions today truthfully, accurately, and completely?"

"No, Mr. Chairman. We don't have adverse interests. To the contrary, the more credits Power Systems generates, the more money I make from the trades." Some members of the committee chuckled in reaction to Frisk's comment.

"Fair enough," responded Senator Kane. "Who would like to begin the questioning?"

The mminority leader of the Committee, Senator Robert Orlean, was the first to take advantage of Senator Kane's offer. "Mr. Frisk, I have here before me a copy of your testimony before this committee a few weeks ago. Do you recall that testimony, sir?"

"Yes, I do."

"At that time, you talked about the so-called carbon market. Is that market maturing to any degree?"

"Yes, it is. The Climate Exchange started trading at the end of 2003. So, the first full year of economic data is for calendar year 2004, in which the Exchange traded just under 50 million tons of greenhouse gases, mainly carbon dioxide."

"Mr. Frisk, I'm sorry to interrupt your presentation," said Senator Orlean, "but I'd be interested to hear—and I think the other committee members would likewise share in my interest—of what those trades mean in dollars and cents."

"At an average cost of, say, $15 per ton, that comes to $750 million dollars worth of business we conducted in 2004."

"That's huge!" shouted one of the other senators, causing Kane to give him a glare. "Sorry about that Mr. Chairman and Mr. Frisk. The number caught me off guard. I wasn't expecting something of that magnitude."

Frisk responded. "Keep in mind, members of the committee, that the number I gave you is the total value of the trades. It's not the amount of money The Climate Exchange makes. I'm just a simple broker, taking only a small percentage out of each transaction." Several members of the committee and the public laughed when they heard this comment.

"Understood." Senator Orlean reacted immediately, obviously getting concerned that the discussion was going afield of where he wanted to go with the questioning. "Let me step back, Mr. Frisk, if I may?" Frisk responded with a nod. "I'm interested in how the Exchange works. One of the things we are attempting to do with the Climate Stewardship Act is establish a definitive set of standards for a national 'cap and trade' program for greenhouse gases, much like what is established under The Kyoto Protocol. We need your advice and guidance on what the language of the law should be to ensure a successful program. Tell me, how does one go about establishing credits?"

"Well, the best example I can give you is Power Systems, considering it was the major contributor of greenhouse gas credits to The Climate Exchange. I can only go on what I know from experience. I understand the Power Systems facility in Philly is no longer operational, but it serves as a good example nonetheless."

"That's fine with me, Mr. Frisk," responded Orlean, looking over to Kane for some form of acknowledgment, which never came. "Go right ahead."

Brendan Frisk pulled out a file from the pile of documents in front of him, drawing Senator Kane's attention. It was as if Brendan Frisk was ready for the question, almost as if it was scripted. Kane looked over at Orlean, who responded back to Kane with a smile. "The first thing you need to consider is a how to verify the credits. In other words, you need some system of measuring how much greenhouse gas a specific source is emitting to the atmosphere. I talked about that part of the process at the earlier hearings before this Committee. Next, you need a verifiable method of measuring how much of that total amount of greenhouse gas that source controls from getting into the atmosphere, by whatever method."

"How did you do it at the Power Systems facility in Philadelphia?" asked Orlean.

The question seemingly caused Senator Kane to shift in his seat, almost as if it triggered a memory of the events surrounding the Tacony facility shut down. It was at that moment Senator Kane noticed Sean Murphy sitting in the audience. *What the hell's he doing here?* Kane thought to himself. *Something's up!*

Frisk responded to Senator Orlean's inquiry. "Funny you ask that, sir. I've been dealing with a lot of questions about Power Systems lately." Kane was now visibly nervous. "Anyway, I required Power Systems to install a Continuous Emissions Monitor on its Tacony plant exhaust system. It provided a 24-7 record that. . . ."

"Senator Orlean," interrupted Kane. "I've decided not to allow this testimony. We all know that the Power Systems facility has been shut down by the EPA because of alleged violations of the Clean Air Act. I don't think it's appropriate for this Committee to be relying on testimony regarding a facility that is no longer operational."

"I beg to differ, Mr. Chairman," responded Frisk.

"Excuse me, Mr. Frisk, but you don't get to 'beg to differ,'" said Kane in his inimitable style. "This is our hearing, not yours."

"Mr. Chairman," responded Orlean anxiously, "I think we should hear what this witness has to say." Senator Orlean looked around the dais for the consensus of the other committee members. It was unusual for the Chairman to stop the testimony of a witness at a hearing. So, it wasn't unexpected to see all of the committee members nodding in acknowledgment of Senator Orlean's opinion. "Go ahead, Mr. Frisk. Please continue."

"As I was saying, the Continuous Emissions Monitor was a device on the Tacony plant exhaust pipes to measure the amount of carbon dioxide in the waste gas."

"But I thought, Mr. Frisk," asked Senator Orlean, "that the Power Systems Tacony plant is a 'zero emissions' facility? How can there be any carbon dioxide in the exhaust gas? In fact, I expected to hear you say there was no exhaust gas at all from that plant."

"That's how it started out, Senator, but it changed early on," responded Frisk.

"What do you mean it changed?" asked Senator Orlean.

"I suggest, Senator Orlean, that you ask the chairman about that event. He knows first hand what happened whereas I only know about it from documents and the like." Senator Kane was glaring intensely at Brendan Frisk, who by this time was staring straight back at him.

"That's okay, Mr. Frisk. I'd like to hear your story for the time being. What do you mean about 'documents and the like?'" asked Senator Orlean.

"Well, soon after Power Systems started operating the Tacony plant, it shut down. I'm not sure exactly why, but it shut down. The shutdown came at a time when the company was trying to get me to certify credits to the Exchange. I know from experience that those credits meant big money to the company. So, as you can expect, the shutdown presented a real problem. It was a substantial loss of expected revenues to the company. I knew the company was planning on making some physical modifications to the plant as quickly as possible to get it up and running again. If I recall, it took about two weeks time."

"Mr. Frisk, I don't mean to interrupt you," Senator Orlean said, "but I think you are getting a bit off track. You mentioned at the outset 'documents and the like.' What document are you talking about?"

"Sorry about that, Senator. The history is fuzzy to me, simply because of the passage of time. So, it helps me to review it as I go. Anyway, what I recall next is that after the company got the plant running again, Senator Kane approached me to restart the negotiations on the credits. As you can expect, I was nervous given the fact that the plant was just coming off of a difficult time."

"What do you mean when you say you were nervous, Mr. Frisk?" asked Orlean.

"Any marketplace is only as good as the value of its products. My product is pollution. I have to be sure that the pollution traded on my marketplace has true value. What I mean is, unlike other commodities, you can't touch and feel the pollution traded on The Climate Exchange. It's not like going to the mall, if you follow me. The members of my Exchange that buy greenhouse gas credits rely on me to make sure that the credit represents real pollution, or I should say the credit represents a real pollution reduction. So, I have to follow strict methods of verifying the credits, which gets me back to the Continuous Emissions Monitor. After the Power Systems plant shutdown, I demanded the company produce something to confirm for me that it was authorized to restart."

"I assume, Mr. Frisk," observed Senator Orlean, "that gets us to the documents you were talking about before."

"Exactly. I told Senator Kane I needed something in writing from the EPA showing me that Power Systems had the authority to modify the Philly plant."

"Senator Orlean," interjected Kane. "We must stop here. The information that Mr. Frisk is about to discuss is subject to confidentiality restrictions, and he knows as much. Not only that, but the Power Systems technology is a proprietary system. If this witness introduces testimony about the engineering or operational aspects of the Power Systems facility in Philadelphia, he will be facing a lawsuit from the company."

"Mr. Chairman, I appreciate what you're saying," responded Orlean. "But I think that's an issue for this witness to decide. It's his risk, not this committee's. What I mean is this committee cannot be sued simply for listening to testimony, even if that testimony turns out to be in breach of some confidentiality restriction. Mr. Frisk, I believe you were talking about modifications to the Power Systems plant. You have heard the chairman's concerns about confidentiality restrictions. The decision is yours, sir, whether or not to continue testifying about those plant modifications."

"I understand, Senator. I'm willing to continue because I disagree that anything I'm about to discuss is privileged and confidential. As I was saying, I demanded that Power Systems give me concrete evidence of its authority to modify the exhaust system at its Philly plant and begin operating again."

"Mr. Frisk, what were the exhaust modifications?" asked Senator Orlean.

"Power Systems," Frisk answered, "had to start bubbling its exhaust gas into the Delaware River. I understood it to be an accepted form of carbon sequestration from my experience with other projects, but it was unusual for a company that touted itself as a 'zero emission' facility to shift suddenly to carbon sequestration as a means of creating greenhouse gas credits. So, that shift in approach is what made me nervous. I needed something to cover my ass, pardon the expression. Keep in mind here that at the time I was negotiating with a company that was going to be the main source of credits on my Exchange. I couldn't take any unrealistic chances just given the volume of Power Systems credits that were going to be traded. I am directly responsible to member companies on the Exchange for inaccuracies or mistakes in the trading information. That's why I asked for something in writing."

"And did you get what you asked for, Mr. Frisk?" asked Senator Orlean.

"Yes, sir, I did. I have a copy of it here. Let' see, where is that thing?" Frisk mumbled as he fingered through the files in front of him. "Ah, yes, here it is, a Consent Agreement between the EPA and Power Systems."

"Mr. Frisk, would you be so kind as to pass that up to the committee so we can have a look at it?"

"Sure. Glad to," Frisk answered as a hearing officer collected the document from Frisk and carried it over to Senator Orlean.

"Mr. Chairman," said Orlean, "at this point I think we should hear from another witness who was not scheduled to testify today." Orlean's comment caught all of the committee members off guard, not the least of which was Senator Kane.

"What are you talking about? This is highly unusual, Senator Orlean. In fact, I don't think our committee rules allow us to hear from unscheduled or unannounced witnesses. No, I'm not going to allow it, and I think we've heard enough from this witness. As you can see from the document he just handed you, Power Systems was a legitimate operation. I don't know that Mr. Frisk's testimony has been all that helpful to us. So, I think we should wrap it up with him."

"Mr. Chairman, I don't understand why you would be inclined to rely on convention when we are soliciting testimony to help us build a good and workable bill. You don't even know who the witness is and you are setting up a barrier. I don't understand, Mr. Chairman. Just so the members of the committee know, the director of the EPA's Office of Air and Radiation is here today. His name is Steve Cooperhouse. He has information relevant to the Power Systems facility in Philadelphia and can expand on the testimony of Mr. Frisk here."

"This is bullshit, Orlean." yelled Senator Kane, which caused the other members of the committee to jump in their seats. "I know exactly what you're trying to do here and I'm not going to allow it. You're turning this honorable committee into a kangaroo court, and I'm your target. This is an abomination! Senator Orlean has obviously been swayed by the lies and deceit that have been spread all over the press about me lately by another person here today, Sean Murphy. He is sitting in the back, there," Kane said as he pointed in the direction of Sean Murphy, who, in his typical rebellious style, lifted his hand to wave at Kane. It infuriated him. "For the record, Mr. Murphy attempted to bring a criminal action against me and failed miserably. The reason he failed is because I did nothing wrong. This farce today is just a last ditch effort to make some kind of case against me. I won't stand for it. I've already put Mr. Murphy on notice that I intend to file a civil rights action against the Department of Justice and him personally if he does not relent. Sitting here today, I'm convinced that I have no choice now but to carry through with that threat."

After a few seconds of complete silence, one of the other, and more senior, committee members spoke up. "Mr. Chairman, I'm confused, which by the way happens a good deal at my age." His comment broke the silence with laughter. "One minute we are hearing from the good Mr. Frisk about greenhouse gas credits and then the next minute you and Senator Orlean are arguing about another witness. Then, we're hearing an argument from you that you did nothing wrong. Frankly, I'm lost. I'm not sure we were even finished with Mr. Frisk," the elderly senator said as he smiled and nodded at Frisk. "As most of you know, I am not one to stand on formality. In fact, I'm just an old country lawyer."

The members of the committee laughed and Senator Orlean said, "show us your suspenders, then," to which the elderly senator leaned back in his seat, pulled aside his suit jacket, reached under his bright red suspenders with his thumbs and pulled them away from his chest. When he released the suspenders, everyone in the hearing room heard them slap back against the elderly senator's body, causing the room to break out in laughter.

"As I was saying," the elderly senator continued, "I don't like to stand on formality. Hell, I wouldn't know or understand formality if you hit me over the head with it." The audience chuckled lightly a second time. "But, I do know one thing, and that is how to show courtesy to people, whether they are our invited guests or not. So, I think that, because this nice young man from the EPA came all the way from Philly this morning, we should be courteous enough to hear from him." The elderly senator looked around the dais after he was done speaking to see if everyone else was in agreement. They were, except of course for Senator Kane, who was angrily staring at Sean Murphy and Steve Cooperhouse in the audience.

"Well, then," said Senator Orlean, "I think the committee is in agreement. . . "

Kane, finally breaking his gaze, interrupted Orlean. Kane shouted as he stood up, "I don't care what the other members think. This is my committee and I will decide what we do and do not hear from witnesses. You need to check yourself, Senator Orlean. Nobody asked that you run this show today. This is my baby and I'll decide who testifies, thank you very much."

"Senator," replied Orlean, "you need to sit down."

"Kiss my ass," Kane shouted as he walked hurriedly across the dais toward Senator Orlean, who now was likewise standing.

"What?" Orlean asked jokingly with a childish tone to his voice. "Are you gonna beat me up?" Before he knew it, Senator Kane was rushing toward him and taking a swing. All the members of the committee, and a few security guards as well, rushed toward the two senators, who by that time had come off of the dais and were wrestling between it and the witness table. When the tussle was over, Senator Kane was being led out of the hearing room in handcuffs by two security guards.

Senator Orlean shouted to Kane as he and the security guards approached a private exit, "You better get used to those handcuffs, Kane." It was at that point the other members of the Committee realized Senator Orlean was orchestrating something for the committee and the public to hear. Understanding this consequence, Orlean wasted no time getting back onto the dais and calling Steve Cooperhouse as a witness. Rebecca Lockhart filled in the seat next to Sean Murphy, left vacant when Steve moved to the witness table.

"Mr. Cooperhouse, thank you for being here today," Senator Orlean said as he straightened his suit jacket and then his hair. "Sorry for the interruption."

"No problem. I'm friends with Sean Murphy, so I'm used to that kind of stuff. Happens all the time." Sean had invited some of the Philadelphia media to the hearing. The few people in the audience who were aware of Sean's reputation laughed at Steve's comment. "Senator Kane likes Sean Murphy about as much as he likes you, Senator Orlean." Everyone laughed.

"Well, Mr. Cooperhouse," Senator Orlean responded, "I took one for the team today. You can thank me later. Let's proceed, then. Mr. Frisk, if you could stay at the witness table with Mr. Cooperhouse, just in case we have additional questions for you." Frisk nodded and Steve Cooperhouse was sworn under oath, after which Senator Orlean began the questioning. "Mr. Cooperhouse, please tell the committee about your background and experience."

"I am the director of the Office of Air and Radiation for the EPA's regional office in Philadelphia. I am responsible for all regulated air emissions projects in Delaware, District of Columbia, Maryland, Pennsylvania, Virginia, and West Virginia. I have held this position for just over ten years now, but I have worked at the EPA in one capacity or another for nearly thirty years."

"You're familiar with the Power Systems Tacony plant, correct?" asked Senator Orlean.

"Yes, sir, I am, but not until just recently," responded Steve.

"What do you mean by not until just recently?" asked Senator Orlean, obviously now acting as the unofficial chairman of the committee.

"Power Systems was not subject to our permit requirements because the Tacony plant did not emit any air pollution, at least as originally constructed. The Tacony plant wasn't under my jurisdiction when it was built."

"So, how did you learn about the plant?" asked Orlean.

"Interestingly, a stiff showed up in the Delaware River a few months back. It just so happened that this dead guy was the environmental compliance manager for the Power Systems Tacony plant. One thing led to another and Sean Murphy had me headlong into an investigation of the plant."

"Were you the Air Director back in 2000, which I believe is the date of the Consent Agreement that Mr. Frisk supplied?"

"Yes, sir, I was," answered Steve.

"And did you negotiate that Consent Agreement with Power Systems on behalf of the EPA?"

"No, sir, I did not."

One of the other committee members sat up and asked, "Come again?"

"I said I did not negotiate that Consent Agreement."

The same committee member asked, "Then someone else in your office must have negotiated it, correct?"

"No sir," Steve responded. "A Consent Agreement of this magnitude would not have left the EPA without my involvement."

The same committee member asked further, "What are you saying, Mr. Cooperhouse?"

"This document is a fraud."

"Mr. Cooperhouse," the same committee member asked, "I trust you understand the significance of your testimony?"

"Yes, sir, I am completely aware of its significance."

"Then please explain," interrupted Orlean, "for the committee, when you say the Consent Agreement is a fraud."

"Well, Sean Murphy and I were talking with Mr. Frisk a few days ago and we learned that he had this document in his files. I did not recall having any case with Power Systems, so we asked Mr. Frisk to send us a copy of the document. It was a standard form of Consent Agreement that my Office uses in enforcement actions. Interestingly, the document had my signature on it."

"Then why do you claim it to be fraudulent, Mr. Cooperhouse?" demanded one of Senator Kane's allies on the committee.

"Because, sir," responded Steve, "upon closer examination, it became abundantly clear that Senator Kane had contrived this document simply to persuade Mr. Frisk to start negotiations on Power Systems greenhouse gas credits on The Climate Exchange."

The same Senator demanded, "What made it 'abundantly clear' to you that Senator Kane was perpetuating a fraud here?"

"I'm glad to answer that, Senator. If you will just bear with me a second, I have some visual aids with me today that may be of some help." Sean Murphy moved forward to assist Steve in setting up a laptop computer and screen, making it obvious to the Committee members that this effort had been carefully orchestrated in advance. After a minute or two, an image popped up on the screen. Sean Murphy, walking back to his seat, gestured to a security guard to dim the lights. "Members of the Committee, what I am showing you here is a copy of the signature page of the so-called Consent Agreement between Power Systems and the EPA. Direct your attention, if you will, to the upper left hand corner of the page." A series of numbers were barely visible. Steve clicked a few buttons on the laptop and a highlighted section of the page appeared on the screen, at which point a series of numbers was visible: 0002155557943-0004251998000.

Senator Orlean asked the next question. "Mr. Cooperhouse, can you make any sense of these numbers. Do you know what they mean?"

"I do have an explanation, Senator. Whenever you send out a telefax, the receiving machine automatically prints out a series of numbers to cover things like the originating or source telephone number, the telephone number at the receiving end and the date the telefax was sent."

"So, can you interpret these numbers?" asked Senator Orlean.

"When I first looked at this signature page, I thought the '215' meant a Philly exchange, which would mean that set of numbers is a telefax number. So, I did some digging and confirmed that one of the fax machines in the Office of Air and Radiation uses 215-555-7943."

"What about the other series of numbers?" Senator Orlean asked.

"This is where the story gets interesting. My best guess is that it represents the date the telefax was sent: April 25, 1998."

"1998! That doesn't make sense," interrupted one of the committee members. "Based on what we've heard from prior testimony, the Power Systems Tacony plant wasn't up and running until much later, like 2000. What would Power Systems be doing negotiating a Consent Agreement with the EPA in '98?"

"That's exactly my point, Senator. I think this page with my signature comes from another document altogether. Maybe even another Consent Agreement."

"So, what are you're telling us, Mr. Cooperhouse?" Senator Orlean asked.

"Members of the Committee, I firmly believe Senator Kane drafted his own Consent Agreement probably using as his guideline the same kind of document from another Office of Air and Radiation file, and then simply pirated the signature page from a 1998 agreement with my John Hancock on it."

"That theory seems kind of far fetched to me," another of the committee members commented.

"Actually, sir, it's very easy for Senator Kane or any other person for that matter to get a Consent Agreement that I signed in another case. All he or she need do is file a Freedom of Information Act request. Just about every Consent Order ever negotiated by the Office of Air and Radiation is identified in the public record. Not only that, but the EPA has an obligation to publish notice of Consent Agreements and seek public comment and input. So it's not hit or miss. Every Consent Agreement I ever signed has been disclosed to the public and can be identified quite easily. After that, it's just a matter of asking the EPA for access to that particular file under the Freedom of Information Act. All someone would have to do to get the signature page from a Consent Agreement is ask the EPA for a copy of the document and pay the copying charges."

One of the committee members asked the obvious question, "Can you tell from what EPA file Senator Kane may have pirated this signature page?"

"I have a fairly good idea, Senator. I had my staff go back through the Freedom of Information Act requests received by the EPA in and around the time that Senator Kane would have been fabricating this document. The problem is the EPA gets thousands and thousands of those requests in every year. Tracking down one is the proverbial needle in the haystack. Unfortunately, we did not find any with Senator Kane's name on it, but I also asked my staff to track the name of Senator Kane's law firm. Sure enough, we hit a request from the firm back in early 2000 and it was the only one from that law firm for that year. The request was for a file—the name of which I can't recall off the top of my head—that had a final Consent Agreement with my signature on it. I'm bringing up on the screen for you now a copy of the signature page from that document." All of the committee members focused on the screen and pondered Steve Cooperhouse's theory. Then Steve Cooperhouse imaged a screen where both signature pages were side by side. They looked exactly alike.

One of Senator Kane's allies on the committee commented, "I don't know. I'm not convinced."

Senator Orlean responded. "C'mon, Bradley. This evidence is overwhelming."

"Overwhelming is too strong of a description for me, Senator. Suspicious, yes, but not overwhelming."

"Then I suggest," Senator Orlean answered, "that we have Senator Kane come back and answer to this charge of fraud."

⊲ ⊲ ⊳ ⊳

Senator Kane was no longer in handcuffs when the D.C. police returned him to the hearing room. About an hour had passed since Steve Cooperhouse concluded his testimony and most of the committee members had left the hearing room for other business. Senator Kane was directed by the security guards to take a seat at the witness table. He did so and immediately began to tap his stubby fingers on the hardwood top. Peering around the room, Kane connected eyes with Sean Murphy sitting in the back of the hearing room with Rebecca. Sean noticed that Kane's aggression had eroded to fear. After ten minutes or so, the committee members had reconvened on the dais and Senator Orlean began the questioning, after Senator Kane was sworn in.

"Tell us about your employment with Power Systems."

"I'm the Vice-President of Governmental Affairs."

"How long have you held that position?"

"For about six years now."

"What are your duties and responsibilities as the Vice-President of Governmental Affairs?"

"Well, the electric power generation industry is highly regulated, especially on the environmental front. So, my job is to make sure the company has the necessary governmental approvals and permits to operate."

"Anything else?" Senator Orlean asked.

"Believe me, that's plenty enough responsibility," Kane answered.

"How about the company's greenhouse gas credits? Were you responsible for negotiating carbon contracts on behalf of the company with The Climate Exchange?"

"Yes. Because of my law firm's corporate contracting expertise, that work came my way too."

"After the company started up the Tacony plant, there were some operational problems, correct?"

"Yes, that's correct," responded Kane.

"Did you have any involvement in remedying those operational problems?"

"Everybody in the company had some level of responsibility. We were panicked because the company was losing money hand over fist."

"What exactly was your job in terms of getting the Tacony plant back up and running?" Senator Orlean asked.

"Well, I don't know that I ever got any specific instructions or anything like that. The idea was for everyone to work together to do whatever was necessary to get the plant back on line as quickly as possible."

"Tell me about this Consent Agreement," Senator Orlean demanded as a hearing officer handed Kane a copy of the document. Even though Kane was expecting the question, his face went blank nonetheless. He spent a good deal of time looking at the document, flipping pages back and forth.

"The president of Power Systems, John Braddon," Kane started, "was going berserk about the plant shut down. He told me that I was being paid for my political influence and that I should use it to get the plant restarted."

"Is that true, that you were being paid for your political influence?" Senator Orlean asked.

"Hell no. I brought much more to the company than that. But even so, any company, in order to be competitive nowadays, has to have some kind of lobbying power in Washington. It's a fact."

"I appreciate that, Senator," Orlean responded and then started flipping through the pages of the Consent Agreement to the end of the document. "That your signature there, Senator, on the last page?"

Kane took some time to move to the end of the document. "Yes, it is."

"Senator, the Director of the Office of Air and Radiation of EPA's Region II just testified. He says the EPA never entered into a Consent Agreement with Power Systems. He says this document is a fraud. A fraud perpetrated by you. What is your answer to that allegation?"

Kane again took his time before answering. "As I was saying, Braddon was hysterical about the shutdown. His investors were losing something on the order of a hundred thousand dollars a day. So, he told me to do whatever was necessary to get the plant restarted. After a few days, I told Braddon about the engineer's conclusion that the plant would not restart unless we vented the exhaust. I also told him that doing so required a permit under the Clean Air Act that could take up to eighteen months to obtain. His response was to ask whether we could 'finesse' something in the short term while the application for the permit was working its way through the process. I explained to Braddon that other companies in this kind of a predicament regularly entered into Consent Agreements with the EPA to cover that kind of situation. So, I recommended that we go use that process. The next day or so, I got a call from Braddon that he had signed a contract for the modification of the plant exhaust system. When I told Braddon that work couldn't begin until I had a Consent Agreement, he said that it was cheaper to operate in violation of the Clean Air Act."

"What do you mean?" Senator Orlean asked.

"He decided that paying the $25,000 a day fine under the Clean Air Act was cheaper than the loss the company was suffering waiting around for a permit or Consent Agreement. C'mon guys, this is nothing new. Companies make that kind of judgment call every day."

"Did this Mr. Braddon know that the company and its officers could be prosecuted criminally for that decision?"

"I assume he did. He was a sophisticated man."

"How do we get in touch with this Mr. Braddon?" asked Senator Orlean.

"You don't. He's dead. He had an accident at his beach home a few weeks ago," Kane answered.

"You still haven't explained, Senator Kane, how your signature got on this Consent Agreement," Orlean inquired.

"I was getting to that, if you would just give me a chance." All of those present in the hearing room noticed that Kane was now squirming. "I knew what Braddon was doing was way out of line. When I broached the subject with him, he said that Robert Stark was likewise bothered by inconsequential details."

"Who is Robert Stark, Senator?" Orlean asked.

"No, who *was* Robert Stark. He was an environmental compliance manager for the company who showed up very dead—murdered in fact—after telling John Braddon that he was going to blow the whistle on Power Systems."

"What are you saying, Senator Kane? This Mr. Braddon had something to do with Robert Stark's murder?"

"I can't be sure, but that's the message I read into his comment. It scared hell out of me for sure. I decided that the safer thing to do was to create that Consent Agreement so we had something to give to The Climate Exchange and get the company's credits activated."

"So you admit," Orlean said bluntly, "that what you did with this Consent Agreement was not only a violation of the Clean Air Act, but also an outright fraud?"

"No doubt, but I did it at the express direction of John Braddon, who was my superior and who, as far as I was concerned, had threatened me to do exactly what I did. What I did, I did under duress."

"Is there anyone who can corroborate your story, Senator?" Orlean asked.

"Only John Braddon," Kane responded with a shrug of his shoulders.

"That's what I thought you were going to say," Orlean said and then pondered his next question. "What would you say if I told you that John Braddon testified before a federal grand jury that you were the mastermind behind the exhaust system modification?"

"I'm not surprised," Kane answered, "that John Braddon may have testified against me. Think about it. It was his only chance. I'll bet the Department of Justice offered Braddon some kind of immunity. Okay, then. Braddon fabricates a story naming me as the bad guy in exchange for protection against criminal prosecution.

I'm sure he would have said anything once he realized that what he did could have put him behind bars. In fact, if the Department of Justice had come to me first, I might have done the same thing. Hell, I fabricated the Consent Agreement, right? Why not do the same thing in exchange for protection against a crime?" Kane leaned back in his chair knowing that the hammer was about to fall.

Senator Orlean made his move. "I'm suggesting this Committee make a motion to seek Senator Kane's resignation. Do I have anybody who will advance that proposal?"

"So moved," answered one of the committee members.

"Seconded?" asked Orlean.

"Seconded," answered another committee member.

"All those in favor?" asked Orlean. The entire committee responded "aye," including all of Kane's allies.

Senator Kane spoke up. "You can seek my resignation, but I won't step down voluntarily. Take whatever action you think is appropriate, but rest assured that I will put up a fight."

CHAPTER 31

Sean was grateful that Brendan Frisk had tipped them off to the fact that the Senate Committee on Public Works and the Environment was planning a hearing on the Climate Stewardship Act. Once Steve Cooperhouse figured out that the Consent Agreement was a hoax, Sean immediately set out to expose Senator Kane as a fraud. Sean decided to use the upcoming Senate hearing as a possible forum to accomplish his goal. He had called his long-time friend on the committee, Senator Orlean, who, like many others in the Senate, had no love lost for Senator Kane. When Senator Orlean heard the story, he welcomed the opportunity, and agreed that Brendan Frisk's testimony would be a good way to expose Kane's fabrication. For three days before the hearing, Senator Orlean met with Sean Murphy, Brendan Frisk, Steve Cooperhouse, and Rebecca Lockhart to devise the strongest possible presentation against Senator Kane. They were all quite nervous about the likelihood of success of their plan and whether keeping it silent the way they had would upset the other members of the committee.

Now that the hearing was over and the strategy had gone pretty much as planned, except for the part where Senator Kane had attacked Senator Orlean, they all breathed a sigh of relief. After Senator Kane left the hearing room, this time without the need for handcuffs, Senator Orlean met with a number of the other members of the committee to explain why he had kept silent about the plan against Senator Kane. He advised them that because of Kane's political strength, and based on the advice of Sean Murphy, surprising Kane with the testimony about the Consent Order was probably the better thing to do. He apologized for keeping his fellow senators in the dark but convinced them that the result they had achieved proved it was a successful strategy.

Senator Orlean then met with Sean, Steve, Rebecca, and Brendan following the hearing to apprise them of the fact that the committee would be issuing some form of press release about the day's events. Although, Senator Orlean was sure the media would be all over the hearing. "After all, it's not every day that two United States senators actually duke it out. You all know I could've kicked his ass." When they had finished laughing at Senator Orlean's assessment, Sean asked what the Senate would do, if anything, in light of Kane's testimony.

"Kane talked real tough at the end of the hearing there didn't he? 'I'm not resigning!'" Orlean mimicked. "I think Senator Kane has bigger things to worry about right now. I'm sure his law partners will have some tough decisions to make. My guess is he will probably be asked to resign from his firm. Plus, I suspect his actions will be reported to the Board of Bar Examiners. He could lose his license to practice law."

Steve asked Sean, "So, how do you feel now that Senator Kane is probably all washed up?"

"I don't know," Sean answered. "I'm having mixed emotions. On the one hand, I feel good about having exposed the fraud. It will bring some integrity to the process in the end, I'm sure. On the other hand, I feel sorry for the old coot. Blame it on my Christian duty of mercy and forgiveness."

Senator Orlean responded, "Folks, I don't think you need to feel too sorry for Senator Kane. Even if he gets disbarred, I know for a fact that he is sitting on a huge pot of money. He'll be just fine. If he just gracefully bows out, no one will be interested in him anymore. And that's what I think he'll do."

"You know what, Senator," answered Sean, "you're absolutely correct. I refuse to feel sorry for Kane. He got what was coming to him. It's a round world. I truly believe that. Kane's been dumping on others for so long that it was just a matter of time before he got dumped on. Yeah, I think Kane got what he deserved. Almost, anyway, I think."

"What do you mean?" asked Orlean.

"Well, people had a strange habit of showing up dead in this case." Rebecca and Steve nodded in acknowledgment. "First, there was Robert Stark, then Tom Roth, and finally John Braddon. Kane knew that Stark was going to blow the whistle on Power Systems. Braddon's secretary told me so. I'm not so sure about Tom Roth, but I remember the environmental guy there, Bob Morrone, saying something about having to call Kane if anyone from the EPA showed up for an inspection. I wouldn't be surprised if Kane knew about Tom's last visit to the Tacony plant. Plus, Braddon's secretary told me that all Power Systems employees, including Kane, knew that Braddon was vacationing at his beach house."

"Wait a minute!," Orlean interrupted. "Are you trying to say that Senator Kane is a murderer?" He began laughing heartily, to the point of almost choking. When Orlean regained his composure, he said, "You've got to be joking, right? Folks, Senator Kane as a corporate evildoer I agree with. Kane as a murderer, though," he started to laugh again. "You have to excuse me, but that has got to be one of the funniest things I have ever heard."

"I don't understand, Senator," Sean said.

"C'mon guys," Orlean responded. "Kane is a bad man, but he wouldn't have the guts it takes to commit murder. Look at the way he folded today under questioning at the hearing. Anybody who can commit murder would have been able to withstand a lot more than that scrutiny we gave Kane today."

"I'm not convinced, Senator," said Steve. "Sean makes a good point. Kane had a vested interest in seeing that power plant continue to operate. So, if he knew this guy Robert Stark was going to blow the whistle on the company, he had motive. Same thing with Roth and Braddon. The circumstances of their death is eerily linked to Kane."

"Folks, I've been in the Senate for many years with Kane and worked closely with him on the committee. I can see him going in the wrong direction for financial reasons. There's no way, though, that he had what it takes to commit murder. Let me ask you this. Are all of these cases you mention definitely classified as murders?"

"That's a good point you make, Senator," replied Sean. "Only the case of the former environmental compliance manager is a definite murder. The other two, Roth and Braddon, have been identified as accidents."

"There you go, then." Orlean said. "Trust me when I tell you that when you work as closely with a case as you folks have, for as long as you have, a lot of things can appear to be more than just coincidence. My guess is that the murder of this . . . what's his name. . . ." Sean reminded Senator Orlean of Robert Stark's name and position with Power Systems. "This Stark's murder, I'll bet, is totally unrelated to his plan to blow the whistle on the company, and the other two deaths are not murders at all. Just wait and see. Give yourselves a little time and distance from the case with Kane and you'll see how remote his actions are."

"You're probably right, Senator," Sean answered.

CHAPTER 32

Sean Murphy was troubled by a sense of unfinished business following the events at the Senate hearing. Sean spent the better part of the train ride back to Philadelphia trying to accept as final Senator Orlean's assessment of the coincidence, and nothing more, of Robert Stark's murder and the accidental deaths of Roth and Braddon. By the time Sean arrived back at his office, it was after 7:00 P.M. and his secretary had left him a package of telephone messages that needed returning, the idea of which was overwhelming. It was obvious from the number of calls he had received that the news of Senator Kane's demise at the committee hearing was in full play. At that hour, though, most of the people would have left the office and attempting to return them would have been futile. So, he decided that he would take care of them first thing in the morning, but the departing topic with Senator Orlean caused Sean to pick up the telephone and make one call before he left the office.

"Hello, Sands here."

"Charles, you're still in the office," Sean answered. "At least a few of us government attorneys feel a moral obligation to work late."

"Is this Sean Murphy?" asked Charles Sands, not entirely sure of the voice on the other end of the line.

"You got it, bud. How's the prosecuting business?"

"Messy, as usual. But busy. I heard you had an interesting day, Sean."

"News travels quickly, ah?"

"Indeed it does, my friend. Indeed it does," Sands responded. "So, what can I do for you, Sean?"

"Well, it's been a while since we last talked. I was just interested to hear if you came up with anything on that Power Systems employee you pulled out of the Delaware. Remember, Robert Stark?"

"Yeah, I remember him. My forensics people tell me that his body was probably dropped in by the base of the Tacony-Palmyra bridge and it drifted upriver to the point where he was found. He was dead a few days, maybe even a week. We got no leads from the body. So we started the usual investigation. I think I already mentioned to you that we met with his family. All of them said he had no enemies. He was kind of a loner. He hung out at home a lot—a real movie buff. His family told us that he had a regular routine of watching classic movies, pretty much every night, including on weekends. He didn't hang out at any bars, no girlfriend . . . nothing."

"So do you have any theory?" asked Sean.

"The only thing my forensics people can come up with is that this guy Stark was the target of some random armed robbery."

"Charles, the guy had a cargo hook in his back. You don't rob someone with a fucking cargo hook."

"I know, I know. One other thing we did was to follow up on the family's suggestion that Stark's murder was the subject of retaliation for 'ratting' out his company."

"But I thought you said your investigation indicated that Stark never went through with it," Sean reminded Sands.

"That's right," Sands said. "At the time, anyway."

"What do you mean?" Sean asked.

"Well, we had absolutely nothing to go on. So, I had one of my investigators go to the EPA offices with a picture of Stark that we got from his family. He showed the picture to all of the security guards. One of them recognized him, but couldn't say for sure that Stark came into the EPA office."

"I don't understand," Sean said. "Either Stark was there or he wasn't."

"Sean, it's never that easy. You know that better than anyone else. The security guards at the EPA offices probably see hundreds of people a day come through the security check point. The guard who recognized Stark's picture couldn't say for sure that he had been in to the EPA office or if the guard recognized Stark for some other reason."

"What about a visitor sign-in sheet?" Sean asked. "Doesn't the EPA require all visitors to sign in at the security check point?"

"Yes, they do." answered Sands. "But the rule of signing in is apparently honored more in the breach than in the compliance. So, anyway, we checked the sign-in sheets and didn't see any record of Stark's signature. My guess is, if he was ratting out Power Systems, he would have signed in under an alias."

"So, that was the end of the EPA part of it?" Sean asked.

"Not exactly. We figured that, because the security guard recognized Stark's picture, we would take the investigation down one more level."

"I don't follow," Sean responded.

"We showed Stark's picture to each of the directors in the office, thinking that if Stark had important beans to spill on Power Systems, it would have been at the director level."

"Did anyone recognize him?" Sean asked.

226

"No. So, that was the end of the EPA part of it."

"Is your investigation concluded then, Charles?" asked Sean.

"We have only one other possible lead," Sands answered.

"What's that?"

"We checked the video tapes from the cameras anchored on the Tacony-Palmyra Bridge. My investigators looked at the tapes for about a two week period in and around the time that Stark may have been murdered. The difficult thing is that the cameras are anchored in a way that you really can't see much outside the bridge lanes, but one camera has an angle that covers the south side of the bridge because of the on-ramp from Interstate Ninety-five. That angle gives you a glimpse of the river on the south side of the bridge. One of the tapes has a record of a late model Ford pick-up truck pulling up to the river just after 1:00 A.M. on a Sunday morning. Let's see, if I recall correctly, this would be the Sunday morning right after Stark was reported missing by his family, just about a day after. You can see from the video that a man gets out of the driver seat and starts throwing a bunch of debris into the river. You know, tires and wooden pallets, a few fifty five gallon drums. Right at the end, though, he throws a large rolled up carpet into the river. From the looks of it, the carpet weighed a lot."

"How can you tell that?" Sean asked.

"Well, my investigators tell me that this guy in the pick-up appears to be a pretty big dude. He was having no trouble with the tires and the drums. Then, when he picked up the carpet, or whatever it was, he fell backwards. He almost fell into the river. Then he leaned over and started to drag the carpet along the ground and you can tell from the video that he was really straining. He finally got it into a position where he could kick it into the river."

"This guy sounds like a midnight dumper. That's it," Sean commented.

"I'm not done. My investigators checked the area where this pick-up was located and found a ball point pen with the Power Systems insignia on it."

"No shit?" Sean blurted.

"No shit," Sands blurted back. "So, we're thinking that maybe Stark was murdered, wrapped in this carpet, and then dumped in the river by this pick-up truck driver. That's why we're trying to I.D. the pick-up truck. It's been difficult, though. The way the driver parked the truck, you can't get a good look at the license plate. Not that we would've been able to read it off the video, but we can't even get a start from a plate. So, we're using some of the other information available to us from the video. But I've got to be honest with you, Sean. I'm not holding out a lot of hope that we're going to get anywhere. The camera is not intended to cover that area. It's more of a situation where we lucked out because of the unusual angle of this one camera."

"Anything else?" asked Sean.

"Well, one of the routine things we do is check phone records. In the case of Stark, we reviewed both his home and office phones. Sure enough, his home phone showed a call to the EPA office two days before he was reported missing. It was around 2:30 P.M. So, he must have left his office and went home to make the call, which seemingly supports the theory that he was blowing the whistle on the company. Otherwise, he probably would have just used the office phone."

"Can you tell who he called at EPA?"

"No. Not really."

"Charles, what the hell does that mean?"

"All we can determine is that Stark called the Office of Air and Radiation. Unfortunately, the main line for that office within the EPA services about twenty five employees. So, we can't tell who within the office Stark was attempting to reach or whether or not he spoke with anyone in that office."

"Did you question the employees about whether they recognize Stark's name or recall speaking to him?"

"No, we haven't done that yet. Other pressing business, you know. I've had about ten new murders since Stark's. September was a busy month for murders. "

"God bless you, Charles. All right, then, good luck with your investigation. Let me know if you come up with anything or if you need my help in any way. Okay?"

"Will do. And congratulations to you and your team on breaking open that thing with Senator Kane."

CHAPTER 33

Rebecca spent a good deal of time poring over her Power Systems file before the Senate hearing. Documents from the file were scattered across her desk and on the floor next to it. When she got back to her office after the Senate hearing, the mess was too much for Rebecca to leave. She hated coming into a disheveled office in the morning. So, even though it was getting late, Rebecca decided to clean up before going home for the night. The last group of documents she gathered up off the floor, which was an indication of their lesser importance, was the seminar booklet and other materials from the "Carbon Expo" Rebecca had attended in Sydney, Australia. She was surprised to see that several months had passed since that trip. *Time flies when you're having fun,* Rebecca thought.

She flipped through some of the brochures, one of which was a collection of photographs taken during the expo. Rebecca hadn't noticed the photographs before, probably because she was exhausted by all of the seminars and discussions she had during the three day expo. Rebecca's saturation with the topics of greenhouse gases, global warming, and the carbon market had compelled her to stuff all of the expo materials in her suitcase without looking at them as she was leaving Sydney. Reflecting on them now, Rebecca was anxious to see if the photographer had taken any pictures of her. After flipping through a few pages, Rebecca came across a shot of her talking with Byron Russell, the British gentleman who told her the tragic story about how Enron caused the collapse of the Minnesota paperboard manufacturing plant. *He was a nice enough chap,* Rebecca pondered, making herself laugh at her feeble attempt to make the thought sound British. *Let's see if there are any other shots of me.* Rebecca continued to flip through the photographs. Toward the end, Rebecca noticed another group of pictures with Byron Russell and some of the other representatives of the European Union that she had met. One of the pictures in particular caught Rebecca's eye. *I recognize that guy.* She looked closer. *So, that's who it is. I didn't know he was at the expo.* Rebecca picked up the telephone and dialed. After four rings, the voice mail message kicked in.

"Hello, you have reached the office of Steve Cooperhouse. I am not in right now, but if you leave a message, I'll be sure to get right back to you."

After the tone, Rebecca said, "Steve, it's Rebecca Lockhart. I guess you went right home from Thirtieth Street Station. I'm too compulsive. I stopped in the office to clean up. I didn't know you were at the Carbon Expo in Sydney. I was there too. I saw a picture of you with Byron Russell. I spent some time talking with him and some of his colleagues in the European Union. Give me a call when you get in tomorrow. I want to compare notes about what you thought of them and how you think they are going to react to the Tacony plant shutdown. My recollection is that this guy Byron Russell had a huge chunk of money riding on carbon futures contracts for Power Systems credits. He's probably going to lose his shirt now that the plant is shut down. All right, talk to you soon."

As soon as Rebecca hung up her phone rang. She answered expecting it to be Steve Cooperhouse returning her message. "Hello, Steve?"

"No. It's your *boyfriend*."

"Sean. Hello, sweetie. I just left a message for Steve. I realized he went to that Carbon Expo in Sydney. Remember that trip I took."

"How can I forget? You billed me thousands of dollars for it."

"And I enjoyed every free minute of it. So, what's up?"

"I'm finishing up here—wiped out, you know. Are you coming over my place tonight?"

"I'd love to, but no. I have some house cleaning to do tonight. My place is a mess."

"Okay. I'd fight you about it, but I'm just too damn tired."

"Good. Go to bed early and get a good night's rest."

"How about I pick you up tomorrow morning and we grab some breakfast before work?"

"That sounds wonderful. You are such a dear. So, I'll see you around 6:00 A.M."

"Yep. See you then."

When they hung up, Rebecca turned her attention back to the few remaining documents on the floor by the foot of her desk. She stared at them for what seemed an eternity, not wanting to bend down to pick them up, which was the numbness setting in after a long day. There, at the bottom, was a sub-file containing the results of some research she had asked one of her young part-time associates to do on the European Union and Byron Russell following the Carbon Expo. Rebecca realized that she had never bothered analyzing the information. She summoned the energy to lean over, grab the sub-file, and opened it up. Flipping through documents, she noticed a lot of repetition of the things she had learned at the expo. In fact, the bulk of the documents were related to the outcome of the expo, one of which was a report on the fact that a number of contracts had been executed for carbon sequestration in Brazil and Canada. Rebecca then started to read a memorandum that the associate had prepared.

MEMORANDUM

To: RLockhart
From: DMacey
Re: European Union-Byron Russell

You asked that I gather background and biographical information on a Mr.
Byron Russell, who you met at the Carbon Expo in Sydney, Australia.
Mr. Russell is a graduate of Oxford University and resides in London,
England. He has a number of diverse business interests, including most
recently acting as a participating member of the International Petroleum
Exchange ("IPE"), which deals in, among many other things, brokering
futures contracts in the carbon market. The IPE recently joint ventured
with The Climate Exchange out of Chicago under which arrangement
greenhouse gas credits will be marketed to the members of the European
Union that are subject to the mandates of The Kyoto Protocol.

A Lexis/Nexis search revealed that Mr. Russell, and some other mem -
bers of the European Union, had been asked to participate in a task force
organized by the United Nations back in the late 1990s to investigate the
means by which to implement the "cap and trade" approach to controlling
greenhouse gas emissions contemplated by The Kyoto Protocol. I per -
formed a Freedom of Information Act review of the publicly available
records from the meetings of that task force. Interestingly, the transcript of
one of the meetings in 2000 contained a discussion of the operational prob -
lems encountered at the Power Systems Tacony facility. The following are
the relevant excerpts from that transcript:

Chairman: We understand the Power Systems facility is a technological
hallmark for the control of greenhouse gases and will serve in coming
years as a major contributor of credits to the carbon market.

Mr. Russell: That is correct, sir, and the members of the European Union
are encouraging Power Systems to begin using its patented furnace out -
side of the United States. My sense is the carbon market will evolve and
mature like any other market. In other words, the greater the supply of
greenhouse gas credits the lower the cost to the consuming members,
including most importantly those in the European Union that must
begin making plans to meet the requirements of the Kyoto Protocol.

Mr. Cooperhouse: While I agree with your assessment, Mr. Russell, you
should understand that the Power Systems electric generating facility,
which is under my jurisdiction as the director of the Office of Air and
Radiation at the EPA, has encountered some kind of unexplainable
operational problem. What has been reported to me is that the furnace
keeps shutting down involuntarily. The company is trying to find a rem -
edy as we speak. As of right now, though, the plant is not operational.

Mr. Russell: That report is truly disappointing to hear, Mr. Cooperhouse.
I'm not sure if you're aware, but the greenhouse gas credits generated

by Power Systems are going to be very important to many European countries' efforts to meet their requirements under The Kyoto Protocol. In fact, future credits from the existing Power Systems facili - ty are already dedicated to the European marketplace under certain carbon futures contracts. So, please keep us apprised of any develop - ments, especially if and when Power Systems finds a cure. In the mean - time, is there anything the company can do to get the facility restarted?

Mr. Cooperhouse: I don't know, but I'm glad to hear any suggestions, sir.

Mr. Russell: Perhaps we could meet with the owners of the Power Systems facility to see what help we may be able to offer.

Mr. Cooperhouse: I think a meeting is a good idea under the circum - stances. I wasn't aware of these futures contracts that you mentioned. I would like to get some more background information on those con - tracts and understand how they may be affected by Power Systems' cur - rent operational problems.

[END OF TRANSCRIPT]

A similar review of EPA records shows that a Mr. John Braddon of Power Systems met with Mr. Cooperhouse and Mr. Russell about a week after this task force hearing. Unfortunately, the EPA file had only two documents: (1) a sign in sheet with their names and the date of the meeting and (2) a Consent Agreement from a 1998 EPA enforcement action that, oddly enough, had nothing to do with Power Systems. My sense is that the Consent Agreement was simply misfiled by the EPA, which, in my experi - ence, happens all the time. The file contained no meeting minutes or other record to indicate what was discussed. So, I will need to speak with one or more of those in attendance at the meeting to gain an understanding of what was discussed. However, I did not want to take that step until I received further direction from you, especially on the issue of whether or not the research I am doing is privileged and confidential.

Let me know if you have any further research needs in this case.

❧ ❧ ❧ ❧

By the time Rebecca was done reading the memorandum, it was nearly 7:30 P.M. She knew from her last call to him that Steve Cooperhouse was not in his office, but figured she would leave another voice mail message anyway.

"Steve, I was just cleaning up my Power Systems file. I read for the first time a memo prepared by one of my associates. I understand now how you know Byron Russell. The memo discusses the global warming task force that you and Byron Russell participated in. It also mentions a meeting that you had with Russell and John Braddon. I was surprised to read about that meeting. I don't recall you ever mentioning it. I'm sure you told Sean about it, but I was just interested to hear what you talked about with Braddon and Russell. Apparently it had something to do with the Tacony plant shutdown. Well, sorry for the long message. Sean and I are getting together for breakfast tomorrow morning. I'll get an update from Sean then. Have a good evening and I'll talk to you soon."

Rebecca placed the Power Systems file in a cabinet, except for the memorandum, which she slipped into her briefcase.

◁ ◁ ▷ ▷

Although she had planned some chores around the house, Rebecca elected instead to slip into her sweat pants and sweatshirt and sink into her family room couch. She turned on the television and, after channel surfing for a few minutes, hit on Alfred Hitchcock's *Notorious.* No matter how many times Rebecca saw the movie, it always attracted her undivided attention because of the powerful kiss shared by Ingrid Bergman and Cary Grant when he arrives to rescue Ingrid from her murderous husband and mother-in-law. The scene had just finished, causing Rebecca to tear up slightly, as it always did, when her doorbell rang. Rebecca wiped her eyes on the sleeve of her sweatshirt as she walked to the door. Rebecca moved the door curtain aside to check who was there, as she always did and then, recognizing the face, unlocked the door and opened it.

"Steve, what are you doing here?"

"Well, I got your voice mail messages," he said, as Rebecca stepped aside to let Steve in. "I just thought I would stop by and talk with you about them."

"You didn't have to do that. It's nothing important."

"Is everything okay, Rebecca? It looks like you've been crying."

She laughed and answered. "Oh, yeah. It's that stupid movie *Notorious.* The kissing scene makes me cry every time." She and Steve laughed together and he handed Rebecca a handkerchief. "Thank you. Would you like something to drink?"

"Sure," Steve answered. "So you went to the Carbon Expo, too?"

"Yeah."

"And you met Byron Russell?"

"Uh huh. I talked with him and a few other members of the European Union at a cocktail reception on the last day of the expo."

"What'd you guys talk about?"

"Oh, let's see. It's been a while." Rebecca paused to think as she went to the refrigerator. "Is beer okay, Steve?"

"Sure. Sounds great."

"Byron Russell . . . Byron Russell." Rebecca said as she poured beer for both herself and Steve. "What the hell did we talk about?" Rebecca asked rhetorically. "Oh, right. I mentioned to him that I was assisting the Department of Justice with an investigation of the carbon market and the Power Systems facility. He told me this dreadful anecdote about how Enron was responsible for the demise of this little manufacturing plant that employed pretty much the whole population of a town in Minnesota."

"Yeah, I heard that one, too," Steve acknowledged.

"So, you know this guy Russell pretty well?"

"Yes. I've served on a global warming task force with him for a number of years."

"Right, right," she said, as both of them sipped their beer.

"Did Byron mention the carbon futures contracts?" he asked.

"Yeah, as a matter of fact he did. I was intrigued by the concept. Sounds like he takes on a lot of risk with those contracts," she said

"You have no idea," he replied.

Rebecca turned back toward the sink to put more beer in her glass. "You know, Steve. I was surprised to see that you had a meeting with John Braddon and Byron Russell about the Power Systems facility around the time it was having those operational problems. You never mentioned it to me. What did you guys talk. . . ." Rebecca turned back to offer Steve more beer. Clenched in his quivering hands, pointing at Rebecca, was a silver revolver. Steve had a look of panic on his face, with his eyes stretched wide open and sweat beginning to form on his forehead. "Steve, for Christ's sake, what are you doing?" Rebecca exclaimed.

"Keep it down, Rebecca. I don't want to hurt you."

"Steve, you're scaring me. Please put the gun away," she pleaded. Rebecca's heart was racing and pounding in her chest. She started to breath heavily and her legs became weak. She leaned forward onto the counter between her and Steve.

"Don't move," he cautioned. "I've never done this before, Rebecca. I don't want to hurt you."

"Then take the gun out of my face for the love of God," she pleaded again, as tears began to roll down her pale face.

"I can't do that. You know too much, Rebecca," he said.

"Know what?" she shouted back at Steve. "I have no idea what you're talking about!"

"I told you once to keep it down. Don't make me tell you again." The tone in Steve Cooperhouse's voice was notably sterner and more fierce than before.

"Okay, okay. Whatever you say, Steve," Rebecca answered submissively. "Please Steve, help me to understand."

He began to cry and removed his left hand from the gun to wipe the tears away. "It's those fucking carbon futures contracts! And that asshole Byron Russell. Oh shit! I never should have done it!"

"Done what Steve? Please tell me. Put the gun down and tell me."

"No! Just shut up. We have to get out of here Rebecca. We're going to have to take a ride. Where's your car parked?"

"No, Steve. Please no. Don't do this. Tell me first what it is that I'm supposed to know."

"I never thought it would go this far," he said.

"Steve, what do you mean by 'it'? Please tell me," she pleaded.

"We'll talk as we drive. There's a longshoreman you need to meet."

"No, Steve," Rebecca said through the uncontrollable sobs.

"You couldn't leave well enough alone. I had everyone convinced it was Senator Kane. God damn it! This shit is way out of control. I never . . . NEVER . . . thought it would go this far. Son-of-a-bitch!"

"Steve, please, if you would just talk to me," she said. "Maybe I can help."

"Shut the fuck up! Let's go. Move it. I want to get this over with."

Rebecca started to pray, "Hail Mary, full of grace, the Lord is with thee. Blessed art thou. . . ."

"I told you to shut the fuck up and move it. Now do it!"

They walked to the front door of Rebecca's house. The porch was pitch black. She walked out first with Steve behind, the gun pressed into Rebecca's lower back. With his other hand, Steve grabbed tightly onto Rebecca's long blond hair and nudged her toward the stairs. As she stepped down onto the first stair, Rebecca heard the sound of pounding footsteps rushing toward them.

Steve felt a piercing blow to his ribs, causing him to fold up into a fetal position. His hands involuntarily clenched into a fist. Steve felt his body flying through the air and heard the shot ring out. He could not breath. When Steve opened his eyes, Sean Murphy was poised above, his fist already on its downward path to Steve's face.

Sean rushed over to Rebecca, who was lying unconscious on the concrete walkway at the bottom of her porch steps, blood trickling from her stomach.

CHAPTER 34

When Rebecca awoke, she had that strange sensation of not knowing where she was. She looked above her head and noticed two intravenous bags. Rebecca slowly traced the tubes with her eyes from their origin at the bags to the point where they entered her left arm. Rebecca shifted in her bed and felt the searing pain in her stomach. She looked to the right and the sunlight streaming through the window forced her to squint. Her mouth was extremely dry. As Rebecca moved her head to avoid the sunlight, she noticed Sean in the chair next to the window, fast asleep. "What the hell is goin' on?" Rebecca said in a low whisper, her body so weak she couldn't muster up the energy for a normal voice. "Where am I?" Sean began to stir. "Sean? Sean, where am I?"

"Be quiet, sweetie," Sean answered, wiping the sleep from his eyes. "You're in the hospital, Becca."

"Did I do something wrong?" she asked.

"Everything's okay, Becca. Be still. Give yourself a few minutes, okay?" By this time, Sean had moved over to Rebecca's hospital bed and was standing over her, stroking her head.

Rebecca struggled to keep her eyes open. "I'm so weak, Sean."

"That's okay. Close your eyes, Becca. Everything's okay. Just relax."

"I'm so thirsty."

Sean grabbed a can of ginger ale on the table next to the bed and opened it up. He put a straw in it and placed it in front of Rebecca's mouth. "Here, honey. Here's some soda." Rebecca, keeping her eyes closed, leaned forward to drink and grimaced in pain. She fell back into her pillow and moaned. "Okay, take it easy," he said. Sean moved the straw over to Rebecca's lips and touched them lightly with it. She opened her mouth and started drinking. "Go easy, Becca. I don't want you to make yourself sick." After a few sips of soda, Rebecca opened her eyes again. "Look who's back," Sean said with a big smile on his face. Rebecca summoned a grin and went back to drinking.

"Sean, what happened? How did I get in here?"

"Let's not worry about that right now. Let's just get you better, okay?" Rebecca nodded and drank some more.

CHAPTER 35

Sean and Rebecca departed the marina just before sunrise on the last Saturday in October. It was an annual end of season fishing trip to the Delaware Bay that Sean had been taking with Steve Cooperhouse for the last ten years or so. However, with Steve in police custody, Sean needed another first mate. Sean had promised Rebecca when she was in the hospital that he would tell her the whole story once she was feeling better. Even though Rebecca's belly was still sore from the bullet wound, the two to three hour trip from Philadelphia to the Delaware Bay was a perfect opportunity for her to gain Sean's undivided attention.

The air was chilly, crisp, and still, just the way Sean liked it. The tide was up, and especially high because of the full moon, but moving out, which meant the trip down river would be swift. Soon after they were underway, the sun rose over the Jersey side, bringing into view on the west side of the river the multitude colors of the changing foliage lining the banks north of the city.

"So, Becca," Sean said, "are you ready for Halloween tomorrow? I know how you go hog wild over the kids."

"Yeah, as ready as I'm going to be, I guess. Being in the hospital slowed me down, but I had some time at home over the past few days to decorate and buy candy."

"Did you see I got you a big pumpkin for your jack-o-lantern? I left it on the side of the porch."

"Yes, yes. Thank you so much. It'll be the first thing I do when I get up tomorrow morning."

As they passed underneath the Betsy Ross Bridge, Sean noticed a pair of bald eagles circling overhead.

"Looks like we may be able to take them off the threatened and endangered species list soon."

"What are you talking about?" Rebecca asked.

"The bald eagle, you big dummy," Sean quipped at Rebecca jokingly, pointing up overhead to the birds.

"Oh, yeah, right. Sorry about that."

Sean continued, "We have done such a good job of bringing them back from the brink of extinction that we may finally be ready to take them off the list. Rachel Carson would be proud."

"You are so weird, Sean."

"I'm serious. Rachel Carson's book *Silent Spring* raised the national consciousness about the loss of bird species, including our national bird. I mean, think about it. We almost killed off our national bird. How freaking pathetic is that?" Sean was fired up by this time.

"Okay, you're right," Rebecca said as she glanced up. "Wow, they are beautiful, aren't they?" Sean pulled back on the throttle for a second and they both gazed up as the eagles flew overhead. They outlined an imaginary circle, occupying a point in space directly opposite one another. Despite their height above the water's surface, Sean and Rebecca could hear their high pitched call clearly and distinctly. After a minute or two watching, Sean put the boat back in gear and continued heading down river. They glided over the glass-like surface in silence for a good deal of time. The tree-lined banks gave way to the bulkheads and concrete revetments heralding their approach to the Philadelphia waterfront. Rebecca broke the silence.

"So, now that I'm feeling well again, Sean, you promised to tell me all about what I missed."

"You definitely feel better, right?" Sean asked. "You just got out of the hospital. I didn't think your coming on this trip was a good idea. It can be a bumpy ride this time of year. You may get jostled around today. Although, it looks like we may luck out and get a quiet day."

"Yes, I feel fine, Sean. My belly hurts a little, but I took my pain medicine. So, I'm good to go."

"You know, Becca, I can kiss that 'boo-boo' on your belly and make it feel all better."

"I'll bet you can, Sean."

"I can't promise, though, that I'll stop at the. . . ."

"SEAN! Stop it."

"Sorry, I got caught up in the moment there. So, you want to know what happened, huh? Where do you want to start?"

"The last thing I remember is coming out onto my porch with a gun pointed in my back. Steve was nuts that night. He kept saying something like I knew too much. Weird stuff. I was petrified."

"I bet you were," Sean said. "I would have been too. Let's see. Where should I start?" Sean paused to ponder his own question. "That night is probably as good a place as any. I really wanted to see you badly that night, if you know what I mean. The way things worked out with Senator Kane at the hearing had me riding on Cloud Nine. I was feeling somewhat . . . oh . . . anxious I guess would be the right way to describe it."

"Okay, okay. Move on please," Rebecca demanded.

"Well, you know me, Becca."

"Yes, Sean, I know you. You're in a constant state of hormonal overload. The hearing with Kane had nothing to do with it."

"You're probably right. Anyway, remember I called you at the office to see if you would come over my house?"

"Yes," she replied.

"We made plans for breakfast?" he asked similarly.

"Yes," she replied again.

"I figured screw it, I would go to your place. When I walked to the front door of your house, I noticed the television was on, but I didn't see you sitting on the couch. I thought you might have fallen asleep, and I didn't want to wake you by knocking on the door. So, I walked to the side window to get a better look at the couch. That's when I saw someone in the kitchen. I walked around to the back door and saw Steve holding the gun. You were leaning on the counter top, looking like you were about to pass out. I couldn't believe my eyes."

As Sean was talking, they passed the mouth of the Schuylkill River and the Philadelphia Navy Yard, stopping along the way to observe the immensity of the moth-balled destroyers. Then it was on to one of Sean's favorite parts of the trip. Just south of the Navy Base, Sean placed the boat in idle and let it drift with the current. Before long, he saw one coming.

"Here we go, Becca."

"What? What are you talking about?" she asked.

Sean reached his hands up in the air as a monstrous 757 came in for a landing at the Philadelphia International Airport. They could feel the percussion of the engines as the airplane whipped by overhead. Sean screamed at the top of his lungs, his voice slowly becoming audible with the declining decibels from the jet engines. When it was all done, Sean put the boat back in gear and continued on the journey. Rebecca shook her head, smiling the whole time.

"So, I watched for a few minutes and debated what to do. I wanted to bust into the kitchen, but I was afraid that it might set Steve off and cause someone to get hurt. Then, Steve started leading you to the front of the house. I figured that would be my chance to intervene. I crept up the stairs leading from the portico to the porch. It was only a few seconds later that you emerged with Steve following you. I couldn't see anything because it was so dark, but I could tell from the shadows that Steve was behind you and he had a hold of your hair. Frankly, I didn't know he still had the gun aimed at you."

"He had it jammed in my back," she said.

"Yeah, I realize that now, but I didn't know at the time. Anyway, instinct set in. It had been a long time since I hit someone like that, but it came back to me just like riding a bike. I bolted across the porch and lit his ass up! Shattered two of his ribs, you know. I heard them breaking when my shoulder hit them."

"Sean, please stop. I can't stand it when you talk like that. Please move on."

"Sorry. You know how I react to a good hit. Geez, the last time I hit anybody like that was this running back from Iowa. Popped his shoulder right out of the socket. His arm was just. . . ."

"SEAN! You're making me sick to my stomach."

"Never mind. After that, I introduced Steve to the Murphy way of life. Knocked him out and broke his jaw in the process. Felt like I was back in the old neighborhood. Typical Saturday night at the Murphy house on South Sixth Street."

"Okay, then," Rebecca interrupted as a means of getting Sean back on track. "How about the more important part of the story? What the hell happened? Why did Steve have a gun pointed at me?"

"Let me finish. I'll get to that part soon. Like I said, I didn't know he still had the gun on you. When I hit him, he accidentally squeezed the trigger and shot you in the lower back. The bullet went right through you."

"Not exactly. I lost my spleen and some of my intestine."

"Oh, suck it up. Those organs aren't that important. Hell, people sacrifice their spleen all the time. I remember this one time. . . ."

"Sean, I don't want to hear about how you hit someone so hard that he lost his spleen." Sean shrugged his shoulders. "Plus I lost intestine, Sean, not just my spleen."

"Okay, I'll give you that. You lost a lot of blood too. We almost lost you there, Becca. That's why I didn't want to talk with you about this while you were in the hospital. I needed you to get better."

"You 'needed' me?" Rebecca inquired with a touch of sarcasm in her voice.

"Don't be so. . . . Yes, of course. Now you know. I need you, okay. Can I continue?" Sean said with an equally sarcastic tone.

"Go ahead," she answered smiling the whole time Sean was stammering.

"Well, Steve was hospitalized with a broken jaw so he couldn't talk for a while. Charles Sands and I visited Steve the day after he was hospitalized. Even though he couldn't say it, I could tell that Steve was not happy to see me."

"I'll bet," Rebecca said. "Why did Steve pull a gun on me like that? What did he mean about my knowing too much?"

"The short answer, Becca, is that Steve was unwittingly caught up in the fraud surrounding the Power Systems operation."

"No way," Rebecca responded.

"Regrettably, yes. Much more so than even Senator Kane."

Passing beneath the Commodore Barry Bridge, the oil refineries dotting the banks of both sides of the Delaware River slowly began to give way back to natural foliage, heavily populated with a wealth of bird species. For the first time since moving south of the Philadelphia waterfront, Sean and Rebecca could see stretching out in front of them the vast, almost unending, wall of autumnal colors. "Maples are the first to turn," Rebecca observed as she pointed out to Sean the bright red leaves offset against the primarily yellow background.

"Explain it to me, Sean. How did somebody like Steve get caught in that web?"

241

"Money."

"Money?" Rebecca asked, obviously surprised by Sean's response. "Steve Cooperhouse? Money? That just doesn't sound right, Sean," Rebecca commented.

"Actually, Becca, I wasn't as surprised as you are. Don't get me wrong. I've known Steve my entire adult life and I love him dearly. He was always good to me. But I know he struggled for a long time with his inability to reach a certain financial success. He came from a well-to-do family. In fact, I know Steve's father was always pushing Steve to change professions or do something else with his life because the government offered a paltry salary. Not only that, but Steve was used to living according to a fairly high standard. His position with the EPA just wasn't paying very well. I know Steve was constantly looking for ways to use his experience and even his position at the EPA as a means to make more money."

"How's that?" Rebecca asked.

"In his position, Steve was privy to the latest environmental technologies, and there are a lot of them. What I mean is many new environmental technologies require the EPA's approval before they can hit the marketplace. And every new environmental technology, without fail, is touted as being the next best thing since sliced bread. You know, guaranteed to make unprecedented profits. Steve would get sucked in. He was always investing in new environmental technologies that would come along. I remember one time this madman from Arizona bought an old mine."

"You mean like a gold mine or something like that?" Rebecca asked.

"Yeah, but I can't remember exactly what was being mined. Anyway, the mine is not what this guy was interested in. It was something known as 'mine tailings.' As I understand it, based on what Steve explained to me, after the raw ore is mined, it is processed and the waste product left behind is called 'mine tailings.' This madman supposedly came up with a way to recycle the 'mine tailings' and use the material in building roads and airport runways. He sold Steve on the idea and, before you know it, Steve handed this guy $45,000 in cash to become an equity partner in this Arizona business enterprise."

"Let me guess how this one turned out," Rebecca interrupted. "After a couple of months, the company was no longer in existence and neither this madman nor Steve's money could be found."

"That's right. I remember that one pretty well because of the amount of money Steve lost, but there were many more of those situations. I'd venture a guess that in the thirty years or so that Steve was in the EPA he called me at least once a year with another 'great opportunity.' Steve would call me every time a new opportunity came along that he thought would be a money maker, you know, to give me a chance to get a piece of the action. Steve is a wonderful scientist, but he is not a businessman. I don't say that to demean him in any way. Hell, I'll be the first to admit that I'm not a businessman. The difference between me and Steve, though, is that Steve thought he had this business sense. But he didn't. Steve lost more money on these 'hare-brained' business schemes than. . . . Well, suffice it to say he lost a good deal of dough over the years."

"So, I assume that Steve was asked to invest in this Power Systems company?" Rebecca surmised.

"Not exactly. Not like the other situations, anyway, where Steve had a legitimate investment in a company that simply failed. What happened here was much worse, and Steve was in deep water before he knew what was going on. When Steve was finally able to talk again, Charles Sands and I had a long conversation with him. He didn't resist or try to put up any kind of legal fight. I think he knew that he was in a world of shit and the only way out was to cooperate. Turns out that Steve worked very closely with this guy from England, Byron Russell. He and Steve first met as members of a global warming task force that was established by the United Nations back in the late 1990s. The main purpose of the task force was to establish methods for participating countries to comply with the requirements of The Kyoto Protocol. Even though the United States was not a participating member, the United Nations wanted a representative from the U.S. on the task force, I guess along the lines of wishful thinking."

"What do you mean by that?" Rebecca asked.

"The United Nations wants to encourage the United States to ratify The Kyoto Protocol. Asking the United States to have a representative on the global warming task force is just one of many tools that the United Nations was and is using to persuade ratification by the U.S. Anyway, getting back to Steve, he met Byron Russell as part of this task force. Soon after they began working together, the IGCC technology became a topic of discussion for the task force. It was trying to encourage the development and use of the technology as a means of electric generation world-wide because of the reported 'zero emissions.' As you can expect, the task force viewed this novel technology as a panacea for the mandates of The Kyoto Protocol."

"You mean, all of the greenhouse gas credits that would be generated by using this technology on a broader scale would give countries subject to The Kyoto Protocol an easy method of complying. Is that right?" Rebecca asked.

"Yes. Rather than restricting industries on carbon dioxide emissions and other greenhouse gas emissions, countries subject to The Kyoto Protocol could just purchase credits generated by these 'zero emissions' facilities."

"And," Rebecca began to speculate, "I assume Byron Russell and Steve Cooperhouse picked up on the financial windfall that would be coming to those investing in the ICGF technology."

"Not quite. Well, Byron Russell did, but Steve wasn't aware of the opportunity as a result of his activities on the task force. This is where the Power Systems situation is a little different than some of the other stupid financial situations Steve got himself into in the past. Here's what we learned from Steve's interrogation."

"You interrogated Steve?" Rebecca asked.

"Actually, I couldn't do it. This whole situation was too painful for me. So, I left the interrogation up to Charles Sands. I sat in on it, though. Steve told us that, during one of the task force meetings, the Power Systems technology came up for discussion. Steve mentioned to the task force the circumstances of the Tacony plant shutdown. Byron Russell suggested to Steve that they get together and discuss how to assist Power Systems in getting the Tacony plant operational again. Here's where the story gets good, Becca. Byron Russell had already huge dollars into carbon futures contracts when the Tacony plant started to experience problems. Plus, Byron Russell apparently knew about Steve's willingness to make investments in environmental technologies. He obviously did his homework. Byron Russell mentioned to Steve that there were serious bucks to be made in these carbon futures contracts, a number of which Russell had already negotiated with The Climate Exchange. It's obvious that Byron Russell's intention in meeting with Steve and Power Systems representatives was to protect this investment he had already made in the carbon futures contracts, but Steve didn't see that. He was blinded by an opportunity to make a quick and sizeable profit. So, this whole situation boiled down to Russell viewing Steve as an easy target to accomplish the goal of protecting Russell's investment."

"I don't follow you, Sean."

"We subsequently learned from documents supplied by Brendan Frisk that Russell had tens of millions invested in these carbon futures contracts with The Climate Exchange and they all were involving the Power Systems credits. When we got hold of the contracts, we learned that Russell stood to make almost twenty times the amount of his investment. I'm talking huge sums of money. But, with the Tacony plant out of operation, Byron Russell was going to lose everything. So, Russell had a meeting with Steve and John Braddon right after the Tacony plant started to have the operational problems. It was Russell's team of experts that came up with the idea of a modification to the exhaust system. He convinced Steve and John Braddon to allow the exhaust system modification to take place quickly in exchange for an equity share in the profits from the carbon futures contracts that Russell had negotiated with the Exchange. It was at this meeting that Russell, Steve, and Braddon conceived the plot of using a fake Consent Agreement."

"But," Rebecca interrupted, "Senator Kane admitted that the fraudulent Consent Agreement was his idea."

"Not quite. Remember Kane's testimony at the hearing. He said that John Braddon was putting pressure on Kane to do something to get the plant up and running again. Steve told us that John Braddon actually put the idea of the Consent Agreement in Senator Kane's head. Kane was an easy fall guy, too; his profit was linked to the amount of credits sold. So, Kane stood to make a good deal of money on these carbon futures contracts also. Kane tried to testify about John Braddon's pressuring him at the Senate hearing, but it didn't go too far. At the time, we thought Kane was the bad guy."

"Are you saying our focus on Senator Kane was wrong?" Rebecca asked.

"No. He made a huge mistake and got what he deserved, but he was unwittingly sucked into Russell's scheme. In other words, Kane was not the sole bad guy that we thought he was when we put together that hearing with Senator Orlean. Steve told us that he came up with the idea of a Consent Agreement at the meeting with Braddon and Russell. After that, it was just a matter of putting Kane on the right trail, which apparently Braddon handled exceedingly well."

"By the way, what happened with Kane?" she asked.

"He did just as Orlean predicted. He resigned from the Senate and his law practice. He's probably in the Cayman Islands chasing trim."

"Sean, you're such a pig! So, let me see if I follow. Steve gets enticed by Russell's offer, and he conspires with Russell and Braddon to cover up the modification to the exhaust system. Kane turns out to be the sucker in the whole scheme?"

"Yep."

"Why did Steve stay so active in the EPA investigation, though? You would think he would have shied away from getting too involved."

"Just the opposite," Sean corrected Rebecca. "Think about it. By staying close to the case, Steve was able to watch you, me, and Tom Roth closely to see if we had uncovered anything about his conspiracy with Russell and Braddon. We never really did uncover anything, so Steve's strategy worked. Plus, if you look back at the investigation, Steve was always pointing us in the direction of Senator Kane, which is something I jumped all over because of my boneheaded need for revenge. Steve orchestrated things to perfection. But then all hell broke lose when Robert Stark came in to meet with Steve."

"Stark met with Steve?" Rebecca asked, the surprise in her voice distinct and clear.

"Yes. I was surprised to hear that too. Remember, we suspected Stark was going to blow the whistle on Power Systems from the letter they found on his home computer, but it never went any further than that. Steve admitted that Stark came in to meet with him, which confirms a suspicion Charles Sands had."

"How's that?" Rebecca asked.

"Sands was having no luck with his investigation of Stark's murder. So, he started going through some routine procedures, one of which was to show Stark's picture to the EPA security guards. One of the guards recognized Stark's picture, but couldn't be sure. Our guess is that Stark presented himself to the security people under an alias. Stark told Steve that he discovered the exhaust system modification during the course of some routine system maintenance Stark was overseeing. Stark blew the whistle. Steve told us that he called Braddon and told him about Stark's report. The next thing Steve knew, Stark showed up dead. Not just dead, but murdered. It wasn't hard for Steve to connect the dots. He knew that either Braddon or Russell was behind it. More likely Russell, in Steve's view. Plus, after Stark's body was discovered, Russell called Steve directly and said something to the effect that nothing further should come up, which scared the hell out of Steve."

"Sean, what about Tom Roth?" Rebecca asked. "Didn't you hear from the Bucks County Prosecutor that his death was under investigation because of suspicious circumstances?"

"That's right. Here's where it gets tough for Steve. Even though he wasn't actually *told* about a plan to 'off' Robert Stark, there was no question in Steve's mind when Stark showed up in the river that either Russell or Braddon, or both, were responsible. The connection was too compelling because of Stark's knowledge of the exhaust system modification. Steve admits it. Anyway, as you may recall, shortly after Stark showed up dead, I pulled Steve into the investigation of the Power

Systems facility because of the environmental issues that Charles Sands discovered in the company's file. Steve admitted that when I came to him, he had suspicions about Stark's murder and that Russell and Braddon may have been responsible, but Steve said he had to act as though it was business as usual. He was nervous about what had just happened to Stark. At this point, Steve knew he was in over his head. So, he put Tom Roth on the case, thinking that it's what I would've expected. And Steve is right about that. Whenever I got Steve involved in a case, I always expected him to put his best people on it. Plus, he had been assured by Russell that nothing further was going to come of the case. Steve never expected Tom Roth to discover what he did, but that's the way Tom Roth operated. He had an instinct for those kinds of things. Steve panicked when Tom discovered the pipe trench and called Braddon, who I believe must have called Russell. By this time, Russell was keeping a daily watch on our investigation, according to Steve. Actually, Steve told us that he was reporting hourly on some days to Braddon, including the day that Tom Roth visited the Tacony plant and found the pipe trench."

"So, what you're saying is that Russell is responsible for Starks' and Tom Roth's death?" inquired Rebecca.

"I think so, but Charles Sands hasn't put together any conclusive evidence of that theory yet. Sands tried to get Russell in to the United States for an interrogation, but he refuses to submit. He is represented by counsel now so Sands is having a difficult time getting access to him. Sands is good, though. I'm sure he'll eventually break that situation down. He has some video tape evidence regarding a pick-up truck by the Tacony-Palmyra Bridge dumping what might be Stark's body into the river. Hopefully, Sands will be able to make an identification of the driver and link him back to Russell."

"What about Braddon?" Rebecca asked.

"Steve thinks Byron Russell had Braddon killed too. So does Charles Sands, although that one is for the authorities on Long Island. I know that Charles Sands is sharing all of his information with them. My guess is that, when Braddon testified before the grand jury against Kane, which obviously was a scheme to deflect our attention from the real culprits, Russell had the protection he needed. He had no further use for Braddon at that point and Braddon was a continuing liability. You know, someone who could 'dime out' Russell if necessary. It's just a theory."

"I hear what your saying," Rebecca answered. "But if that's true then Russell would have done the same thing to Steve, right?"

"I suppose, but I think Russell viewed Steve as less of a liability than Braddon. I suspect Braddon knew a lot more than Steve.

"So, why did Steve come after me?" she asked.

"After the hearing, you called Steve to mention something you had found in your Power Systems file."

"Yeah, I noticed from the Carbon Expo stuff that Steve knew Byron Russell, who I had met for the first time at the expo. Come to think of it, Russell mentioned to me that he knew somebody from the EPA. Must have been Steve he was talking about. I also found a memo that mentioned a meeting between Steve, Russell, and Braddon. So, I called Steve to ask him about that stuff."

"That's what set him off," Sean observed. "When Steve got that message, he called Byron Russell. He told Steve to sit tight and Russell would have you taken care of . . . 'quickly and quietly,' I think was the phrase Steve used. As odd as this may sound, Steve wanted the craziness to stop at that point. He knew by this time, with what happened to Starks, Roth, and Braddon, that Byron Russell was going to harm you in some way to shut you up."

"But when I called Steve, I didn't know he was conspiring with Russell!"

"I know that. The problem is Steve didn't know you were unaware when you called. Your message was the proverbial straw that broke the camel's back. Steve immediately became suspicious that you were on to him. It may have had something to do with the way we pulled the rug out from under Senator Kane earlier in the day. It went down so easy, you know. So, Steve's knee-jerk reaction to your message was that he was next in line and we were trying to set him up."

"What you're saying, Sean, is Steve pulled a gun on me for my own protection? Is that right?"

"I know it sounds crazy, Becca, but that's what Steve says. And, I gotta tell you, I believe him. When he thought Russell was planning something bad for you, just like Stark, Roth, and Braddon, Steve lost control. He actually came to your house to get you out before Russell could do you any harm. Steve didn't think he had the time to explain everything to you and convince you to leave the house. So, he came up with the hare brained scheme of threatening you as a means of getting you to leave the house. Steve told us that he wanted to explain the situation to you, but the more immediate thing to do was to get you to a safe place. He had no intention of harming you. He was ready to confess."

"Sean, I have a bullet hole in my stomach. Don't tell me Steve had no intention of harming me."

"Unfortunately, I think you have me to blame for that. I wasn't thinking, Becca. Like I said, instinct took over. Before I knew it, I was slamming by shoulder into Steve's rib cage. He accidentally squeezed the trigger when I hit him. He really didn't intend to shoot you, Becca. Hell, I don't think Steve even really knows how to use a gun."

"So, where's Steve now?" Rebecca asked.

"He's in Graterford Prison," Sean answered, "awaiting arraignment. The Bucks County Prosecutor was originally planning on bringing attempted murder and conspiracy charges against Steve. I don't think that's likely, though. I know they have been talking about giving him a break for his cooperation."

"What do you think he will be charged with?" Rebecca asked.

"Hard to say, but because of what happened at your house, he was not granted bail. The judge viewed Steve as a likely risk of flight. Given Steve's state of mind recently, I tend to agree with the judge on that one. My guess is he will certainly be charged with federal crimes. I don't think he'll be charged with anything related to Stark's murder, or Roth and Braddon, assuming the investigators come up with some leads that they were also killed. Everyone seems to believe Steve that he had no knowledge of any murder plot. At the end of the day, Steve will probably plead out to some federal crime and do some probation. It will be a long time before he can find a descent job again, if at all."

"At the outset, Sean, you said Steve did it for the money. How much?"

"That's the rub," Sean answered. "He never made a dime. Byron Russell promised to give Steve a percentage of the profits from the carbon futures contracts, assuming that at some point they would start paying out, but they never did start paying out because the Tacony plant shut down. So, Steve will never see any money. The flip side of that is Russell is going to lose everything. He used those carbon futures contracts as a means of leveraging money for a host of other investments. Without those contracts, Russell's financial empire is crumbling."

"So, what's next Sean?"

"What do you mean?"

"For you, what's next?"

"Well you know I announced my resignation." Rebecca nodded in acknowledgment. "I didn't like the way the Attorney General submitted to Senator Kane's pressure. It was the first time that ever happened to me, but that was enough. I can't work for an agency that's so politically whimsical. A lot of people told me to blow it off, especially considering it was the first time it ever happened. But I don't operate that way."

"So what are your plans?"

"I offered to stick around for a month, assuming they need me to finish up some of the larger cases I'm handling."

"Were they surprised?" Rebecca asked.

"Hard to say. I know the other attorneys in the office and my secretary were shocked. But, I don't think the attorney general was surprised. As soon as he heard that I had continued the Power Systems investigation against his direct order, he wanted me out. I'm done anyway."

"What do you mean by 'I'm done?'" Rebecca asked with a clear sense of frustration. "I hate it when you talk like that, Sean."

"I've accomplished everything I can in this position. Things are becoming repetitive."

"How can you say that when you just brought down a corrupt United States Senator and broke open a huge conspiracy in the air pollution trading market? Aside from the hole in my stomach, that was the most exciting case I've ever worked on," Rebecca commented.

"Agreed," Sean answered. "But that case is the exception to the rule. Most of what I do nowadays is just 'same old, same old.' Plus, I'm not convinced that what I'm doing with the Department of Justice is the right thing."

"There you go again. What the hell do you mean by that comment?"

"I don't know. Enforcing all these environmental laws. I'm not sure it's making an impact."

"Bullshit, Sean. We just saw two bald eagles flying over the Delaware River, which, if you recall, was a cesspool when you and I were kids. The only thing flying over the river back then was airplanes, cutting through impenetrable smog."

"I know, I know. But I'm talking about something different. It was easy to clean up that mess. It was so bad that any effort, no matter how small, was bound to yield noticeably good results."

"So what are you talking about? What is this 'something different?'"

"It's hard to explain," Sean said quietly.

"Try me," Rebecca retorted.

"Well, the late '70s were truly the golden years for me. Everything was still fairly new in the environmental protection world. Actually, Steve and I spent most of our time together shutting down steel mills in Pittsburgh. But then I spent most of the '80s fighting with Philadelphia lawyers over the Federal Superfund. Most of the money in Superfund went to legal costs and not much on actual cleanup. Then, in the '90s, there were times when I was sitting around the office with nothing to do. There was almost no environmental enforcement activity for stretches of a year or so some times. This Power Systems case was a welcome challenge. On balance, I don't know that my work has resulted in a measurable benefit. Plus, I can't stand the politicization of the environmental process."

"How's that?" Rebecca asked.

"I'm no good at politics, Becca. You know that. Politics take a lot of finesse. I'm a bull in a china shop, most of the time anyway. In this environmental world, you have to have political smarts to be successful."

"Yeah," Rebecca acknowledged, "I agree with you there."

"It seems like environmental protection is in a great stall," Sean said. "And it has been for a while now. It is a topic that has become nothing more than a political football. Every election year we hear new ideas about environmental protection strategies, but nothing different ever happens. It's been a long time, Becca, since something as monumental as the cleanup of the Delaware River. We are simply resting on our laurels now." Sean paused a second and then continued. "But that's not the only thing."

"What do you mean?" responded Rebecca.

"I'm tired, Becca . . . tired of . . . fighting. It seems like that's all I've done since I was a kid . . . fighting. I can recall growing up and having a fist fight once a week . . . hell, at least once a week. Next thing I know I'm in courtrooms everyday fighting Fortune 100 companies and their high power attorneys." Sean paused a second becoming obviously upset by what he was about to say. "Even my marriage was a battle, Becca. God knows I loved Mary, but life with her was a constant battle between the miscarriages and then losing little Kristin. Maybe it's my age or something. I don't really know. But I look back on my life, Becca, and I don't recall a single week going by where I wasn't in some kind of raging fury. James Joyce wrote in *Dubliners* that it's 'better to pass boldly into that other world in the full glory of some passion, than to fade and wither dismally with age.' Lord knows I believe in that way of thinking and I've tried to live my life that way, Becca, but I just don't seem to have the energy any more."

"Well, Sean, I can't say I understand what you are feeling, but I have to admit you look tired, probably for the first time since I've known you." Rebecca watched Sean as he piloted the boat, an activity that seemingly gave him at least some minimum amount of peace. "Sean, you should take advantage of this time you have to think about what you want to do with the rest of your life. You're still young." Sean smiled as Rebecca continued. "Think back to when you were a kid. Is there something in your youth that you always wanted to, but just never had the chance?"

Sean pondered Rebecca's question for a few seconds and answered with a grin on his face. "Well, Becca, I always thought I would have made a great rock star." They chuckled together for a long time.

As they entered the Delaware Bay, an easterly breeze swamped them with brackish air. Sean and Rebecca lifted their heads and sucked in a chestful of it, slowly releasing the salty mix after a thorough cleansing of their lungs. Sean idled the boat engine, walked to the bow, and tossed the anchor into the water. The sun, now bringing much more warmth than when they departed the marina, caused them to remove the sweatshirts they had been wearing for the ride. Sean baited both his and Rebecca's hooks and cast their lines into the water. A good sized striper leaped from the water and snagged a snack. They smiled at each other with the expectation that today would probably be a good day.

AFTERWORD

Environmental protection in the United States, in the form of governmental legislative "command and control," has its roots in the *parens patriae* doctrine, which means the state acting in its capacity as the legal guardian of persons or things, such as natural resources, that are incapable of caring for themselves. *Parens patriae* evolved, in the limited area of natural resource protection, into what is commonly known as The Public Trust Doctrine principally as a result of an 1877 United States Supreme Court decision in the case of *McCready v. Virginia*. There, the State of Virginia was attempting to prevent a resident of a neighboring state from planting oysters in Virginia's tidal waters. The Supreme Court, upholding Virginia's right to exclude non-residents from this oyster planting practice, held that natural resources are the equivalent of a common property right of the citizens of a state and that the government, as a sort of "trustee," must regulate the use of this common property right for the benefit of those citizens ("[The grant of power over the fisheries] remain under the exclusive control of the State, which consequently has the right, in its discretion, to appropriate its tide-waters and their beds to be used by its people as a common for taking and cultivating fish. . . . Such an appropriation is in effect nothing more than a regulation of the use by the people of their common property."). Embodied in The Public Trust Doctrine is thus the assumption that the "state," or government generally, is best equipped to implement measures designed to protect the environment and all its biological inhabitants.

The first bold congressional step incorporating The Public Trust Doctrine into codified law was the adoption of the River and Harbor Act of 1894, which authorized the Secretary of what was then known as the Department of War to "prescribe rules for the use, administration, and navigation of the navigable waters of the United States as in his judgment the public necessity may require for the protection of life and property. . . ." As originally adopted, the River and Harbor Act included provisions specifically dealing with "pollution of the sea by oil," and "pollution

251

control of navigable waters." Like the United State Supreme Court's motivation in the decision of *McCready v. Virginia*, the aim of the pollution control provisions of the River and Harbor Act was not so much the preservation of natural resources as it was the protection of commerce: the federal government realized that pollution of navigable waters was interfering with the flow of interstate commerce.

While much of this historical body of Public Trust Doctrine law is founded on the principle of protecting a citizen's economic or business interests flowing from natural resources, and not merely protecting the environment as a goal itself, this doctrine nonetheless served as a perfectly well-oiled springboard for Congress when it decided to adopt a broad ranging federal environmental legal system in 1970. Unlike predecessor policy and law, which was mainly economically slanted, this new legal system had as it its principal goal protection of the environment and its natural resources. However, the economic fabric underlying The Public Trust Doctrine poured over into this federal environmental legal system in the form of a "right to pollute." That is to say, although not expressly stated, Congress recognized that, according to historical public policy and law, the citizens of the United States "own" the environment and all of its natural resources and thus should be permitted to degrade the environment to the extent economically necessary. Indeed, to this day, with a few rare exceptions, consideration of any new environmental law includes a cost-benefit analysis, which weighs the projected economic impact on regulated industry to comply against the projected environmental benefit to be gained by the public as a result of the proposed legislation. If the case can be made that the economic cost of complying is too significant, the proposed environmental law will either be scrapped or its standards whittled down and relaxed to the point where the projected economic impact is lessened. While this process may be subject to criticism, especially by the "deep ecologists" who believe we should let the natural word revert back to control by the bugs and bunnies, it acknowledges an inevitable fact of life: we must pollute to live.

What this new environmental legal system did was to put into the hands of a large government bureaucracy—specially and expertly staffed with scientists, policy makers, and, of course, lawyers—the question of how much we need to pollute to live. As with any large government bureaucracy, without particular fault on anyone's part, it didn't take long for the laudable goal of environmental protection to fall into the same dismally unfriendly categorical topics as taxes, welfare and social security. Environmental protection simply became another government mandated program, despite the good and honorable intentions of those involved with the day-to-day efforts of implementing the environmental laws . Agencies tasked with protecting the environment fell prey to the same pitfalls as any other government agency: insufficient funding, understaffing, and too much work. This unfortunate dynamic, combined with overly zealous regulation in certain circumstances, resulted in either inaction or improper action a good deal of the time.

Given these inadequacies, it wasn't long after the establishment of this national system of environmental protection that it became bogged down in the courts. Environmentalists file suits against the government claiming that it is not carrying out the mandates of the legislation, and that the environment is suffering as a result, whereas the regulated community challenges virtually every new rule that government adopts to satisfy the environmentalists. In the meantime, courts are stuck in the middle struggling with the proper equitable balance needed to achieve the original intents and purposes of the environmental laws and regulations, which simply is to stem the tide of pollution.

What is pollution, anyway? Webster's Dictionary defines it as "an undesirable state of the natural environment being contaminated with harmful substances as a consequence of human activities." But, what is undesirable or unwanted to one person may not be undesirable to another. Some people like to live in the city and others the suburbs. Some people like camping while others prefer a comfortable hotel stay. Some people prefer tea to coffee. In other words, pollution, or the experience of pollution, is just as subjective a concept as is any other daily event that effects us personally, and anything that is, by definition, subjective is virtually impossible to regulate governmentally. Courts consequently wind up trying to satisfy both sides of the table by rendering decisions that the courts believe are fair and equitable.

A good example of this strained situation is the federal Superfund Law. Officially titled the Comprehensive Environmental Response, Compensation and Liability Act, it was established in 1980 in reaction to Love Canal, New York, which was a liquid waste disposal area for the Hooker Chemical Company. The company's historical dumping activities became front page news when a number of residents that had occupied homes built on top of the dump became ill. Hooker Chemical Company was ordered to clean up the pollution caused by the dumping activity, which Hooker challenged legally on the basis that its disposal activities were perfectly lawful at the time they occurred. While the legal challenge took many years to resolve, Hooker Chemical Company eventually paid to clean up Love Canal, which is now probably one of the cleanest spots on the planet. The lessons learned from that incident led to the development of the Superfund Law. It says that anyone who disposes of waste at a site that eventually turns out to be a contamination problem must fund the cleanup of the site, even if the party disposing of the waste is not at fault at the time of the disposal event.

Unfortunately, for the first ten years or so after its enactment, Superfund was nothing more than a battleground for lawyers because of its broad reaching liability provisions. Courts were constantly wrangling with the question of what Congress intended by Superfund's concept that the polluter pays. Although the Superfund Law, as originally drafted, contemplated that a single party disposing of waste can be liable for the entire cost of a cleanup of an abandoned waste site—otherwise known as strict liability—courts have deviated substantially from the original language of the statute. Applying principles of equity, courts have held that a more reasonable reading of the Superfund Law is to allocate or spread liability across all parties contributing waste to the contaminated site. Accomplishing this groundbreaking allocation scheme, however, took substantial time, effort, and money, including funds that otherwise could have been used to remediate many of these abandoned waste sites. Only after twenty years or so of contentious litigation to establish these equitable principles did money start to channel into funding actual cleanup as opposed to establishing college annuities for generations of lawyers' children.

Adding to this quagmire is the fact that government's implementation and enforcement of environmental laws has not been without fault. One of the reasons for this difficulty is that environmental laws are not always perfectly drafted. In fact, ambiguity is the rule rather than the exception. Reasonable minds can thus differ as to what a particular environmental law requires, which means parties inevitably need to resort to the court for an interpretation of the environmental law. This process unnecessarily increases the time and expense of environmental compliance. Another reason behind the government's faulty implementation and enforcement of environmental laws arises from the fact that, typically, with each change of administration comes a new leader of environmental agencies. Because of the prosecutorial discretion built into most, if not all, environmental laws, different administrations will interpret and enforce those laws differently. The uncertainty resulting from government's consequently unpredictable decisions can have a damaging effect on the marketplace.

After more than thirty years of history now, this environmental legal system is changing, at least in part, from one of government "command and control" to one of market-based strategies essentially free of government interference. Critics of the existing "command and control" environmental legal system argue that the marketplace is better equipped to advance environmental protection initiatives on the theory that financial incentives are available to those market participants that achieve ever greater levels of pollution reduction. The success of this market-based approach to environmental protection will no doubt be tested in the emerging "carbon market," which, unlike most market-based strategies so far, will indeed be a global market.

Experience dictates that you consider the desirability of the ends before rashly and hastily implementing the means. All too often we rush headlong into a new program with the best of intentions, not realizing or appreciating what the outcome will be, only because we fail to take the time to explore the consequences. Hopefully the lessons learned with Enron, Inc. and Worldcom will guide this emerging market in a direction of integrity and strength.

No doubt environmental protection has become a household concept since the publication of Rachel Carson's *Silent Spring*, but what once had the broad appeal of "mom's apple pie" has now become a topic of contentious political debate and whimsy, not to mention the hostage of pop science. Environmental protection has become big business, too, subject to all of the concomitant vagaries and pitfalls. At the end of the day, one must wonder whether the current state of affairs is what Rachael Carson had in mind when she declared her call to arms.